About the author

Born in Newcastle in 1942, Arthur Clifford was educated at Rugby School and Newcastle University. He went on to train as a teacher and subsequently taught in schools in Uganda, Scotland and England. In the late 1990s he retrained as a TEFL teacher and taught English in Siberia, Budapest and Romania. He is a keen mountain climber, having climbed in the Andes and Siberia, and scaled some of the world's most famous peaks, including Mount Ararat and Kilimanjaro. As a teacher, he led expeditions to Peru, Turkey, India and East Africa. He lives in Durham.

FAR, FAR
THE MOUNTAIN PEAK
A BUMPY JOURNEY

Arthur Clifford

The Book Guild Ltd

First published in Great Britain in 2018 by
The Book Guild Ltd
9 Priory Business Park
Wistow Road, Kibworth
Leicestershire, LE8 0RX
Freephone: 0800 999 2982
www.bookguild.co.uk
Email: info@bookguild.co.uk
Twitter: @bookguild

Typeset in Sabon MT

Printed and bound in Great Britain by CPI Group (UK) Ltd, Croydon, CR0 4YY

ISBN 978 1911320 913

British Library Cataloguing in Publication Data.
A catalogue record for this book is available from the British Library.

Introduction

This book continues the story of John Denby. His early life has been told in the first volume of "Far, Far the Mountain Peak". John was the accidental result of a frenzied love affair between Giles Denby, an up-and-coming university lecturer with strong left wing views, and Mary Ponsonby, one of his students. It was consumated during a "Ban the Bomb" protest march. Deeply involved in the "progressive" agenda of their 1960s plate glass university in a northern industrial town, neither he nor Mary could be bothered with a bawling and messy baby and young John was bundled off to live with his rich grandparents in their opulent London suburb.

There he lived a pampered and sheltered life, sent to a posh, upper class prep school and engulfed in a world of Christianity and model railways.

Then, suddenly, at the age of eleven, disaster struck and his cosy world was shattered. His grandparents were killed in a road accident and he was sent back to his parents in their northern industrial town.

Having been spoilt by his grandparents, he was utterly unable to cope with his parents' cold and hostile attitude. Their "liberated" life style and ostentatious atheism bewildered him. Sent to a new experimental school in a deprived sink estate, he was thrust into a maelstrom of delinquent and criminalised pupils. Here he was rejected, horribly bullied and subjected to a gruesome rape with a bicycle pump by a senior pupil.

Deeply traumatised, he fled to London in a vain attempt to get back into his old happy life. After a series of adventures he was returned to his parents and sent to a small private school started by Dorothy Watson, a teacher with a mission to rescue youngsters who couldn't cope with the local bog standard comprehensives. Unable to have children of her own, she semi-adopted him as her own son. After more traumas he finally began to make progress. In the course of all these ups and downs he learned to lead a double life, telling lies and deceiving people in order to survive.

Now as, he enters adolescence and sex kicks in, he faces a new and deadly challenge…

Read on to accompany young John on his "Bumpy Journey"…

Places and Characters in the Story

Places

Boldonbridge: a big industrial town at the mouth of the River Boldon in northern England. Once famous for its ship building it has fallen on hard times and awaits renewal.

Greenwood: a decayed industrial suburb of Boldonbridge. Once the beating heart of industrial Boldonbridge, it is now the haunt of down-and- outs and criminal gangs.

Moorside: an affluent middle class suburb of Boldonbridge.

Greenhill: the new experimental comprehensive school in Greenwood to which John was sent on his arrival at Boldonbridge. Notorious for its violence and indiscipline.

14 Gloucester Road: Giles Denby's ultra-modern house in Greenwood, specially designed by a progressive architect to demonstrate his commitment to "working class culture".

Beaconsfield School: the small private school in Moorside to which John is sent after his attempted escape to London. It is an all boys school.

People

Dr. Giles Denby: John's father, a leading social historian and passionate left winger. Now an influential member of the Labour Party.

Mary: Giles' wife and John's mother: she has left Giles and disappeared into Africa doing "progressive good works." John hates her.

Dorothy Watson: Headmistress of Beaconsfield School. A would-be missionary, who after a disillusioning time teaching in Uganda and the traumatic break up of her marriage to Lawrence, has started Beaconsfield School in an idealistic attempt to rescue pupils who have failed in the local comprehensives. Unable to have children of her own, she has informally adopted John as her own son. She keeps him in her own house during the week and sends him back home at weekends. She finds him difficult and has has doubts about him. During a hiking trip on the Isle of Rhum she actually physically assaulted him. She is devout Christian.

Roderick Meakin: Deputy Head of Beaconsfield School. A grizzled old war veteran with the Military Medal, he has "seen it all and done it all". Trapped in an unhappy marriage, he finds teaching the Beaconsfield kids a welcome therapy. The boys call him "Mekon". John hero worships him.

James Briggs: P.E. teacher at Beconsfield School. Having failed as a teacher in a local comprehensive, he is secretly ashamed of having to work in a private school. He despises John as a spoilt upper class brat. He is a "Saved" and fundamentalist Christian who believes that every word in the Bible is literally true.

Annie Coburn: Giles Denby's housekeeper who looks after 14 Gloucester Road for himwhile he is in London. An old fashioned "heart of gold" Geordie, shedotes on John.

Bob Steadman: Curate attatched to the local Moorside Church. Highly intelligent and a an accomplished scientist and theologian, he is bored stiff by his dreary suburban parish. He finds teaching the the Beaconsfield kids a welcome relief from fussy old ladies. John hero worships him.

Michael Connolly: Beaconsfield pupil from a disastrously dysfunctional background. John's first friend at the school. Has serious learning difficulties.

Danny Fleetwood: Beaconsfield pupil. Lively and bouncy, he is John's best friend.

Martin Davidson: "Army Barmy" Martin. Beaconsfield pupil. Obese and of limited intelligence, he lives in a military dream world. Hates John because has exposed him as a fraud and supplanted him.

Sam Hawthorne: Beaconsfield pupil. Disastrously dyslexic… Abandoned by his father.

Fred Macdonald: Beaconsfield pupil. West Indian lad from Barbados and the only boy to rival John's intelligence and ability. Close friend.

Billy Nolan: Beaconsfield pupil. Bad lad and school ner-do-well. John's enemy.

Billy Lees: sad and hideously abused waif and stray who was John's only friend at Greenhill. He disappeared into the wasteland of Greenwood, John feels guilty because he was too scared to come to his aid while he was being beaten up by his classmates.

Robert Napier: a hopelessly delinquent young criminal sent to Beaconsfield School in the vain hope that he could be reformed. Sent to a young offenders institution when his nefarious activities were discovered.

1

The Enemy Within

Girls: Another Species?

It began slowly the following year and was all about girls.

So far girls hadn't figured much in John's life. There hadn't been any girls at Rickerby Hall and the only ones he'd met had been at parties given by his classmates. They were odd, inferior creatures who wore silly dresses and did soppy things like playing with dolls. Proper boys didn't have much to do with them.

At Greenhill the girls had terrified him. They were vicious predators who used their superior strength to destroy anything remotely weak. They were best squeezed out of your mind. Yet real women – not his mother, Mary, because she wasn't a real woman! – were kind and gentle things who were nice to you and cuddled you like that nice policewoman in London and that fat Martha he'd met at Giles' weird parties. That girl at Greenhill on that dreadful Friday had, also, been kind. So girls weren't all horrible. But they were a dangerous and alien species, best avoided – until eventually they changed into nice, kindly women.

Of course, he'd always assumed that one day he would fall in love with a beautiful girl and get married. After all, that's what everybody did.

Delicious Lad's Stuff

That September Mrs Watson got the local doctor in to give his 'little talk' to Form Three. Mysteries came clear and a whole new world opened up, an exotic and deliciously 'dirty' world which was real 'lad's stuff'.

'God, I was *innocent*!' John exclaimed to Danny one Saturday evening as they played with the trains round at Gloucester Road. 'And to think that I didn't know what benders did! I mean, going up bums and that, it's disgusting!'

'My Dad just hates benders!' Danny added vehemently. 'He says they should have their balls cut off and be locked up for life!'

'Quite right, too!' replied John, 'That bloke in the Lake District two years ago! God, if I'd known what he was really after I would have killed him!'

'Benders' duly took their place among the Nazis, the Argies and the Wimps as the least permissible forms of animal life. Even worse – if that were possible! – were the loathsome old men in dirty raincoats who wanted to 'bum' little boys.

'My Dad says they should be publicly hanged at Tyburn,' declared Danny.

'Yeah!' added John, 'Publicly exterminated, like you do with rats!'

Only a Matter of Time

In Form Three, girls suddenly became the height of fashion. Everybody started to have girlfriends. John didn't know any girls and wasn't really interested in them either. Indeed he found the whole idea of the sex act disgusting, about as revolting as the things that benders did. The endless talk about sex bored him rigid, but to keep up his 'big bold lad' image he had to pretend to be interested. In place of a real girl friend he found a copy of the *Sun* and announced that he was passionately in love with the bosomy and bare-bottomed female he discovered on Page Three. Like his story of being expelled from Greenhill for hitting a teacher, the ploy worked: 'Denby! He's a real sex maniac, him!'

Soon, however, he believed that he really would start to like girls and would have to stop pretending. He was a normal boy, after all. And as the doctor had said, it was 'only a matter of time'.

A Demon Taking Control

But things didn't turn out as they should have done. Instead something bewilderingly unsettling began to happen. Slowly, by imperceptible stages, he found himself becoming interested in other boys' bodies, especially those of the younger and slimmer ones. The 'forbidden zones', especially the 'nether regions', began to fascinate him. He found himself staring at small boys as they bent down and longing for them to drop their trousers and let him see the exquisitely shaped backsides that lay hidden underneath.

The feeling came in waves. Some days it wasn't there and the whole business disgusted him. Then suddenly a madness seemed to take hold of him and he would be filled with a craving to do... well, the filthy things that benders did! At the time it didn't seem filthy at all. It seemed as normal and as natural as having a drink of lemonade. More than that, even. Much more. It was the most wildly exciting thing in the world. In these moments he seemed to become another person, as if an alien had entered his body and taken control of him, the sort of demon you read about in science fiction stories. Then the fit would pass and he would be filled with shame and disgust. Only little kids were interested in bums and that, but instead of growing up, he was becoming a little kid again. He simply couldn't understand it.

After games he found himself lingering in the showers, especially when the younger boys were showering, his eyes fixed on places where they should not be fixed. It began to be noticed, especially by the ever-vigilant Briggs.

'Come on, Denby,' he would say in a loud voice that all could hear, 'Just what do you think you're looking at?'

Slowly the incidents mounted up. With a scarcely concealed relish, Briggs noted them down – chapter and verse – and duly informed Dorothy.

'I'm worried about young Denby. He's always lurking in the changing room ogling at the juniors when they're showering. Frankly, I think he's turning into a dangerous homosexual.'

'Nonsense!' she snapped, 'I know you don't like him and you're probably just imagining it.'

Drifting into Danger

Blissfully unaware, John was drifting into danger; almost as if he were asleep in a dinghy which was being borne down an increasingly turbulent river towards an abyss. Trouble began in a round-about way.

Billy Nolan was now a swaggering Fifth-Former. Ducking out of every difficulty that came his way, he'd set himself up as the school rebel, refusing to work, refusing to play games, refusing, indeed, to do anything remotely constructive. It was so much easier to laze about, smoking fags, reading porno mags and swilling the odd slug of vodka, so much easier than to struggle away with things like maths and woodwork. Even when you *did* try your best you only achieved a very modest success, and people like stuck up little snob Denby always did better than you, and let you know about it, too! But refuse to work, set the Maths teacher, Polly Parrot, squawking round the room, dodge games, smoke fags in front of the juniors on the playing field... that paid dividends. And how! You became a real *hard*! The juniors admired you, some of the teachers were even a bit scared of you.

Nobody could do anything with him. About once a month his father would come up to the school and present a Grand Remonstrance: 'You ain't done nuttin' for my lad! Nuttin' at all in all the five year wot 'e's bin 'ere!'

Dorothy would call in Meakin and Briggs and a new strategy would be worked out to try to get him to play games or go on an adventure weekend. It never worked. Made captain of the rugby team, he simply refused to turn up. The fact was that Billy liked being bad. As the 'rock-hard bad lad of Beaconsfield' he was in paradise. He was King of the Corridors. The bleak world beyond Beaconsfield that world where you had to work for a living and needed qualifications and skills if you were to avoid unemployment that just didn't exist.

The only fly in the ointment was that little snob, Denby, who openly called him a thickoid and a wimp. He would like to kick him in, but he didn't dare to. Denby could fling a hefty punch and, what was more, he had all of Form Three behind him. Hatred smouldered.

One day it transpired that Billy had been forcing the First Year boys to buy cigarettes at exorbitant prices. He was duly hauled up before Mrs Watson.

He was openly defiant. 'I ain't done nuttin' wrong, me! They jus' gives us money so that I can help me Dad when he runs short. He's unemployed you know!'

'But you are deliberately encouraging small boys to smoke and that is wrong.'

'It ain't half as wrong as wot your Denby does! He's a bender wot bums little kids!'

'Nonsense!'

'No it ain't! He's your little pet ain't he? Jus' because he's posh and talks posh you gives him all the prizes an' that and you keep him at your house!'

'That's because his father and mother have left him. I'd do the same for you.'

'No you bloody wouldn't! Cos' I'm not posh like him! And I'll tell you a thing! The lads is getting' right pissed off with 'im an all! Always bloody Denby, ain't it! Even if he's right bender wot bums liddell kids! Why not bloody us, for a change?'

With that he stormed out of the room and slammed the door. Adolescent in a temper tantrum. Teenager out of control. School's failed with him. Dorothy Watson, you're a failure.

'I Think There is Something You Ought to Know'

A crisis meeting was held with Meakin and Briggs.

'We can't go on like this!' sighed Dorothy. 'If Billy Nolan won't toe the line we'll just have to get rid of him.'

'Like Robert Napier,' said Briggs pointedly.

'Yes, like Robert Napier, I'm afraid. I mean, he's corrupting the juniors. The things he said about John Denby...'

Briggs seized his chance. 'He may have a point there.'

'Oh?' said Meakin, puffing on his pipe. 'What's your favourite pupil gone and done now?' (A long-standing antagonism was reviving.)

Ignoring Meakin, Briggs addressed Dorothy. 'Well to be perfectly frank, Mrs Watson, the way that you openly favour that young man is causing problems among the seniors. They resent it.'

'Oh do they now?' A spear was stuck into Dorothy's soft underbelly and it hurt. What was more her precious credibility was under attack. She set her face into a grim 'how dare you?' expression and switched on the X-ray eyes. Frosty silence.

Undeterred, Briggs pressed home the attack. 'I'm afraid they *do*. After all you *do* keep him in your house. Why not poor old Sam Hawthorne? He's just as deserving. And Denby gets all the prizes, doesn't he? I mean it's Denby, Denby, Denby, all the time. He's not the only kid in the school and the other kids are beginning to resent him.'

'He gets the prizes because he *is* better than most of them,' declared Meakin hotly.

'Yes!' added Dorothy, greatly relieved by Meakin's coming to her rescue. 'He's a very positive influence in the school. A real role model for the boys.'

'You *really* think that?'

Briggs complacent smile needled Dorothy. 'Yes I *do*!' she retorted hotly. 'And what's more, it's my duty to manage this school as I see fit! If you don't like the way I run things, Mr Briggs, you can always go elsewhere!'

'I'm not disputing your authority, Mrs Watson,' replied Briggs with just the smallest touch of glee. 'But there's something I think you ought to know.'

Out, yet again, came the business of his ogling at junior boys when they were naked in the shower after games, embellished this time with further incidents.

'Are you saying he's a homosexual?'

'It does look rather like it, doesn't it?'

'Mr Briggs, I shan't believe it until I've got solid evidence, and not a lot of schoolboy smut. That subject is closed.'

'I take your point. But this *is* a Christian school and we can't possibly be seen to condone homosexuality. The Bible is quite clear on that matter.'

With that the meeting ended. The Billy Nolan problem was left unresolved.

Seeds of Uncertainty

On the way home Dorothy began to have second thoughts. 'Pompous bluster worthy of Lawrence at his worst! The rational Professional began to challenge the Emotional Woman. But maybe Briggs *did* have a point? Maybe Billy Nolan *did* have a point? After all, it *was* true. She *did* favour John Denby... too much perhaps?

No! She'd been through all this two years ago. John was a good and very positive boy who had repaid her kindness with interest. Forget about these smutty rumours put about by inadequate seniors who were jealous of him. Stand by your protégé in his hour of need! Be strong! Yet, a tiny seed of uncertainty had been planted.

The following week a timorous and red-faced First Year knocked on her study door. 'Please, Miss, I'm sorry to disturb you,' he mumbled, 'But it's very embarrassing.'

'Yos, don't be afraid, what is it?'

'It's that Third Year boy, Denby. He keeps looking at me in the shower. I mean, he's always there. It's embarrassing.'

'Don't worry, I'm sure it's nothing.'

Dorothy fervently hoped it *was* nothing. But the little seed of uncertainty began to germinate.

A Time Bomb Ticking Away?

In the event, Billy Nolan was reprieved after a Final Warning. He even managed to apologise for his boorish outburst. The awful reality of losing his little kingdom and being cast out into the hostile world beyond Beaconsfield managed to penetrate even his limited consciousness.

Meanwhile, blissfully unaware of the dangers closing in on him, John drifted lazily on in his metaphorical dinghy. He began to be obsessed with Danny. It slowly dawned on him that he was quite ridiculously beautiful: that slender, muscular and superbly shaped body, that soft velvety skin, the elegant curve of his exquisitely shaped backside. It was all too good to be true. Showering after rugby became the longed-for high point of the week, a chance to glimpse – oh, so fleetingly! – those naked splendours. When the Demon entered him he was filled with a wild and ecstatic craving; but when it left him he felt as squalid as a little kid who'd messed his pants.

Then the dreams began. The doctor had said that they would dream about girls. But, while other boys dreamt about girls, he didn't. Instead it was Danny, always Danny. Danny naked in the shower, Danny naked on the rugby field, Danny cavorting naked round his bedroom at Gloucester Road and asking him to do... *that*!

He was at Mrs Watson's house when it first happened. He woke up to find the sheets sticky and disgusting. That was bad enough, but, oh God, if she'd known what he was dreaming about!

One night he had a particularly vivid dream. He was at Greenhill on that dreadful Friday, naked in the hands of the baying mob. It should have been a nightmare, but it wasn't. Instead it was wildly and deliciously exciting in a way that he had never known before. The Demon possessed his everything. And it wasn't Freddy Hazlett's bicycle pump that was going into him. It was Danny. Danny naked and wonderful. And, what was more, he John Denby, Denby the big bold lad of Form Three, was *enjoying it*, enjoying it with a frenzied, searing joy that he'd never known before! He woke up suddenly to find himself engulfed in a sticky white glue. He'd messed Mrs Watson's sheets again! It was all so degrading! God, if she knew what he'd been dreaming about! If *Danny* knew!

Nobody, he decided, must know of this. Absolutely nobody. Like Greenhill, like the walloping Mrs. Watson had given him on top of Askival during that mountain hike on the Isle of Rhum, it must be consigned to oblivion. Dropped into the fire and burned to a nothingness.

But it wouldn't burn. It remained there, whole and unscathed, ticking away like a time bomb.

All Topsy-Turvy

One dreadful day the bomb exploded. It was a wet Wednesday afternoon and they were showering after rugby with Briggs. It was late March and the playing field was a grassless swamp of sticky mud, which meant that they were exceptionally dirty. The showering took a long time.

The Demon had entered him that day. All through the game he had become increasingly entranced by Danny's glorious body, especially by the treasures of the hidden zone which loomed tantalisingly under the small and very tight shorts that he was wearing. The longing became a craving.

Then, as Danny had strolled unconcernedly into the shower with all those hidden treasures at last revealed, that craving had flared up into an all-consuming flame. In an ecstatic trance, he followed him in. The warm water, which flowed sensuously over his cold, muddy body, seemed almost like petrol, which fed and enhanced the already roaring flame.

Suddenly, his wildest hopes came true. Danny dropped the soap and bent down to pick it up. Everything he'd been longing for was there before him. In a crazily ecstatic moment the Demon took hold of him. His "thing" was massive and erect and squirting stuff as never before. And it happened.

Normality returned with a devastating crash. Danny reacted violently: '*Gerroff yer fucking bender! Sir, Mr Briggs, sir, the bender's shafting me!*'

He swung round and punched John violently in the face. Blood flowed.

An excited crowd gathered. '*Fight! Fight! Hey, lads, Denby's a bender!*'

A stunned John fought back and together, amid shouts and yells, they rolled onto the floor as the warm water poured over their tangled limbs. Mayhem broke loose.

A frantic Briggs exploded onto the scene. The one thing he most dreaded was happening: wild disorder in his tightly run domain. If he couldn't instantly control it, his self-confidence as a struggling PE teacher would be irreparably damaged.

'*Stop it at once! I say stop it! What's going on here?*'

To his immense relief the tumult died down and the two boys disentangled themselves. A sort of silence descended.

'What's all this about?'

'He bummed me!' hissed a white-faced and seething Danny, 'He's a hom! He bummed me!'

Briggs felt a surge of exaltation. Religious exaltation. Yes, even the hand of God! Vindication. As a Saved Christian, he'd always *known* that young Denby was bad. Here at last was that firm evidence that old Dolly was always wittering on about.

'Is this true, Denby?'

A dazed John just stood and gaped. It was all so unreal.

'Well?'

'Yes it is!' cut in Martin, who was hovering like a vulture over the wounded carcass of his hated rival. 'Yes it is. I saw him do it, the dirty bender!'

A chorus of jeers broke out from the assembled crowd.

'All right, lads,' said Briggs in an unusually gentle voice. 'You lot get dressed now. I'll deal with this character. Denby, you wait here.'

While a bewildered, shell-shocked John shivered alone in the shower, the crowd dispersed in silence. As they left the changing room a babble of excited talk exploded.

'Cor, I never thought he was a bender!' 'My Dad's going to go apeshit when he hears of this!' 'Wait till Billy Nolan hears of this, he hates Denby and he hates benders.'

'Now then Denby,' said a gloating Briggs. 'You can get dressed and come with me. We're going to see Mrs Watson.'

'Am I in serious trouble, then?' asked John, finding his voice at last.

'I should say you *are*!' answered Briggs in a firm and confident voice.

'But it was an accident. I didn't mean it. It just sort of happened.'

'Don't try to wriggle out of it. I've been watching you all term. You've been planning this a long time, and just because you were John Denby from Rickerby Hall you thought you would be allowed to get away with it. You have committed a deliberate homosexual assault on another boy and that's one of the worst things anybody can do.'

'But —'

'Read your Bible, young man. Genesis, Chapter Nineteen. It's all there. Homosexuals are among the damned. Hitler was bad enough, but even he wasn't as bad as a homosexual.'

Dumbly John followed Briggs along the corridor to the door of Mrs Watson's study.

'*Fucking bender!*' Danny screamed at him as he left the school.

It was crazy. Topsy-turvy. Only an hour before, Danny had been his best friend. Now they were mortal enemies. It was like a road accident. Normal before. Crazy afterwards.

Briggs knocked on the door and opened it to reveal a normal-looking Mrs Watson sitting at her desk marking a pile of exercise books.

'Yes, what is it?'

Triumphantly, Briggs delivered his long-cherished and long-rehearsed announcement. 'This boy has just committed a serious homosexual assault on young Danny Fleetwood.'

Taken aback, Mrs Watson just gaped. It was such an unexpected bombshell.

'Well?' she managed to say, looking at John.

John remained speechless. What could he say? He hadn't consciously done it. It was the Demon inside him. It had just happened to him.

'Frankly, Mrs Watson,' said Briggs, 'I think this merits

expulsion. I think you should, also, contact the police. This young man is a danger to all the young people in the area.'

An embarrassed silence.

'I think you'd better go home, now, John,' said Mrs Watson eventually.

'This is Meant to be a Christian School'

'Can you fetch Mr Meakin for me, Mr Briggs?' Dorothy said as John slunk out of the room. 'This matter needs serious consideration.' Sensing a major assault on her credibility, she went into Formal Headmistress mode. Guns were loaded. Grenades were primed.

Meakin duly breezed in amidst the usual clouds of pipe smoke. 'What's today's disaster, then? Arson, rape, terrorist attack? Murder, perhaps?'

'It's more serious than that,' said Briggs as they sat down on the settee.

With the triumphant air of a scientist announcing a major discovery that proved his much-derided theory right, he launched forth. The whole business was lovingly described in all its sordid detail, chapter and verse, with nothing left to the imagination. The long build-up from the beginning of term, the stream of incidents reported to him by other boys, the actual deed, the witnesses who could prove its reality beyond the faintest shadow of doubt... a bravura performance worthy of *Rumpole of the Bailey*, of which he was an ardent fan.

'Yes, I know this must be very distressing for you, Mrs Watson, especially after all that you have tried to do for that young man,' he concluded with a victor's magnanimity. 'But I have always felt that your benevolence – doubtless well meant, don't get me wrong! – was, shall we say, somewhat misplaced. I always knew that that young man was bad and, well, now I've been proved right.'

'So where do we go from here?' asked Meakin aggressively.

He couldn't stand Briggs at the best of times, but this complacent triumphalism was unbearable.

'I think it's obvious. We can't keep him, can we?'

'You mean expulsion?' said Dorothy quietly.

'Frankly, yes.'

'Oh come on, Jamie!' expostulated Meakin. 'That's a bit over the top!'

'That's what you think!' declared Briggs vehemently. 'But this is meant to be a Christian school, in case you didn't know it. And homosexuality is explicitly condemned in the Bible. Leviticus, Chapter Eighteen, Verse Twenty-two: "You shall not lie with a male as with a woman: it is an abomination." There you have it. The word of God. If you're a Christian you must accept it.'

Having delivered his knock-out blow, he folded his arms and sat back, confident of victory.

'Oh, for heaven's sake!' snorted Meakin, 'We're not living in the seventeenth century! Times change, you know.'

Both looked at Dorothy for support. She remained silent. Deep waters here.

Then, plunging on, Briggs spoke up. 'All right, let's get modern, shall we? Can you imagine what will happen if we don't act decisively? This school's already got a bad enough reputation as a dustbin for deadbeats. I see it all the time when I try to arrange sporting fixtures. It will go all round the town that Beaconsfield is a school that allows older boys to sexually molest younger ones. It will be the end of us. The council will close us down – and rightly so, too! Anyway, as I've said before, Denby shouldn't be here. We're not here to mollycoddle upper-class dropouts. Our remit is among the deprived inner-city kids.'

'But,' interrupted Meakin, 'he's the only one with any real potential!'

'That's exactly why he should go! He's a tempter who'll

lead the others astray. The Devil isn't a silly old thing with horns and tail, you know! He's beautiful and very clever.'

'You're not saying that the kid's the Devil in disguise, are you?'

'Not in so many words, but I am saying that, as the bright and able purveyor of homosexuality, he's doing the Devil's work!'

Borne aloft on the wings of his rhetoric, Briggs ploughed on, filled with the Holy Ghost, as he fervently believed. 'I mean, have you thought about the future? Sooner or later Denby will be hanging round public toilets and molesting little boys. He'll be hauled in by the police, up in court, and the press will get old of it and cause us no end of trouble! And when he grows up he could even start murdering his victims – they all do that, you know! It'll get into the papers and onto television and people will start saying, "Look what Beaconsfield produces!" And they'll be right. I know you meant well, Mrs Watson, but by getting involved with that young man you've landed yourself right in it. I'll be absolutely frank. If I were you I'd cut my losses and get rid of him *now*! *Now*, before it's too late. You'll only regret it if you don't. It's no use being sentimental.'

The torrent ceased while Briggs paused to catch his breath.

'And I'll tell you another thing,' he continued, breaking the embarrassed silence, 'You'll be having Mr Fleetwood up first thing tomorrow morning.'

'That randy old tomcat!' sighed Meakin. 'He's a fine one to get on his high horse about sexual morality!'

'He's promiscuous, I'll grant you that,' replied Briggs, 'but he's absolutely right about homosexuality, especially when it involves child abuse.'

'I'm going to have to think all this over very carefully,' said Dorothy eventually.

'Well, all I can say is that tough decisions have to be made,' declared Briggs. 'This is no time to be weak or emotional.'

That hurt. A humiliated Dorothy ended the meeting.

That evening Briggs went down to the Tabernacle and described the day's events. Filled once more with the Holy Ghost, he 'spoke in tongues'. A spontaneous service of thanksgiving followed.

Worse than Hitler?

John crept back to Mrs Watson's house where he stayed on weekdays. He was in a daze. Apparently he had done something awful. The trouble was that he couldn't see why it was so awful. A smutty, embarrassing accident had happened. But, then, such things were always happening with kids – like being sick in cars and needing the bog in the middle of the city. He hadn't hurt anybody. He hadn't stolen anything. Yet, according to Briggs, he was even worse than Hitler who had killed six million Jews. It didn't make sense.

But that strange exaltation that had gripped him and had pushed him into doing such an embarrassingly dirty thing? It was so mysterious; and so frightening in the way that it took hold of him.

And now, because of it, he was in the shit. Everybody was screaming at him. Danny was calling him a bender. Even little Michael was calling him a shit-stabber. It was all so crazy, so crazy, indeed, that it probably hadn't really happened. In any case, the whole thing would probably blow over. If kids went mad, the adults always calmed them down and made them see sense. After all, adults were sane. When he'd gone and peed in his sleeping bag in Scotland two years ago, Mrs Watson had brushed it off as an unfortunate accident. That was all this was, an embarrassing accident, as if he'd gone and peed himself in Morning Assembly.

He went into the spare room that Mrs Watson had given him as a bedroom and did his maths homework. Then he put on a video. Later Mrs Watson arrived, looked into the room to see that he was there, and went away without saying a word. She didn't even cook supper for him; not, of course, that he felt like eating anything after the trauma in the shower. Still, it was a bit odd. Unsettling, even.

Only One Answer

The fact was, Dorothy didn't know what to say to him. She, too, was in a daze. As a biology teacher she knew all about the testosterone surges that occurred in adolescents. She'd seen plenty of it at Greenhill: all those sex-crazed boys and girls copulating furiously in the toilets, cupboards and bicycle sheds. And girls, she knew, could be worse than boys, maturing earlier and, especially at Greenhill, turning into sex-obsessed maniacs. She'd had strong urges herself. Her affair with Lawrence had been a passionate and carnal one. Even now the embers of that lost love could flare up.

All that was normal. Comprehensible. But homosexuality wasn't. It was something outside her experience. Theoretically she knew about it: at best as an unpleasant disease, at worse as a deliberate and squalid self-indulgence. She was not a fundamentalist and Briggs's simplistic dogmatism repelled and embarrassed her. But it wasn't only the Old Testament fire-eaters who condemned homosexuality: Saint Paul did, too, and, as a committed Christian you had to take Saint Paul seriously.

Besides, she had problems enough with the adolescent volcano that was her school without homosexuality entering the already deadly mix of inadequacy and incipient loutishness. Briggs had a point. If she allowed homosexuality to flourish unchecked it could run riot and bring all that she had so painfully achieved crashing down in ruin and ridicule. It definitely was no time to be weak or emotional. Yes, chuck out the bad apple before it could ruin the barrel.

No problem if that bad apple had been Billy Nolan. How

she would just love to be rid of that useless ducker and diver! But *John*! *Her* child, her protégé, her discovery who was sitting in her very own spare room and who was so positive and so full of the good qualities that the rest of her school lacked! That was something else.

Two years ago she'd resolved all her doubts. John was a good-hearted and wholesome boy who needed her help and would richly reward her for it. A gift from God, indeed! But was he *really* what she fondly imagined him to be?

The vision loomed up before her. A homosexual predator lurking in public lavatories and molesting small boys. Always in trouble with the police. Always in court. Getting into the newspapers. Dragging her down into the depths. Prison. Sordid repercussions. Aiding and abetting a child molester. Dolly, you fool!

With it came another disturbing thought. Why had she been so fond of him? Not just because he was an orphan in need of help. Face it, Dolly old girl, it was because he was *cute*: that lovely smile, those big appealing eyes, that glorious mop of blonde hair. You'd let yourself fall for him! Soon he would mutate into a dangling and spotty adolescent. He would cease to be cute. Would you be so fond of him then? You're just an Emotional Woman, aren't you!

All through the year there had been that drip, drip, drip from Briggs, making the hole in her confidence that little bit bigger. Now this bombshell. Briggs had openly accused her of being weak and emotional. That sealed it. She would have to prove once and for all that she was a *strong* and steely *professional* able to make tough decisions. There was only one answer.

An Evil Germ

The next morning John walked to school. He felt light-headed. He'd eaten nothing since lunchtime the previous day and he hadn't spoken to Mrs Watson since that awkward meeting in her study. Things were certainly out of joint. But... well... with a bit of sense they would get back to normal again.

As soon as he entered Assembly there was an ominous hush. The boys of Form Three immediately moved away from him, leaving him isolated as if he were radioactive. Whenever he approached anyone they backed off. Beaming and smiling, he greeted Danny. But, instead of smiling back, Danny screwed up his face and snarled, 'Fuck off bender! I'm not standing next to you!'

At that the senior boys started hissing like a heap of vipers. 'Bender.' 'Hom.' 'Shit-stabber!'

He was bewildered, dismayed, frightened. This was something new and alarming.

As they waited outside the maths room for the first lesson, the whole class placed their backsides firmly against the wall. 'Watch out, lads!' cried Danny. 'The bender's here!'

So it went on all morning. Nobody would sit near him. Even Mekon seemed oddly cold and distant. A black doom fell on him. It was Greenhill again: no longer a big, bold lad, but back to being an evil germ. Mad. Everything had gone mad!

Out on the field during lunch break a mob gathered round him. As at Greenhill, he was trapped. A swaggering and swashbuckling Billy Nolan approached him.

'Denby, we don't like poofters here, do we lads?'

A roar of approval went up from the mob.

'And we don't like suction pumps what smarms up to teechas, neither!'

Another roar of approval from the mob.

This was terrifying. The whole school was against him. It had obviously been planned. He'd always thought he was popular. He'd no idea that his success could have stoked up this venomous resentment. With Army Barmy Martin, yes, but not with people like Michael and Fred. A ghastly revelation.

'Right, Billy, lad, let him 'ave it!'

Billy brandished his fists. This was Billy's big day. Briggs had been telling him that, after his near expulsion, he ought to show his gratitude by doing something positive for the school for a change. So when a deputation had come to him asking him to 'sort out Bender Denby', he had seized the opportunity – with relish! Here was his chance to finally get even with the little snob. Alone, and without his gang to help him, he would be easy meat. And what could be more positive than bashing up a shit-stabber? After all, Briggsy had told him shit-stabbers were vermin, hadn't he? By kicking Denby in good and proper, he would be a good lad for once!

John was cornered. The trapped rat. The fox before the slobbering hounds. But never again crumple up as you did at Greenhill! These are human beings: they bleed. Billy Nolan is a big, cowardly, bullying slob who picks on weaker people. Go for him. Either smash him or go down fighting.

A savage punch straight onto Billy's big, flat nose. Blood flowing. Another punch on the mouth. Another in the stomach. Enemy reeling from the unexpected ferocity of the attack. Billy down. Kick him savagely with all the frenzy of accumulated hatred. No Geneva Convention stuff in this war.

'*Ow*! *Help*! *Lay off yer bender*!'

Crowd cowed. See Michael Connolly jeering. Smash him in the face. More blood. Tears, too.

Then Briggs blew the whistle for the start of afternoon school. As the crowd trooped in, John noticed a change in the atmosphere. He was no longer the complete pariah.

'Well done, John,' whispered Fred. 'You put up a great fight. You're not a poofter, are you?'

He'd won a battle, and in schoolboy eyes a fight had all the aura of a medieval trial by combat. Those who won were right… just like Greenhill! There was a glimmer of hope. It had been terrifying to discover how suddenly you could become an outcast, but now the worst of the storm seemed to be blowing over.

'Not you, Denby,' said Briggs as they filed along the corridor. 'You're to go to Mrs Watson's study.'

That was a further reassurance. A talk with Mrs Watson. His Mum. The bedrock of sense in this crazy world. She'd straighten things out. Suddenly he felt like a little boy. God, he actually wanted a cuddle from his Mum; that reassurance that the world really was sane after all.

'No School can Survive with People Like You In It'

But as soon as Briggs ushered him into the study, he got a shock. It wasn't his smiling, cuddly, shaggy sheepdog of a Mum who faced him. It was Mrs Watson, Headmistress of Beaconsfield School, seated behind her desk, glaring at him with her Medusa eyes. Briggs sat down on her left, and with Mekon sitting on her right, he was facing a hostile interrogation group. No hugs or cuddles here. An image from the war stories he'd read flitted through his mind: the Gestapo grilling a British pilot shot down over Germany. It was like having a bucket of icy water tipped over you.

'John Denby,' said Mrs Watson in a cold, hard voice, 'this is a most unpleasant thing that I now have to do, especially after all the progress that I thought you were making. But, in view of what Mr Briggs has told me about you, and particularly after what you did to Danny Fleetwood in the shower yesterday, we cannot keep you at Beaconsfield School any longer. Neither can I have you in my house. You are to go back to your home in Gloucester Road. I will contact your father and he will find you another school.'

John gaped in utter bewilderment. Death sentence? He couldn't have heard properly.

'What?'

'You heard. We can no longer have you at Beaconsfield School.'

The death sentence was repeated.

Silence.

Slowly the realisation burrowed through the layers of John's disbelief. Then the awful truth dawned on him. The black pit beneath him was revealed. The abyss. What he had always secretly dreaded had happened. Assaulted by those he confidently believed were his protectors. Like that time in the London police station when they'd told him that Mrs Bowles wasn't at Oaktree Gardens any more and that they didn't want him back at Rickerby Hall. His life shattered. That avalanche of icy boulders crashing onto him just as it had done when his grandparents had been killed.

Involuntarily, the tears started to trickle. Despite himself he became a snivelling little infant. 'Oh God! Oh God! Please, no! I was so happy here. What will happen to me?'

While Briggs's face wore an expression of righteous triumphalism, Mrs Watson and Mekon sat in embarrassed silence.

Suddenly John's temper blazed out. 'I thought you were my Mum who liked me!' he yelled at Mrs Watson. 'Now you're chucking me out for no reason! I mean, what have I done? *It was all a silly accident!*'

'Just a silly accident? Is that how describe it?' said Briggs in a cool, confident voice. 'I've been watching you closely. Don't try to tell me that you hadn't planned this whole thing out very carefully. You have calmly and quite deliberately committed a dirty and depraved act. For your own gratification you have sexually abused a fellow pupil and, just because you were John Denby from Rickerby Hall prep school, you thought you could get away with it. Well, you can't.'

A pause followed while John gaped in bewilderment. What the hell had Rickerby Hall got to do with it?

Briggs continued, 'You're bad, Denby, *bad*. No school can survive with people like you in it.'

'But —' This was mad.

'But *nothing*. You've planted the seed of sodomy, which is a disease. If unchecked it will contaminate the whole school and destroy it. You're a sodomite. You know what God did to Sodom and Gomorrah? Read your Bible. Leviticus, Chapter Eighteen, Verse Twenty-Two. "You shall not lie with a male as with a woman: it is an abomination." You are an abomination, Denby.'

'All right, Jamie,' sighed Meakin, looking uncomfortable. 'We can do without a sermon.'

'John Denby,' declared Mrs Watson, 'You're to go back to Gloucester Road. We'll get your things sent on from Fern Avenue.'

The Only Lifeline

Shell-shocked and with tears running down his cheeks, John stumbled out of the room. Mercifully, all the boys were in lessons so there was nobody to jeer at him in his degradation. He was able to slip unmolested into the street.

It was one of those balmy days which are not yet spring, but which promise a recovery from the long, wasting disease of winter. The warm, friendly sunshine and the soft, mellow brick of the comfortable old buildings seemed to mock him.

Now what? A burst of wild anger was followed by a feeling of helpless despair. The plug had been pulled and his whole world was spiralling down the drain. He'd been a good and promising lad. Now he was bad; worse than bad – *evil*. 'No school can survive with people like you in it.' Worse even than Hitler. Why? Mad. Crazy.

He desperately wanted to talk to somebody who was *sane*.

But *who*? Who was sane in this great big loony bin? Then he remembered Bob Steadman. He was always kind and friendly and, unlike Briggs, he was a proper vicar. He'd always got on well with him. But then he'd thought he got on well with Mrs Watson and look what had happened! What if even Bob wouldn't listen to him? A vague notion of suicide, misty as yet, began to form in the depths of his mind.

It wasn't far to Bob's place in Queen's Road. He'd been there several times before and he knew the way. As he walked briskly through the red brick streets, the calm, watery sunshine and the soft blue sky seemed to reassure him. Maybe the world wasn't completely mad after all.

Soon he was in the street of tall Edwardian houses. Built to house lower-middle-class clerks and petty shopkeepers at the turn of the century, there were no trees or gardens, just harsh red brick and front doors that opened directly onto the pavement. With the sandstone mullioned windows and the ornate lintels, the street lacked the naked cut-price utilitarianism of Gloucester Road, but it was definitely a step down from the leafy opulence of Fern Avenue where Beacobsfield School was.

Faced with the doorbell marked 'Steadman', he had a moment of panic. What was he to say to him? With Bob Steadman he'd always been the big, tough *lad*: last summer it had been he who'd forged the way up through the crags that encircled the lordly summit of Sgurr na Ciche at the far end of lonely and roadless Loch Nevis: and how Bob had praised him for it! But now he had been reduced to a squalid little retard. Worse even, a dirty little shit-stabber. It was as bad as going up to a teacher and telling him that you'd messed your pants. What *would* Bob think of him?

Eventually he managed to press the bell and the buzzer sounding as the door unlocked indicated that Bob was in. Now for it! He opened the door and clambered up the white-painted and carpetless staircase to the bachelor den on the top floor under the roof. The fresh-faced, bushy eyebrowed young vicar opened the door and, beaming as always with bonhomie, effusively welcomed him.

'Ah, John! Great to see you! Now what can I do for you?'

The words just wouldn't come.

'Shouldn't you be at school? You've been crying. What's happened?'

No reply. Just trickling tears.

'Well, come in and tell me about it.'

Just a Dirty Little Bender

Steadman's den, never noted for its orderliness, was more than usually untidy. Papers and books were strewn over the armchair and settee and covered the floor like the results of a tornado. In one corner stood an easel with a half-finished oil painting on it – a wild mountain landscape, probably a derivation of Loch Nevis – and, beside it, an old chair adorned with a sticky, multicoloured palette, a pile of half-squeezed tubes of oil paint and several jars containing paint brushes of varying shapes and sizes. The whole room reeked of turpentine. All of it was a visible sign of Steadman's frustrated creative impulses. It was some time before he managed to clear a big enough space on the settee for John to sit on.

He'd never seen the kid in this state before. He felt encouraged, even a little excited. Here, at last, was a chance to use those 'counselling skills' he'd so assiduously acquired on one of his many 'social awareness' courses.

John sat down timorously.

'Well, what's it all about?'

But John just sat there. Still the words wouldn't come. To his intense embarrassment the trickle of tears became a stream.

Faced with a brick wall, Steadman slipped into his

bedroom and phoned Beaconsfield. He got Miss Curry, the reclusive school secretary who inhabited a little den next to Mrs Watson's study. It was a secret room, a sanctum unknown to the boys of Beaconsfield. Out of charity, Mrs Watson had employed her, but due to financial constraints, only part-time. This, old Curry resented, and by way of revenge she refused to have anything to do with the staff or pupils of the school. She was gruff and surly as she answered the phone.

'I've got young Denby round here. He's in a real state. What's happened to him?'

'He's been expelled.'

'Good lord! Can you tell my why?'

'No I can't. It's not in my remit.'

With that she put the phone down.

Expelled from a place like Beaconsfield? That took some doing. And the prize pupil, too. Steadman felt excited. Young Denby must have done something pretty gruesome. Drugs? Grevious Bodily Harm? Murder even? This was going to be interesting.

He returned eagerly to the sitting room, shoved some papers off the armchair and sat down opposite John.

He spoke calmly and gently. 'So you have been expelled from Beaconsfield. What have you done?'

There was no reply. The boy turned away and looked at the floor. The big teardrops made a puddle on the carpet.

Steadman had always liked this skinny, goggle-eyed little thirteen-year-old with his mop of white hair, so full of life, so creative, so appreciative. He had to stop himself favouring him too much. Now that he so obviously needed his help, he felt flattered and paternal. But in situations like these you got nowhere with direct questions; he'd learnt that much.

'Make yourself comfortable,' he said eventually. 'I'll get you a cup of cocoa and, when you're ready, you can tell me all about it. Sugar and milk?'

A vague nod.

Steadman disappeared into the grubby chaos of his small kitchen and busied himself with filling his electric kettle and rinsing out some dirty mugs that had sat in the sink for the past four days.

Meanwhile John studied the white-painted bookcase which occupied most of the wall in front of him. It was crammed full of all sorts of interesting books; not the sort of things you'd have expected a vicar to read. There were vast, weighty tomes about biology, chemistry, genetics and human genes, psychiatry. Then, lighter and more populist things: *White Holes: The Birth of the Universe?*, *The Case for Atheism*. And very interesting books about exploration: *Across the Dark Continent* by Henry Morton Stanley, *The Albert Nyanza* by Samuel Baker, *Missionary Travels* by David Livingstone.

Forgetting his misery, he got up to take a closer look and discovered books about mountain climbing: *World Mountains* by John Cleare, *The Big Walks* by Richard Gilbert. Then his eye caught a title called *Young Explorers*, also by Richard Gilbert. Curious, he pulled it out and flipped through the pages. It was about schoolboys climbing big mountains in far-off, exotic places: Iceland, Morocco, and even the Himalayas. He'd always imagined that only specially selected supermen went to places like that, people like Lord Hunt, Sir Edmund Hillary and Chris Bonnington. He found a photograph of a ferocious fang of rock called Kolahoi and then a photograph of a schoolboy standing on its airy summit. A wave of longing flowed out of him. That schoolboy was what *he* wanted to be like: tough, bold, able to scale fearsome mountains. But he never could be: he was just a dirty little bender and shit-stabber. Overwhelmed with shame and self-disgust, he replaced the book and sat down.

'Is that all?'

Steadman eventually returned with a steaming mug of cocoa.

'Now, when you're ready.'

John sipped the soothing liquid. How could possibly mention *that*? It was so degrading. But... well, it had to come out some time! Screwing himself up tight, he prepared the ground.

'Promise not to get angry. Please! Don't shout at me! Don't hit me. Promise!' Oh God, it was back to being the dirty little weed who'd pissed his sleeping bag that night in Scotland two years ago! He was even using the very same words! The shame of it!

'Of course not.'

Silence.

'You're absolutely sure?'

'Absolutely.'

'Well, it's very bad. Very, very bad.'

'It's not a matter for the police is it? You haven't gone and killed somebody, have you?' That *would* be interesting!

'No, it's much worse than that. Much worse.'

'Well?'

'It's so embarrassing. I'm so ashamed. So ashamed.'

'Go on.' This was getting juicier by the minute!

With a huge effort of will, which reminded him of a power-driven wrench which fastened the nuts onto the wheels of cars in a garage, John told his story. It was awful, excruciating. Admitting to this man, your hero, the man you so desperately wanted to impress with your gung-ho manliness, that you were an unpermissible biological mutation. Worse than filling your pants in Assembly in front of the whole school...

'I mean... I... well... I went and shafted him. I didn't mean to. It just went and happened. Danny's my best friend. Now he hates me. Now they all hate me.'

Silence.

'Is that *all*?'

Silence. Tears flowing.

A Little Theology of a Different Sort, From a Frustrated Missionary

Steadman's first reaction was disappointment. No high drama. No redeeming of a murderer's soul. No weaning off drugs. No grand Dostoyevskian saga of sin and repentance. Just a silly little bit of adolescent smut, the sort of mucky triviality that was best hidden behind a locked lavatory door. Oh, the banality of it all!

'And why do you think that's so bad?' he said eventually.

'Well, it's disgusting.'

'But so are most bodily functions. As a trained biologist I know all about the animal side of human beings. We're risen animals. We carry a lot of our animal behaviour with us. It's neither good nor bad. It's just there.'

'A biologist? I thought you were a vicar.'

'I am. But I was a research biologist before I took holy orders. But, tell me, why do you think that what you've done is so bad?'

'Well, it's sodomy and Mr Briggs says it's so bad that it cannot be forgiven. God sends you to hell for it. Even Hitler wasn't as bad as that.'

'And just how does Mr Briggs know that?'

'Well, he's a Christian. He's been saved. He reads the Bible and he knows what's right and wrong. He goes to the Tabernacle in Ellesmere Road.'

Steadman leant back and sighed deeply. 'The Tabernacle?' he spluttered. 'Not *that* lot!'

John had touched an exposed nerve here. Professional status, territorial imperative, or just plain wounded vanity, call it what you would: it was all there. As a theology student Steadman had spent long hours – years even – chewing over the subtleties and inconsistencies of that extraordinary ragbag of violence, bigotry, racism, moral grandeur and deep human insight called the Bible. What did this word actually *mean*? Had its original impact been blurred in its translation from Hebrew into English via Greek and Latin? Linguistics, as he well knew from those intellectual drubbings at theological college, could be fiendishly complicated. Besides, the ancient Middle East was so utterly different from the modern world that it needed all the wiles of a trained anthropologist to even begin to penetrate it. How much of this passage was influenced by Egyptian Wisdom Literature and how much by Babylonian myth? He'd spent years on a PhD thesis on the relationship between the Pharisees and the Essenes, and having lost his way in a linguistic and anthropological jungle, had been forced to lay it aside for a while. Only last month had he completed it and submitted it for appraisal.

Yet down at Ellesmere Road, those self-elected 'saved saints', simply swept aside the entire notion of scholarship. The whole Bible business could just as well have happened in a modern suburb of Boldonbridge. Forget about history and anthropology: throw it all in the bin! These people were lethal. They reduced everything to banality. They could destroy all he wanted to achieve. They could even destroy him.

He became testy. 'Now listen to me, young man,' he snapped. 'They're not scholars. I *am*. The Bible isn't a once-and-for-all series of instructions. It's a very human document. It's the ancient world talking to you. It's full of all sorts of contradictions and misunderstandings.'

'But isn't it the word of God?'

'Not quite. It's words *about* God. It's human beings groping their way towards God. Like you might do in a dark corridor when there's no light. You know the general direction, but quite often you go the wrong way and trip up. There's deep wisdom there, but you've got to know where to find it.'

'Oh?' John was becoming genuinely interested.

'I mean, take the story of Adam and Eve. Of course it's not literally true. Any fool knows that. It's a Mesopotamian creation myth. But there's deep thought lurking in it. In the Garden of Eden, Adam and Eve are small children, animals really. They frolic about and live for the moment. They are unaware of death and suffering. But when they eat from the tree of knowledge, they grow up and become aware of death and suffering. But they have been given the power of God. They have the ability to do something about it, but equally they can use that power to destroy themselves. But I digress. It's an intellectual's failing, you know.

'Now, back to you. You're thirteen years old and you've had a testosterone surge. It happens at your age. Your body suddenly pours eight hundred per cent more of the stuff into your bloodstream, and it can send you crazy. It's like having a swill of vodka on an empty stomach. It can be difficult to control yourself, especially if – like you – you don't know what's happening to you.'

'But doing it with another boy?'

'That's fairly normal. Inside you there are chemicals, some of which make you heterosexual – that's what most people call normal – and some which make you homosexual. The mix varies from person to person. Some people are more one way than the other. Often youngsters go through a homosexual phase until the chemicals even out. It's nothing to be ashamed of. It just happens. What you've got to do is learn to control it. Sexual urges are like violence and alcoholism. We've all got them, but for the sake of society as a whole, we've got to keep them in check. They're a bomb inside you. They can blast everything to bits. I mean just think what would have happened if Danny had been a girl and you'd got her pregnant? Then you really would have been in trouble.'

'But, if it's normal, as you say, then why is everybody so angry with me?'

'Firstly, because they are pig ignorant and don't know anything about it. Secondly, because they have similar urges themselves and are frightened of them. They conceal their fear behind a mask of aggression. And thirdly, because of their primitive instincts. Here's a biology lesson for you, Jonny boy. People – especially kids – are very like chickens. Aggression is part of their make-up. It's necessary for survival if you are a caveman living in a small hunter-gather group on the dangerous savannahs of tropical Africa. Also they have an innate tendency to destroy anything among them that is weak or different; necessary to keep the gene pool up to scratch. It might have helped our ancestors to survive, but in the modern world it is very dangerous and can destroy us. It is a cause of war and crime. A convenient shorthand for it is Original Sin. It's in all of us.

And, Jonny boy, you *are* different from the others. I've often wondered why you are at Beaconsfield. You talk differently from the others, and that can cause hostility for a start. Also, you're abler than the others, better at things than most of them, and they resent that. When things go wrong you're a natural target.'

'But why does Mr Briggs hate me? I've always tried to be good. I don't muck about in the PE lessons like some of the other kids. I always do my best for his rugby team. Not like Billy Nolan who just fools about. You'd think he'd like that. And he's always going on about Rickerby Hall, that posh prep school I was at. I mean, what's that got to do with anything?'

'My dear fellow, people often hate you not for anything that you've ever done, but because of what you are. Mr Briggs has been taught at his teacher training college that the upper classes who send their kids to posh prep schools are the enemy. So, having come from Rickerby Hall, you are the enemy.'

'But that's pathetic!'

'Of course it is, but that's what the world is like. At the posh public school I was at we hated all state school pupils. Why? Because they weren't us. People have to have something to hate. Hatred is a great bonding force. It makes for social cohesion. After all, Hitler needed the Jews. I'm afraid you'll have to get used to it. But don't worry too much, the present thing will blow over. It's you today, it'll be somebody else tomorrow.

Anyway, sex isn't the only thing in life. Not unless you're very stupid, that is, and you should feel sorry for people like that. Life can be very hard for them. But you're lucky. You've got a lot going for you. Put your energy into things like sport and mountain climbing. Don't get obsessed with sex. And, a final word, just remember that if God didn't exist, we'd have to invent him just to save ourselves from ourselves.'

Silence followed. All very reassuring. John had never thought of this before. A step into the adult world – the forbidden fruit from that tree of knowledge?

Then suddenly he slipped back into childhood. He became that small boy of two years ago on that Scottish campsite who'd had a nightmare and run into Mrs Watson's tent, frantic for attention. It was as if he'd been climbing up a steep hillside, grasped at a rock near the summit, only to go tumbling down to the bottom.

'Yes, but what's going to happen to me?' he wailed. 'I've been expelled and my father will send me back to Greenhill where they'll beat me up like they did before. I'm so frightened! I'm so frightened!'

He began to sob like a small child. 'I thought Mrs Watson was my mum. I thought she liked me. But now she's turned against me. I've no one. I might as well throw myself in the river!'

'Throw myself in the river!' Corny, melodramatic plea for attention? Yes! But, nevertheless, Steadman was loving it.

After a brilliantly promising academic career, he had gone into the Anglican Church determined to achieve great things. A vision of his hero, John Henry Newman, had floated before him. But he would go further. In this increasingly secular world, he would reconcile science and religion. He would staunch the flow of unbelief by proving the validity and necessity of Christianity. It was a mission for which he had been specially chosen. Heady stuff, indeed; but things hadn't worked out that way. He'd found himself shunted into a dreary suburb, surrounded by banal and unreceptive minds. Sidelined. Marginalised.

'You're a real brain box,' the man who lived in the flat below him had said one day, 'So why are you doing a job like this? I mean vicars are way out of date now. All this God stuff is only for old ladies and the odd nutter. Intelligent people don't waste time on it.'

Now here was his chance to prove his usefulness. To prove that, far from being an outdated superstition, Christianity really *did* matter. That hint of suicide added just that extra bit of spice. He could get somewhere with this kid. It could be the start.

But there was something else lurking there, something he hardly dared to admit even to himself. This boy was *attractive*. And quite possibly 'one of us'. But control yourself, my man! Down that path lies ruin: exposure, ridicule, prison, labelled as a paedophile, shame and degradation. Help this poor creature, yes, but resist the Demon that whispers unmentionable things into your ear; or, rather, stirs up testosterone in awkward places.

'All right! All right!' he said to the attention-seeking heap of misery on the settee. 'We'll sort things out. You're not alone. There are people who'll help you. Meanwhile you just stay here while I do a little arranging. Feel free to look at the books. There's some that might interest you.'

When the boy tried to embrace him, he pushed him gently aside. Physical contact could set off a chain reaction that might have unforeseen results! Then he went into his bedroom and picked up the telephone. First he rang Dorothy Watson to find out what was going on.

No Longer an Emotional Woman?

At that precise moment Dorothy Watson was suggestible. Walking home through the calm and friendly sunshine that afternoon, she'd been fixed in 'Mrs Watson, Professional Teacher' mode. Realistic, hard-bitten, fully in control of her emotions. Having taken a tough decision, she'd felt relieved; proud of herself, indeed, as if she'd just passed a difficult exam. Nobody could call her an 'Emotional Woman' now. If only Lawrence could have seen her!

She entered the silent house. Looking into John's room, she found it empty. He had gone, leaving an unmade bed and a scatter of books and videos on the floor. Then she saw the book about world railways that she'd given him for his birthday and a lump came into her throat. In the hall outside she noticed the expensive plate he'd given her that celebrated Christmas two years ago… and then the even more expensive plate he'd given her last Christmas and next to it his painting of Loch Nevis and a fantastically sheer Sgurr na Ciche that she'd had specially framed. All part of the irretrievable past, now! Her child, her only child, the one she'd longed for and cherished… gone, leaving a silent and empty void behind him. Suddenly she burst into tears.

Then the telephone rang. It was Steadman.

'Look, I've got young Denby round here. He's in quite a state. What's going on?'

'Hasn't he told you?'

'In a muddled sort of way, yes. But, frankly, isn't it all rather an over-reaction? I mean, the whole business seems rather trivial to me.'

The condescending tone needled her. Steadman was a great vicar, but he was so pushy, so tactless... give him half an inch and he'd take five miles. If you weren't careful, he'd end up running your school for you. It was a matter of credibility.

The 'Hard-Bitten Professional' mode began to revive. 'Mr Steadman, I really can't have homosexuality in my school. In the opinion of my staff....'

'You mean in the opinion of James Briggs.'

'Well, he was the one who saw the incident.'

'And you take his views seriously? A mere PE teacher from St Martin's College?'

Vintage Steadman, this! Under his breezy bonhomie there lurked an intellectual snob of formidable proportions. First-class degree from the University of Cambridge versus certificate from St Aiden's Teacher Training College. Hackles rose.

'Mr Steadman, as Headmistress of Beaconsfield School, I have to take hard decisions in the interests of my school. It is my duty to run this school as I see fit.'

'And you think it's fit to destroy a fatherless and motherless thirteen-year-old who's had a silly accident, do you?'

This was too much. Steadman overstepping the mark as usual! Dorothy slammed the receiver down.

End of Argument. Or Was It?

End of argument. Or was it? That insight with which she had been blessed – or cursed? – began to nibble away at her. Why was it so difficult to run a small school? She'd had a ghastly day. That morning she'd had an indignant and self-righteous Mr Fleetwood sounding off in her study: 'My boy. My lad. I can take a lot of things, Mrs Watson, but not benders or child abusers. You really gotta *do* sommat!' And so on for over an hour.

Had she been a weak and emotional woman by letting him ramble on like that? Him, a brassy and coarse garage owner who flogged dubious second hand cars to gullible would-be machos who fancied themselves as budding Fangios? And, what was more, let his thirteen-year-old son watch luridly pornographic videos?

Oh Dolly, you weak woman! Massaging your ego by picking on a soft target like little John Denby! You're no better than Billy Nolan who picks on vulnerable juniors to get a bit of corridor cred! Call yourself a headmistress!

She spent that night in floods of tears.

A Matter of Credibility

She was sleepy and headachy all the following Friday. She made no mention of John's expulsion in Morning Assembly. In the break, Briggs cornered her.

'Isn't it time you made a formal announcement about it? I mean it's a serious question of discipline. Mr Fleetwood... '

'I'm not sure it's necessary to labour the point.'

That worried Briggs. Was she starting to go soft on Denby?

Answer: yes. But she wasn't going to admit it in public – 'credibility', you know.

Assailed by an Ecclesiastical Gorilla and its Mate

She'd hardly arrived home that evening before the telephone rang. It was the Bishop of Boldonbridge. Immediately she stiffened, like a private soldier when he sees a general. The Bishop was no frustrated and struggling young Cambridge graduate. He was an important member of her governing body and a considerable – if very controversial! – force in the city. At crucial moments in the past he had been one of her most stalwart supporters. She couldn't afford to get onto her high horse with him.

He was direct and aggressive. 'I've got young Denby staying with me. It seems you've thrown him out. What's going on?'

Desperately, she tried to defend herself. 'Well, he was sexually interfering with other boys. I simply cannot allow this sort of thing to go on in my school. I must insist on standards.'

'Quite so! Quite so! But, even if the lad *was* abusing other pupils – and having interviewed him myself, that's far from being proven, *very* far! – isn't Beaconsfield School there to help youngsters with problems? I had thought that was its purpose.'

'But homosexuality is more than a problem. When it involves abusing children it's a perversion, a crime. It's something for a psychiatrist.'

'Oh for Heaven's sake!' the Bishop exploded. 'And you call yourself a biology teacher!'

Donald Macnab, Bishop of Boldonbridge, had never felt the need to be tactful. Indeed, he was something of a bully who enjoyed flaunting his strength, both physical and mental. He was a man of Causes. The relevance of Christianity in the modern world was the main one. But it was rather too abstract and needed a more tangible Cause to highlight it, just as William Wilberforce had had the negro slaves. The problem had been which Cause to choose. So many of them had been appropriated by others. Amnesty International had cornered the political oppression business. Whales and pandas were best left to the World Wildlife Fund. In the end he'd picked on gay rights, prompted on part by his experiences as an army officer in charge of young soldiers in Northern Ireland.

But it was vital that a Relevant Church should do more than just talk about it. He was heavily into politics. Inspired by Len Bowman in London, he'd teamed up with Jonnie Pearson, the local Liberal Party activist, to create a similar Rainbow Coalition in Boldonbridge- 'inclusiveness', caring for the casualties of a callous Thatcherism; oppressed minorities fighting back. Even the 'scientific socialists' and professional atheists up at the university found this package hard to resist. Women priests, gay marriage? So what if the benighted Neanderthals of the Tabernacle frothed and fumed? It was just what he wanted. Donald Macnab positively relished a good fight.

It wasn't long before he had Dorothy reeling on the ropes. One after another the polemical bombs of a decade of campaigning exploded in her face. Didn't she *realise* that in Britain alone there were ten million homosexuals? What was statistically significant could hardly be called a perversion, could it? Was she aware of the latest genetic research, which indicated that... And so on for at least ten minutes, non-stop.

In vain she tried to defend herself. 'Be reasonable, please! I really cannot be seen to turn a blind eye to the activities of a promiscuous homosexual who debauches my pupils. I have to consider the other boys... and the opinions of the parents.'

'Debauches other boys? That's hardly true, for a start! Get the facts right, woman! Yes, let's stick to proven facts! All right, hate the sin – if it really *is* a sin! – but at least try to love the sinner. Now, when you took him on, I was impressed. Yes, deeply impressed. A sign of true Christian commitment. I strongly supported you with the governing body and the local education people. But, for heaven's sake, woman, you can't just drop him when he's become a bit inconvenient. I know a lady who's always buying puppies. It's all lovey-dovey when they're small and cute. But as soon as they get big and awkward she dumps them in the doggie home and buys another one. That's you, isn't it? Lovely when he is small and cute, not so good when he starts growing up. A puppy is not just for Christmas, it's for life, in case you didn't know it! I never imagined that you were a petty bourgeois sentimentalist.' (Having done a PhD on the relationship between Communism and Catholicism in Nicaragua, Donald Macnab was well versed in Marxist jargon.)

Eventually even he had to pause to catch his breath. A battered Dorothy had hardly picked herself off the floor before she was bowled over by another blast.

'Dorothy,' a shrill feminine voice trilled into the phone. 'How *could* you? Yes, just how *could* you?'

This was Isabel, the Bishop's wife – and also his rival – who had commandeered the second telephone in the house. She, too, was into Causes. Her's was 'neglected children'. To this end she spent her time gathering up the waifs and strays from the 'deprived areas' of the city, especially from Greenwood. But unfortunately these waifs and strays always refused to play the docile and appealing role allotted to them. They effed and blinded, ran round smoking cigarettes, and left disgusting messes in the toilet. Worse still, they stole and were not only sexually precocious, but sexually carnivorous, always ready to make advances and, even at the tender age of ten, well versed in all the arcanae of 'child abuse' which they exploited with all the skill and precision of a trained fighter pilot. Definitely not what an 'oppressed minority' should have been like.

But John Denby was apparently completely different. 'A *wonderful* boy! So polite, so considerate, such perfect manners. And so *creative*, too! Oh, Dorothy how *could* you be so unfeeling?'

When, after five or so minutes, the bombardment finally spluttered to a finish, the Bishop started up again. 'Anyway, I'll be having a word with Professor Hindmarsh. He's a big noise in matters sexual in case you didn't know it, and he'll put you right on a number of things!'

Hauled up before the Beak like a schoolgirl who hadn't done her homework? She, the Headmistress! It was so humiliating.

'Yes, yes,' she gasped as she put the receiver down. 'Thank you very much for your advice.'

Voices from a Lost Child

But be *strong*, Dorothy! Don't let domineering men manipulate you! You're a proper professional. Stand by your principles. After a moment's reflection she marched resolutely into John's room, determined to start clearing it out.

In a previous age she would have said that she'd seen his ghost or heard his voice. As soon as she opened the door she felt his presence: the unmade bed, the scatter of clothes she'd bought for him, the book on world railways she'd given him for his birthday lying open on the carpet. Her lost child! Her only child, given her by God and then betrayed by her! She burst into tears.

She went into the living room and sat down. There looking at her was the framed photograph of Margherita Peak. 'I'd love to go to the Ruwenzori Range. You haven't any more pictures have you?' She may not have heard that voice in the material world outside herself, but she certainly heard it in her mind. The eager, high-pitched tone was there, word for word. So was the bright-eyed and fascinated face. He was around her all the time.

So it went on all weekend. Wherever she went, he was there. Questioning her. Accusing her. On Sunday afternoon she decided that she needed a good, deep read to take her mind off him. So she picked up *Jane Eyre*, the book which had swept her off her feet as a sixteen-year-old and which still had a powerful hold on her.

The old magic worked and soon she became absorbed to the exclusion of everything else. Until she came to the bit where the voice of the wounded and deserted Rochester called her through the ether, 'Jane! Jane! Jane!' How she'd wept over this passage as a teenager! But now, did she hear John's pleading voice in the room? 'Miss! Miss! Miss!' She half believed that she did.

By Sunday evening the stately ship of her 'Unsentimental

Professionalism' was full of holes and leaking badly. Would she ever get her wayward protégé back again? What *was* happening to him?

2

Strange Adventures

'He's Nice Really'

The answer was: quite a lot. John had been going through a bewildering series of mutations. As Steadman had made his long and involved phone calls in the bedroom, he had sat on the settee enveloped in shame and self-disgust. *One day I'll be famous; yes, famous as a bender in jail!* He couldn't bear even to *look* at the books on the shelves in front of him. They simply reminded him of what he wanted to be and never could be.

Then Steadman had bounced back into the room full of beaming bonhomie. 'No problem, John! The Bishop's going to put you up till we've got this business sorted out.'

John let out a sigh of alarm and despair. 'Oh my God, not *him*!'

The Bishop had a fearsome reputation. Mekon had mentioned a school in a remote and irredeemably savage part of Uganda, which he'd brought to heel by 'drastic methods': thrashing, floggings. And there was talk of a stint in the army and intelligence operations in Northern Ireland involving 'third-degree' interrogations. He'd glimpsed him once during a Sunday service in the cathedral, a huge, towering figure with a great booming voice, shaggy eyebrows, a bristly chin and hair coming out of his ears. Alarming. Awesome. He'd make short work of shit-stabbers. John felt like crawling under the settee and hiding there like a frightened puppy.

'Oh don't look like *that* about it!' exclaimed Steadman. 'He's nice really. He likes you.'

John wasn't convinced.

Is This Man Really a Bishop?
After a while the doorbell buzzed.

'Come on, up you get!' said Steadman.

'Please, do I *have* to? Can't I just stay here?'

'Oh come *on*!'

That doom-laden Greenhill feeling returned as he crept downstairs; the terrified soldier hauled up before the firing squad. In the warm sunshine outside, everything changed. A vast, scruffy man in rumpled jeans, a grubby sweater and muddy trainers hailed him from beside a bright red and lovingly maintained sports car.

'Ah, John, old man! Come and get in!'

Only by looking very carefully did John recognise the frightening figure he'd seen two months ago, awesomely mitred and robed in the cathedral.

No chidings, no recriminations, no formal floggings with a rhinoceros hide whip... at least not *yet*. Instead the engine revved frantically and with a roar from the exhaust the car surged off into the watery sunshine. Ducking and diving his way through the traffic, the man was obviously a skilful driver; hardly what you would have expected a vicar to be, let alone a bishop. Soon they were out onto the bypass, bowling down the open road. A bemused John noticed that they were doing nearly 100 miles an hour. Wasn't the speed limit 70 mph? Weren't bishops meant to obey the law? Or was this man really a bishop? He certainly didn't look like one.

All the while the man kept up a stream of talk. 'I've heard a lot about you, John Denby... dab hand at art, I'm told... quite a mountain climber... hold the rugby team together. We'll soon sort you out. Mind, do keep your bits under control... causes no end of problems when you don't.'

Mutations. No longer a shit-stabber, but a big, bold lad again?

'Come on, let's go for a spin! Isabel, that's my better half, won't let me go fast. Dead boring driving her, always nagging on about the speed limit. But with you it's different.'

The car surged on through the evening sunshine, overtaking everything in sight. The Bishop's talk relapsed into aeronautical metaphors, World War II vintage. 'Coming on his tail now... Got him! Down he goes!... Next one, big bomber in sight.' (A big, lumbering, articulated truck.)

Suddenly the car slowed down. 'Police car coming up at six o'clock on my tail! Won't do for a bishop to get done for speeding. The *Daily Mail* would just love it, and so would the *Guardian*!'

Exhilarated by the speed and the rush of cool air, John felt an almost physical change coming over him. It was almost like a metamorphosis in a science fiction video. A proper lad once more, he chatted away about rugby matches, Sgurr na Ciche, railways and the Ruwenzori Range. He was surprised and gratified to discover that – unlike Giles, that other terrifying ogre – the man actually seemed to be interested in what he had to say. Always, of course, he was ultra-careful to remember his manners. He was desperate to make a good impression. After today's catastrophe he needed all the allies he could find.

Haunted House?

Eventually they turned off the motorway and drove through an opulent tree-lined suburb full of big, detached Edwardian houses, some brick, some stone and all set in spacious, leafy gardens. Swerving through an ornate cast iron gateway, the car swept up a drive flanked by sombre yew trees and skidded to a halt amid clouds of dust and gravel.

John eyed the house with trepidation. It was about the ugliest building he'd ever seen, a grotesque gothic pile made out of harsh red brick, all spikes and spindly turrets and adorned with randomly scattered glazed white tiles of the sort that you found in public lavatories. It was the kind of place you saw in horror films about vampires.

'Yes, it is a bit of an old morgue, isn't it?' declared the Bishop, noticing his surprise. 'But it's what they've given me to live in. It's my *palace*, would you believe it? Designed by a bloke called Josiah Richmond in the eighteen-eighties. Great fan of Ruskin's. Swallowed all he had to say hook, line and sinker. Consumptive. One of those beautiful young geniuses who die young. This is his monument. And what's your monument going to be, young man? Not something like this, I hope!'

John followed the Bishop up some sandstone steps and through a formal entrance consisting of a pointed white-tiled arch and a big brown door covered with weird floral and heraldic designs. He found himself in a cavernous stone hall, panelled in dark wood, with an ominously threatening hammer beam ceiling lowering down above him and dimly lit by stained glass windows in gothic arches. A big, old-fashioned wooden table stood in front of a vast, empty fireplace flanked by a couple of sinister-looking gargoyles with vicious fangs and long, sharp claws. The floor was of bare grey flagstones. The place could have been specially created as a set for a Dracula film. He half expected a vampire to emerge at any moment from one of those big wooden doors at the far end.

Which almost did seem to happen when suddenly one of them creaked open and a tall, bony, beaky-nosed woman swept up to him. (God Almighty, what *was* this apparition? Had it emerged from some coffin hidden in the creepy depths of this sinister building?)

'Ah, Isabel!' boomed the Bishop. 'This is him, John, our latest trophy, another addition to our collection!'

The aquiline woman's Medusa face twisted up into a ghastly grin. Help! Perhaps she really *was* a vampire! You never know what's going to happen on crazy days like this!

'Oh John!' she exclaimed in a high-pitched voice as she rushed up and embraced him. 'You're all right now! All your troubles are over!'

John writhed. Treated like a little kid! But remember your manners! If people are being nice to you, be nice back to them. With an immense effort he managed to smile sweetly and submitted to the knobbly and suffocating embrace. Mercifully, she didn't grow fangs and bite his jugular vein – at least not *yet*, but when the sun went down, who knew what might happen?

'*Do* come in and have some tea,' she cooed. 'You must be awfully hungry after your terrible day!'

He switched on his ingratiating smile. 'Thank you very much indeed. It really is most kind of you. But, first, please can I wash my hands?' Back into 'good little boy' mode – ugh! But necessary for survival.

'I'll show you to the toilet!' an educated voice brayed out from behind him.

He turned round to see a thin young man – almost a walking broomstick – with a long horse-like face, deathly white and crowned with a mop of straggly black hair tied up in an untidy ponytail. Draped over his skeletal frame were baggy blue jeans and a grubby black T-shirt, much the worse for wear. He seemed to have suddenly appeared from nowhere and looked uncannily like a walking corpse that a vampire had drained of its blood. Christ, was Dracula himself going to burst through one of those gothic doors to accompanying flashes of lightning and peals of thunder? Perhaps!

Before he could reply the creature grabbed his arm and hustled him away down a long, red-carpeted, brick-walled corridor. Opening another of those big wooden doors, he ushered him into a kind of mini chapel with stained glass windows and a rib-vaulted ceiling. Inside, instead of an altar, there was a massive Victorian lavatory, a real masterpiece of nineteenth-century sanitary engineering: all white china, floral patterns and polished wood, and surmounted by a complex array of gleaming metal pipes. It was set on a little podium and you approached it as to a throne. In the eyes of its designer it was clearly an altar to the God of Sanitation, one of those seminal Victorian achievements you read about in the more boring chapters of history books.

'Golly!' he ejaculated, almost stunned by the vision. Desperate for a pee – for, with all the traumas of the day, his natural functions had been forgotten and his 'liquids' had accumulated to bursting point – he tried to shut the door. But the creature-vampire, zombie, or whatever it was,- prevented him by putting its foot in the way.

'We have no closed doors in this house, John, dear.'

'Dear'? (What was going on here?) 'But, please, I need the toilet.'

'Go ahead. There's nothing to be ashamed of.'

'But can't I close the door?'

'No you can't.'

The 'thing' seemed determined to watch him having his pee. For a moment he hesitated and then sheer biological necessity overcame any embarrassment. When he pulled the ornate, china-tipped chain he unleashed a veritable Niagara of slooshings and gurglings and rushing torrents of water, proclaiming far and wide the user's virtuous dedication of cleanliness.

In the midst of the cataclysm the Bishop's voice suddenly boomed out. 'Ah, *there* you are! I thought for one ghastly moment that Cedric had carried you off to his den! Can't have that!'

Guest of Honour... and Odd Company

He was ushered back to the hall and then through the wooden door from which Isabel had emerged, and on down another corridor. This one was painted white, carpeted and in good repair.

'These are our living quarters,' declared the Bishop. 'No point in trying to colonise the whole wretched barn. Can't afford to. We've made this end habitable. Say a prayer every night to prevent the rest collapsing on us.'

They entered a light, airy dining room. The wooden panelling was all painted white and the big, gothic picture windows opened out onto a spacious and well kept lawn surrounded by trees. It was a profound relief after the haunted house gloom of the entrance hall. There before him was a long table, laden with all manner of gastronomic delights: ice cream, meringues, sticky buns, jammy doughnuts and huge bottles of Coke. Hovering over it like a vulture was Isabel.

'Ah, John, dear, you must be so *hungry* after your ordeal. This is all for *you*! Sit down and eat as much as you want.'

From a dirty little outcast to a guest of honour! Weird. Weird. Suddenly he remembered that he hadn't eaten properly for the last thirty hours and that he was desperately hungry. But before he attacked that gorgeous pile of meringues, he remembered his manners. Not just habit, however, but necessary for survival. So before he sat down, he ostentatiously offered Isabel the plate of meringues.

'This is most kind of you. I really appreciate it. But, please, after you.'

Her pointed face creased up into its vampire leer. 'Oh, thank you, John. You are *so* considerate.'

So it went on for the next half-hour. Every time he moved on to the next plate of goodies he made an elaborate point of offering it first to Isabel and then to the Bishop. Grease the wheels! Grease the wheels! And it seemed to be working – with Isabel, at any rate. Soon she was eating out of his hand. The Bishop, of course, was another matter.

Meanwhile he noticed that Cedric, sitting at the far end of the table, was staring at him.

'Cedric, would you like a doughnut? They're delicious.'

There was no reply. The long, corpse-like face continued to stare at him.

Suddenly a door at the far end of the room opened and another apparition appeared: a wildly untidy young man in filthy jeans and a strange sheepskin waistcoat, barefoot and with big, staring eyes. A long, beaky nose protruded from an anarchic tangle of brown hair and beard, looking like a chick peeping out of a bird's nest.

'Ah, *do* come in, Jason!' cooed Isabel. 'It's tea time.'

'Time,' said the apparition in a calm and clear voice. 'Time? It never is time is it? Time for the uprising? Time for renewal? Yes!'

Then, like a ghost, it disappeared through the door again.

John was unsettled. 'Another addition to our collection.' What other grotesques – vampires, living dead, undead or whatever – lurked in this extraordinary place? Didn't bear thinking about. But he was too polite to say so.

'Don't worry about Jason,' said Isabel reassuringly. 'He's a bit strange at times. He's just having one of his turns today.'

'Don,' she added turning to the Bishop and speaking

in a new authoritarian voice, 'have you remembered his medications?'

'Thanks for reminding me!' growled the Bishop, dashing out of the room after him.

'Jason's our only son,' Isabel whispered to John. 'He's been having a few problems lately.'

The meal eventually ended, with John feeling bloated. He ostentatiously thanked Isabel and made an elaborate show of helping to clear the table.

'Can I help with the washing up?'

'That would be most kind of you.'

Now that Ma Watson had ditched him, he was desperate for a new mum; one who he could trust and who wouldn't chuck him out on a whim. So pile on the treacle by the bucketful! Weighed down by a mountain of plates, he followed Isabel into a large, old-fashioned kitchen, all wooden tables, stone slabs and gigantic 1950s Aga cookers. He duly filled a huge sink with hot water and then, with an orgiastic frenzy of washing-up liquid and Brillo pads, attacked the ever-increasing pile of crockery she produced.

His hands were still warm and soapy when she led him off along a dusty corridor and into a sprawling workshop type of room at the far end of the house. On a couple of long wooden benches was a jumbled mass of glue pots, paint pots, brushes, scissors, pencils and stacks of paper, some white, others coloured.

'John, I *know* you are very creative! We *so* need a frieze for the Easter Service at the cathedral. I wonder if you could help?'

It was just what he wanted: a chance to lose himself in an interesting task and forget about his troubles. And, more important, to impress these people who were his only hope. The trauma of the day had sharpened his mind and he plunged in with frenetic energy. After three hours he had produced the required 'Up to Date and Modern Crucifixion', a vast collage of a thing with an SS Panzer division on the rampage, complete with burning buildings, Stukas, barbed wire and a gas chamber, and in the background three large black crosses on a hill, silhouetted against the smoke-filled sky. Then, seeing some old tins and cigar boxes lying around, he made an ancient, balloon-funnelled steam locomotive and doused it with black enamel paint. It symbolised the struggling poverty of the Third World. It was well past ten o'clock when, with grubby and paint-stained hands, he presented his creations to Isabel.

'Oh John!' she cooed. 'You are *so* clever, so *creative*! So *talented*!'

This one's a pushover, much easier than Ma Watson ever was! So keep working on her. From dirty little bender, to pathetic cry baby, to honoured guest and now to acclaimed artist? What an extraordinary day!

An Unforgettable Bath... and Apparitions

It was bedtime.

'You'll be wanting a bath, darling,' said Isabel. 'Here's a towel and some soap and I'll show you the way.'

With that she led him along to the entrance hall – gloomier and more cavernous than ever in the darkness – and up the big stone staircase with its Castle Dracula-style balustrade that swept grandiloquently up from it, and then along a shabby, red-carpeted corridor that branched off to the left. As he followed her down the dusty tunnel, he noticed Cedric's lugubrious, corpse-like face staring at him from behind a threadbare red curtain.

Opening a large, heavy door, Isabel ushered him into a small, white-tiled room filled to capacity with a vast museum piece of a bath.

'Here you are, darling,' she said. 'Now be careful with the

taps. They're rather stiff and the water's very hot. You see, the thermostat doesn't work properly. When you've finished, come back downstairs and I'll show you to your bedroom.'

With that she swept away, leaving him to puzzle over the complexities of the immense piece of Victorian hydraulic engineering that confronted him. First he had to close the door. For some weird reason it seemed to prefer being opened rather than being closed and it was only after a considerable battle with its ancient and rusty hinges that he finally managed to shut it. Then he noticed that there was no way of locking it, which was awkward! But, being fixed into 'best behaviour' mode, he obviously had to do as Isabel had said and have a bath. So he quickly undressed and, climbing out of his school uniform and folding it up neatly, placed it carefully on the ornate towel rail.

Now he faced the awesome mysteries of the antique waterworks before him. Eventually he discovered that by pressing a big brass lever you put the plug into the bath. Then he attacked the two huge porcelain-capped taps. The bath itself was a colossal iron vat big enough to wash a horse in. Standing on tiptoe, he found he could just reach the far tap. As Isabel had said, it was stiff and it required all his strength to twist it. Suddenly a geyser of boiling hot water exploded out of it, nearly scalding him and momentarily blinding him in clouds of steam. After further frantic wrenching he managed to get some water out of the cold tap and was able to fill the cavernous trough with a suitably temperate mixture.

Getting into it was quite exciting: a mini-mountaineering expedition which involved trying not to take a header onto the stone floor while you hauled your leg over the smooth and slippery edge and dropped into the steaming maelstrom below. Finally, however, he slid into the deliciously warm water and luxuriated in its soothing balm: the answer to all his troubles.

Suddenly there was a scraping and groaning sound as the

big wooden door creaked slowly open. Through the billowing clouds of steam there emerged… Cedric! Caught starkers! The sheer embarrassment! Frantically he grabbed a conveniently placed flannel and tried to cover his more 'biological' bits.

Cedric's corpse-like face loomed up as he knelt down and gripped the sides of the bath. In a soft and purposely soothing voice he began to speak.

'I know all about you. You *must* understand that you're not bad. You're good. Very *good*! It's beautiful. Truly beautiful.'

What *was* this thing – vampire, zombie, or whatever – on about?

Cedric paused and then continued, 'You're just more fully aware. A deeper and more beautiful person. So let's celebrate your beauty…'

Then a long and skinny arm reached out like a squid's tentacle and a cold hand gripped John's left elbow while the other arm moved down towards his thighs. Desperately John struggled as he fought a losing battle to keep the flannel in place. Mounting alarm made him drop the 'good boy' façade.

'*Gerroff!*' he screamed. '*Gerroff! Leave me alone! I don't like it!*'

Just then a bomb seemed to explode. A stentorian bellow blasted out of the corridor, '*Let him go Cedric! He's not for you!*'

The Bishop, a towering, thunderous figure, all bulging muscles, black hair and bushy eyebrows, burst through the clouds of steam. Cedric released John and cringed against the wall. It was like that scene from the horror film when the hero confronted Dracula with a crucifix.

'But I *need* it!' wailed Cedric. 'I've *got* to have it!'

'Maybe, but not with him!'

'Look Don, it's not sex, it's *love*!'

'Rubbish! Come on out!'

'Have a heart, man! It's like the sacrament at Holy

Communion. Physical expression of a spiritual reality. Christian love. What you're always on about!'

'Cedric, we've been through all this before. You can't have it with kids.'

'But you have it with Isabel so why can't I have it with him?'

'Because she's an adult and he's a boy.'

'That's not fair! It's discrimination.'

'Look, if you lay a hand on him it'll be back to prison again! Flan and that lot will be waiting for you. Remember what they did the last time?'

'You wouldn't grass on me, would you? Not me. You're a Christian.'

'Oh come on *out*!'

'No! No!'

Cedric curled himself up like a naughty child who wouldn't drink his milk. Whereupon the massive and burly Bishop grabbed his shoulder and dragged him towards the door.

'Stoppid! Lemme go!' squealed Cedric as he threw a vicious punch into his assailant's side.

A colossal blow from the Bishop felled him in an instant. Whimpering weakly, he was picked up and heaved out into the corridor.

'All right, John,' the Bishop boomed through the open door. 'You can finish your ablutions in peace.'

John cowered in awe. Message understood: whatever you do, don't mess with this bloke. He duly finished and clambered out of the great iron trough, dried himself and dressed. Bright and shiny, he made his way along the corridor. On the landing, suddenly and like an apparition, Jason, the Bishop's son, appeared out of the gloom.

'Are you ready?' he said in a calm and measured tone.

'Ready?'

'Yes, ready. It's time to start now. The Military Revolutionary Committee has unanimously voted to start the rising. If we don't act now, History will never forgive us. We're scientists. We know.'

'Sorry, but I don't understand.'

'No, of course you don't. Kamenev, you're weak. Part of the problem. Not part of the solution. It'll all burn. It's only cardboard, you know.'

Bewildered, John hurried downstairs.

The Bishop met him in the hall. 'I see you've had an encounter with Jason. Don't worry about him, or about Cedric for that matter. They're just poor lost souls. We look after society's casualties here.'

Society's casualties? So he wasn't that special after all! Just a younger version of Cedric or that strange, deluded wraith on the landing? How he had fallen! But they're being nice to you and, anyway, they're your only hope, so keep pouring on the treacle.

'It was a lovely bath. Thank you so much for helping me out with Cedric.'

In the dining room he found Isabel brandishing a tray of meringues and sticky buns. 'Help yourself, darling. This is your supper. And would you like cocoa, Horlicks or Ovaltine?'

Sweet smile. 'Thank you so much. You really are very kind. I'd love some Horlicks if it isn't too much trouble.'

He duly stuffed himself with the meringues, and luxuriated in the hot, creamy drink.

'Now I'll show you to your room.'

'Make sure you lock the door after you,' said the Bishop as Isabel led him upstairs.

It was back along the corridor, past the bathroom and into a small, modernish room at the far end. He squirmed as Isabel hugged and kissed him; he wanted to be a *lad*, not a soppy little kid! When she finally got round to going, he bolted the door firmly. God alone knew what other 'casualties' might be lurking unseen in this incomprehensible place! Stripping down to his underpants, he draped his clothes over a big wooden chair and climbed into the spacious, old-fashioned bed.

What a crazy, lunatic day! Where *was* he going? He seemed to be on a wild helter-skelter, plummeting down to he knew not where. On Tuesday he'd been a normal lad, secure and thriving. Then suddenly the ground had given way beneath him. It was uncannily like that day when his perfect Gran and Grandad had been torn from him. And just what *was* he? A big, bold lad? Pea-brained retard? Irredeemably awful shit-stabbing pervert? Brilliantly creative and promising young student? But, oh God, if he were to end up like Cedric or that grotesque apparition on the landing who seemed to think he was Lenin or something... ! Suddenly the sleep of exhaustion overwhelmed him.

Mutations: A Delicate Piece of China

He woke up to see bright sunlight streaming in through a large curtainless window. For a time he gazed at the unfamiliar room with its modern white radiator and wash basin and old-fashioned flowery wallpaper, quite unable to remember where he was. Then it all came back to him. Expelled from Beaconsfield. Cast into outer darkness. A disgusting bender. Despised by all his mates. And rightly so.

He felt like crying – indeed, a tear did trickle – but then he remembered that big boys didn't cry and just lay there wishing he were somebody else. However, practical considerations eventually took over. Should he get up? Should he wait till he was called? What was the right thing to do? Whatever else happened, he *had* to keep on the right side of these strange people; especially that big, terrifying ogre, the Bishop. They were his only hope.

In the end biology clinched the issue. He needed the bog, more desperately with every passing moment. So he hurriedly dressed and quietly opened the door. A quick decco. Coast clear. No sign of Cedric or Jason. Then a quick scuttle downstairs. This time he locked the toilet door and eventually emerged to the accompanying Niagara-like roar of the waterworks. Mission successful.

In the corridor he met Isabel. More gushing, more excruciating hugs, more kisses, and he was ushered into the dining room.

'What would you like for breakfast, darling? Cornflakes? Weetabix? Grape Nuts? Chocolate spread? Peanut butter?

Another mutation. This time he was a delicate piece of china that had to be carefully wrapped up, like those plates he'd bought Ma Watson for Christmas.

Another Mutation: Grovelling before the Beak... Plus Weird Confidences

Then everything changed. Thunder and lightning. Green light. Entry of the Devil into the kiddies' pantomime. The Bishop burst into the sunlit room, grubby and be-jeaned as if he was a workman who'd just finished digging up the road. A vast gorilla of a man, he towered over an alarmed John.

'*You*!' he growled. 'Into my study now! You've got a bit of explaining to do!'

John's insides seemed to melt. Not a piece of delicate china now, but a delinquent schoolboy hauled up before a terrifying Victorian schoolmaster of yore. He remembered Cedric cowering against the bathroom wall. His turn now! God, what had he *done*?

Trembling and feeling slightly sick, he followed the Bishop into a large, sombre and very gothic study; the sort of place you read about in books like *Tom Brown's Schooldays*.

The Bishop sat down on a big leather chair behind a large wooden desk. John remained standing in front of it. The great shaggy eyebrows seemed to bristle and the black hairs that came out of his ears to quiver, as the huge face creased up into an angry scowl.

'Now then,' he said with restrained aggression, 'I've been onto young Steadman again and, frankly, the story you told him doesn't make sense. You wouldn't be chucked out for one silly incident in the shower. Not out of a place like Beaconsfield anyway. There must have been more to it than that. So come on, let's have the truth.'

John gaped speechless, like a mouse scared motionless by an advancing python.

The Bishop continued. 'You'd better face facts, young man. You're in a mess. I'm what's standing between you and being taken into care. In case you don't know what that means, it means being dumped in a home full of Geordie yobbos who'll beat you up because they think you're posh, and being sent back to that Greenhill disaster, which is what your father wants. Where, I gather, you had a pretty ghastly time of it.'

He fixed John with an even more aggressive stare. 'So don't start trying to play me along. I can always put you over that sofa there, arse in the air, and lay into you with that rattan cane in the corner. And if you don't like it, you can always go back to Greenhill. Do I make myself clear?'

John continued to tremble; he felt himself starting to dissolve.

The monologue proceeded. 'You probably thought I would be a pushover, didn't you? Smile that sweet smile of yours, say please and thank you and all the rest of it and you'd have me. Well you got it wrong, didn't you? I'm not your usual soggy, wet-necked, easy-oozy, lovey-dovey old vicar. Before I took Holy Orders I was in the Paras; learnt a thing or two sorting out terrorists in Ulster.

'Then I was headmaster in Uganda, in the far north east where the Mburong people live. Warriors. Cattle thieves. Not a proper man until you've killed somebody and eaten his genitals. Before you could hope to control them you had to get their respect. And do you know how you did that? By passing their test of manhood. That meant going out into the bush armed with a spear – no guns, please note – and killing an elephant. I know you shouldn't kill elephants, but I'd no choice. Having passed that test I could begin to get the place in order. No use reasoning with them. Violence was what they respected. Superior physical strength. So it was wield the sjambok. Once I'd got them where I wanted them, I could start on a bit of Christian love. Not before.

'It's all in the Bible, you know. Shouldn't scare the kiddies with hellfire, that's what the line is today. But think what those old Israelites must have been like: crude, violent thugs, many of them. No use talking lovey-dovey guff to them. Had to scare them with hell fire to get them to behave. Even Jesus had to bring in a dose of hellfire when he was faced with bandits and terrorists, and blokes whose idea of fun was to go and gloat at a good crucifixion. Got to make 'em a bit scared. Then they might start listening to you.

'So, don't you go thinking that that smile of yours works with me. I've dealt with hard men. I know all there is to know about Original Sin. So what exactly *have* you been getting up to at Beaconsfield? You've a choice. Go back to Greenhill and let them beat the living daylights out of you. Muck me about and end up arse in the air over that sofa. Or tell me the truth.'

The old Greenhill feeling descended on John. It wasn't like those escape stories he read in which secret agents defied the tortures of the Gestapo. Your whole flabby body swelled up and took over, reducing you to a wobbling jelly. Sobbing like a small child, he spluttered out his story again.

'Please, please. Don't hit me!' he snivelled. 'I *did* tell Mr Steadman everything. Cross my heart. Swear to God! I want to be good. I hate being bad. But well, it just happened…'

'*What* "just happened"?'

'I started to think dirty thoughts. About boys, not about girls as I should have done. I don't know why. And then I had these dreams. It's like an alien taking you over. You go sort of mad. It all happened so suddenly with Danny in the shower. I'm so ashamed! So ashamed!'

Complete collapse. The big bold lad exposed as a pathetic little baby. God, what *did* this man think of him, the man he so desperately wanted to impress?

Actually, had he known it, he *had* impressed the Bishop. Don Macnab was a man out of his time. The wild frontiers of the Victorian Empire were where he really belonged. Of his choice, he'd spent his life among hard and desperate men. The world of the Bible can't have been very different: wild, warlike tribes, rapacious amoral tax collectors, brutal warlords; no use being all lovey-dovey with a seasoned thug like King Herod. His mentor was that old warhorse of the Raj, General Charles Napier who'd conquered Sind: flog 'em first, let 'em know who's boss, and then ladle out the kindness. Worked in Ulster; worked among the Mburong. But this kid wasn't like that. He wasn't basically violent. A little firmness, yes, but be kind to him and you'll have him. No need for sjamboks or the third degree with him. He'd learnt that much. He was desperate for a bit of help. So help he'd get. A practised interrogator, he switched personalities and became a kindly old uncle.

'All right! All right! I believe you. I know you're telling the truth. You're not daft enough to lie. You know which side of the bread the butter's on.'

He leant back and the great craggy face broke into a warm smile. 'We'll get you back to Beaconsfield, never fear. But first I'll have to sort that ridiculous Watson woman out.'

God Almighty, was he going to lay *her* over the sofa and set to work with the rattan cane? Quite possible.

'*You* a problem!' he continued. 'I wonder what she'd make

of poor old Cedric? Incidentally, young man, I set that business in the bathroom up specially for you. Just to let you know what it's like to be chased by a sex-mad freak. You didn't like it, did you? You were scared stiff, weren't you? So think what it must be like for your victims. No use just *telling* you. Got to learn it at first hand. Then it really sinks in.'

John's degradation had made him ready to confess everything. It was a sort of catharsis, a cleansing. 'I wasn't expelled from Greenhill for hitting a teacher like I told them at Beaconsfield. I ran away because of what Freddy Hazlett and his gang did to me. It was *horrible*.'

'Yes,' nodded the Bishop, 'I heard about that. So let it be a warning to you. And, whatever you do, don't end up like Cedric.'

'But can't anybody help him?'

'Not really. You can only help those who want to be helped. Cedric doesn't. He's very clever, you know, a philosophy and mathematics student at university. But he's totally without willpower. God doesn't put you into Hell, you know. It's where you put yourself. Still, you've got to love 'em all, even when they don't want to be loved and can't see the point of it. Like being a soldier under orders. Anyway, all that's by the way. You like steam engines, don't you?'

'Yes.'

'Well, today's my day off and we're going to drive one. Mind you, any rubbish out of you and I'm perfectly capable of throwing you into the firebox. Could pass it over as just a sad accident!'

'You've driven steam trains before?'

'Yes, while I was in Africa. I wangled my way on to one of the big garrets that went up the line from Mombasa to Kampala. Getting them up the gradients out of the Rift Valley, that *was* engine driving! Well, *tempus fugit* as they say. We'd better get going.'

'But what am I to wear?' said John. 'I mean, I'm still in my school uniform.'

The Bishop eyed the neat little mannequin in his bright red blazer, white shirt and clean grey trousers. 'No, we can't have you going dressed like that. Wait a minute, Isabel's got a lot of stuff she's collected for her "neglected children" jumble sale. I'll see what she can find.'

'Just the Picture You're Looking for'

On cue, Isabel went into a fluttery action. After a prolonged session of rummaging in boxes at the far end of the workshop, punctuated with more excruciating hugs and kisses, John finally entered the dining room draped in a pair of oversize jeans, held precariously in place by an old leather belt and half hidden in a tattered red sweater that reached down to his knees – some of the fruits of her 'good works' on behalf of 'the despised and neglected of capitalist society'.

As she delivered the finished product to her husband, she noticed John's tear-stained face. 'Don,' she said in an accusing tone. 'You haven't been bullying him, have you?'

'Nothing out of the ordinary, dear. Just straightening a few things out.'

'That's your word for it, is it? One day you'll go too far and get into trouble with the law!'

The Bishop eyed the scrawny rag doll in front of him.

'I must say he does *rather* fill the bill as one of your neglected children, doesn't he?' he said. 'He could be just the picture you've been looking for.'

'*Absolutely*!' declared Isabel, 'You've given me an idea. Wait till I get my camera.'

'What's all this?' asked a bewildered John as she scuttled out of the room.

'Just one of her obsessions. She needs a suitable photograph to illustrate her appeal in the parish magazine.'

'But why me?'

'When she tried to photograph some street kids from Greenwood all they did was stick their tongues out and make obscene gestures with their fingers. Not very appealing, but you, Jonny boy, look the part and you play the part.'

'But that's cheating.'

'Not really. It's just the way propaganda works. Most of the pictures you see in your history books have been faked, like the famous storming of the Winter Palace in 1917.'

Isabel returned, brandishing a large, and obviously very expensive, camera.

'No, John darling, don't try to comb your hair. Ruffle it up a bit. That's right. Wait a minute. We could do with a few tears.'

She stuck her fingers into a nearby vase of flowers and duly added them to his cheeks.

'Now come into the garden where there's some light.'

They walked out onto the lawn.

'We'll have you standing in front of the brick wall, there. A *suggestive* background, don't you agree, Don? No! No! No! Don't *smile*! Look sad. That's it.'

Click. Click. Click.

Throughout it all John squirmed. It was so *embarrassing*! If the lads at Beaconsfield find out...! And what if Cedric were to get hold of the photos and start masturbating over them? Or send them to *Gay News* or something? Didn't bear thinking about! But, since Thursday's catastrophe he just had to go with the wind – wherever it blew him. So do as they say and keep smiling.

A Hell's Angel Now?

'All right, Isabel, that'll do,' said the Bishop. 'Time to start, Jonny boy!'

They walked round to a red brick hut on the far side of the house that served as a garage.

'Wait here,' he said as he disappeared behind the brown-painted double doors.

A moment later he emerged dressed in black leathers and wheeling a vast red motorbike. Once more, John gaped. Just what *was* this extraordinary man? A Hell's Angel? Or a sixties rocker escaped from a time warp? Who knew?

'Ever had a ride on one of these before?'

'No.'

'Well here's a new experience for you. Great things, motorbikes! Get the adrenaline going. I may be a bishop, but I can't be holy all the time. Drive me mad.' He became conspiratorial. 'And here's another thing, young man. It's a good way of burning up all that testosterone which makes lads like you go and do daft things in showers. And, by the way,' he added with a wink, 'when we get to the Radmore Railway I'm not the Bishop of Boldonbridge, I'm your Uncle Don, a retired engine driver. If some of the blokes there knew I was a bishop, one half would get all deferential while the other half would get all class-conscious and resentful. I can do without the proles versus the toffs show. I get too much of it in my work.'

He began to reminisce, becoming oddly confidential, as if he needed to unburden himself to a sympathetic listener. Why me? thought John, why me?

'Got to be able to change your identity from time to time, you know. That's how I wangled my way onto the footplate of those big East African Railways garrets. Wouldn't have done for a headmaster out there to have been seen driving a train.'

'Why not? I thought that it would be the thing to do.'

'Not among the Mburong. Headmaster there's the big magician who gets you the good exam results that get you a cushy office job. Can't be seen to do manual work or he stops being the intellectual with magic. So I turned myself into a Boer – helps being a good linguist, you know – white farmer up from the dreaded South Africa. Went down a treat with the

Hindu engine drivers. World's greatest snobs. Caste system. White man higher caste than black man..'

'And another thing,' he added as he donned a big red crash helmet and handed a second one to the awe-struck John, 'I believe there's some damned silly law about not letting kids ride behind you on motorbikes. So, if the police see us, you're my wife; get it? Right, on you get. Hang on tight. Don't worry if you're a bit scared. You've every reason to be!'

With that the big machine burst into a thundering, vibrating life and they roared off into the weak spring sunshine. Wind, fear, wild excitement, the adrenaline of pure speed. Hanging on desperately, John was vaguely aware of hurtling through tree-lined suburbs, over the river, up through the steep terraced houses of Southside and away over the green hills beyond. Soon he glimpsed the untidy industrial city sprawling down the valley beneath them like a ragged old tartan rug.

Eventually they skidded to a jerky halt. Shaking slightly and greatly relieved to feel solid earth beneath his feet, John dismounted. Removing his helmet, he saw a neat, almost toy-like red brick railway station with 'Radmore Heritage Railway' emblazoned on it in big gold letters. They marched over to a large red brick shed beyond it. Inside were three glitteringly clean saddle tank engines, one blue, one red and one green, resplendent in their gleaming paint and bright red buffer beams. John's heart leapt.

They hung their helmets on a row of hooks and, having removed his leathers, the Bishop led the way into a little office. Immediately he started talking in broad Geordie to the man behind the desk.

'Tick us off, will yer? I'm nummer fower. Yin's me nephew like. From doon sooth like so he talks a bit posh like. OK if Ah tak 'im wee us on the footplate?'

'Well... the safety regulations, you know...'

'Hadaway, he'll do nowt daft, him! An' Ah'll tek the rap if 'e does owt – after havin' skelped 'im proper like!'

'OK.'

They went outside to find Number Four, another immaculate little saddle tank engine, shiny black this time and lined in gold. Bob, the fireman, had been getting it ready and smoke was coming out of the chimney. They climbed up into the cab.

Trains, Glorious Trains

What followed was a glimpse of paradise. John was immediately accepted as one of the crew, helping Bob and shovelling coal into the fire at his behest.

'More over there, son! We don't want no holes or we'll be sending most of it up the chimney and lose pressure. There. That's right.'

The thrill of leaning out of the cab window with everybody looking at you as the engine chugged into the station pulling a single coach. Not a shit-stabber John now. Not pathetic little cry baby either, but an adult member of the footplate crew.

'Now me bonny lad, you can do a brirra drivin'.'

The excitement of standing, gloved hand on the regulator, looking through the spyglass at the advancing track. The sudden surge of power as you opened the regulator a little. The stream of technical jargon that made you feel that you were part of an elite: 'A little more cut off now… Watch the slipping. A bit of sand… Gently now.' That feeling of omnipotence as you, yourself, controlled the live, fire-breathing dragon. The dirt. The smell of smoke.

'You've Gone and Landed Yourself in it'

'Thanks a bomb!' he spluttered when it was all over, 'That was *wicked*! Mankey!'

They climbed onto the motorbike and he prepared himself

for the adrenaline-filled mixture of fear and exhilaration that was the ride home.

But before they started the Bishop turned round and glared at him. 'You've had your fun,' he barked, 'and now you've got to earn your keep. Tomorrow's work day. Isabel's grabbed you for her weekly Good Deed. It's your own fault. You've gone and landed yourself in it.'

A spurt of fear rippled through him and he blushed bright red. What *now* with this unpredictable gorilla of a man?

'I'm terribly sorry. I, er… didn't mean it!'

'No! No! *No*! You haven't done anything *wrong*! Quite the opposite. You've gone and charmed her. You're quite a change from the usual bag of dropouts and deadbeats that she collects. She wants you all to herself tomorrow. You're earmarked for her Waifs and Strays do. Hope you know something about croquet, because you're in charge of the croquet match. I can only pray that you manage to stay sane.'

With that bombshell the Bishop's charger burst into thunderous life and they roared away: wind, speed, fear, thrill.

'He's All Yours Now'

They'd hardly skidded to a halt in the Bishop's drive before Isabel swooped.

'Don, where *have* you been? You haven't been driving *trains* again, I hope? Leaving me to prepare for tomorrow all alone! And I've had a terrible time with Cedric! He drank a *whole* bottle of methylated spirits. I *do* wish you would keep that garage door locked, darling. I've spoken to you about it *so* many times! Well I had to ring for the ambulance and they've taken him into the detoxification unit at the General Hospital.'

The gush momentarily died down as she recovered her breath. Then she eyed the grubby, soot-smeared John. 'What *have* you been doing to him?' she exclaimed. 'You haven't been making *him* drive trains have you? You *know* how *dangerous* that can be! One day there'll be a terrible accident and we'll *all* land in prison.'

'Well he's yours now,' said the Bishop when the tirade eventually fizzled out. 'I've got to get some work done.'

With that he wheeled the motorbike into the garage.

'You Must Wash Properly'

Isabel frog-marched John into the house, like a little boy who'd been rolling in the mud. Laden with towels and bottles of shampoo, she hustled him up to the bathroom.

'Now you *must* wash properly. I mean *properly*! *All over*! You *must* get this filthy coal dust and soot off you. It gives you *cancer*, you know! Yes, *cancer*! So get out of these dirty things! *Now*!'

For a ghastly minute he thought she was going to undress him and sponge him down like a little baby. Even his armour-plated 'good boy' act could hardly have survived that humiliation. Fortunately once she'd managed to get the taps to work – as awkward as ever – she swept out into the corridor and left him in peace. Without Cedric hovering in the near distance he was able to enjoy a long and glorious wallow in the warm soapy water.

Eventually he clambered out, dried himself and scuttled along to his bedroom where he found his school uniform, which Isabel had laid out neatly on his bed. Finally, resplendent in his red blazer, white shirt and striped tie, he headed for the dining room.

On the landing he met Jason. He was standing in a 'commanding' pose, his left arm outstretched and his right arm making pointed didactic gestures.

'You!' he barked. 'Finland Station! You, Nevsky Prospect!' He eyed the newly washed and glowing John. 'Kamenev's weak! History is looking to *you*! Yes, to *you*!' he repeated aggressively.

'Yes, yes, yes,' replied John as he scuttled down the stairs.

'A Very Civilised Game'

In the dining room Isabel subjected him to a rigorous examination – neck, hair, behind the ears...

'Yes, you'll do,' she finally said. 'Now tomorrow I've got a group of deprived children coming for tea. You *will* help, won't you?'

Required answer: 'Yes.' So he smiled sweetly and said, 'Of course I will.'

'Oh John, you are so *good*!'

Yet another excruciating hug and kiss followed.

'What do you want me to do?' he asked when she eventually released him.

'You're to take charge of the game of croquet.'

'Croquet? What's that?' The name stirred distance memories that he couldn't solidify.

'Surely they taught you croquet at school?'

'No.'

'Good gracious! I thought *all* proper schools taught croquet. It's such a *civilised* game! Well, come outside and we'll have a little lesson.'

As he followed her into the garden and round to a tree-lined lawn at the back of the house, it came back to him. A history trip in the summer term at Rickerby Hall to some boring old stately home. "Hairy Mary", the loony Latin master, had been in charge and had tried to contain the growing anarchy by 'having a game of croquet... A *very* civilised game.' It had resulted in a glorious Battle of Hastings with the long wooden mallets acting as swords and lances and the wooden balls as cannon balls fired by an alien spaceship caught in a timewarp. They had been chased back to the minibus by a furious tourist guide, and when they had returned to Rickerby Hall, Mr Cotton, the headmaster, had blown a mega fuse.

A tedious hour of hitting balls through metal hoops ensued. The contrast between that lost paradise and his present dire predicament made him want to go away and cry. He had to fight back his tears and try desperately to appear lively, interested and grateful.

As they went back inside, Isabel issued a warning. 'The Bishop's in his study preparing his Sunday sermons. You are *not* to disturb him. He can be very fierce when he's in a temper.'

John didn't need to be reminded of that fact.

In the Kitchen

Saturday morning consisted of helping a frenetic and hyped-up Isabel prepare the 'deprived children's tea': a matter of running round the kitchen with vast tray-loads of meringues, stirring huge bowls of exotic cake mix and putting them into the oven, decorating enormous ice cream concoctions with Smarties, and trying to squeeze them into the small and overcrowded fridge without damaging them.

All the while Isabel kept up a stream of exhortations. 'We *must* make a very special effort for these children. You see they've had so *little*! They have been so *abused*! They will be *so* grateful. You *will* do your best for them, John, won't you?'

Expected answer: 'Yes!'

And when it was given with gusto it was followed by an effusive gush. 'Oh, John, you are *so* kind and *so* thoughtful! Really, that Watson woman...!'

Definite political possibilities here, but tread carefully. Adults are so unreliable: all over you one minute, going up in blue smoke the next.

By mid-morning the dining room table was a gorgeous cornucopia of gastronomic goodies.

The 'Deprived Children' Arrive

Morning slid into a fine and balmy afternoon.

'The children will soon be here,' declared Isabel, looking at her watch. 'We must go outside to meet them.'

As they waited by the main entrance, a white minibus with 'Boldonbridge Christian Volunteers' emblazoned on its sides came careering up the drive and skidded to a halt amid clouds of dust and gravel. Immediately the back doors opened and vomited out an anarchic bundle of youngsters: tall, short, fat, thin, boys and girls, mostly bejeaned but some in leather jackets, some with shiny shaved heads, almost all with fags hanging out of their mouths. Whooping, yelling and screeching, the tumult poured over the lawn and scattered itself among the trees at the far end near the wall. A huge, brawny gorilla of a youth, fearsome with his shaved head, bare tattooed arms and dangling cigarette, wrenched the head off the stone sundial in the middle of the lawn and hurled it aggressively over the drive.

John felt his bones dissolve into mushy putty as the old Greenhill fear gripped him. These creatures were not children, nor had they ever been. They were dangerous and untamed predators. Did some adults *never* learn elementary facts?

Twisting her beaky face into what was supposed to be a beatific smile, Isabel marched resolutely up to the driver, a young man in a denim suit who was busily lighting a cigarette.

'I'm Isabel,' she cooed. 'Welcome to Fairfield House.'

The driver acknowledged her presence with the barest grunt and continued lighting his cigarette.

'Please,' she said, after an awkward silence. 'Could you gather the children together?'

More striking of matches was followed by a long inhalation of smoke, which duly emerged from his nostrils.

'Not my pigeon,' he eventually condescended to grunt.

'I'm only the driver and I'm not being paid overtime, you know. They're your problem.'

Isabel turned to John, her face still fixed in its beatific smile. 'John, darling,' she purred, 'Perhaps *you* would go and fetch them back for me?'

Which was, of course, the very last thing that John wanted to do. A glance down the lawn revealed terrifying anarchy. While half of the mob seemed to have disappeared round the back of the house, the remainder were cavorting about, shrieking and yelling. Some seemed to be fighting, a couple even appeared to be having sex: openly and in front of everybody and everything without the barest hint of shame. He might as well jump into a pool of hungry crocodiles. He felt himself melt.

But, reality! He needed Isabel and the Bishop to save him from… Greenhill and that seething mob in front of him! No choice but to obey. He felt like a First World War soldier ordered to attack an enemy trench. Disobeying orders meant a firing squad and the certainty of death; obeying orders meant only the risk of death. He marched as resolutely as possible over the lawn.

Seeing a gaggle of what seemed to be girls pulling up some daffodils – though with the unisex jeans and the shaven heads determination of gender was not easy – he approached them.

'Er, please could you come back to the minibus?'

'Wee's the posh git then?' one of them screeched as she (or, maybe, he) continued the work of destruction.

But three of them – a couple of what were probably girls and a dark-haired, pointy-faced creature who was obviously a boy – eventually wandered back to the minibus. Not dead yet! Partial success, even. Feeling slightly encouraged, he walked round to the back of the house to 'take charge' of the game of croquet.

When he got there he found that some kind of a fight –

play or otherwise – had broken out. The big lump who'd bust the sundial was in the midst of a boiling mass of arms and legs, having what seemed to be a sword fight with the wooden mallets. No possible sense in entering that maelstrom! But three mallets were lying unused on the grass beside the four balls. Screwing up his courage to bursting point, he picked up a mallet and a ball and approached a couple of boys who were slouching round with fags in their mouths and vaguely watching the big fight.

'Would you like a game of croquet?' Invitation to suicide. Stick your head into the hungry crocodile's mouth.

To his gratified surprise they didn't immediately react to his alien accent.

'Reet,' one of them said, 'Whadder yer dee with them things like?'

'Well, you hit the balls with them and try to get them through the hoops. Like this.'

He gave the ball a smack. Mercifully it went through the requisite hoop. It seemed to arouse a modicum of interest and a desultory approximation of a game began with the sword fight providing a noisy backdrop. After a while it petered out. 'Dead borin' this.'

Suddenly, something seemed to happen. The cacophony of voices – the deep male bellows and shrill female screeches – rose to a crescendo and the whole adolescent tsunami went surging round to the front of the house.

A bewildered John was left standing alone amid a debris of uprooted daffodils, empty fag packets and even the odd broken beer bottle. God, the Bishop would go apeshit when he saw this mess! And *he* wouldn't half cop it, too! 'You're in charge of the game of croquet.' Those two broken croquet mallets were *his* responsibility! 'I can always put you over that sofa there... lay into you with that rattan cane.' The pain! The sheer humiliation. Could he stand it without crying like a little baby? Only one solution: find Isabel and set to work on her before that great God of Thunder – or whatever it was – descended from the clouds!

He scurried round to the front of the house. There was nobody there so he crept inside. Opening the door of the corridor that led to the dining room, he froze. A colossal din hit him with an almost physical force. Bovine bellows, piercing screeches and great volcanic eruptions of wild, uncontrollable laughter; that 'yob laughter' of Greenhill, which was the Devil breaking loose. Above the hullaballoo Isabel's voice could be heard squealing with anguished pleas. '*Do stop it, boys and girls! Please sit down!*'

He was going to have to enter that boiling cauldron. It was back to being the First World War soldier who had to choose between the certainty of death or the mere high probability of it. He felt his insides twist into knots as he opened the door and plunged into the seething chaos.

The whole artistically arranged table of gastronomic goodies – the fruit of all that diligent morning labour – was a bomb site chaos of squashed meringues, half-eaten doughnuts and gobbets of tipped-up ice cream lying around looking like polar islands in a brown sea of spilt Coca-Cola. Around the wreckage the heaving mass of youngsters seemed to have split into two rival teams, busy pelting each other with lumps of jelly and the remains of the trifle, so lovingly created by Isabel the previous night.

Seeing John, Isabel rushed over to him. 'John, darling, *please* can you tell them to behave. They just *won't* listen to me!'

Kamikaze mission. The Polish cavalry ordered to charge the German tanks. He approached the big skinhead who'd bust the sundial and the croquet mallets. 'Please could you sit down?'

Entirely predictable response: '*Aw fuck off yer posh twat!*'

To an accompanying explosion of yob laughter, the bowl

containing the remains of the trifle was dumped on his head. Unable to see where he was going, and with the cold slime seeping down his neck and under his shirt, he lurched around like a drunk. At the mercy of the unbridled savagery of the mob. What next? Punches? Kicks? Even stripped naked? Oh God!

Suddenly he felt himself blunder into a massive body. As if he had pressed the plunger of a detonator an enormous bellow exploded out, '*Gee ower the lotta yers!*' Pure, coarse Geordie. Silence followed.

Removing the bowl from his head, John found himself staring up at the colossal figure of the Bishop. Immediately he cringed.

He watched, awestruck, as a gladiatorial contest began. At stake was the control of not only the dining room, but of the whole house. Seeing his dominance threatened, the big skinhead flung a handful of jelly against the wall in ostentatious defiance.

The Bishop responded in a soft and gentle voice. 'Ah telled yer ter gee ower, didna?'

'Fuck off!'

'Tharz naebeddy tells us ter fuck off, son.'

The skinhead's face twisted up into an ugly leer. 'Ah will an' all an' wet the fuck are ye gannin' ter dee aboorrit?'

'Reet! Let's 'ave yer then!'

Before an avidly expectant audience the Bishop's massive pile-driver fists laid into his opponent. One! Two! Three!

With the custard and the jelly still dribbling icily down his neck, John became almost analytical as he observed the way that the fists carefully avoided sensitive areas like the face and hit the chest and the sides. After a few minutes the reeling skinhead was picked up and pinned against the wall.

'Had enough, son? Wanna wee bit mooah like?'

'Ah reet! Ah reet! Gerroff will yer!'

The audience stared in stunned silence as the defeated gladiator was dropped ignominiously onto the floor. John noticed an immediate change in the atmosphere. It was almost as if a light had been switched on in a darkened room, revealing a whole new scene. Before there had been scornful defiance. Now there was respectful cooperation. Trial by combat again. His fight with Billy Nolan. That school kid world where might was always right. Why couldn't adults ever see this obvious fact?

'Now clear the mess off the floor the lottayers.'

John watched in awed wonder as what had only a few minutes ago been a pack of ravenous wolves meekly obeyed, picking most of the debris off the carpet, placing it in semi-orderly piles on the table.

The Bishop became avuncular. 'Good on yers, lads an' lasses! Yer can come again like, yer's always welcome, but mind, divvent ye start geein' us any shite, else Ah'll 'ave yers!'

He eyed the crestfallen skinhead, 'Yer a canny fighter, you, but mind, Ah can take yers àny time, son, so divvent mess wi' us like. Gerrit?'

The youth smiled and shook his hand. 'We's is proper mates noo!' he said.

A speechless John gaped as the Bishop led the motley crowd out to the waiting minibus. The sheer power of this man! The control! Whatever else he did he had to keep on the right side of this elemental force of nature.

Wiping himself down with the edge of the tablecloth, he hurried out to meet him as he came back into the house, 'Please, sir, I'm terribly sorry about the mess on the croquet lawn. I tried my best. Honest I did! But... well, they just wouldn't listen to me.'

He cringed, expecting a punch, or, at the very least, an angry bellow. But to his bewildered surprise, the ferocious giant's face melted into an avuncular smile. God! You never knew what to expect from some adults, especially an adult like this one! So unpredictable!

'No need to apologise! Of course you did your best. Any fool can see that. Only an idiot would have expected you to handle that lot.'

Missile fired in Isabel's direction? Be careful. Don't get caught in the crossfire. Try to keep both parties sweet!

Suddenly – and even more unpredictably – the Bishop started confiding in him, seemingly telling him things that he couldn't tell other people, let alone his wife. Why *him*, a pathetic little shit-stabber? Most odd!

'Don't think I *like* getting physical, young man. It's a loss of control. Failure. But it's a sad fact that the only thing a large part of humanity respects is violence. Taxi drivers know it. They've a saying: "String 'em all up! It's the only language they understand!" Rather more truth in it than some people would have us believe. They just don't *want* to face it, that's the trouble. Isabel doesn't, as you've probably noticed. But I know better. So, I suspect, do you, young man. Your experience at Greenhill hasn't been a complete waste of time. It's taught you reality.

'You saw what happened in the dining room, didn't you? Two elephants fighting for dominance, just as they do in Africa. Contemptuous defiance at first, but when I sorted that young thug out, I got respectful obedience. I became leader of the herd. Same among the Mburong in Uganda. Only there, those young bloods had fibre and discipline. Not like this lot. Most of them are just pathetic, gutless, slaves to their own craving for bodily sensations. Of course it's not really their fault: bad genes, poor environment, a deadly mix. And that's where Christianity comes in: get a grip on your self destructive cravings, aim high. But you've got to win their respect first, and that can mean violence,

I'm afraid. Can't get the wife to see it, though. I'll be getting some stick for thumping that young hooligan. Just you wait!'

They entered the dining room. Ostentatiously John began to attack the mess on the table, spooning up the mounds of spilt trifle with his bare hands and putting the mess into the bowl, which had so recently been on his head, stacking up what remained of the meringues and piling up the plates that weren't broken. As predicted, Isabel waded into her husband.

'Really, Don, did you *have* to hit that boy? It was assault, and you could get prosecuted, you know!'

'But what else was I supposed to do? Let him beat the living daylights out of little Jonny boy here?'

'It's violence, Don, violence, the one thing I'm trying so desperately hard to combat.'

'But can't you see that there's no other way with people like that?'

'I can't and, what's more, I *won't*!'

'Really, dear, you'd do better sticking to old ladies and stray cats. Leave the young thugs to me.'

'And let you brutalise them? *Never*!'

Stalemate. A frosty silence ensued.

'By the way,' she eventually said, changing the subject and adopting an anxious tone, 'Have you seen Jason today? He's gone all silent and morose. I do hope he's not going to have another of those dos! I really couldn't stand it! Not *another* one!'

Suddenly she caught sight of John. 'Oh, John, you have been *so* brave this afternoon and *so* helpful! *Do* tell me: you're not violent, are you?'

'No! No! I'm not violent. I *hate* violence!' But only when I am the victim of it, but don't muddy the waters by telling the truth. Won't do any good.

As a reward he was hugged and allowed to stuff himself with the edible remains of the feast, and was presented with three large bottles of Coke which had somehow managed to survive the afternoon's holocaust intact.

A Night to Remember; Wimp or Hero?

A blissful bath was followed by bed. Having drunk two of the three bottles of Coke, John found it difficult to get to sleep. For a long time he lay tossing and turning, his mind full of the images of yet another weird day. The proven superiority of physical strength. His own abject humiliation at the hands of the skinhead. His fear – nay, terror! – of the mob. How he wished he could be as strong and masterful as the Bishop. Awesome, terrifying, but so unpredictable. That strange tendency to confide in him as if he were an adult companion and not a thirteen-year-old boy.

When eventually he did doze off the Demon entered him. There he was, naked. There was Danny, naked… He suddenly woke up to find himself in the darkness with the bed all sticky. The Bishop's bed! The shame of it! Couldn't it *ever* stop?

He got up, knelt by the bed and prayed, 'Please God, please stop this. I don't want to be a shit-stabber; sorry about the language, but you know what I mean. Please make me good. Make me dream about girls. Make me normal like the other lads.'

In the middle of this he suddenly realised that the large intake of Coke had done its worst and that he needed a pee, and pretty damned urgently too! God would have to wait a moment or two.

Still in his underpants, he switched on the light, unlocked the door and crept out into the darkened passage. Immediately he sensed that something was wrong. There was an unfamiliar acrid smell and a dense fog hurt his eyes and blurred his vision. A dull, flickering glow was coming from the landing. Curiosity made him forget about the need to pee.

Reaching the landing, he gasped in amazement. Thick

smoke was billowing around and made him cough. Bright red flames were licking their way up the curtains on the window and running along the banisters like Christmas streamers. So that's what it was: fire! Fires just didn't happen in his world and for a moment he gaped in confusion.

Suddenly he saw a large figure looming up through the swirling murk. It knelt down and proceeded to sprinkle some liquid from a bottle onto the carpet and then to start flicking a cigarette lighter it held in its other hand. A brilliant yellow flame raced over the carpet like a luminescent snake.

He crept closer and saw... Jason!

'Jason, what *are* you doing?'

Slowly Jason stood up. Through the flickering gloom John could see that he was stark naked; not repulsively naked, but almost noble, like a Greek statue with his muscular, well-built body.

'It's time,' he said in a calm, measured voice, 'Time. The Military Revolutionary Committee has occupied the Peter and Paul Fortress. This time I'm getting it right. Stalin is too rude. He doesn't know how to use his power properly. Trotsky is too arrogant. There's nobody, so I'm starting all over again.'

He emptied more liquid from his bottle, this time on a different bit of the carpet and, bending down, flicked the lighter. Another snake of yellow flame wriggled across the floor.

'Jason, you're setting the place on fire!'

'Of course I am. This house is part of the old pre-revolutionary world. It's made of cardboard. It must be burnt down and replaced with a proper stone building.'

He stood up and faced John. 'You're in my way, aren't you? You've come to steal my inheritance. You think you can replace me, don't you? But you can't. You, too, are in the dustbin of history. You must burn like the house.'

Dropping the lighter, he lunged at his shoulder and pulled

him down. Then John saw him reach for the lighter and felt a cold liquid run stinging down his bare back. What the hell was this naked weirdo doing?

Suddenly it hit him. The man was mad – crazy! – and was going to set him on fire! With the strength of sheer terror he struggled frantically, and with his bare foot, aimed a desperate kick at his assailant. It hit its mark – a bull's eye, straight into Jason's large, well-developed genitals. With an agonised yell he relaxed his grip and John struggled free.

Run! Run! Run, rabbit, run! Run where? Down the stairs… into the hall at the bottom.

Jason was following him. 'You can't escape!' he shrieked. '*Nobody* can escape! It is the Law of History! It is written!'

Chased by a nightmare monster – was he dreaming all this? – he dithered a bit and then, seeing that the door was open, dashed down the corridor that led to the dining room. The monster was close behind him. Seeing the door of the Bishop's study open, he dived in there. Had to hide somewhere… The curtains hadn't been drawn and moonlight flooded in through the windows, enabling him to see the big desk before which he had so abjectly trembled the other morning. On it he saw a telephone. Lucky choice! Salvation. Terror made him lucid. He picked it up and dialled 999.

Footsteps in the corridor getting nearer… Loud voice: 'You can't escape! I'm coming!'

He knows I'm in here! Oh for fuck's sake get on and answer the bloody phone!

A slow, weary voice: 'Horton Police Station. What is it?'

Falsetto gabble and high-pitched squeal: 'It's the Bishop's house! The Bishop of Boldonbridge, Fairfield House! It's on fire. There's a loony loose! He's trying to kill me! *hurry*!'

The door opened wider. He's coming in! I'm trapped!

'I know you're there! You're trying to kill my father, aren't you?'

John dropped the telephone, ran round the desk, dived under the big swivel chair and squeezed into the leg space between the two sets of supporting drawers.

The light flicked on. Suddenly everything was frighteningly clear. Beyond the big leather armchair, which partially blocked his view, he could see Jason's big, hairy legs approaching his hiding place. Nearer and nearer...

'I've got you now!'

Nearer still. Heart thumping. Body turning to jelly. Body out of control... Suddenly the pee poured out of him, violently and uncontrollably, down his left leg and out onto the white carpet in front of the desk where it formed a steaming, yellow lake. The shame! The degradation! Little boy messing himself!

Triumphant voice: '*There* you are! You've pissed yourself like Zinoviev before his execution! You *are* Zinoviev!'

John leapt up. There before him on the other side of the desk, naked and muscular, was Jason, panting like a savage dog. For a moment they stared at each other. Then Jason lunged towards the left-hand end of the desk. Instinctively John lunged towards the right-hand end. Jason made a grab at him, sending a tray-load of papers fluttering over the carpet as he did so. Frantically John dashed for the door, knocking over a big standard lamp in the process, which fell with a crash. By sheer good luck – the hand of God or whatever? – Jason tripped over it and landed on the floor with a thump. That gave him thirty precious seconds – and how each second mattered! – to escape. But where? Where? Outside into the garden where he couldn't be trapped. French windows of the dining room would be locked, so off to the entrance hall. Run! Run! Run! Down the corridor. Smoke. Flickering red light. Heat. Into the hall. Oh God! Smoke. Bright red flame on stairs. Front door not locked. Footsteps behind him. Loud voice: '*You can't escape!*'

Out into the sharp, stabbing cold of the night. Cold air

stinging like a whiplash on his wet, piss-soaked legs. Dash over the gravel... hard stones hurting my bare feet. Onto cold, wet lawn... Into the pitch-black tangle of the bushes at the far end. Desperate struggle with the hard, unyielding and spiky branches. Crack! Crunch! Crack! He's bound to hear! Then down on my knees. Crawl into a dark hollow under the anarchic trellis of branches. Freezing mud chills me. Wriggle round to get a look at the lawn. Huge figure of Jason towering like a statue, silhouetted against the red flames flickering brilliantly out of the landing window, like strobe lights at a disco.

Lie still. Fierce cold making me shiver. Panting. Gasping for breath. Whole body quivering.

'I know you're there! You can't usurp my rightful place. I'm my father's son. Not you!'

He's coming nearer. Body taking over completely! Oh God, I'm shitting myself! Frantic removal of underpants averts total catastrophe. Leaving a pile of crap in the Bishop's garden: how utterly pathetic! I should be a hero, rescuing the Bishop and his wife and putting the fire out, not leaving turds in the garden!

He's nearer now. Oh come quickly, police! *Do come*!

Did Guy Gibson shit himself when he led the Dam Busters on their celebrated attack on the Möhne and Eder dams? No, because Guy Gibson was a proper man, a *real* hero and not a dirty little shit-stabber.

Oh police, *do* come! He's reached the bushes...

Then lurid pandemonium. Wailing siren. Blazing headlights. Big fire engine roaring up the drive. Police car with blue lights flashing. Deliverance.

Fire engine into action. Ladders up. Hoses out. Water pouring through landing window. Brilliant flames disappear. Jason running back into the house.

John ran out onto the lawn, waving his arms furiously.

'Sorry to disturb you, but there's a lunatic loose!' he yelled at the policeman who got out of the car, 'He's setting the house on fire. He's trying to kill me!'

'Where is he?'

'He ran back into the house. The Bishop and his wife are still in there.'

'You'd better sit in the car. Stay there and don't get out.'

All this in a crazy, flickering motion, like a video being fast-forwarded.

He sat down in the front seat of the car. Enormously relieved. As if a painful boil had been lanced. Safe. Alive.

Then the shame. His pissed underpants were wetting the car seat. If they should notice it…! And when the Bishop found that puddle in his study. Not to mention the pile of turds under the rhododendron bushes. Oh God! Squalid, dirty little shit-stabber!

A sort of order eventually emerged from the chaotic darkness. Lights went on. Jason emerged form the front door, handcuffed and his nakedness covered by a blanket, escorted by two burly policemen who seemed to be talking to him gently and agreeing with everything he said.

The big, genial policeman opened the car door. 'All right, you can come out now.'

Timorously he followed him back into the house. In the hall he was confronted with an apparition. A huge monster of a man was there, all bulging muscles and quivering hairs – indeed, if you could call it a man. It was more like a towering gorilla on the rampage, the famous 'missing link' perhaps, or the eternal caveman of yore; all that was missing was the club and the unconscious wife draped over its shoulder. It was, in fact, the Bishop, reverting it seemed to primordial type or to some previous incarnation deep in prehistory. A pair of ragged pyjama bottoms and a tatty old dressing gown were his meagre concession to civilisation.

He glowered down at John. 'Just what *have* you been getting up to?'

John cringed and darted behind the protective bulk of the policeman. Oh Lord, what *now*?

'All right! All right,' said the policeman, going into his 'crisis management' role and relishing the chance to put all those hours of tedium spent on 'courses' into action. 'Don't go for him. I know it's all been a great shock to you, but if it hadn't been for his quick reactions and responsible behaviour there could have been a very nasty fire and fatalities. He's the one who alerted the Fire Brigade, and in the nick of time, too.'

'Oh? What happened, then?'

'You tell him, young man.'

John emerged from behind the protective bulk of his defender. 'Well, I... er...'

The words wouldn't come.

'Come on, don't be frightened.'

'Well, I was walking along the corridor when I saw Jason on the landing. He was all weird and was sprinkling petrol or meths or something all over the place and lighting it. Then he attacked me. So I ran and telephoned the police.'

'And just *why* were you wandering round the house at night, not even dressed?' The Bishop seemed to resent his being rescued; adults were so *odd*! He should have embraced him and hailed him as a saviour; after all, that's what happened in books and films.

John blushed bright red. 'Well, er... I needed the toilet.'

'Oh, come on now! You don't expect met to swallow that one do you? You don't need the toilet in the middle of the night at your age! You're not an old man with diabetes, are you? So what was your little game, then?'

Another mutation: this time from squalid little retard to evil, scheming juvenile delinquent. This fearsome caveman seemed determined not to believe him.

'But I *did* need the toilet, honest!'

Suddenly – and almost on cue – another apparition appeared. Isabel came sweeping down the stairs in a long white nightdress, her long straggle of mousy hair streaming out behind her, her beaky nose protruding from her wild, intense face like the tip of a spear. Boadicea, riding into battle in her chariot of yore.

'*Please*, Don, *do* stop it! John's a hero! He's saved our house!'

She embraced and kissed him. Yet another mutation: hero now! What next?

'I suppose you *could* put that slant on it,' growled the Bishop aggressively. 'Pretty unlikely though.'

Strange man, this! Save souls, help the poor and needy, rescue the drowning. But the drowning weren't allowed to rescue themselves, let alone rescue *him* if he fell into a river! By saving the house from burning down he seemed to have annoyed him. What *were* you supposed to do?

'But Jason!' exclaimed an anguished Isabel, releasing a red-faced and squirming John. 'What about *him*? It's not his fault, you know. He's having one of his turns.'

'You can set your mind at rest,' replied the policeman, relishing his role as the competent professional dealing with the crisis. 'We won't charge him. We're taking him to St Margaret's Hospital where he'll get medical attention he needs.'

'He won't be sent to prison, will he?'

'Of course not, but under the Mental Health Act he'll have to be detained in a secure unit. Now, we'd better have a proper statement.'

'Well, we can't give a statement standing here,' growled the Bishop, eyeing the firemen who were still clunking around with hoses. 'Come into my study.'

They filed in. The Bishop switched on the light and angrily

surveyed the devastation: the broken lamp, the telephone swinging gently on its cord as it dangled over the edge of the desk, the scatter of papers all over the floor. The eyebrows tightened threateningly. 'Strewth!' he growled. 'Those are my Sunday sermons I'll have you know!'

He turned on John. 'What *have* you been doing in here? Playing rugby or something?'

John could only gape in silence.

The Bishop marched over to a big brown cupboard from which he extracted an empty bottle of whisky. 'I see somebody's been at the whisky!' he said with a hint of triumph.

Then he saw the puddle on the carpet, bright yellow and stinking away. Ostentatiously he screwed up his nose. 'And what's your explanation of *that*?' he said, pointing to it.

John felt himself shrivel up. Why did he have to draw attention to *that*, for Heaven's sake? He seemed determined to humiliate him. Why? To show off to that policeman, perhaps, by parading those interrogation skills he'd learned in Ulster? He was as bad as a small kid.

'It wasn't me, honest! It was Jason!'

'Don't lie to me. Look at your drawers.'

Squashed flat. The insect under the boot.

The assault continued. 'You've been stringing me along, haven't you? I'll tell you what really happened. When you thought we were all safely in bed, you sneaked downstairs didn't you? Had a little poke round to see what you could steal. Fiddly fingers opened the drinks cupboard, didn't they? Couldn't resist a pull at the whisky, could we? Then Jason comes along and you invite him to join your little party on condition that he won't grass on you. Right? But it all gets out of hand. Can't hold your drink so you pee on the floor. Then you smoke Jason's fags, and the whole place catches fire.'

John felt himself melt. A snowman on a sunny summer's day, that sinking feeling of despair. This was crazy. How could he convince this great ogre of the truth? And what *was* the truth anyway? For all his whirling mind could tell, the Bishop's concoction could well *be* the truth. Despite himself, he began to snivel.

'Oh, Don, *do* leave him alone!' cried Isabel, rushing to his rescue. 'You've got him all upset! You're not dealing with terrorists in Newry, you know!' she added vehemently.

Further mutation. This time a suspected terrorist breaking down under interrogation.

Then the policeman, calm and assured, intervened: 'No, no, no. It wasn't like that at all. The kid's not drunk. Jason was stinking of the stuff. My men will confirm that. He was the one who was setting the place on fire. He said so himself. He had a bottle of petrol in his hand. The fire was started by petrol, that's what the firemen say.'

'And as for *that*,' he continued, pointing at the puddle, 'that's further evidence. The kid was obviously scared witless. It happens when people are scared, even to soldiers, you know. Luckily he managed to stay sane enough to phone us. You've got a lot to thank him for. Now let's have the statement.'

The Bishop grunted and harrumphed – like a volcano that wanted to explode but had decided not to – as John stumbled through his story, bit by semi-coherent bit.

Standing there in his sodden underpants, next to his own puddle, with tears trickling down his cheeks, he felt utterly degraded. Piss pants, shit pants, cry baby! If the lads at Beaconsfield could see him now! He'd die of shame! In his fantasies he'd been Denby the Dauntless, the airman shot down over Nazi Germany, defying his interrogators and braving their most ferocious tortures. 'Vee haff vays of making you talk!' Maybe, but they don't work with Denby the Dauntless! Now, reduced to *this*!

He got the feeling that he was really a kind of football, tossed around between the three adults for their own purposes:

the Bishop's to show off his interrogation skills, Isabel's to parade her caring and concern, the policeman's to display his cool professionalism in the face of heated emotion.

As he finally staggered to the end of his story, the Bishop's face broke into what was meant to be a reassuring smile. 'Well, I suppose I'll *have* to believe you, after all.'

'Now, your side of the story.'

'Not much to say. An infernal racket woke both of us up. Smelt burning and rushed down to see what was going on.'

He turned to John. 'Bishop's Palace saved by small boy's weak bladder,' he said grumpily. 'There's a headline for the newspapers.'

John winced. The man seemed unable to lay off him. Obviously he found any sort of gratitude demeaning.

Then the guns were turned on Isabel. 'Frankly, darling, I *do* wish you'd listened to me about Jason. I told you something awful would happen if we kept him here. He's beyond our help. I wish you'd face up to the fact.'

'But he's our *son*! Our *only* son!'

'Quite so, but this mess is going to cost us a pretty penny or two. And I doubt if the insurance will want to pay up. Well, after I've tidied up the room a bit and retrieved what you've so graciously left of my Sunday sermons, that is' – sharp glance at John – 'I'm off to bed. I've got a big day tomorrow. I'll leave you to clean up His Nibs here. Hope the bathroom's still working.' Another sardonic glance at John.

The police and the firemen finally left.

God has a Funny Way of Doing Things

Isabel led John into the kitchen. Sitting him down on a wooden stool, she draped a blanket over him and began to crash round with mugs and kettles.

'I think you could do with a little refreshment after your terrible ordeal, darling.'

When she eventually handed him a mug of steaming Horlicks, she suddenly burst into tears. 'Oh, John, how can you *ever* forgive us? We take you into our house and a madman tries to kill you! And then my husband tries to blame *you* for it!'

The cold night air, the roller-coaster of emotions, the adrenaline, the squalor of his uncontrollable bodily functions, the shame... it all made him clear-sighted. In his degradation he felt a sense of comradeship with a fellow sufferer. Poor, poor woman! Her only son a murderous lunatic!

'Please don't feel like that!' he exclaimed. 'Please don't! I admire the way you're looking after Jason. Most people would have chucked him out. But in spite of all he does, you stand by him. It's so *Christian*! Please, that's not crap. I really mean it.'

'Oh, John.'

As she hugged him the superlatives poured out in an avalanche: 'Strongest... best... kindest... bravest... most noble.'

He writhed. God, how he just hated this cuddling! He so wanted to be a proper *lad*, not a baby!

When eventually she released him form her octopus-like embrace, she suddenly became all confidential, even slightly conspiratorial. In a low voice she started telling him things that clearly she didn't tell many people; least of all, perhaps, her husband. Why *me* of all people? She doesn't fancy me, does she? Quite a thought!

'Jason's our only son, you know. He was the child of many prayers, *many* prayers! I had such a difficult pregnancy, I nearly lost him. He was premature, you know. But he was such a *wonderful* child. Such a *joy*! So promising. So full of life and so *clever*. He could read at four, you know and he got twelve O Levels when he was only fifteen. He was a wonderful sportsman, too. He was a champion boxer and played rugby for the county. He won an open scholarship to Oxford. We were *so* proud of him. *How* we thanked God for him!

'Then everything started to go wrong. He began to go all strange. He stopped talking to people and just sat in his room at Oxford for days on end doing nothing. Then he was found in the street, sitting on the pavement and staring at a tree for hours on end; and in the pouring rain, too! One day he ran naked through the park saying that Stalin was chasing him and trying to set his clothes on fire.

'It was so *distressing*! His tutor said he was having a nervous breakdown because of overwork and stress. There were stories of *drugs*! Why? Why did it happen? Perhaps Don was being too hard on him. He was so engrossed in his own affairs – his army work, that school in Uganda, you know – that he didn't have enough time to talk to him. Don means well, but he can be such a *bully*! I'm sure you've seen that. He has to *dominate*. Whatever Jason did, it was *never* good enough. He was always wanting *more*. Excellence just wasn't good enough. Don just can't understand human weakness, I'm sure you've discovered that! Maybe he was even a bit jealous of him because he was so clever; he doesn't like rivals, you know.

'By the way, he knows that you saved the house and, in a way, he's angry with you because you've upstaged him. That was why he was bullying you and cutting you down to size. He was always doing that to Jason whenever he did well at something. I should have stood up to him more and protected Jason, just as I've tried to do with you.

'But the psychiatrist said nobody was to blame. He said Jason was simply suffering from schizophrenia. That's a disease, you know. But why does God send these diseases? It's so *cruel*! And, maybe, I *was* to blame, after all. One of my brothers was schizophrenic and they tell me that the disease is hereditary. So I shouldn't have brought poor Jason into the world at all. But now that he's here I must stand by him, whatever he does! I pray all the time for God to cure him and end his suffering.'

The torrent eventually dried up. They sat in silence for a while, he on his wooden stool and she on the edge of the kitchen table.

Suddenly a blind fury blazed up in John. 'Don't blame yourself!' he almost shouted. 'You're good, kind and noble! You're *far* better than that Watson bitch! Whatever Jason does, you stand by him. Not like her! One silly little accident – which I couldn't help! – and she throws me out! *I hate her! She's a cunt!*'

He paused, alarmed at what he'd gone and said.

'Sorry about that,' he mumbled, 'I shouldn't have used dirty language. I just got… well… carried away. But, what's going to happen to me? I'm so worried. I've got no one!'

At that Isabel seemed to glow, almost to become phosphorescent: 'John, you've got *me*! I'll look after you. You can be *mine*!'

'You know,' she added looking beatific, 'I think God has set this whole business up just to give me another child! That's the only explanation for it.'

So God had been responsible for shafting Danny's bum in the shower. And how would Briggs answer that one? God had been responsible for his needing a pee that night, for the puddle in the Bishop's study, for the – as yet undiscovered! – pile of turds at the bottom of the lawn and for the disgusting state of his underpants. God had an odd way of doing things!

Another suffocating hug. He seemed to have found another protector – good politics! But, oh, he was so ashamed of himself, sitting there in his pissed knickers letting himself be kissed like a baby. If anybody should get to know of it…!

Finally he managed to disentangle himself. 'I'm tired. I think I'll have a bath and go to bed. Thanks for everything.'

He went upstairs past a sodden black mess. The stairs and the landing were still intact, but charred and sooty. The window was broken and the curtains had been reduced to dirty black rags. Everything stank of burnt cloth, smoke and sodden wood. The Fire Brigade had arrived just in time. A few moments later and the whole landing and staircase could have come crashing down. A terrifyingly narrow escape!

The bathroom was undamaged and the taps still worked. As he slipped off his sodden underpants, he noticed to his shame and disgust that he'd hadn't just pissed them: there was unmistakable evidence of the scatological disaster under the rhododendron bushes at the bottom of the lawn. Washing them was a degrading and repulsive business. Could he *never* escape from the human body – *his* body, in particular! – and its squalor?

In the bedroom he draped the dripping article over the radiator and climbed into bed in the nuddy. Not something he'd ever done before. Priority task for tomorrow: get some clean clothes from Gloucester Road.

Sleep descended. Blessed oblivion.

Underpants

John awoke to see his underpants. There they were on the radiator, brilliantly illuminated by the sun shining in through the window. In the half-real world of semi-consciousness they seemed to be talking to him.

'Sussed!' they sneered. 'Sussed to a crust!' Can't dream about girls. Dreams about boys instead. Hard man Denby? Sod that for a lark! A loony freaks out and chases him round the house, and what does he do? Pisses himself, that's what, and all over the Bishop's carpet, too! Then – wait for it – he goes and shits himself like a little kid. And that's not all. Oh no, Just as soon as the Bishop bollocks him he starts to cry. Christ, what a wimp!

They didn't want you at Greenhill. They didn't want you at Beaconsfield either. Nobody wants a dirty little shit-stabber. Except Isabel, that is. And do you know why she wants you? Just because you *are* totally pathetic, that's why. You'll be her little kitten. You'll never grow up. And if ever you do try to grow up, the Bishop will lay you over that armchair and whack your bum with that rattan cane of his, just like a little kid. You'll go mad and end up like Jason.

He lay there for a while, hoping to go back to sleep and sink once more into oblivion, and when that proved impossible, wishing he was somebody else. Even Billy Nolan.

Practicalities: Escaping from an Octopus

Eventually more immediate problems took over. His clothes were grubby and sweaty and he had to get some clean ones. That meant a trip to Gloucester Road. Reluctantly he got up, dressed in his school uniform and went out into the passage. As he squelched his way along the sodden black ash and past the dripping and sooty walls, the smell of dampness and burnt cloth filled his nostrils. God, last night *had* been a close run thing!

He found Isabel in the dining room. She was obviously in what Michael Connolly – a considerable expert in such matters – would have called 'a right state'. She was still in her dressing gown. Her face was white and tear-stained and her hair was all awry. She looked as if she'd had an encounter with the electric chair or a high voltage power line.

'Oh, John darling, *do* sit down and talk to me! I've had *such* a terrible time with Don!'

He sat down at the table next to her and was engulfed in a torrent of words.

'Don blames *me* for the fire. And for the bad behaviour of the children yesterday. I don't know *what* I'm going to do!

Really I don't. But if *you* hadn't been so *brave* I just don't know *what* would have happened. Really I don't.'

Eventually she ran out of breath and the flood momentarily ceased.

'Look,' he said, managing at last to get a word in edgeways, 'it's Sunday. Hadn't I better go to church?' Both politics and sincerity here. Keep the Bishop sweet, yes, but, at the same time he felt desperately in need of a bit of help from on high. Something. Anything.

'Oh *no!*' she replied with vehemence. 'It's *much* too late for that! It's past twelve o'clock and Don's been gone for nearly four hours!'

'Sorry, but I must have slept in.'

'Please don't *apologise!* You just *had* to have a good sleep after all you did last night. I spent *all* last night trying to explain it to Don.'

The torrent burst forth again with renewed vigour, sweeping all before it. It was quite a while before it eventually began to peter out in a series of gurgling little eddies. Head-shakings followed. 'I don't know. I really don't know,' she sighed, and then fell silent.

'Please,' he finally managed to say, 'I must go back to Gloucester Road to get a change of clothes. I mean, this lot are getting pretty yukky.'

'Don't *you* go! Don'll get them for you when he comes back.'

'Please don't bother him. He must be terribly busy. I can get the bus into town. It goes from the end of the road. It's no sweat.'

He felt desperate for air, like a drowning sailor dragged down into the depths by a giant octopus.

'Oh, but you *can't* go alone. I mean, what might happen to you?'

Bloody hell, couldn't he even get on a bus by himself?

'Please, I'll be all right. I do it every day. Anyway, both you and the Bishop have so much else to think about today.'

To his relief she gave way. 'You are *so* considerate! *So* considerate! Now *do* be careful. I feel so *guilty* about letting you go like this. You *will* be careful, won't you? I mean if anything should happen to you, I'd *never* forgive myself!'

Animal Crudity: A Gazelle in a Pride of Hungry Lions

The bus at the end of the road took him into town, where he was able to get onto the Greenwood bus. Getting out at the top of Gloucester Road, the bright blue sky and the warm, gusty wind gave him a sense of liberation. Free at last from the grasping tentacles of adults. He could be himself now! He marched purposely down the hill.

Then the underpants – or whatever it was – started again. Be yourself? But *what* self? He had no right to wear that red blazer, had he? He wasn't a Beaconsfield lad any more. He'd been chucked out. It was Sunday and Mrs Coburn would be looking after the place as she always did at weekends. Was he going to tell *her* that he'd been booted out for being a shit-stabber? No way! For a start, she wouldn't understand; and if she ever did... the shame of it! Worse still, she probably knew already. 'We'll get your things sent on from Fern Avenue.' He was going to have to cobble up some semi-plausible farrago to get round that one, and hope that she'd be daft enough to swallow it. He was very fond of her and he hated having to deceive her. Oh, the mess he was in!

'Wee's the fuckin' hom then?'

A high-pitched Geordie screech made him jump.

He glanced ahead to see a group of youngsters blocking the pavement ahead of him: male, female, dirty jeans, grubby miniskirts, woollen hats pulled down over the eyes, ferocious scowls, several shaved heads... a pack of predators on the prowl. In his distraction he had gone and forgotten Rule

Number One of Greenwood survival: camouflage and low profile. In his Beaconsfield school uniform he was as glaringly conspicuous as a gazelle in a pride of hungry lions.

With a tingling sense of fear rippling through him, he crossed the road, studiously avoiding any eye contact. Forget about old Granny Coburn. It was into survival now.

The pack followed him. It was a boring Sunday afternoon and he was obviously a welcome diversion.

'Why man, it's wee Jonny boy, wor Sam's liddell mate!'

He looked round to see the beaky-nosed girl who'd brought Sam Hawthorne round to Ma Watson's place on that famous Christmas two years ago. A big, sex-mad bully of a girl, she had scared him almost to death. It was her all right, no doubt about it, but bigger and more aggressive than ever. His guts seemed to twist up inside him as he broke into a panic-stricken run.

The pack surged around him. Soon he was pinned up against a wall, the gazelle surrounded by the slobbering lions.

'What's the hurry son?' screeched the girl, 'Divvent yer wanna say "hello" like?'

'Er, hello,' he mumbled in the desperate hope that this might be the hunk of bloody meat that might satisfy the advancing pack.

Instead, it merely seemed to fuel the feeding frenzy. The mob surged closer. Trapped! That old Greenhill feeling of sogginess when fear dissolved your bones.

The girl eyed him: 'Eeeeee yer've growed a canny bit.'

A brief silence followed; that silence before the crash of thunder that comes after the distant lightning flash. Frantically he tried to push his way through the ring of sweaty bodies.

'Have yer broken yer duck yet, son?' somebody said.

'Er, what do you mean?'

'Hadaway, 'ave yer done it yet?' laughed a bald-headed youth, his leering face twisted with pent-up aggression.

'What?'

'Hadaway!' shrieked a girl in a dirty T-shirt and a leather miniskirt. 'How long's yer cock?'

John blushed bright red and made another attempt to break free. It was no good. Struggling furiously, his arms were pinioned behind his back. Emitting great peals of yob laughter, which made his innards shrivel up, the mob frog-marched him into a little side alley.

'Divvent be shy, son,' said the beaky-nosed girl. 'Gee us a look!'

'No! No!' This was awful!

'Eeeee, lads, 'es ower shy like! Pull 'is pants doon and we'll 'ave a good look!'

Ghastly doom! 'No! No! Not my pants, *please*!'

Don't be a dickhead, Jonny boy! You can't expect any mercy from these people. Not a hint of it. You're the Christian thrown to the lions. You're the afternoon's entertainment. You of all people should know that. Get *real* lad! Get *real*!

While grubby hands pushed him firmly onto the ground and held him down, the beaky-nosed girl undid his belt and heaved down his trousers and then his drawers. A huge roar went up as his white nether regions were exposed. Despite all his efforts he began to cry. He closed his eyes as he was pushed down onto the hard, knobbly ground. He felt a hand grabbing his thing.

'Eeeeee! It's just a liddell pencil!'

'There'll be nowt commin' oota that but piss!'

'Why no, man! Ah'll see if it gans like!'

He felt his thing being manipulated. He became two people. One, John Denby, was horrified, appalled, disgusted, utterly shamed. The other was the Demon, which was actually *enjoying* it, especially when hands groped towards his back end; a wild, ecstatic, unholy joy.

Opening his eyes, he saw that the beaky-nosed girl had

pulled down her jeans and her knickers and was kneeling with her legs astride him. Momentarily glimpsing the grey, mouldy flesh of her groin and the dirty mass of black hair in it, he closed his eyes again in revulsion and disgust.

The Demon engulfed him, taking over his all… and it happened with a juddering, ecstatic rush. A wild, savage roar went up, like a sheet of flame.

'Eeeeeee! It gans after all!'

He felt his trousers and his underpants being hauled off over his feet. Despairingly he pleaded, 'No! *No! No!*'

He opened his eyes to see the mob whooping away down the alley, waving his trousers in the air. In spite of all his efforts to be a proper lad, he wept with an uncontrollable anguish. The despairing anguish of a small child. His whole being, his whole world was in ruins. Nothing left. And if anybody should *see* him like this! Degraded. Squalid. Totally awful. Giles's contemptuous words of two years ago came back to him. 'So *that's* what they thought of you.' Because John Denby was a pathetic little shit-stabber who deserved it.

Eventually he picked himself up. To his enormous relief he saw his trousers and his underpants lying at the end of the alley. Frantically he hurried over and dressed himself. Then he made a dash for safety of Number 14.

An Awkward Encounter

As soon as he opened the door he ran into Mrs Coburn.

'Eeeee pet,' she sighed, 'Warst tha bin? Ah been waiting for yers all yesterday.'

Next problem: what to tell her? In desperation he mumbled something about visiting a friend.

'Yer meet o' tard us, pet! Here Ah were gerrin' yer teas an' that an' yer nivver torned oop! Ah mean what kept yers? An' Ah divvent like ter see good food wasted me. No wi' all them bairns starvin' in Africa an' that.' (One of Annie Coburn's hobby horses, this.)

'Sorry about that!'

'An' worraboot yer washin'? Ah mean neebeddy's given us nin!'

He felt a spurt of relief at this, a flash of light at the end of the tunnel: nothing had been sent on from Fern Avenue. So she obviously hadn't heard. That gave him a breathing space.

'An' why, look at the state o' yers! What 'ave yer bin deeing like? Fightin' an' that?' Motherly concern here. But, oh God, she'd noticed! He couldn't possibly tell her about *that*. It was *shaming*! It had to be consigned to oblivion. It hadn't happened. Never. Not ever.

'Oh. Er… nothing.'

'And why, yer've bin cryin' an' all!'

He made for the ladder, desperate to get to his room. But old Annie Coburn wasn't going to be fobbed off as easily as that, not where 'wor bairn' was concerned anyway. She went into 'wise old grandmother' mode. 'Ah knaa worrit is, pet. It's luv, ain't it? Yer divvent need ter tell us. Yer's bin seein' yer lady luv an' yer've quarrelled. Yer divvent need ter tell us. Noo, when Ah forst met me man like…'

There followed one of her long, rambling stories. He listened as patiently as he could. He *did* like her; she was so kind and generous, and kindness was the one thing that he just couldn't resist. But, oh God, she was so *irritating*! *Coronation Street*, women's magazines, soppy love stories: these were the parameters of her universe. Still, if she wanted to believe it was all a question of 'Love' (and wish to God that it was!) then let her get on with it. It got him off the hook. There was no need to cobble up a semi-plausible construction of fibs. What he would have to say to her when she finally *did* learn that he'd been chucked out of Beaconsfield for being a shit-stabber – as she surely must! – well, that would just have to wait!

Eventually the convoluted tale fizzled out. 'Well ye gan an' wash yersel.' An' when yers finished like, gimme them things what yer've gorron what wants washin.' An' when yer ready, pet, Ah'll give yer yer teas. Yer want feedin' up ye.'

With a sense of relief he clambered up to his room. His television, his model planes, his railway… they all seemed to welcome him back to normality. Then the underpants started up again. *His* railway? *His* television? Were they really his now? When Giles heard of this latest disaster he'd almost certainly chuck him out, just as Ma Watson had done! Indeed, he'd probably done so already. His only hope was Isabel. He'd have to get back to her double quick. 'If anything should happen to you I'd *never* forgive myself!' Well, happen to him it had, but he couldn't possibly tell her about *that*! Couldn't tell anyone!

He suddenly felt dirty and defiled, especially round those nether regions, which had been so coarsely fingered. He went down the ladder and into the bathroom. Stripping off, he glimpsed his skinny white body in the mirror. God, how he hated it! A pathetic, humiliating body that didn't work properly! Why couldn't he trade it in for a better one that didn't push him into excruciating situations?

He duly washed, changed into scruff order and handed his dirty things to old Coburn.

'That blazer'll be wantin' dry cleanin,' she said. 'Can't have yers gannin ter skyerll in that. Why, Mrs Watson wouldn't half be playin' war.' God, if she knew the *truth*! 'Noo howay an' eat yer teas.'

She propelled him to the table. Its famous 'total working-class honesty' had long since been hidden under a flowery table cloth she'd bought with her own money with 'Good luck from Blackpool' on it: 'Can't have folk eatin' off yon thing. Ain't proper like! I'm not common, me!' Today it was covered with plate-loads of the cakes and sticky buns that she loved to make, and a huge, steaming plate of egg and chips.

After the melodrama in the alley he wasn't hungry, but she'd been so kind that he felt he had to make a big effort to eat as much as he could. He did his valiant best and thanked her profusely, making full use of the deadliest weapon in his social armoury, his ingratiating smile.

It duly worked. 'Eeeee, yer's a luverly lad, ye!' Diplomatic fences repaired for the time being. Now back to work on Isabel, his only hope!

Rearranging a Few Facts to Create a Hero... The Essence is True?

He found Isabel waiting for him outside the front porch.

'John, darling, where *have* you been?' she exclaimed, looking at her watch. 'You're very late,' she added aggressively. 'Did anything happen to you?'

'No! No! I'm fine!'

'Are you *sure?*'

Gads! Was she telepathic? A witch with a crystal ball who could see across cities and through brick walls?

'No! No! Honest. I'm perfectly all right. Nothing happened to me.'

No way was he going to tell *her* what happened it that alley! Quite apart from the awful embarrassment, just imagine the sheer hassle that would ensue if she found out! Didn't bear thinking about!

'Well, that's a relief, anyway.'

She seemed almost resentful to find him safe and sound. He got the impression that she would have preferred a disaster, to reinforce her chosen role as his sole protector. A big, soppy hug and kiss followed. Back to being a pet kitten again.

'Now then,' she cooed as he disentangled himself from her octopus-like embrace, 'I've got somebody who wants to see you.'

Tremor of anxiety: what now?

'It's about last night.'

'Please, no! I've told you everything. I told the truth. Swear to God!'

'Oh don't get like *that* about it! He's a reporter from the *Boldonbridge Journal*. I've told him *all* about you. Yes, about how *brave* you were. He wants to interview you.'

'Cripes!'

What to tell him? About Jason running round starkers? About the puddle on the Bishop's carpet? About the pile of shit under the rhododendron bushes? All this in the newspapers for everybody to laugh at? His mind seemed to seize up as she led him along the corridor.

'And this is our young hero, is it?' said a crisp young man as they entered the dining room. Draped with cameras and what seemed to be the very latest electronic gear, he looked like a futuristic Christmas tree.

'Now sit down and tell us all about it,' he said to John. He produced a notepad and a biro, which he held in quivering anticipation.

John's mind remained blank. Switched off. That pile of shit under the rhododendron bushes! Soon the Bishop would find it – it was just the sort of thing he *would* go and notice! It was a bomb waiting to explode...

'Come on, don't be shy!'

He looked helplessly at Isabel.

'He's very shy,' she said reassuringly to the reporter, 'and he is so *modest*, you know!'

More silence.

'All right, darling, I'll tell him. You woke up to smell burning, didn't you?'

'Yes.'

Please don't start on me needing a pee and running round in my underpants, or Jason being starkers! Is there any end to this run of disasters?

'And then you had to fight your way through the smoke and flames, didn't you, darling?'

'Yes.'

'Come on, tell us about it,' said the reporter. He needed some copy to fill the empty pages of his notebook: professional necessity. Even professional survival.

'Well, er...'

Helpless look from Isabel. 'He's *so* modest, you know.'

Suddenly the penny dropped and John cottoned on. Both the reporter and Isabel needed a lurid story – for whatever reason, it didn't matter – and literal truth wasn't that important. So a lurid story they would get. Embellishing facts was something he *was* good at: that old business of telling lies, inventing your own reality and getting yourself to believe it.

'When I went out into that passage I couldn't see anything for the smoke. It was like being in one of those poisonous fogs that aliens send down when they want to conquer the world. It hurt my eyes, yes, it blinded me for a moment. I felt I was choking to death. Then I saw the flames. They were really quite pretty, you know, like Christmas streamers. I was only just able to get downstairs. The flames were running along the banisters like evil little snakes chasing me.'

'Yes, go on! This is great!'

Before he could continue an excited Isabel broke in. 'Any *normal* person would have saved themselves by rushing out into the garden, but you didn't, did you darling? You stayed cool and collected and telephoned the fire brigade!'

'Well, what else could I have done? I couldn't let the whole house burn down, could I?'

'And then what happened?'

John paused. This was the awkward bit. He could hardly tell the man about crashing round the Bishop's study, knocking the lamp over and peeing on the carpet, could he?

And certainly not about cowering under the rhododendron bushes and shitting himself with fright! The pause continued.

'Come on, darling!' said Isabel, eventually. 'Don't be too modest! Then, despite the flames and the danger, you rushed back up the stairs and warned me and the Bishop. And in the nick of time, too!'

This had never happened! He'd run out of the house in a wild panic. In any case, the Bishop's bedroom was up a different flight of stairs and he hadn't a clue where it was. But, well, the tale was taking on a life of its own. And if that were what Isabel wanted, let her have it, and with interest; compound interest and not just simple interest either!

'Yes, I had to be quick. There was so little time. But, you know, what was really scary was having to barge into somebody else's bedroom in the middle of the night. You just don't do that sort of thing...'

'And, especially not with a man like my husband!' interrupted Isabel with some vehemence. 'When he's angry he can be... well, like a *cave man*! Don't you agree, darling?'

'Yes, he can be a bit scary when he's in an episweat! Waking him up was even more scary than the fire! It was, well, like waking up a monster in a cave. I was really bricking myself.'

This just slipped out and immediately he regretted it. 'But he's awfully nice really!' he added hastily. 'And I really like him you know!'

Scribble, scribble, scribble on the notepad.

'But you *did* manage to wake us up!' declared Isabel. 'And in spite of my husband's temper – and, you know I *really* thought he was going to *eat* you! – and you *did* warn us in time!'

Scribble, scribble, scribble on the notepad.

Inwardly John sighed to himself. What a load of garbage he was spouting! And, if ever the Bishop were to hear of it, he would blow at least twenty gaskets – probably more! And rightly so, too. Talk about biting the hand which fed you! Madness. Just what *was* Isabel's little game in getting him to talk all this nonsense? That feeling of drifting helplessly down a foaming river.

'Well, let's have your photo. No, don't look so solemn. Smile!'

He managed a sort of grotesque leer. You could hardly call it a smile.

'That's it. It'll all be in Tuesday's *Journal*.'

Better lie low on Tuesday, then. Keep well clear of the Bishop.

Forebodings

Monday came, clear and sunny. Before anybody else was awake, John slipped out into the garden. There, under the rhododendron bushes were Saturday night's turds. Bright and fresh, they lay there like the smoking gun in a murder trial, as yet undiscovered, but waiting to proclaim his shame to the whole world. Frantically scrabbling round among the dead leaves and rotting twigs, he buried them, consigning his humiliation to oblivion. Like yesterday's business in the alley off Gloucester Road, they did not exist. Never had existed.

Thankfully the Bishop was absent and he passed a restful day in the workshop painting pictures and making collages to illustrate Isabel's various causes. Losing himself in an orgy of creativity, he tried to forget his troubles. Live for the moment. All that matters is the anguished face you are drawing and those piles of discarded milk cartons and Coke cans that you are turning into a bombed city.

But it was no use. His troubles just wouldn't go away. What was to become of him? What would the yobbish inmates do to him when he arrived at the care home? What would happen to him at Greenhill when they learned – as surely they must – that he was a shit-stabber? More immediately, what would happen if that idiot of a reporter went and printed all that rubbish he spouted last evening? The Bishop would go apeshit, for starters! And he'd be right, too. He'd been so kind in helping him out; what a way to repay that kindness! He'd chuck him out.

Nag! Nag! Nag! It was like having a heavy rucksack on your back, always digging into your shoulders and chafing your spine.

'So I Am a Caveman, Am I?' More Grovelling and an Unexpected Outcome

Tuesday came. Sunday evening's landmine duly exploded. He was at breakfast, trying to do justice to the vast bowl of Weetabix that Isabel had thrust in front of him, when suddenly the Bishop burst into the dining room. In off-duty scruff order, eyebrows bristling, hairs in his ears upended and quivering, and brandishing a copy of the *Boldonbridge Journal*, he was in full caveman mode.

Take cover! Big storm on the way! But nowhere to hide!

'Just what *is* this?' he boomed, dumping the paper down on the table.

John shrivelled up. Oh Lord, that reporter's gone and done it and he's seen it! He just *would*, wouldn't he!

'Go on, look at it.'

A frightened glance at the paper confirmed his worst fears. 'BOY HERO SAVES THE LIFE OF "CAVEMAN" BISHOP' screamed the headline. Beneath it, prominently displayed, was a photograph of himself wearing an idiotic smirk. He scanned the article and picked up the phrases 'cool and calm'... 'braving showers of sparks'... 'fighting through fierce flames and poisonous fumes'... 'Bishop'... 'a bit like a caveman with a club'... 'saved him in the nick of time'.

Oh no! That reporter really has done it! Dropped me right in the shit!

'And you told them all *that*? So I am a caveman, am I? I suppose you think that's frightfully funny? Your idea of a joke?'

John stared at the breakfast bowl, wishing that the sodden heap of Weetabix was a mountain range into whose unexplored fastnesses he could disappear for ever.

'It's a load of rubbish, isn't it?'

No response. What the hell *am* I to say? I didn't set this one up, Isabel did. But how to cool this rampaging monster down? I *know* I should be grateful to him, and I *am*! But, oh God, he scares me shitless! And where the hell is Isabel? Crashing round in the kitchen and leaving me to face the music all on my own!

He felt himself going soggy.

'You're a little liar, aren't you? And cunning with it.'

The Bishop folded his arms and became 'the tough interrogator', a role he obviously relished.

'I've been doing a little bit of thinking. You set the whole business up, didn't you? Don't tell me that you needed the toilet in the middle of the night. Oh no! You were doing your Beaconsfield Shower Act, weren't you? That's why you were cavorting round in your underpants. You saw that Jason was susceptible to your charms and you thought you'd have a bit of fun. Tart about. Get him all worked up. Not difficult, I'm afraid. But it all got out of hand, didn't it? Ended in tears. Now you've invented this little farrago to cover your traces and get a little kudos as well. Go on, admit it!'

The floor giving way beneath me and sending me hurtling down... to where? To what? Now I really am in the shit. What *did* happen on Saturday night? I don't know. Does anybody know? It could have been like he says it was. How do I know that it wasn't?

Desperate plea: 'Please, I didn't! Honest, I didn't! Swear to God!'

Is he going to start on me with that rattan cane? The humiliation! But I'll just have to grit my teeth and bear it. No choice. He's probably going to have me sent back to Greenhill.

Despite himself, and to his enormous shame, he began to cry. He knew he shouldn't. Proper lads didn't cry. But it just went and happened.

Then deliverance came crashing through the door as Isabel exploded into the room. '*Don, leave him alone*! You *know* it's not true! If you must know, I told the *Boldonbridge Journal* about the fire. I told the reporter everything that is in that article!'

'But it's simply not true!'

'In the details, perhaps not. But the *essence* is true. If it hadn't been for John, the whole house would have been burnt down, and us with it! Why can't you see that? You seem determined to deny obvious facts.'

Another of those awkward silences. The two antagonists eyed each other. Eventually the Bishop backed down with a bad grace. For Donald Macnab, accepting any kind of defeat was about as palatable as swallowing a bowl of liquid cement, especially defeat at the hands of his wife. Digestion of unpleasant realities took time.

He turned his guns onto the squashed mess that was John. 'All right, you can stop snivelling. I'll believe you. I was just stirring the pot a bit to get you to face up to what people will start saying if you let yourself get big-headed. Anyway, I've got news for you.'

'Oh?' John felt a spurt of alarm running through his body like an electric shock.

'You're leaving us this morning.'

Doom! You've messed your nest!. They're chucking you out! Yobbos. Greenhill.

'Oh, please, *no*!' he gasped. 'Please give me another chance!'

'Don't be an ass! It's all been sorted out. Watson's having you back. You're back at Beaconsfield again.'

An overwhelming feeling of relief. Curtains drawn back. Sunlight flooding into the darkened room. Heavy rucksack falling off your back. Uncontrollable surge of emotion surging up. Those yukky tears started again.

'Thank you! Thank you! I'm so pleased.' Sniffle... Wiffle....

'Don't thank *me*!' snorted the Bishop. 'Thank God. He's the one who makes people want to help the likes of you. So what are you going to say to him, eh?'

John knelt down on the carpet. 'Thanks, God. Thanks a billion! I really *will* try to be good. I'm so grateful!'

The Sermon on the Motorway

The Bishop drove him back to Fern Avenue in his souped-up BMW. In the few calm intervals of the adrenaline-filled, fighter pilot style battle with the traffic, he delivered an impromptu and disjointed sermon.

'Go on, woman, can't you see the light's green! Get your car into gear!... Let all this be a lesson to you, young man... That's right! At *last* you're moving!... Whatever you do, don't forget about God! You're going to need him. Don't end up like your ridiculous father... Driving an Audi and he's only doing thirty, for heaven's sake!... Yes, I know I'm being tactless – 'unprofessional' they call it! – but it's no use ducking reality. You get his line: God's a fairy story, a load of garbage. *He* can do without God, but *you* can't... Come on, man, it's no use trying to chase me! I've got a BMW and you've only got a little Metro. Unequal contest, so don't fret! There, that's got him!... Remember the camel going through the eye of a needle. For "rich in money" substitute "rich in talent, rich in achievement, rich in friendship". That's your father... Go on, you idiot! Move over! You shouldn't be doing thirty in the outer lane... Blind to reality he is. You, my man, aren't like that. Your proclivities – and, I'm afraid, Professor Hindmarsh says, they could be permanent – are going to be a problem for you in this sex-obsessed age. Most people won't understand you. A lot will despise you. The do-gooders will consider you a freak, a sort of endangered species to be cotton-wooled like a panda... Condescended to look in your mirror, have you, madam? Well done! You're learning! You're learning!... I wouldn't get too closely involved with the so called "Liberated" hippies, if I were you. Narcissic exhibitionists, many of them, Think of poor old Cedric. Not your scene, my lad! You'll just get labelled, pigeon-holed. Won't do you any good. Anyway, to get back to the point, you know what it's like to be on the wrong side of the boot. And that's wisdom. Not something your father knows or is ever likely to know. Clear road ahead... Off we go! Whoa! There's the police! Can't be caught doing ninety! You know it's quite possible that the Guy Upstairs could have made you gay for one of his odd little schemes. God's a crafty old bastard, you know! Devious, underhand, springs things on you out of the blue.'

Not that Little Toad Again!

Perhaps God had arranged things for him. Or, maybe, it was just another of those mundane chains of circumstance. Who knew? Anyway, that Monday morning Dorothy had arrived at school to find a letter waiting for her on her study desk. Awesomely official and on House of Commons notepaper, it was from Dr Giles Denby MP, no less.

Nervously she read it. Dr Denby was 'appalled by the inhumane treatment' of his 'cherished son, John', etc., etc., etc. This was a new departure. Apart from the direct debit, which paid the school fees – a decidedly impersonal business, handled by his secretary – this was the first time in over eighteen months that he had condescended to communicate with the school.

Just what had caused this sudden eruption of parental concern for his superfluous son? God, perhaps? A sudden conversion, the Road to Damascus and all that? Hardly likely. Or, if at all, in a very roundabout sort of way.

On the Wednesday afternoon Giles had ignored Dorothy's message on the answer phone. He had much more important things on his mind: a visit to Yorkshire to support the striking miners, the craven attitude of the T.U. C, what to say at Prime Minister's Question Time...

The following Friday, Maggie Wright – who was now his partner and full-time secretary – handed him the letter formally expelling John from Beaconsfield for the homosexual abuse of a fellow pupil. It contained all the gory details; chapter and verse lovingly supplied by Briggs.

'Giles, I really think you ought to read this.'

His first reaction was exasperated anger. Not that little toad *again*! He'd fondly imagined that with him installed in Ma Watson's house the whole business had been settled. Out of sight. Out of mind. Swept comfortably under the carpet. But – oh no! – he couldn't conveniently disappear, could he? He had to keep messing things up, hadn't he? Christ, why couldn't he just go and jump in the river or something? That would solve a lot of problems.

He shook his head dismissively. 'He'll just have to sort this one out for himself. I don't know what I'm supposed to do about it.'

Then Maggie fixed her large, watery eyes on him. She was a quite irresistibly lovely creature – that exquisitely shaped body, those wonderful bulbous breasts, that glorious flood of silver hair, that velvety skin... and that impishly appealing smile, which was such an improvement on Mary's analytical stare. And she was so calm and rational, too. Softly and gently persuasive.

'You're quite right, darling. But he's a sad little scrap, isn't he? It's not *his* fault that he's inadequate.'

'I'm not here to deal with petty bourgeois inadequates.'

'Aren't you? Isn't that what the Rainbow Coalition is all about? Concern for the casualties of Thatcherism?'

'He's hardly that. Spoilt brat, if you ask me!'

She sidled up to him and sat on the edge of his desk, every so often shifting her superbly shaped bottom to emphasise a point.

She entirely agreed with him, but... well... Didn't he realise what all this could lead to? He was a firm supporter of Len Bowman's Rainbow Coalition of Oppressed Minorities: blacks, Asians, deprived youngsters, so-called druggies... that alienated proletariat that would ignite 'objectively necessary social change'. And this *did* include gays, didn't it? What would happen if it were to leak out that his own son was being persecuted for being gay and he was doing nothing about it – as it most certainly would? The Tories would have a field day for a start. And, more to the point, what would Red Len himself have to say about it? He wouldn't be exactly overjoyed to learn that Dr Giles Denby, that champion of the underdog, had callously ignored his own son, would he?

Giles heaved a resigned sigh: 'Yes, I suppose you are right! I hadn't really thought of it in that way. But, Christ Almighty, he *has* landed us in it, hasn't he?'

Maggie edged closer to him and wiggled her bottom deliciously. Christ, she was *so* beautiful! Couldn't she take her knickers off *now* instead of keeping him waiting till after midnight as she usually did?

'No, darling,' she cooed, 'He's given you a wonderful opportunity.'

Here was his chance to show to the world what a truly caring and compassionate parent he really was. The champion, indeed, of *all* persecuted youngsters wherever and whoever they were. Red Len would just eat that!

The ice melted. The warm glow of righteous indignation filled Giles. (Briggs would have said it was the Holy Ghost.) How right she was! Now that he didn't actually have to be next to his wayward son – and endure his squeaky voice, inane conversation and baby-nappy smell – he became quite fond of him. Strictly in the abstract, of course. What a glorious opportunity to parade his socialist ideals before the Unbelievers and, also, to put that stuck-up petty bourgeois baggage, Ma Watson, firmly in her place – *down* into her place! Then and there, he dictated an 'outraged' letter.

He was 'appalled by the insensitive and inhumane treatment' of his 'cherished son, John'... When he had 'so reluctantly' entrusted her with his care he had naturally assumed that he was dealing with 'a properly trained professional'. Never for one moment had he imagined that she was the sort of person who would let herself be dominated by a man like James Briggs. And as for 'kow-towing to a semi-educated car salesman like Fleetwood', and, moreover a person who let his son watch pornographic videos...! (And for this spicy titbit he had to thank the ever-assiduous Martha Merrins; God, or Providence, rot the old bag!) Well! She was nothing but a 'weak and pliable woman' who listened to 'bird-brained religious bigots' and 'sleazy businessmen'! He, at any rate,was 'not prepared to countenance the persecution of minorities, be they black, brown or gay'. He was 'seeing a solicitor', and, if this matter was not satisfactorily resolved, would 'not hesitate to sue the school'. In the meantime, he was taking the matter up with the Boldonbridge Education Committee and was seriously questioning the whole business of local authority support for Beaconsfield School....

'It's Pretty Obvious, Isn't It?
A stunned Dorothy called Meakin into her study.

'Read this, Roderick. What *are* we going to do?'

Meakin read through the letter. 'Well, it's pretty obvious, isn't it?' he said.

'Obvious?'

'You'll just have to have him back. Should never have been expelled in the first place, if you ask me.'

'But will that be possible? Will the boys accept him? They're very hostile to homosexuals, you know. And what about Mr Fleetwood?'

'I'll sort that one out. I'll get the seniors together and spin a line about the dangers of ogling at porno mags and Page Three of the *Sun*. Hypes you up so much that you lose control and go and do daft things in showers. So, don't go for old Denby when he comes back. It could be you next time. Even old Fleetwood might swallow that one.'

A Visitation from the Almighty

That afternoon Professor James George Hindmarsh, M.B, B.S, PhD, DSc, F.R.C.S, F.R.S, etc., etc., descended on Dorothy in all his professional and academic splendour; perhaps the nearest thing that ordinary mortals might get to an actual visitation from the Almighty. He duly put her right on a number of things, and not very tactfully, either.

That evening Dorothy had telephoned the Bishop. 'Yes, we'll take him back.'

'So Proud of You'

When the Bishop's BMW finally screeched to a juddering halt in Fern Avenue, Dorothy rushed out to greet them. She was no longer Mrs Watson, Headmistress and hard headed professional, but Dolly, big, warm, affectionate shaggy sheepdog Dolly. Very much the Emotional Woman.

She embraced John, clasping him tightly to her breast as if he were a cherished puppy, which had got lost and been found again; which in a sense he was.

'Oh John!' she gushed. 'You don't know how pleased I am to have you back again! It's all been a terrible misunderstanding. But it's all water under the bridge and we're back to normal.'

Overwhelmed with relief, John responded in like fashion. 'Thanks! Thanks! I *am* going back to Beaconsfield, aren't I?'

'Of course, of *course* you are! Mr Meakin has talked to the boys and it's all been sorted out. And I see from the *Journal* that you're a hero! I'm so *proud* of you!'

So she gushed on for five or more minutes.

3

A New Start?

A Proper Lad Now

It was the start of the Easter holidays and a blissful period followed. It was the warm euphoria of sheer relief, relieved of that anxiety that had been weighing you down. And, also, the relief of being freed from the cloying tentacles of Isabel and from that terrifying high-explosive landmine, the Bishop; inspiring you with hope and confidence one minute and blasting you into grovelling smithereens the next.

Dolly continued to gush over him. He was invited to the Town Hall and given a Merit Award for his 'bravery' and duly appeared on the local television. The terrified little wimp who'd peed on the Bishop's carpet and shat himself in the garden was no more. It was cool, caring, unselfish and fearless John instead.

But what *was* the truth? Which was the real John? Did such a thing as Truth actually exist? It all depended on which facts you chose to mention. It seemed that you could create your own truth.

Which was what he proceeded to do over the business of Danny in the shower. He'd got so sexed-up by gawping at all those bare female bums on Page Three of the *Sun* that when he'd seen Danny's bare bum in the shower... well, he'd just exploded! He wasn't called 'Dirty Denby' for nothing, you know!

All Back in Place?

So all was back in place. Or was it? Some truths seemed to be unalterable, firmly fixed no matter how artfully you juggled the facts. The dreams continued. But always about boys and never about girls. The Demon was still there. 'Your proclivities... I'm afraid they could be permanent.' Time had changed things and was pushing him down an unknown river.

Then there was that awful Wednesday afternoon tribunal. *That* was another unalterable fact: warm, friendly and loving Dolly, always so sympathetic and understanding, suddenly turning cold, pitiless and unforgiving. Could it happen again? Very probably. It was like a meteorite hurtling down from a clear blue sky, wholly unexpected and wholly devastating. Things were not the same as before. Trust had gone.

For Dorothy, also, things could never be quite the same again. She'd duly swallowed the nasty medicine that the Bishop and Professor Hindmarsh had poured down her retching throat. She now understood that homosexuality was not a deliberate crime, but a normal part of the human condition. For those so afflicted it posed serious problems in a sex-mad and homophobic world: rejection, harassment, loneliness, self-disgust and perhaps even suicide. Was *she* equal to the challenge of guiding a homosexual youth towards a stable and productive adulthood? Wasn't she aware that God could well have set the whole situation up just to test her mettle? Was she going to be like that young man in the Bible who, faced with a tough challenge from Jesus, had gone 'away sorrowful because he had great possessions'? Not monetary riches in her case, but her so-called professionalism and her complacent self-esteem. As a Christian, of course she wasn't!

But… deep down, she still found the whole notion of homosexuality strange and unnatural- indeed, deeply repulsive. What John had done to Danny in that shower was both incomprehensible and downright revolting. It took all her self-control to accept it let alone forgive it.

If only it had never happened! It was all such a brutal disappointment. She'd allowed herself to fantasise about John's getting married and giving her grandchildren to enrich her declining years, and banish for ever the awful prospect of her sinking into an empty and unwanted old age. Now this hope was probably gone. Try as she might, she could never quite look at him in the same light again.

Problems Remain

It all came to a head over supper one evening.

She suddenly looked at him with an intense stare: 'John, you must *never* do a think like that *ever* again.'

John stared sulkily at his mince and dumplings. 'What are you on about?' he eventually muttered.

'You know perfectly well. That business with Danny Fleetwood in the shower. You've no idea of the trouble you caused.'

Sullen silence.

'John, I am talking to you.'

More sullen silence.

'Well, what are you going to say to me?'

Eventually he condescended to answer with a sulky mutter:, 'Look, do we *have* to talk about this? I thought you said it was water under the bridge.'

'Yes, John we *do* have to talk about it. I want you to promise me that you'll never do a thing like that ever again.'

(Have you any idea of what you're asking for? All afternoon I've been thinking of Danny. Danny starkers. Danny's bum. Can't help it. It just happens... like spewing!)

Eventually he managed a semi-audible mumble, 'All right, I'll try.'

'Try isn't good enough. I want a definite NO.'

Suddenly his temper blazed out. 'And if I am bad again, will YOU promise never to do what you did to me ever again? Never! *Never!* *Ever!*'

Her turn to be silent.

The dam broke. Out it all came. 'Expelling me like that! It was heartless! Cruel! I thought you were a kind person who understood kids. But you were like an S.S. officer sending Jews to the gas chamber.'

'Don't be silly!'

'It was horrible being chucked out like that! If Bob Steadman hadn't helped me... I might have killed myself!'

'But you *had* been bad!'

'But if you had been a proper mum who *really* liked me you'd have bollocked me. Sent me to Mekon for a walloping. Not *that*!'

'We're doing away with physical punishment at Beaconsfield. It's old fashioned and barbaric.'

'Not half as barbaric as what you did. That was sadistic. You shouldn't do that sort of thing to kids – especially when they depend on you. I mean why didn't you get Mekon to give me a walloping?'

'That would have been degrading.'

'You've got kids all wrong. We don't mind being thumped. We do it to each other all the time. We expect it. What we hate is mean cold-bloodedness. You know, deliberate cold-blooded cruelty. I did something dirty on the spur of the moment – in a flash – but you planned your cruelty and that's much worse.'

Silence.

Dorothy finally broke the impasse. 'Look John, I know I made a mistake. *Of course* I'll never chuck you out again, but you *must* do your bit. You must try to help me by not doing a thing like that ever again!'

Peace treaty on offer. Remember which side of your bread the butter's on: you *need* Dolly!

'OK. I promise.'

Big smiles all round. Big hug from Dolly.

So back to normal? Not quite. Previous illusions of youthful innocence and adult omnipotence had been shattered. And for Dorothy there was another lingering doubt to nag away at her. 'We don't mind being thumped. We do it to each other all the time.' Was it really so humane to abolish physical punishment for boys? They weren't adults, they didn't think like adults.

A Convenient Rearrangement of Some Awkward Facts

Just before the summer term began, something happened. John was at Gloucester Road sorting out his dirty washing for Mrs Coburn when Danny Fleetwood suddenly burst in, all smiles and matiness. Seeing him, John felt a warm, physical thrill flow through his body – a stirring which should not have happened – and, also, a profound sense of relief. Greeting him effusively, he babbled out the tale he had been so assiduously rehearsing.

'Sorry about that business in the shower... but you know, I'd been hooked on those bums and tits on Page Three of the *Sun* and got myself so sexed up that... man... Any bum gave me a hard one, even yours! Well, you know, you just can't help these things.'

Danny grinned wickedly. 'Yeah, I know. Mekon told us. Dirty Denby, that's my lad!'

'Well, a bloke's gotta do what a bloke's gotta do!'

Explosion of dirty laughter. Fence mended. Ploy's

worked. Thank God Danny doesn't have that much on the upper deck.

Then Danny became serious:. 'Look, there's something we've got to discuss. It's about my Dad.'

Him? Enemy Number One who'd publicly demanded his expulsion and privately his castration? Oh hell!

'You see, he's in deep shit and you're the one who can help him.'

'Of course I will.' Important fence to be mended here.

'It's all a bit difficult.' Danny dropped his voice and became conspiratorial. 'You know a girl called Tracy Bowers?'

'No.'

'Well, she knows you.'

'Oh? How so?'

'Don't you know? She's Sam Hawthorne's bit. She's the one who brought him round to Dolly's Christmas party two years ago. Remember?'

John *did* remember. The beaky-nosed creature who'd debagged him in that alley next to Gloucester Road! God, how had *that* got out? Now the whole world knew of his shame and degradation! Doom! All lost! He went white and felt physically sick. All he could do was grunt and stare at the floor.

'Well she's the local bike,' continued Danny. 'Everybody rides her. My Dad did. You see, he didn't know she was under age when he picked her up at the Rose and Crown. She looks so grown up. Well, now she's preggers – you know, a bun in the oven – and she says it was him. She's going to get the law onto him. And, if she does, he'll get done.'

'Done?'

'Yes, the nick.'

'But what can I do?'

'Say it was you.'

'*Me?*'

'Yes, you. She says you had her, too! She's always going on about it. Posh git, Denby. Couldn't even do it in bed. Had to do it in the street, didn't he? Is it true what she says?'

Quick thinking required here! There's a lifeline dangling in front of you. Grab it while you still can!

He blushed bright red. The whole business had been so excruciatingly degrading! Eventually he managed to nod his head and mumble an embarrassed, 'Yes.'

A long pause.

'OK,' he finally said. 'I'll say it was me if that gets your Dad out of the shit.'

Thoughts whirled round in his head. A wholly unexpected vista was opening up. But if that particular version of events suited everybody, well, let it be 'The Truth'!

Danny's face broke into a wide, radiant smile, a wonderful smile that sent a tingling thrill through the less mentionable parts of John's body. 'Great! *Wicked*! You're a real lad! Dirty Denby! Had it off in the street! Even Billy Nolan hasn't gone that far! Yes, I knew you weren't a bender.'

In the event the whole thing fizzled out. Closely questioned by her probation officer with a view to bringing charges, Tracy proved incapable of remembering the simplest facts, let alone times and dates. Drugs, alcohol, glue, they had all reduced what mind she had (and that wasn't much) to a hopelessly confused blur. When she had a miscarriage the matter was quietly dropped.

A Lucky 'Eruption'

As a reward, Old Man Fleetwood invited John round to his house to watch a blue movie. John found the whole thing quite excruciatingly embarrassing and repulsive, but for the sake of his new-found reputation, he had to pretend to enjoy it.

However, once again, luck was on his side. Danny was having a bath when the show began. 'Howay Danny lad!'

his father bawled along the passage, 'You're missing the best bit!'

A semi-dried Danny bounced into the room stark naked and lay down on the rug in front of John. Everything he'd ever wanted was on display. By surreptitiously eyeing those treasures, he was able to perform at the right moment – and what a performance it was, too!

'I can see that you know what's best in life!' chortled Fleetwood Senior, slapping him heartily on the back when the show ended.

A lucky chance, and, no, you couldn't honestly say that God had laid this one on.

That evening, as he walked back through the purple gloaming to Dolly's place, he reflected on the whole crazy saga that had begun on that fateful Wednesday back in March. All might have come out right in the end, but it had given him a nasty fright. It had shown him just how precarious his position was. It could all so easily have ended in disaster. Still, there was one lesson he had learned – and not for the first time, either! Be careful, watch your step, keep certain things well under the wraps. Absolute truth is a luxury few people can afford. You certainly can't.

Onwards and Upwards, Again

The summer term began. It was back to normal again. Back to an enhanced normality, in fact. He loooked forward to the high summer with its long days, its leafy trees and its liberating forays into the shimmering world beyond.

John found that his reputation had soared. Among the older boys he was 'Dirty D' who'd had it of in a back alley and had been so sexed-up by Page Three of the *Sun* that he'd gone and shafted Danny Fleetwood by mistake. And, having been invited to attend one of Old Man Fleetwood's porno shows, he'd achieved a rare social distinction.

Among the younger boys he was the 'boy hero', who'd saved the Bishop's life, won a Merit Award for his bravery, and actually appeared on television.

Things developed. At last he was old enough to join Major Allen's Army Cadet Force contingent. He was enrolled in the Duke of Edinburgh's Award Scheme and began to work towards his Bronze Medal. He was duly confirmed as a Christian in the cathedral- quivering with scarcely concealed alarm as the Bishop laid his massive hairy hands on him. Was he going to suddenly pick him up bodily and fling him, Cedric-style, into the transept? Quite possible, knowing that humanoid gorilla! At weekends he created friezes and collages for Isabel, which were displayed before admiring audiences in church halls. Onwards and upwards.

'One Day it will All Fall Apart, Won't it?'
But the Demon was still lurking inside him. However hard he tried to be normal, he still continued to dream about boys and to be infatuated with Danny's nether regions. Nightly prayers and supplications made no difference. God just wasn't listening... or, ghastly thought, God just didn't exist at all. And behind it all was the nagging anxiety about the future. Should he go and have another 'accident', he would not be so easily forgiven a second time. He had to tread very carefully.

Especially with Briggs. He'd always found hatred difficult and it took a great deal of provocation for him to find enough energy to sustain it. He desperately wanted to end the vendetta; indeed, that was what Steadman and the Bishop had told him was the proper Christian response. Yet, try as he might, nothing seemed to work. Big ingratiating smiles, ostentatious keenness in the P.E lessons, spontaneous offers to help clear away the hurdles and high jump equipment; it was all greeted with the same monosyllabic dismissal. 'Cor, he really *has* got it in for you!' sighed Fred after one especially brusque rebuff.

At the end of that summer term Briggs left Beaconsfield. Glowing testimonials from Meakin and Dorothy had finally secured him a post in a nearby comprehensive: a proper school, a *real* school, etc, etc., etc. A great weight slid off his shoulders. At long last he would be able to attend the annual students' reunion at St Martin's. For how could he possibly have admitted to his old tutor that he was at a *private* school, let alone told his former classmates?

On the last day of term John made one last try at reconciliation, bouncing up to him, all beaming smiles: 'Goodbye, sir, and thank you for all you've done.'

Briggs eyed him coldly: 'Don't try to soft soap me, Denby. You should know by now that it doesn't work.'

'Sorry, I er...'

'I read you like a book,' he added vehemently, positively spitting the words out. 'You're not what you pretend to be. You're a fraud, and I think you know it. One day it will all fall apart, won't it?'

That hurt.

Living a Lie

But it was no use getting angry about it. Briggs has spoken the truth – and didn't he just know it! 'Dirty D', who'd had it off with a girl in a back alley? Crap. He'd cried like a baby when they'd ripped his pants off. 'Boy hero' who'd saved the Bishop's life? Also crap. Isabel had set the whole thing up for her own devious purposes. He's been a pathetic wimp who'd been so terrified that he'd gone and shat himself like a little kid. And, what was more, Isabel knew it.

He was living a lie all the time. When he'd joined the cadets he'd sworn a solemn oath before 'Almighty God' (no less!) that he would 'live a clean, upright and wholesome life' and reject 'all impurity, most especially homosexuality in all its forms'. Even as he had been speaking those very words he had been casting longing eyes on the slender winsome boy standing next to him. If Major Allen had *known*...! God, however, knew. 'You're not what you pretend to be.' You could say that again.

Even so, he was still the bright and creative lad who soared to the top of his class in all subjects. Not even Briggs could deny that.

A Pet Guinea Pig in a Lovely Cage

Yet even that came unstuck. That summer he attended the annual Cadet Camp at a place called Wasgill up in the Pennines. Contingents from all over the north of England were there, and as a deliberate policy they were all mixed up. For the first few days things went brilliantly. He quickly mastered the intricacies of the cadet rifle, he did well on the rifle range and he soon had a firm grasp of the arcane complexities of section attacks.

The climax of the week was a two-day exercise involving a night operation. As a mark of distinction he was given the light machine gun, a much-coveted assignment, which had caused a certain amount of muttering among the older cadets who resented being upstaged by a newcomer.

Darkness found him in an 'ambush group', crouching in a ditch. It was wildly exciting: lying there, snuggled into the black depths of the wood, wearing a real soldier's uniform, clutching a real live machine gun, adrenaline pumping, all senses screwed up to red alert, waiting for the faint crunch of broken twigs that would herald the approach of the enemy. Above him, erratically glimpsed through the ragged canopy of the trees, was a mass of glittering stars, and all around him the rich smell of damp earth.

Lying next to him was a tall, gangling youth who had been appointed as his 'buddy'. They began a whispered conversation.

'Where are you from?'

'The Stirling Academy.'

'Is that a comprehensive?'

'Of course not! It's a proper grammar school!' A put-down in an unpleasantly supercilious voice, lazy and drawling.

Silence followed.

'And you?' the youth eventually condescended to say.

'I'm from Beaconsfield.'

'You're *not* are you? I didn't think they allowed people like you into the A.C.F.'

'Oh?'

'It's a simple matter of intelligence, isn't it? Only the head cases and dimwits go to Beaconsfield. It's the local dustbin. Everybody knows that.'

'But I'm not a head case or a dimwit!'

'That's what *you* think.'

Another brittle silence.

Suddenly the youth grabbed the machine gun. 'I'd better take charge of this. We can't have an Educationally Subnormal like you handling a dangerous weapon. You'd go and kill yourself. And me, which is more to the point.'

Rather than start a noisy fight John let him get away with it.

That little midnight contretemps clouded the remaining two days of the camp. Word got around quickly and he found himself cold-shouldered: 'Do we have to have *him* in our section? He's too thick.'

Deeply wounding. But it was probably the truth. Youngsters were more direct than adults. They didn't feel the need to spare your feelings. They spoke the unvarnished truth, however painful it might be.

So what was left of the once dashing *condottiere*? Not a lot. He felt like a pet guinea pig in a lovely cage, cherished by its owner, cosseted, fed, lovingly nurtured and carefully shielded from the realities of the outside world.

A Sheepdog on a Leash

What he needed was some big achievement, solid and rock hard, and which nobody could gainsay. There were the exams he would take when he was sixteen; Dolly and Meakin had hinted at several O Levels as well as the usual C.S.E.s. But they were a long way off and, anyway, would he actually be able to pass them? He needed something more immediate. Also bigger. Bigger and more dramatic than the things most people did.

He thought of the Ruwenzori Range. He remembered those glorious slides that Dolly had shown him. Go off to the Ruwenzori and make the first ascent of an unknown peak: that really would be something solid.

But how would he ever get there? He couldn't do it on his own. He'd need an adult to go with him. But who? Who would take *him* of all people, thickoid and shit-stabber Denby?

In August Dolly and Meakin took a group of them to the mountains of Torridon in the north of Scotland. He warmed to those ancient peaks, bold, upstanding and wreathed in shifting clouds, and he longed to go off and explore the hidden fastness of misty, rain-sodden glens that stretched away behind their rocky ramparts. But he was constantly restrained. 'We'll have to go down. Simon's tired and Barry's getting cold. John, can you be back marker and see that we don't lose anybody.' He felt like a sheepdog on a leash.

'What's your Score?'

The following year passed without any disasters. But as time wore on the 'Dirty D' act became increasingly difficult to sustain.

Danny continually paraded his girlfriends to the world, smooching openly with them in the street outside the school and holding hands as they walked into town on Saturday mornings. 'Scored again!' he would say as he erupted into school on Monday mornings. 'How about you, John? What's your score?'

What indeed? John didn't even have a girlfriend, let alone a 'score'. Never had. Never would. So he made up a story about being madly in live with a girl 'down in London' who was 'so fucking pure' that she wouldn't do it. 'It's a real challenge, I can tell you, but I'm working on her. God, she's so horny.' It wasn't very convincing, but at least Danny swallowed it. But for how long? That was the nagging question.

In the meantime he found this endless obsession with sex so *boring*. Once Danny had been so full of fun: into trains, aeroplanes and model making. Now all that had stopped. It was just sex, sex, sex and more sex. All the richness of childhood had gone. He was as boring and banal as his ghastly old father who talked of nothing but porno films. They were drifting apart.

John grew bigger. Still slender and elfin with a hairless chin, but at last his voice was breaking. Outwardly he was 'one of the lads', but inwardly he felt himself becoming increasingly isolated. More than ever he needed that big, far-off mountain.

4

That Big, Far-Off Mountain

At Last, His Great Chance!
Then on a dark, rain-swept afternoon in January, something
happened. It was a Saturday and they'd just finished a weapons
training session with Major Allen at the Cadet Centre. As
he left, he happened to glance at the notice board. It was
the usual forlorn jumble of scuffed and faded typewritten
sheets which 'hereby informed' those who could be bothered
to read them of such things as 'Standing Orders' and 'Fire
Precautions'. But suddenly he noticed a brightly coloured
leaflet hiding in the bottom left-hand corner. Casually, he
examined it.

Amid a splurge of bold letters and dramatic photographs
of smiling youngsters scaling rugged mountain peaks
it announced that the Boldonbridge Youth Outreach
Committee was organising a 'Youth Expedition to North
Africa'. Specifically aimed at 'the young and adventurous'
it promised a 'host of exciting life-changing experiences'...
'the ascent of the highest peaks in the Atlas Mountains'...

'a camel trek through the sandy wastes of the Sahara' ...
'challenging cross cultural adventures'. 'Those interested,' it
declared, 'should apply at once, either to their teachers or to
the Youth Outreach Committee at County Hall, Hackworth
Street, Boldonbridge.'

A hot flame seemed to flare up within him. At last, his
great chance! Not quite the Ruwenzori Range, but still Africa.
A vision rose up before him of camels, burning deserts, palm
trees and vast ranges of dry, rumpled mountains surging off
into a fiery sunset, a wild kaleidoscope of exotic images all
promising great achievements. Pathetic little shit-stabber
Denby would be raised to the level of the great African
explorers like Burton and Mungo Park. He just had to go.

'Look, Sunshine, You've Got it All Wrong'

On the following Monday, as soon as school was over, he
dashed off to the Youth Outreach office in County Hall.
Bursting in uninvited, he found a large man, burly and bald-
headed, writing away at a desk. On the wall behind him were
brightly coloured posters depicting smiling youngsters hiking
over green and sunny hills under uplifting slogans like 'Yes! I
can do it!' and 'Get involved! Go for it!'

As he stood panting at the desk, the man continued
writing. He seemed to be deliberately ignoring him.

'Er, excuse me.'

No response.

'Please... er...'

Eventually the man condescended to look up. He fixed
him with a cold stare, which brought back memories of
Mary's analytical stare. This stare was not aggressively
academic, however, but merely baleful.

'Yes, I heard you the first time.'

'I've come about the North Africa Expedition.'

Another baleful stare. 'Well?'

'I'm very keen. I'm starting on my Duke of Edinburgh's Silver.'

'Uh.' A monosyllabic grunt after which the head went down again and the writing continued.

John's eager smile dissolved into a bemused gape. He felt like a deflated football which had lost its bounce. The last thing he'd expected was this negativity. He was nonplussed. Should he go or stay? He decided to stay.

'I'd love to go on the expedition.'

That, at least, produced a response. The man looked up and fixed him with his baleful stare. 'And just why do you think you're good enough to be selected?'

'Well, I've climbed lots of mountains, and... well, I'm very keen.'

'Uh.'

The head went down and the writing resumed. After a while it was raised again, seemingly irritated to find him still standing there. The baleful stare intensified.

'Which school are you from?'

'Beaconsfield.'

'And you think that gives you the right to be selected do you?'

'Well no. Er...' What the hell was he supposed to say?

'Beaconsfield's a private school isn't it?'

'Well, yes, I think it is.'

'The cream of Boldonbridge isn't it? Rich and thick. It gets all the dropouts who think they can buy their way up the system, doesn't it?'

'But, er...'

Suddenly the man came to life, a bit like a bear disturbed in its den.

'Look, sunshine, you've got it all wrong! This is a *serious* expedition. We only want the best. We can't take inadequates and certainly not people from private schools. You obviously think that just because you're at a private school you have an automatic right to be selected. Well you haven't. We're not here to pamper spoilt upper-class brats. So forget all about North Africa. It's not for you.'

'But —'

'You heard. Off you go.' With a dismissive gesture of his head the man resumed his writing.

John slunk out of the office, utterly deflated. He felt like a frolicking puppy that had been dropped in a bucket of cold water. Ambling disconsolately down the corridor, he saw another poster on the wall showing a group of fresh-faced and smiling youngsters sitting outside a tent. 'Why not join us?' ran the caption. 'You'll be welcome!'

'Welcome?' Maybe, but definitely not if you were John Denby from Beaconsfield School. Anger blazed up within him. What had his being at a private school got to do with anything? It was Briggs all over again: officially there to encourage you to play games, but actually trying to stop you. Or, indeed, his horrible mother, Mary: officially devoted to the welfare of children, but in reality hating their guts. And what had happened to her in the last few years? Hopefully eaten by a crocodile somewhere in Africa. The adult world was full of frauds. His resentment smouldered.

Pouty Adolescence and a Little 'Factual Alteration'

Wednesday evening was Meakin's and Steadman's D. of E. evening. After a practice cooking session in the Geography Room with Trangia stoves, mess tins, dried food and water bottles, Meakin made an announcement.

'Before you go, you might like to know that the education people in County Hall are organising an expedition to Morocco this summer. Each school is being invited to send a list of volunteers. John, this should be right up your street.'

John's subterranean resentment welled up, lava-style, and

produced an angry pout, a curled lip and a sullen sneer: 'That's what *you* think! It's all crap. When I went round to the County Hall office and asked about it, they told me to fuck off!'

'There's no need to be rude, young man!' said Meakin, reacting to the adolescent surliness. 'And mind your language!'

Recently he'd been noticing an incipient loutishness developing in his one-time prize pupil. Was the eager and bright-eyed young thing slithering down into a moody and negatively hostile adolescence? Danny Fleetwood had gone that way; and was young Denby about to follow him? It was starting to look horribly like it.

'Well, what happened?'

Low-key mumble: 'Well they told me it wasn't for private schools like Beaconsfield.'

'That's not what I've been told. Who said that?'

'The man in the office.'

'Oh? And who was he?'

Hostile shrug of the shoulders: 'How should I know?'

'Well, come on, what did he look like?'

'Big. Bald head. Open-necked shirt. Geordie accent.'

Steadman cut in. 'That'll be Dobson, our resident class warrior. What did he actually say?'

'That the expedition wasn't for blokes at private schools.'

Steadman's bushy eyebrows contracted into an angry frown. 'He had absolutely no business to say that. Did he say anything else?'

Now's your chance, Jonny my lad! Nobody else was in the room, so it'll be his word against yours. You can put the knife right in. But play it carefully. Drop the rebellious teenager thing. Play the bewildered innocent. Use your smile. They're coming round.

'Well, er, it's really rather embarrassing. I mean, I don't want to land the man in it...' (Of course I do, but I'm too goddam canny to admit it!)

'Well, get on with it.'

'He said that Beaconsfield was a private school for thicks and that thicks shouldn't be doing things like the Duke of Edinburgh's Award and definitely shouldn't go on expeditions. They weren't for spoilt upper-class brats like me.'

'Yes, go on.'

(This is working well, so hot it up bit!) 'He said that Beaconsfield got the cream of Boldonbridge, rich and thick, and he sneered at me.'

'Yes.'

'Then he told me to fuck off and pushed me out of the door.' (Big embellishment here. Anxious wait to see how it goes down!).

'Those were his actual words? Are you sure?'

'Yes.'

'And he actually laid hands on you, did he?'

'Yes.'

'Was anybody else in the room?'

'No, it was just him and me.'

Steadman turned to Meakin. 'He had no business to say that sort of thing, and certainly not to swear at a boy and manhandle him.'

The two men began a hasty exchange.

'That man!' sighed Meakin. 'He's got such a chip on his shoulder!'

'Not a chip,' added Steadman, 'but a whole blasted tree. Working-class origins. Always been done down. Always been denied his rights.'

'Head of Maths at Morton Hill Community College? That's a plum post. It's hardly being done down.'

'Oh yes it is, in his eyes. Just because he's not the Professor of Mathematics at Oxford he's been denied his rights. Everything's his by right. He should have been picked to make the first ascent of the Southwest Face of Everest, you know, but he was turned down because of his working class origins.'

'Beaconsfield pupils spoilt upper-class brats?' said Meakin shaking his head in mock disbelief, 'I ask you! Sam Hawthorne rich and privileged? But whatever he feels, he shouldn't take his rancour out on kids, that's what I say.'

'But he only takes it out on certain kids,' said Steadman, 'Not on his own group. With them he's very charismatic; in his own twisted way, inspirational. Also, he's a crafty old thing. He wants to corner this Morocco thing for his own people. Good career move. It'll look good on his C.V. when he applies for a headship.'

'Well, he's not going to get away with it, is he?'

'Not if I can help it. But it's not going to be that easy. They've gone and appointed him Chief Expedition Adviser for the region. Heaven alone knows why. He's never been on a proper expedition in his life. Still, it gives him a position of power. Power to do a great deal of damage. Anyway, I'll take him on at the next committee meeting.'

'Good on you, Bob! But be careful. Big ears are flapping and tongues will talk in awkward places. John, you've heard nothing, have you? Or you, Fred?'

'No, sir. Absolutely nothing.'

'Off you go, then.

'Don't worry, John,' said Steadman as he left. 'We'll see that you get to Morocco.'

'And a word of advice, young man,' added Meakin. 'Don't bite the hand that feeds you. You need it more than you realise.'

Aware of his tactical blunder, John thought it best to climb down.

'Sorry I was rude, sir, but that man in the office put me into a right strop.'

To put icing on the diplomatic cake, he then flashed his

'ingratiating smile,:.'Thanks a bomb for all you're doing for me. I really do appreciate it.'

Meakin went home relieved. So the old Denby was still there. The bright flower hadn't withered under an arid adolescent sun. Properly watered, it could still blossom.

Lies, Lies, Lies

John walked back to Dolly's place elated. Clouds were parting. The sun was coming out. His ploy seemed to be working. But why, oh why did he *need* to intrigue like this? It should all have been so straightforward. 'Those who are interested should apply to...' 'Why not join us? You'll be welcome!' But it just wasn't like that. Adults were bigger liars than kids. Just look at his 'caring' father! Or at Isabel and the *Boldonbridge Journal*. Or, indeed, at Fleetwood Senior and Tracy Bowers! Of course he'd known she was under age when he'd screwed her! It was lies, lies, lies. Well, he could lie as well as any of them, in fact better than most. A sin? Doubtless, but it was also a matter of survival.

Expedition Politics, and Ideological Problems

Later that month a meeting of the Boldonbridge Youth Outreach Committee took place at County Hall. Representatives from the local schools and youth groups were seated round a table. As Chief Expedition Adviser for the region, Dobson occupied a big chair at the far end.

Mellor, the secretary, looked up from his pile of papers, and spoke up. 'Next item on the agenda, the proposed Morocco Expedition. Selection of members. Applications from schools and youth groups.'

He glanced expectantly at Dobson who cast a bleak glance at the assembled group and nodded his head.

Mellor proceeded, 'It was decided that each group should nominate two candidates, preferably of both sexes. When we've got the list of nominees we can start the training programme and make the final selection. So, names please. Mr Barnes, that's Highgrove Comprehensive, isn't it? Well, who've you got?'

'Four possibles. Two boys. Two girls. Here are their .C.V.s. The girl, Julia, is very promising.'

Round the table the nominations went, each representative presenting more candidates than the requisite two, and each candidate supported by the very best of reasons as to why they should be selected and others not.

'Very able lad this. Great footballer. Nine O Levels. Real powers of leadership. Father a coal miner.' (And Dobson nodded approvingly at this evidence of a proper pedigree.)

Steadman's turn came. 'I've got two candidates. One of them's very promising.'

Right on cue Dobson uncoiled himself; once more the slumbering bear roused in its den.

'Not so fast, Mr Steadman, not so fast.'

Steadman paused and raised his eyebrows.

Dobson glared bleakly at him. 'Where's your group from?'

'Beaconsfield. You know that.'

'I'm sorry, but we can't take Beaconsfield people.'

'That's news to me. And just why not?'

'Well, Beaconsfield's private, isn't it?'

'In one sense, yes, but many of the boys are paid for by the local authority.'

'That's neither here nor there. It's still private and the Outreach Committee isn't here to subsidise the rich and privileged.'

'But you can hardly call Michael Connolly rich and privileged. I'll read you his C.V..'

'Don't bother. In case you didn't know it, the Outreach Committee has got to maintain standards. We can't let rubbish through.'

'I'm not asking you to let rubbish through.'

'Yes you are. Beaconsfield is where all the wasters end up. Can't handle a normal school so you go there; so long as Daddy can pay for you, that is.'

'That's not quite true.'

'All right, I'll take your point. What shall we call your people then? How about the cream of Boldonbridge, rich and thick.'

A little wave of obsequious laughter rippled round the table. Steadman winced. Dobson was so banal; he actually seemed to think that hoary, dog-eared old adage was witty! It appeared that John had been telling the truth after all.

'Now wait a minute.'

'All right, then,' replied Dobson with just a flicker of a smile on his glum face. 'Let's be democratic, shall we? We'll take a vote. Shall we have Beaconsfield people on the expedition? Those in favour?'

Only Steadman raised his hand.

'And those against?'

A mass of hands immediately went up. A few hesitated, feeling a little guilty. This really was a little unfair, definitely against the stated principles of the Outreach Committee, which expressly forbade any discrimination on grounds of race, religion and – yes! – social background. But, well, Dobson had a point and more importantly, as Chief Expedition Adviser for the region, he had the power to make or break your group. Getting your people onto the Morocco Expedition was a test of your worth as a group leader, the sort of thing that headmasters noticed. Keeping Dobbie sweet wasn't just a matter of ethics. It was a wise career move, and you couldn't afford to be too sentimental where Number One was concerned. Simple professionalism.

The flicker on Dobson's face broke into a broad smile, all the more gratifying for being so rare. He looked at Steadman.

'That's settled then.'

Steadman left in disgust.

Anything but Settled

But as far as Steadman was concerned the matter was anything but settled. War had been declared, and war was an exhilarating break from the boring trivialities of his suburban parish. It was a chance to hone those underused military skills of his. A chance to champion the underdog, and to be *seen* to champion the underdog. A chance, moreover, to stress the relevance of Christianity in the modern world.

He worked out a plan of campaign. Should he appeal to the Bishop? There was heavy artillery there. But, on reflection, he decided it was best not to. The Bishop could get onto his high horse about homosexuality... and any mention of John's homosexuality would wreck everything. Donald Mackay was hardly renowned for his tact. Instead, he wrote an impassioned letter to County Hall.

For three weeks nothing happened. Eventually, out of exasperation, he telephoned them. After all sorts of referrals to this department and that extension, an anxious voice condescended to reply. Yes, the council had every sympathy with him. *Of course* they took his point. But, well... the Youth Outreach Committee relied on the unpaid voluntary work of people like Brian Dobson, and he *was* doing sterling work, you couldn't deny that. So they couldn't possibly afford to offend him. 'I'm sure you'll understand.'

Steadman didn't 'understand': or, rather, he understood just too well. There things rested for a while.

'The Lives of Children at Risk'

In the end chance came to the rescue; or was it fate, or perhaps event the hand of God? Who knew? The Youth and Community Safety Committee got involved. After all, what was it there for if not to ensure the 'safety' of the Boldonbridge Youth and Community? An expedition organised by the Youth Outreach Committee, no less, was clearly in their remit. And, youth swanning off into the wilds of North Africa could hardly be deemed 'safe', could it? Hackles rose. 'The lives of children' were at risk. Something had to be done. The proposed expedition went under the microscope.

But unfortunately, all seemed to be in place. The leaders were all 'properly qualified', especially Brian Dobson, the 'Senior Coordinator'.. For who could possibly be better qualified to lead a youth expedition than the 'Chief Expedition Advisor' for the region? So, alas, there was no comfort for the would-be 'children in danger' crusaders, not even a crumb.

Or was there? Suddenly, somebody remembered that people in North Africa didn't speak English. And, worthy as they undoubtedly were, none of the designated expedition leaders spoke a word of any foreign language. Neither had any of them ever set foot in North Africa. It just wouldn't do, would it?

In short, the expedition couldn't possibly be allowed to proceed if this were not remedied. Unless an additional leader with the requisite skills could be found, it would have to be cancelled. Sad, very sad. The Youth and Community Safety Committee 'deeply regretted' having to say this, but where 'the lives of children' were at stake, they had no choice. Victory for the Youth and Community Safety Committee.

But then it transpired that there *was* in fact one local youth leader who filled the bill: The Reverend Bob Steadman. In his younger and wilder days he had backpacked his way round Morocco, tramping over the Atlas Mountains from end to end, living with Berber shepherds in remote and inaccessible valleys, and becoming fluent in Arabic and picking up a working knowledge of Berber as well. As a matter of fact, he was also fluent in French.

Steadman was duly approached, and agreed to join

the expedition. Dobson was 'disgusted', but was given an ultimatum: it was either accept Steadman or no expedition – which, being fully translated, meant egg all over his face. The Chief Expedition Advisor for the region incapable of leading an overseas expedition? It was a middle-class put-down, a direct assault on his working class origins, a deep personal insult. But in the end he had to 'eat shit' and accept Steadman.

For his part, Steadman agreed to accept Dobson as expedition leader, but he insisted on bringing his two Beaconsfield lads along.

'That's out of the question, I'm afraid,' was the sulky response, 'This is a serious expedition and we've got to keep standards up.'

'Take it or leave it, Dobbie.'

Dobson took it; with a sullen grunt, of course. But every cloud is apt to have its silver lining. He'd acquired one more grievance, to be lovingly polished up, treasured and added to his cherished collection.

'Officially Selected to Join the Expedition'

'Well, John,' said Steadman after the Sunday service, 'you and Mike Connolly are going to Morocco, after all. You've been officially selected to join the expedition.'

John lit up like a floodlight, flashed his ingratiating smile and clasped Steadman's hand. 'Thanks, Bob,' he spluttered. 'Oh, thanks! I'm so pleased! 'You're so kind to me,' he added. 'What can I do to thank you?'

'Just do your best and don't let me down,' Steadman replied. 'Prove that you're just as good, if not better, than the other kids. That'll be more than enough! And there's something else,' he continued. 'How good's your French?'

'Well, I learned a bit at Rickerby Hall, but I was never very good at it. Anyway, it was yonks ago and I've forgotten most of it.'

'Well, that can be remedied. Come round to my place on Friday evening and we'll start some lessons. You can be expedition interpreter. None of the other kids'll speak a word of any foreign language. That I know for certs! There's a role for you.'

There was, of course, another – far less mentionable! – way that John could say thank you. But Steadman quickly erased that satanic thought from his consciousness.

A Gorgeous Puppy – But Changing into What?

Elated John rushed round to Fern Avenue to see Dorothy.

'Miss! Miss! Me and Mike have been chosen to go to Morocco!'

Dorothy lit up: 'That's wonderful, John! Wonderful!'

Then she did something that she hadn't done for a long time. She hugged him. The truth was that, throughout the year, she'd been having renewed doubts about her protégé. Once he'd been a gorgeous puppy, so full of creativity and childhood wonder. But now he was changing – and changing into *what*? He was still pink and hairless, but he was no longer cute. He had become scrawny and gangling, with a husky voice and blackheads in his once cherubic face. A sullen and argumentative streak was developing. Was all that childhood exuberance draining away into a morass of adolescent surliness and banality? Danny Fleetwood had already gone that way, so why not John? And in his case it would be even more depressing. Not just a teenage lout slipping out of control, but a *homosexual* teenage lout!

Try as she might to rationalise it, that 'shower affair' had shaken her. But here was reassurance. Chosen to go on a hazardous expedition with the elite of the city. Picked, not by people like the Bishop who had an obvious axe to grind, but by an impartial tribunal. What an honour! What an honour for Beaconsfield School! What an honour for *her*! She hugged John again.

Positive Behaviour Gets Positive Results

At Assembly the next morning Dorothy made an announcement. John Denby and Michael Connolly had been chosen by the Boldonbridge Youth Outreach Committee to go on a tough and demanding expedition to North Africa. It was a triumph for the two boys and a great honour for Beaconsfield School. When the requisite applause had died down she delivered a little homily about how positive behaviour gets positive results.

John walked on air.

Not that Simple

But things weren't that simple. Steadman had been careful not to tell Dorothy the whole truth. The backroom machinations had been carefully concealed from her and, moreover, Dobson was not beaten yet.

A week later he phoned Steadman. 'Yes, you can rest assured that your expedition expenses will be paid. But, I'm afraid we cannot subsidise your two lads.'

The tone grated on Steadman; he could just picture the triumphant leer at the other end of the line. Battle was renewed.

'And just why not? They're just as deserving as the other kids, aren't they?'

'In *your* eyes, perhaps, but I'm afraid that's not what the Committee thinks. They aren't prepared to spend money on kids from private schools. Anyway, they just haven't got the funds. They're overspent as it is.'

Socialist Rectitude

Steadman duly phoned Dorothy. 'I'm afraid we've hit a snag. The Committee says it can't fund our two lads. Something to do with bureaucracy and private schools. Also, it seems that they're running out of money.'

'I suppose that's only to be expected,' she sighed. 'But

not to worry, I'm sure Dr Denby will pay up. He usually does. Anything to get shot of his son. I'll give him a ring tonight.'

But Dr Denby wouldn't pay up.

Maggie Wright happened to be away visiting her sick mother and was not there to soften his hard ideological edges. So when Dorothy rang he was in full 'socialist rectitude' mode. No, he couldn't possibly subsidise his son, or Michael Connolly either, for that matter. As Labour member for Boldonbridge West he could not possibly be seen to give favours to relatives. That would be nepotism: corruption, in case Dorothy found the word too difficult to understand. If the local Youth Outreach Committee didn't think they were worth subsidising, he would abide by their decision. Anyway, it would do his son good to be brought down a peg or two. He'd been indulged quite enough already, what with his being sent to a private school instead of a proper state school, etc., etc., etc.

Good Samaritan

Dorothy phoned Steadman. 'Bob, what *are* we going to do? I mean, we can't stop the two lads going, not after all that we've said. It would be a terrible blow for them. They have been so looking forward to it.'

And a terrible blow for her, too. Think of the fallout! John reverting to a sullen and hostile teenager, Michael Connolly reverting to the adolescent slob that she so desperately wanted to redeem. All her talk about the 'rewards of positive behaviour' exposed as mendacious hot air.

Steadman was silent for a while. Then he spoke up. 'Well, I suppose I'll have to subsidise them.'

'*You?* How can you possibly afford it?'

'Actually, between you, I and the doorpost, I *can* afford it. I've got a little nest egg, you know…'

He spoke the truth. Unbeknown to all, he had private

means. When he'd been ordained, he'd thought of giving it all to the poor. 'If thou wilt be perfect, go and sell all that thou hast and give it to the poor.' But, on reflection, he'd decided not to. It wouldn't have gone to the poor so much as into the pockets of the self-appointed 'guardians of the poor', all those 'highly qualified' and 'exceptionally able' administrators who 'so merited' the gargantuan salaries they demanded. Not quite what he had in mind. Better keep it yourself and use it at your own discretion. Perfectly Christian this: after all, what use would the Good Samaritan have been to the man who fell among thieves if he hadn't been able to pay his hotel bills?

'Well, that's very good of you, Bob,' replied a relieved Dorothy. 'But, please, let me make a contribution.' She could afford to do this. The school was doing well and numbers were up. Time to be a proper Christian, Dolly, old girl!

'But, for heaven's sake,' she added. 'Let's keep this from the boys. We don't want any feelings of inferiority.'

'Exactly.'

Blissfully unaware of all the backstage goings-on, John's ego swelled. Numbered among the 'chosen'! Chosen to go on a hazardous expedition. Here at last was the solid achievement he so craved. Here was redemption. He flung himself into the preparations with tremendous gusto, assiduously attending all Steadman's French lessons and taking the horrors of French irregular verbs head on.

Hearing that many of his fellow expeditioners would be 'deprived children', in a burst of Christian altruism he gathered together a great heap of discarded clothes and kit to give them. Poor, naïve, innocent John Denby!

Away to the Far-Off Blue Beyond

July 25th. The day of departure. Windy, bright, clear. Away! Away! Away! Away to the far-off blue beyond!

John and Michael arrived at the school, weighed down

by massive rucksacks and attired in full expedition kit: boots, anoraks, jeans, water bottles full of specially Puritabbed water dangling from their belts. John even sported an Australian bush hat that he'd bought as a visible sign of his preparations for the Sahara. A beaming Steadman, similarly arrayed, joined them.

Somehow managing to squeeze everything into her little car, Dorothy drove them down to Heathrow, where they were to meet the rest of the expedition and catch the plane to Marrakesh.

'Now you *will* do your best, won't you, lads?' she said as she dropped them at the entrance to Terminal Two. 'Don't let the school down. We're relying on you.'

With that, she drove back to Boldonbridge. She was a chequered pattern of elation and misgivings. Persistent doubts nagged her. Michael was no problem: under the irredeemably disorganised exterior there was a core of solid common sense. John was the problem. Perform well, and triumphant success would follow. But would he 'go silly' as he had done on that famous first Adventure Weekend in the Lake District back in '82? And this time it wouldn't be an angry farmer sounding off on the telephone about dirty language. It could be the British Embassy at Rabat 'regretfully informing' her about drugs and prison. And – God forbid! – would he go and have another homosexual 'accident' like that one in the shower two years ago? She was in his unstable hands.

'Young People from Deprived Areas', and a Little Ideology

Meanwhile 'his best' was what John was most emphatically doing. Frantically eager to make the right impression, he'd gone into 'enhanced good expeditioner' mode: selfless, energetic, full of team spirit and concern for others. In an altruistic frenzy he rushed round, commandeering trolleys and loading the rucksacks onto them.

Coaxing their laden vehicles through the revolving doors, the two boys followed Steadman into the terminal. It was John's first visit to an airport, and the seething hubbub was wildly exciting: the mountains of luggage, the boiling mass of humanity on the move, the great variety of people – grave men in dark suits, scrubbed and shiny children in brilliant T-shirts, dark-skinned men in turbans, elegant Indian women gliding along in colourful saris... even black men in vivid tribal robes. It was a new world of exotic adventure.

They struggled through the crowds to the agreed rendezvous point at the Mediterranean Airways check-in desk. Having been told that the expedition consisted of 'underprivileged young people from deprived areas', John was expecting to see a bunch of ragamuffin paupers; not quite Oliver Twist style, but of that order. Indeed, that was why he had stuffed so much of his rucksack with the spare shirts, socks and sweaters that he was sure they'd be needing. He was even prepared to part with his anorak should the need arise. (Team spirit... lots of Brownie points in the offing.)

Yet when they eventually reached the check-in desk the only youngsters he could see looked anything but deprived. Positively gorgeous in the very latest and greatest outdoor gear: Gore-Tex cagoules, state-of-the-art rucksacks, glossy new boots... you name it! They could have been a group of tailor's dummies in the shop window of Wilderness Paths. Strutting round in front of them was a lean and spare young man with closely cropped hair. Honed down, immaculately dressed and sporting a large 'Mountain Leader' badge on his spotless safari jacket, he exuded clipped efficiency.

'That must be another group going to Morocco,' said John. 'I thought we were the only one.'

'Whoever they is,' added Michael, 'Somebody's got some money, it must be the Stirling Academy.'

'It's not the Stirling Academy,' said Steadman. 'It's our lot.'

'But you said they were deprived kids!' expostulated a bewildered John.

'So they are. What you're seeing is the visible part of – I quote – "the Boldonbridge Council's Initiative to Combat Poverty and Deprivation".'

He pointed to the elegant young man in the safari jacket. 'And that's Joe Morris, my colleague and co-leader.'

'Well, I needn't have brought all those spare things,' muttered John. 'I suppose I'd better give them to the local people in Morocco instead.'

'I'd hang on to them for the moment,' replied Steadman sagely. 'We could well be needing them before we're through.'

John's surprise was followed by a shock.

A resplendent Dobson stepped forward. He cast a baleful eye at Steadman.

'I see you've got company. I thought we'd decided that these two weren't coming along.'

John felt the temperature drop 20 degrees.

'Oh no,' replied Steadman, exuding a contrived bonhomie, 'they've both been paid for. It's quite above board. Now this is Michael Connolly, the one I told you about. I think you've met John Denby before.'

Dobson turned his baleful stare onto John, nodded his head and turned to Steadman. 'Well I trust *they're* not expecting to be part of the expedition.'

'Oh yes they are. John here is going to be our interpreter.'

'Huh!'

With a resigned shrug of his shoulders, Dobson turned to his group and went into a whispering huddle with Morris. Another grievance had been notched up.

A frosty silence ensued for the next few moments.

Eventually John approached a big, burly youth and extended his hand in welcome. 'I'm John, what's your name?'

Without a word, the lad turned his back on him. Almost

on cue, his mates moved away from him and Michael, leaving them isolated as if they were radioactive. The air temperature plunged even lower.

John shuddered. Something was up, and it wasn't very nice, either. He had a sudden flashback to that ghastly Thursday morning after his 'homosexual accident' in the shower.

He saw Dobson laughing and joking away in the midst of his group, free and easy, relaxed and friendly, a wholly different person. It was like a story he'd read about a bloke who was two different people at the same time: Dr Jeykell who was good and kind, and Mr Hyde who was an evil fiend. But what the hell was it all about? What had he possibly done to deserve this rejection?

Then he remembered. It was obvious, wasn't it? Dodson knew that he was a shit-stabber. They *all* knew, both the boys and the girls. Briggs must have told them. What would they do to him? Pull his pants off and get to work, Freddy Hazlett style, with a bicycle pump? Why not? It was what shit-stabbers deserved, wasn't it?

He turned to Michael. 'They don't seem to want us here, do they?'

Michael seemed unconcerned. 'That's just folk, ain't it?' He paused and then delivered a little Michael-style homily. 'I don't like that Dobson bloke me. I mean he's just like Darran.'

'Darran?'

'The bloke me mam's gone an' shacked up with. Sittin' in the hoos like, livin' off her social security an' that. Feedin' her with dope an' all. Wants me ooota the place. Keeps givin' us the X-ray eyes an' sayin' that Ah oughta look after mesell an' that. Says he's gonna kick us oot if Ah divvent gan mesell like. Well Ah'd like ter see 'im try. He's soft as shit. Ah'd 'ave 'im any day. Yer knaaa John, yer daft you.'

'Oh?'

'Well, yer livin' in fairy land. Yer thinks folk is sensible an' that. They're not like that. Bob's great, mind, but most folk ain't like him. You should *know* that by now.'

That was the gospel according to Michael Connolly. A bleak perspective: don't expect too much; most people are nasty, so be pleased when you find the odd one or two who aren't.

Meanwhile Steadman was at the check-in desk. Having been deputed to get the party onto the plane, he was busy talking to the lady in fluent French and brandishing a heap of passports and air tickets.

Crestfallen, John approached him. 'Bob,' he whispered, 'Can I have a private word?'

'Not now, John, I've got to get everybody onto the plane.'

'But it's urgent.'

'If you need the toilet, it's over there.'

'It's not that.'

Steadman looked up angrily. 'Well what is it then?'

Almost on cue a loud Geordie bawled out from behind. 'The poofter's shat hissell, that's what!'

An explosion of raucous laughter followed. Steadman winced. Trouble already, and they'd hardly even got started.

'Come on, boy, out with it!'

'Could you come over here where the others can't hear.'

Steadman obeyed.

'Seulment un moment,' he said to the check-in lady. 'Je suis un petit peu pressé.'

'Bob, this is embarrassing.'

'Well get on with it, boy, I've got to get this lot into the departure lounge before they start getting out of hand.'

'Nobody's told Dobson about... well, what I did to Danny in the shower, have they? I mean Briggs hasn't been saying things, has he?'

'Good Lord, no! You can set your mind at rest on that one.

You don't think a snob like Dobson would condescend to talk to a bloke like Briggs, do you?'

John felt a great wave of relief, almost as if a painful boil had been lanced.

'But what's all this about?' he added. 'I mean we *are* part of the expedition, aren't we?'

'Of course you are. It's just Dobbie being Dobbie. Don't worry, it'll all work out. Just show them what you're made of. But for heaven's sake don't start losing your temper. O.K., reassured? Now I'd better get back to work.'

The luggage was duly dispatched and the boarding passes issued. They proceeded to the departure lounge.

Synthetic Class War Ahead

Inwardly, Steadman was seething. Dobson was living up to his worst expectations. And this was only the start. Five weeks of synthetic class war stretched out before him in all its dreary futility. What would happen when they reached Morocco? As the designated 'North Africa expert', Steadman had been deputed to arrange things there. Accommodation, transport, guides, mules, camels… that was his remit.

'This expedition will be a new departure,' the blurb on the handouts had declared. 'It will give the young people who are to be our future leaders first-hand experience of a very different culture.' Well, 'first-hand experience of a very different culture' was exactly what those 'future leaders' were going to get. No comfortable Western-style hotels in the modern part of Marrakesh. Not even the sparse and spartan International Youth Hostel. It was to be a pension in the old town run by Moroccan friends of his. It would be sitting cross-legged on cushions, sipping mint tea and eating bits of barbecued lamb with their fingers. And when nature called, it would be off to a squatty toilet with a bowl of water instead of paper. Then it would be Berber villages in the Atlas Mountains, and nomad tents in the desert. John, he knew, would lap it up.

But Dobson certainly wouldn't. It was doubtful if he would even hack the mounds of dried food they'd brought along. 'I'm not chancing myself on the local muck,' he had vehemently declared before they set off. 'Nor the lads neither. We'll have to have food we understand.' Food Dobson 'understood' meant things like sausage and chips and, of course, beer. Well, sausage, chips and beer was what he wasn't going to get. Almost certainly, he'd freak out. It would all, of course, be a matter of 'safety', which being translated into Dobsonese, meant doing things the Dobson way. Stormy waters ahead, but, also, the thrill of coming battle.

But, also, a less mentionable thrill. Having been rejected by the others, John was dependent on him... and that would make him pliable. But don't go down that path! Don't even think about it!

In the Aeroplane: 'Deprived Kids' Have Their Bit of Fun

They boarded the plane. Ignoring the air hostess's repeated instructions to sit in their assigned places, Dobson's group commandeered the back of the plane, filling any empty seats with bags of half-eaten chips and empty crisp packets. It was a case of the young bloods assuming their rightful place in the order of things and carving out an exclusive enclave for the elite. The outcasts, Steadman and his two pariahs, took up their assigned places near the front.

In his excitement John forgot his 'good expeditioner' pose and bagged the window seat. It was his first ever flight and he gazed in awe at the nearby aircraft with their huge, vividly coloured tails, and at the distant ones thundering down the runway and roaring off into the vastness of the sky above.

Then it was their turn. Fasten seat belts. Seats upright. The safety demonstration, which proved that you were doing something dangerous – not quite going to the Moon with Neil Armstrong, but of that order of things... They were moving. The surge of power. Pressed back into your seat as you hurtle down the runway. Airborne. Flying through the sky! Heathrow spread out below you like the town you made for the model railway at Beaconsfield. The Thames, London, the Houses of Parliament... like one of those picture maps you get at a tourist information office. Up through puffy white clouds and into the dazzling blue immensity beyond. On! On! On!

Yes, he'd show them! He'd be worthy of the trust Bob and Dolly had placed in him. He'd wipe out the stain of... well... *that*!

Things settled down. The plane levelled off, a little tube of mundanity alone in a grandiose vastness, suspended and seemingly motionless. Below it was a boundless ocean of white cloud, above it a dark blue void. Seat belts were unfastened. People got up and started walking round. The drinks trolley jangled slowly down the aisle.

'What would you like to drink?'

It was time for John to try out some of the French he'd been learning with Bob.

'Coca-Cola, si'il vous plait... Merci beaucoup.'

'De rien! C'est mon plaisir.'

He'd survived his first encounter with a foreign language! His ego swelled!

Then it was the lunch trolley. The excitement of prising open your steamed metal carton and discovering what was inside; a brief return to the childhood thrill of your Christmas stocking.

The loo queue formed.

Suddenly there was an uproar at the back of the plane, an explosion of loud Geordie voices and peals of raucous laughter. One of Dobson's lads, a great red-headed lump of a youth, came lurching down the aisle and began pushing his way through the loo queue.

Outraged consternation. 'Steady on! It's not your turn! There *is* a queue, you know! Do you mind?'

Slurred reply: 'Gorra get to the bog, me! Gorra!'

Then he vomited loudly and copiously, all down his front, onto the sandal of the man in front of him and into a nearby seat, which luckily happened to be unoccupied.

A bewildered John looked on as pandemonium broke out.

'Oh, for Christ's sake!'

'Bloody hell!'

'He's drunk! What the hell's going on back there!'

'Les Anglais! Comme toujours!'

An angry air hostess approached Steadman. 'He's one of yours, isn't he? I don't see why I should have to clean up this mess!'

'No, he's not mine. He belongs back there, but I'll see to it.'

With that, he marched the soiled and stinking youth to the back of the plane. A great cheer erupted from the 'In' group.

'Good on yer, Kev lad!'

'That'll show the Pakkies!'

Dobson beamed at his crestfallen protégé: 'You're learning, lad! You're learning! The best thing ter dee when yer pissed like is ter throw it all up!'

'That's as maybe!' snorted Steadman, 'But in the meantime somebody's got to clear up the mess over there.'

On cue Dobson went into Mr Hyde mode. A sullen grunt. 'The air hostess will do it. That's what she's paid for, isn't it?'

'She doesn't seem to think so.'

'Huh!'

'Well, you're the expedition leader. You'd better placate her!'

'Huh!'

A resentful Dobson eventually extracted his bulk from his seat and followed Steadman up the aisle.

'Well,' exclaimed the air hostess pointing to the sticky green slurry on the seat. 'What are you going to do about this? I see you've been letting your boys drink alcohol. That's against the rules, you know.'

Dobson nodded in a vague acknowledgement. After a frosty silence he spoke up. 'Well, I'm not mopping it up, if that's what you think.'

'Well get Kevin to do it,' said Steadman. 'He made the mess, didn't he?'

'He's too pissed.'

'Well get the others to help him.'

Suddenly Dobson came to life. 'And just why should they demean themselves by mopping us spew? Yes, I see, it's because they are deprived kids, that's why. Working-class mops up spew. Upper-class doesn't get its hands dirty. That's it, isn't it?'

'You brought class into this. I didn't.'

Steadman felt his temper rising. 'And another thing. You really shouldn't be letting them drink alcohol. The Committee won't exactly clap their hands with joy when this leaks out. The papers could have a field day.'

'But they're *deprived* kids. Why shouldn't they have their bit of fun? They don't get much fun, you know, not like your two over there.'

He threw a contemptuous glance at John and Michael.

'Well, are you going to clean this mess up or not?' said the air hostess, increasingly impatient. 'I've got to collect the lunch trays, in case you hadn't noticed.'

Deadlock. None of the protagonists were willing to lose face.

John saw his chance. Help Bob out of this fix. Show him that you are worthy of him! And collect a few Brownie points as well! Perhaps it might even placate Dobson.

He stood up and squeezed past Michael. 'Don't worry, I'll clean it up.'

'There's my lad!' exclaimed a relieved Steadman. God! How he liked this kid!

'Think that'll get you onto the expedition, do you?' hissed Dobson as he went back to his group.

The air hostess went into the kitchen area and returned with a wet cloth, paper towels and a bottle of washing up liquid.

'*You* shouldn't be doing this,' she said as John attacked the mephitic green sludge.

'De rien,' he replied. 'De rien. C'est mon devoir.'

'Comme vous êtes sympa!'

'Can't stop showing off, him!' growled Dobson from the back.

'Well done, lad!' said a big man in bright Bermuda shorts as John emerged from the toilet, having disposed of the disgusting paper towels and floor cloth. 'Lucky they've got you as their nursemaid.'

As John sat down, Michael started up. 'That Dobson blerk! Now if it hadda bin one o' us like what got pissed and spewed, he wouldn't half 'ave created him. Ain't right! Like me mam's Darran. Gets pissed an' spews all over the floor like. An' she's gorra mop it up else he thumps 'er. Daft cow let's 'im do it an' all.' He eyed John with a sad look. 'Yer shouldn't 'ave done it. Suckin' up ter Dobson won't dee yer nee good, yer knaa. He'll just think yer soft.'

John noticed the way that he was slipping into an exaggerated Geordie – obviously a survival strategy. But was speaking the truth. He *was* being a little suck-up. More than ever, he wanted to be a proper lad! But how he needed Bob, the friend and protector who alone could see him through these stormy waters.

Africa!

Over Africa now. Yellow dusty land below. As the plane turns a glimpse of rumpled brown mountains surging off into a hazy distance. Just as he'd pictured it. Adrenaline rush. Adventure. Redemption.

Bump! Trundle, trundle, trundle. We're down!

Half an hour of impatient confusion as people get out of their seats and start pulling luggage out of the storage lockers. Then out into the blinding sun. Blinking in the brilliant light. Onto the blistering tarmac where the heat assaults you, wave after soporific wave of it.

'Fuck me, Brian! You never said it would be this hot, like!'

'How's we meant ter handle this, like?'

John relished the heat. It was the first big challenge to be overcome, and a chance to prove his worth.

With Steadman in the lead, they trailed through the passport control and customs and set about retrieving their luggage. Dobson's lot were surly and listless; a side-effect of the 'fun' on the plane. Bright and frisky, John saw a chance to win more Brownie points and was soon hauling rucksacks off the carousel.

'Is this one yours? Hang on while I fetch a trolley.'

A big, red-faced girl with long black hair beamed at him. 'Aye, you're a canny lad you. Yer's not posh, is yer? We berra be mates. Me name's Tracy. What's yours?'

'John.'

They shook hands.

A flicker of hope. A gap in the enemy line. Get in and exploit it. But he noticed Dobson glaring at him and set to work with renewed vigour, hauling the remaining bits of luggage off the caroused and stacking them up on more trolleys. Not through the wood yet.

A Little Bit of Culture Shock

They went out of the airport where once again the great waves of heat assaulted them.

'Cor, Brian, how much o' this 'ave we gorra hack, eh?'

A hiatus ensued. Everybody milled around in a confused huddle. Nobody seemed to know what to do next. Steadman was quite deliberately testing Dobson, and stayed ostentatiously in the background.

Eventually Dobson broke the silence. 'Well, where do we go from here?' he said aggressively.

'You're the leader,' replied Steadman. 'It's up to you. You're in charge.'

'Huh! We'd better get to our accommodation. You *have* booked it, haven't you?'

'Of course.'

'Even for these two?' Contemptuous glance at John and Michael.

'Naturally.'

'Huh!'

Silence.

'Well, how are we supposed to get there?'

'We'll have to get some taxis, won't we?'

Steadman pointed to a swarm of yellow cars parked on the far side of the sun-blasted tarmac.

'Can you deal with it, then?' said Dobson.

'Let's give the expedition members a chance,' replied Steadman with a mischievous smirk.

'Hey, you lot!' he said to Dobson's group, 'Can anybody get some taxis for us? You'll have to talk French, mind. I'm afraid they don't speak much English here.'

Silence.

'Anybody speak French?'

Hostile silence.

'These aren't privileged kids, Mr Steadman,' said Dobson reprovingly. 'You can't expect them to have polite accomplishments. They've more important things to do than fiddling around with fancy things like learning French.'

'But they *do* teach French at Morton Hill, don't they?'

'Only to the better-off middle-class kids. The real kids, the deprived kids, haven't time to waste on that sort of triviality. They live in the *real* world, you know.'

Silence.

'Well, John,' said Steadman eventually, 'It's time to parade your frivolous middle-class accomplishments. You sort out the taxis for us. Here's where we are going.'

He handed him a piece of paper with an address written on it in Arabic.

John walked over to the nearest taxi. As a large man, bejeaned and sporting a luxurious black moustache, approached him, he began to recite one of the French exercises he'd done with Steadman. 'Excusez-moi, monsieur. Nous avons besoin de trois ou quatre taxis pour transporter ces gens là à cette addresse.'

He handed him Steadman's paper and continued slowly and robotically, carefully mouthing each syllable.

'Malaigrement, nous avons beaucoup de baggage. Combien pour chaque taxi?'

'Cinquante dirhams.'

'D'accord.'

Phew! Survived the encounter with a foreign language! But, bloody hell, I've probably been done! Fifty dirhams is way over the top. Still, with any luck, nobody will notice. Dobson's lot are dripping with dosh anyway.

He waved to the mob, signalling them to come over.

'There's my lad!' exclaimed a beaming Steadman. Point scored in the simmering war with Dobson.

'What it is to be a privileged private school brat!' grunted Dobson, as he prevented Tracy from getting into the same taxi as John and Michael.

As they drove off, John began to seethe. The 'good expeditioner' act was becoming increasingly difficult to sustain. Couldn't do a bloody thing right with Dobson, could he? Dobson was a shit. No, worse than that, a pool of liquid, stinking squitter! But... reality! Dobson's lot were big and strong. He couldn't possibly take them on. Indeed, they scared him. It was that Greenhill feeling again of helplessness before brute force. So keep a low profile. Keep close to Steadman. Survive!

'Don't fret, lads!' said Steadman, sensing the mood. 'Don't let Dobson get you down. Think of the mountains and what you're going to achieve.'

John cooled down. His excitement returned as they sped towards the city. It was dry, sun-bleached fields at first and then flat-roofed modern buildings that reminded him of his childhood trips to Italy. Then came palm trees, ancient castellated walls, and men in skullcaps and flowing robes...

and then a large open square surrounded by low, reddish buildings bathed in the dusty, yellow light of late afternoon.

'This is the Jemaa el-Fnaa square. That's the famous Koutoubia Mosque over there.'

The cavalcade eventually pulled up in a narrow side-street, hemmed in by red-walled buildings. Everybody piled out of the taxis and retrieved their luggage. Steadman paid the bill.

'That's a bit much, isn't it?' growled Dobson. 'Obviously your little sidekick thinks we're all as rich as he is.'

Another hiatus.

'Well, what now, Brian?'

'Yeah! Where's the hotel you was tellin' wor aboot?'

'Hope it's got a proppa telly like. It's *Coronation Street* tonight.'

'Fuck *Coronation Street*. I could dee wi' a beer, me! There berra be a proppa bar!'

'All right, people!' declared Steadman, taking charge. 'We're going Arab now. It's new experiences. That's the mantra!'

'Mantra? What the fuck's that?'

Steadman led them down a narrow lane – almost a mini canyon – between high, old-fashioned buildings, painted a dull red. At once they entered a cool, shadowy world of deep, twisting alleys, hidden corners and elaborately carved wooden doors. Far above, peeping spasmodically through the enclosing red walls, was a strip of yellow sky. There were no cars, only the odd donkey, and veiled women tripping quietly by. A pungent smell of wood smoke and spices wafted round them. Here – to John at any rate – was the old, untouched world of the explorers.

'Cor, Bob!' he exclaimed. 'This is great! I never thought places like this still existed.'

'Here we are,' said Steadman, pushing open a big wooden door in the blank canyon wall.

They filed in and found themselves in a neatly tiled courtyard in the middle of which was a low wooden table surrounded by richly embroidered cushions. A steep, wooden staircase led up to a balcony which ran round the entire four walls. It was a cool, hushed place, the only sound being the tinkling of a small fountain, trickling away under the spreading branches of a palm tree.

A grave, bearded man in a white robe approached them, followed by a large, leathery woman wearing a head cloth and a long, colourful dress. Steadman began a vigorous conversation with them in Arabic, and then turned to his expectant entourage.

'Sit down on the cushions here, people. They're giving us tea as part of a traditional Islamic welcome.'

John and Michael immediately squatted down on the inviting pile, but the others remained standing, sullen and suspicious. A small boy, white-robed and barefoot, arrived with a large tray-load of jangling little glasses filled with a steaming brown liquid.

'Your first taste of Arab tea,' declared a beaming Steadman.

'Warraboot some beer? I'm reet thorsty me!'

While John and Michael sipped the hot sweet liquid, the others eyed it dubiously. Eventually Tracy and another girl tasted it. Three of the boys tipped it contemptuously onto the ground.

'Now, chaps,' said Steadman, assuming what John called his 'commanding officer' voice, 'accommodation. Mr Dobson's and Mr Morris's groups are upstairs in two large rooms. There's a bog at the far end of the balcony and a shower next to it. John and Michael, you are with me down here.'

The elite dispersed in silence while John and Mike followed Steadman into a long, high ceilinged room. Round the edges of the tiled walls were broad, cushioned benches.

John was entranced. 'Just like the Arabian nights, isn't it, Bob?'

They unpacked their rucksacks and busied themselves spreading their things over their assigned places. Suddenly Dobson appeared in the doorway and the temperature seemed to drop below freezing, almost as if Dracula had gate-crashed a Christmas party.

'Mr Steadman, a word.'

Steadman joined him outside while John and Michael listened to the ensuing dialogue.

'Is this your idea of accommodation for British kids?'

'Yes. Why not?'

'"Why not?" you say! Have you seen it? No air conditioning. No television. I don't know what you call those bench things, but they're certainly not beds. And have you seen the bog?'

'Yes, I've been here before.'

'Maybe you have. But British kids need proper facilities. It's a matter of safety.'

'I thought this expedition was supposed to, I quote, "Give the young people who are to be our future leaders first-hand experience of a very different culture".'

'Quite so, but that doesn't mean disregarding safety.'

'Oh come on! They're as safe as houses here!'

'Obviously you and I have different standards of safety. And what about tonight's supper? The kids need feeding you know.'

'Well, I was going to get Madame to prepare a tagine.'

'Tagine? What on earth's that?'

'A local dish. A big and nutritious stew full of meat, vegetables and dates. It's delicious. But, if they would prefer it, we could take them round the town and try the local cafes. They'd like that.'

'You mean eat the local muck? No way.'

'Look, if you don't like this place, go and find a better one for your group. It'll be pricey, though.'

'Right. Will you come along and talk the lingo? They don't seem to understand anything here.'

'No, you'd better go yourself. I'll stay here and hold the fort.'

'Huh!'

Dobson stalked off, muttering furiously to himself. Steadman returned to the room.

'Big ears flapping, eh?' he exclaimed as he saw John hovering behind the door.

'What was all that about?'

'Just a little bit of culture shock.'

'Oh?'

'Dobbie doesn't like this place. He's gone off to find a better one.'

'But it's great here. We're not going to leave it, are we?'

'Of course not. It's all we can afford. The hotels are all ultra-expensive, and they'll all be booked up, too. This is a popular tourist resort. But, anyway, about supper...'

'Can me and Michael go exploring? I mean, it's going to be boring, just sitting here.'

'Yes, of course. But be careful and remember what I said about not photographing the locals. *Please* don't get lost. Be back by ten.'

'Wicked! Come on, Michael!'

Young Explorers; A Tentative Alliance

In the courtyard they ran into a sullen mob of Dobson's people, milling round the exit. John sensed danger. It was back to Gloucester Road, and that meant a low profile and avoiding any eye contact. He tried to slip past them unnoticed.

'Hey, you!'

Seen. Caught. What now? Debagging? Or something

worse? But don't panic. Steadman's in the vicinity. Keep your cool.

'Yes?'

'Wharst thaa gannin' son?'

'Just exploring. We're going to try the local cafes.'

Tracy spoke up. 'Can I come, too?'

'And me an' all, added a scrawny, pointy-nosed youth with a spotty face.

'Yes, please do,' replied John nervously. Let the whole mob come and they easily do you over in one of those back alleys, but with only two of them you might just have a chance. But it could possibly be an opportunity to drive a wedge into the closed phalanx of the enemy... so grasp it while you can!

They went out into the dark and silent street where the by now black walls towered over them.

'I'm Jim,' the youth said. 'Worra yous two called?'

'John.'

'Michael.'

'I think it's fuckin' rotten the way wor Brian gans on at yer twos!' said Tracy vehemently. 'Yers not snobs an' that. Yers jus' lads.'

'Aye,' put in Jim. 'Yer berra than Kev an' them lot. All they want is beer an' fags. Aye, an' a birra dope, an' sex an' all. But Ah wanna dee sommat me, climb moontins an' that. Not jus' fuck roond gerrin' pissed an' shaggin' an' that. Ah mean, me mam's paid fuck knaas wot ter gerrus here like.'

John put on a Geordie accent and shook his hand. 'Good on yer! We's mates then.'

He felt a surge of relief: there was a gap in the enemy phalanx. To cement the new alliance, he took a photograph of the group. Then they set off down the twisting alley.

Soon they emerged onto the big open square of the Jemaa el-Fnaa. The sun was setting and suffusing everything with a warm and almost kindly orange glow. The place had woken up. Previously, it had been a sun-blasted emptiness. Now it was a seething mass of activity: market stalls, bright lights, robed exotics strolling about, glowing braziers, clouds of smoke, the smell of wood fires, spices and barbecued meat, strange music. It was alive and richly pulsating.

John was entranced. 'Cor, just look at this!'

Wriggling their way through a tightly packed crowd, they discovered a gaunt, turbaned figure sitting cross-legged on a mat, holding a long flute. Putting it to his lips, he began to play, and a strange, haunting melody seemed to float upwards. From a nearby basket a snake emerged and appeared to sway in time with the mysterious notes.

A scene straight out of one of his childhood encyclopaedias! It was too much for an already hyped-up John. 'Cor, a real live snake charmer! Hang on while I take a photograph!'

A bright white flash was followed by an uproar. The music stopped. The turbaned man stood up and started shouting.

'C'est interdit photographer!' somebody yelled.

'Dihrams! Dollars!' somebody else bellowed.

Flustered, John pulled a 10 dirham note out of his pocket and tried to give it to the turbaned man. An unknown hand snatched it from him.

'Plus! Plus! More! More!'

'Howay, John, let's get oota here!' said Michael, now firmly embedded in the Geordie patois he used for survival situations.

Squeezing their way through the crowd, the four of them fled.

A man grabbed John's arm. 'That's the Koutoubia Mosque over there.'

'Yes, it's very beautiful!'

'Fifty dihrams! Me tourist guide!'

John gave him a 10 dihram note.

'Not enough! More! More!'

'For fuck's sake, John!' exclaimed Michael, 'Divvent start given' 'em money! They're just doin' yers!'

'Let's go somewhere else!' added Jim.

They hurried through the jostling bodies and found themselves in another dark and silent alley. Once again, tall buildings reared up, gorge-like, on either side of them, framing a narrow strip of red sky far above them. They had escaped.

'Phew, that was hairy!' gasped John. 'Sorry, team, I should have remembered what Bob said about photographing the locals.'

'No sweat!' said Jim. 'We're still alive! So, let's see where this leads to.'

'Gee, this is ever so exciting!' chortled Tracy.

They wandered off down the black, narrow canyon, finding themselves once more in a hushed world of darkened and twisting alleys. The odd robed figure slipped quietly by. From the occasional openings in the enclosing walls, dim lights flickered. Through beaded curtains they glimpsed shady little dens hung with thick carpets. Above them the sky slowly turned into a dark, velvety blue, spangled with glittering stars.

'I'm starving!' said Michael.

'Me an' all,' added Jim.

'An' Ah didn't eat nowt on the plane, me,' declared Tracy. 'What with Kev gerrin' pissed and spewin' like. Eeee, I'm dying o' hunger, me!'

The moon rose, a big silvery orb in the dark blue sky, poking delicate fingers of light into the slumbering world of black shapes. Eventually they came to what seemed to be a café: a big cave in the alley wall, hung with richly patterned carpets and dimly lit by hissing and flickering paraffin lamps. A clay oven and a glowing brazier occupied one wall. In the middle was a low table surrounded by cushions. With the big clay pots and beaded curtains, the place was a vision of an older and more colourful world to John; but not, perhaps, to the others.

'Let's try this.'

A man in a white robe approached them. 'Voulez-vous manger?'

'What's he saying?'

'He's asking us if we want to eat,' replied John.

'Yeah!'

'Oui, certainment!'

They filed in and draped themselves on the cushions round the table.

'Voulez-vous un tagine?'

'What's that?'

'Dunno!'

'Nor me neither.'

'Well,' said John, 'let's give it a try. We're explorers, after all. Oui, monsieur. Nous desirons manger un tagine.'

Stirrings began. Tea was brought. The man sat down beside them and started a conversation. John interpreted to the best of his limited ability. The man's accent and pronunciation gave him dire comprehension problems, but he struggled on.

What were their names?

John, Tracy, Michael and Jim.

Where were they from?

Boldonbridge.

Was that in London?

No, it was a city in the north of England.

How much did a schoolteacher earn in England?

Eventually the meal came: a big, clay bowl containing a steaming and exotically smelling stew. Spoons were handed round. Hungrily they attacked it.

'Not bad this.'

'Better than I thought it would be.'

'Berra than the crap me mam dishes up, anyway.'

'C'est tres bon!' said John to the man. 'Vous êtes tres bon chef. Je l'aime, et mes amis aussi.'

The bowl was scraped clean.

'We'd better pay the bill,' said John who was by now wallowing in his role as leader and interpreter, 'L'addition, s'il vous plaît?'

'Rien,' said the man, bowing slightly.

'Comment?'

'Rien. Vous ne payerez rien.'

'But... well... That's very kind of you.' This in a bemused, muddled English.

'What's all this?' asked Michael.

'He says he's not charging us anything.'

'Mais nous vous payerez. C'est comme il faut.'

The man then gave a little speech. John failed to understand much of it, but managed to get the general gist of it.

'He says were are young people and it's the tradition of Islam to be hospitable to young people.'

'Merci beaucoup. Merci beaucoup. Vous êtes tellement sympa...'

Addresses were exchanged and they left amid profuse thanks.

'Cor, he were nice, him!'

'Yeah!' said Tracy. 'Not like what Brian said they would be.'

'Dobson's a cunt!' snorted Michael.

'No, he ain't that!' replied Tracy defensively. 'He's ever so nice to us.'

'But why does he hate us? I mean what the fuck's me and John done to 'im, like?'

'Don't ask me,' sighed Tracy, shaking her head. 'But I'll tell yous one thing. He's ower scared of Kev.'

'Kev!' snorted Jim. 'You wanna watch oot for 'im, like! He'll fuck the whole bleedin' lorra us up, he will! Him and

Sandra, an' Jakie an' all! All they wants is booze, drugs an' fuckin'. Why the fuck Brian brought 'em along Ah divvent knaa.'

He began a passionate speech. 'Ter gerron this thing Ah had ter dee all sortsa tests: runnin', hikin' and the like. But Kev did nowt. Sat around smerkin' fags an' that. Yet Brian brings 'im along and treats 'im like a bloody lord! Divvent make no sense.' He shook his head with a resigned fatalism. 'Anyways, Ah'm stickin' wi' you twos, me. Kev'll be landin' in the shite ower soon.'

'There's Going to be a Big Bust-Up Soon'

They eventually found their way back to the pension.

Steadman greeted them warmly. 'Great to see you back safe and sound!'

Excitedly gabbled out the story of their adventures.

'That man he was so nice!' exclaimed John. 'He refused to let us pay for the meal. I've got his address. I've taken lots of photos.'

'Splendid! That's just what I want to see. Now, you lot better get to bed.'

'John,' he added, 'you'd better watch out. Dobbie's after your blood!'

'Why?'

'Well I did wind him up a bit, told him that you'd gone to sell Tracy in the souk. He got his knickers in a fair old twist!'

Before he turned in, John slipped up to the toilet on the landing. The tagine and the brisk walk were having their effect. It was a squatty do... but, well, he was used to squatting now and, primed by Steadman, he'd brought his own supply of paper. Luckily the chain worked reasonably well.

Returning along the balcony, he passed an open door and smelt a pungent, sweetish smell that brought back memories of those Sunday night parties Giles used to have at Gloucester

Road. Casually he peeped in. Through a bluish haze he discerned a group of bodies sprawled untidily on the benches and on the floor. Some he recognised as Dobson's people. Others were strangers: ragged young men, bearded, bangled and with long, matted hair; possibly some of those 'itinerant hippies' about which Steadman had warned him. Empty beer cans littered the floor and everybody seemed to be smoking. In a far corner, apparently oblivious of everybody and everything, a couple of naked bodies were wrapped in a heaving and grunting embrace, big hairy backside wobbling furiously and a white feminine body jerking up and down rhythmically; one of Dobson's girls and a stranger, hard at work, Fleetwood-style. Booze, drugs and fuckin': Jim hadn't been exaggerating.

As he turned to leave, Kev leapt up, grabbed his arm and pulled him up to his chest. Trapped. The Greenhill terror was on him. But try not to show it.

Slurred and aggressive voice. 'Herld on, me bonny lad! Yer've not seen nowt, 'ave yer? So divvent gan grassin' ter yon Steadman blerk. Gerrit?'

He punched him violently in the ribs.

'Oyer! No! No! I'll not grass on you!'

'Berra not, son!'

He punched him again.

'Oyer!'

'There's a lot more where that came from.' With that, he relaxed his grip.

John scuttled off, desperate to reach the protecting wings of Steadman. What *had* he discovered? They were smoking dope, which they'd probably got from those hippies. The idiots! Didn't they know what would happen if they got caught? Steadman had dinned it into him, all right: arrest, a Moroccan jail, beaten up by the guards. And, worse still, trouble for everybody else. Bloody hell, *he* could land in jail, too! And what would Dolly have to say about *that*? 'No! I'll not grass on you!' Don't be daft! Let Steadman know now before it's too late!

As he bounded down the stairs, he ran straight into Dobson. 'Where the bloody hell have you been?'

Blank stare. The words just wouldn't come.

'You don't know, do you? Well, I'll tell you. Off on your own without permission into a dangerous part of the town and gorging yourself on the local muck – and God alone knows what parasites are in that stuff! – *and* inveigling bona-fide expedition members to come with you. If you bloody poison yourself and your little mate, that's your business, but I'm *not* having you endangering the lives of *my* expedition members and undermining expedition discipline either! You shouldn't be here. You're a thoroughly bad influence. Your face doesn't fit. I'm sending you home tomorrow!'

At that, John's smouldering resentment burst out. 'You *can't* do that! I've been selected for the expedition! Mr Steadman says.'

'Huh! That's what you think. Well, you'll be learning a thing or two in the morning!'

Disaster! Dropping the last vestiges of the 'good expeditioner' pose, John wriggled past him and made a dash for the bedroom.

'Bob! Bob! This is urgent!'

A sleepy Steadman emerged from beneath an enfolding sheet.

'Yes?'

'Dobson says he's sending me home. He can't do that, can he? I mean, you won't let him, will you? *Please*!'

'Good lord, no!'

Profound relief. 'Thanks, Bob, thanks!'

Then anger came. 'I mean, what's got into that man? I was going downstairs when he blew a fit on me for going into the town with Tracy and Jim.'

'Don't worry. It's all par for the course. He and Morris went to a hotel and found it far too expensive, just like I said it would be. Then they got sloshed on the local beer.'

'But why pick on me?'

'Because he's jealous of you. You can speak French and he can't. He sees you as a threat.'

'But what have I done?'

'It's not what you've done. It's who you are.'

'That's pathetic! He says I'm a bad influence. Bad influence! You should see what his lot are getting up to upstairs.'

'Oh, and what's that?'

'Please don't say I told you. Kev said he'd do me over if I grassed him up. Please Bob, I know I'm a wimp. But, well, I'm scared of him.'

'Don't worry. I won't tell. Now out with it.'

'Well, they were there with some hippie types, smoking dope...'

'Dope?'

'It'll be hash or, mebbe, heroin,' put in Michael, sticking a tousled head out of his enclosing blanket. 'Me mam uses hash from Morocco and Darran told us to bring some heroin back, an' all. But Ah'm not deein' it! Ah'm not that daft, me!'

'Hmmm.' Steadman nodded knowingly. 'Anything else?'

'Well one of the girls was being screwed by a hippie, right in front of everybody, too!'

'Just as I thought.'

'But the dope? It's against the law. Hadn't we better get the police? I mean, if we don't, we could all get done, like you said! I'm scared!'

'Just you cool down. That's Dobbie's problem, not ours. Give that lot time, give them enough rope to hang themselves. They're daft enough to do it. There's going to be a big bust-up soon. At least half of Dobbie's lot don't like what's happening with Kev, and want to join us lot. That's one reason why

Dobbie wants you out of the way. Like it or not, my man, you *are* a threat to him. In the meantime, rest assured. You're doing fine. So are you, Michael.'

Michael covered himself up and rolled over. Suddenly Steadman embraced John. Both felt a warm – and unmentionable! – thrill sweeping through them. Quickly, and actually frightened by it, they disentangled themselves.

'OK. Bed now.'

John stripped down to his underpants and slipped under a blanket alongside Michael. What a day! And this was only the start.

Expedition Briefing

A hot, sun-soaked morning came. Along with Michael and Steadman, John had a leisurely breakfast of tea, bread and olives, seated on the cushions under the palm tree in the courtyard. There was no sign of the others. As he slipped past their room on his way to the toilet, he noticed that they were still asleep.

Some time after ten o'clock the 'Expedition Briefing' occurred. Slowly, in dribs and drabs, Dobson's group trickled down to the courtyard and sprawled listlessly under the palm tree. When about half of them had arrived the trickle dried up, and a hiatus began. Eventually, like an Advent Angel, Morris appeared, spick and span, crisp and efficient, heralding the approach of the 'One Greater than He'. Finally, looking thunderous, Dobson arrived.

'What's up with him now?' John whispered to Michael. 'Has he found out about the dope and that?'

'Doubt it. He's jus' got a 'angover him. He's bin on the beer all last night, like.'

Seeing Jim and Tracy, John bounced over to them.

With a roar that made some people jump, Dobson suddenly came to life.

'*You*! Over there!'

'*Me*?' asked John in an aggrieved tone, complete with a surly adolescent curled lip. 'Why?'

'Because you're not part of the expedition. And don't answer back!'

'Yes, I am! Mr Steadman says!'

A teenage confrontation was developing. Steadman acted quickly before it could turn violent. He grabbed John's arm and escorted the protesting lump back to where Michael was sitting.

'Not now, young man. Not now!'

Dobson took charge. 'We're not all here. Where's Kevin and Jakie? Somebody had better get them.'

'They're ill. They're staying in bed today.'

Dobson glared at Steadman. Several notches up from the normal baleful stare. 'Ill? Just what I knew would happen if we stayed in a place like this. But, then, some people thought they knew better, didn't they?' He then launched into what was obviously a carefully prepared speech.

'Now, before we start, I've got something important to say. You've landed in a difficult situation which is not of my making.' Glare in Steadman's direction. 'But so far, you've all managed well. Unfortunately you have been let down by our two – shall we say, 'extras?' – who went off into the town, alone and without my permission as expedition leader (another glare at Steadman) and, regardless of the risk, consorted with dangerous locals, and risked their health by eating God alone knows what local muck. Endangering themselves was quite irresponsible enough. What has made it much worse is that they put two of our own team at risk as well. I trust Tracy and Jim will have learned their lesson, and from now on I want no more sneaking off without permission. Mr Steadman, I want your two beauties sent home. *Now*. Before they do any more damage.'

As the peroration concluded, John's temper had steadily boiled up. This was crazy! That excursion last night had been a good and positive thing! Steadman had said so! And what about the sex and drugs he'd seen? Didn't that matter? Fuming, he stood up.

But before he could shout at Dobson, Steadman grabbed his shoulder and pushed him down again.

'Keep your temper, John. Leave this to me. Mr Dobson,' he continued, 'I'm afraid that won't be possible.'

'And why not? Those are my orders as Expedition Leader and I expect to be obeyed.'

'But the flight is an APEX cheapie and the dates are fixed.'

'Well, put them on another flight.'

'Not possible. All the flights are booked up. Anyway, we haven't got the money. So they'll have to stay with me.'

'Huh!'

A pause followed, while Dobson visibly smouldered.

Finally he pronounced: 'As you say, Mr Steadman. But I'm not taking any responsibility for them. They stay with you, and I forbid any of the real expedition members to have anything to do with them. I might as well tell you that when we get home there will be consequences. Serious consequences. Now, it's over to you, Joe.'

Morris stepped forward, carrying bundles of papers. Exuding even more than his usual aura of clipped professionalism, he seemed almost manic. Glancing nervously in Dobson's direction, he paused.

God, thought John, he's like a small kid having to speak to the school at Morning Assembly! He's shit scared of Dobbie, that's for sure!

Eventually Dobson gave a little nod and Morris handed each expedition member a neatly folded map, ostentatiously omitting John and Michael, who went into a huddle with Steadman. There was a pause while one half of the recipients opened out their maps and the other half dropped them onto the ground.

Morris gave another anxious glance at Dobson, who finally condescended to nod his head. He then launched into a carefully rehearsed speech, all in a nervously clipped staccato. Rat-a-tat... a list of facts poured out like bullets from a machine gun.

'Expedition timetable. Phase One. Acclimatisation to climate and culture. That's today. Stay in Marrakesh. Phase Two. Acclimatisation hike. Tomorrow morning for three days. Phase Three. Self-managed ascent of Jebel Toubkal. Four thousand six hundred metres. Three days from Imlil. Main objective of the expedition. Aim: to prove the expedition expertise of proletarian youth.'

More names and facts poured out. John, at any rate, lost track of the avalanche.

'Acclimatisation hike. Now detailed planning. At zero nine hundred hours tomorrow morning we take taxis to Imlil. Locate it on your maps. We spend the night at Imlil in the French Alpine Club hostel. Next day at zero nine hundred hours we start the acclimatisation hike. Look at your maps. From Imlil up to the Tizi Mzik Pass. Down to Tizi Oussem and Taddert. Over the Tizi–n-Techt Pass and back to Imlil. The duration of the hike: six hours.'

Suddenly Steadman spoke up. 'Hold on a minute! Isn't this a bit ambitious? I mean, it's a big pull up to the Tizi Mzik Pass. Two thousand feet plus, and under a hot sun too. And it's quite a drag to Imi Oughlad. It'll take this lot a lot longer than six hours, especially if they're not that fit.' Here he threw a glance at some supine adolescent lumps sprawled on the ground.

Morris threw a nervous glance at Dobson and then scowled. 'Are you questioning my professional judgement?'

'No, I wouldn't dream of doing that,' replied Steadman with a benign smile, 'but in view of the fitness of some of our troops, wouldn't it be wiser to do an easier hike to Tacheddirt? It would break them in gently.'

Again, he indicated the supine heaps on the ground.

At this, Dobson weighed in with the full weight of his leader's authority. 'Mr Steadman, this is a serious mountaineering expedition. You can take your two extras over to Tach-whatever it is, if you want, but they're not coming with us. The real expedition members are going over the Tizi M'Zik Pass. We don't want them held up by a couple of free-loaders who won't be able to cope with serious mountaineering. Understand?'

At this John's temper broke. He stood up and shouted, *'That's not fair! I can cope! I've—'*

But before he could go any further, Steadman grabbed him and pushed him down.

'Temper tantrums won't do you any good. Just *sit down*!'

Dobson glared contemptuously at the seething adolescent heap. 'You watch yourself, sunshine! You just watch yourself.'

Morris resumed his fusillade. 'Equipment. Full mountain kit. Boots. Rucksacks. Any questions?'

Steadman spoke up. 'You haven't mentioned water bottles. It'll be very hot and they'll need Puritabs if they're not to get stomach upsets.'

Morris ignored him. 'Now go and prepare your kit.'

The expedition briefing was over.

'Just Give it Time'

Back in their room, John exploded. 'Dobson's a cunt! I'm going to punch his fucking face in!'

'No, young man, you're *not*!' said Steadman grabbing his arm and flinging him onto the bench, where he landed with a thump. Placing his hands firmly on his shoulders he held him down.

'Gerroff! Lemme go!'

Speaking quietly and firmly, Steadman addressed the quivering heap. 'Go on, take a swing at Dobbie if you like. But what do you think will happen? I'll tell you. He'll just set Kev onto you, that's all.'

'I don't fucking care!'

'You will fucking care when Kev starts on you. He's already got two convictions for Greviouis Bodily Harm.. Now, just cool down. Things are going your way quicker than you think. There're going to be a few chickens coming home to roost fairly soon. Don't go and mess things up.'

'He's right, John,' added Michael calmly. 'He's right, yer knaa. Don't gan an' muck things up. Leave it ter them lot. They're doin' it quite fast enough, them.'

'Just give it time,' said Steadman. 'Give it time.'

John threw a sulky pout. 'And how the hell do you know?'

'I've got second sight. I'm a prophet, didn't you know?'

'Very funny.'

Mysterious Souks, Ancient Mosques

Later that morning Steadman took John and Michael on a tour of Marrakesh. It was twisting alleys, mysterious souks, ancient mosques and an exotic tannery, all of which helped to soothe John's temper.

In the afternoon they returned to the pension where they prepared their rucksacks for the acclimatisation hike.

'We *are* going with the others, aren't we?' asked John.

'Of course!' replied Steadman. 'You don't think that lot could manage on their own, do you? Most of them can't read a map, and none of them speak a word of French.'

Of Dobson's lot there was little sign.

'With any luck they'll have buggered off,' said Michael. 'That means we can get on with things proppa like. I mean do we *have* to have them lot wi' us?'

'There's Sommat Gannin' on'

That evening, Steadman took them out for supper. As they were leaving they ran into Jim.

John greeted him with a friendly smile. 'Jim! Want to come and have supper with us?'

But with an inaudible grunt, Jim pushed past them and scuttled upstairs.

'Well, he wasn't very sociable!' snorted John.

'He's scared, that's what!' said Michael.

'There's sommat gannin' on,' he added sagely. 'Like what you said, Bob.'

Steadman nodded vaguely.

They went to a small rooftop restaurant overlooking the Jemaa el-Fnaa. As the sun went down in an orange glow, and the square below them seethed with sparkling lights and frenetic bustle, they ate a vast and spicy Moroccan meal.

Mugged

It was dark when they eventually returned to the pension. Vague murmuring from upstairs indicated that Dobson's lot were in residence.

'Seems them lot's back!' sighed Michael. 'That's torn it!'

'Just try to be patient,' said Steadman. 'Just wait and see what happens tomorrow.'

Before settling down for the night, John slipped up to the toilet. Emerging from the foetid little cubicle amid the groans and gurgles of the barely functioning waterworks, he made his way along the balcony. Suddenly a massive figure loomed out of the dark. It was Kev. All John's bravado seemed to go hissing out of him, like the air out of a punctured football. He turned round and tried to scurry back to the toilet, with the vague hope of locking himself in.

But a big hand seized his shoulder and swung him round.

There before him was the whole bunch: Jakie, Sandra, and the rest of them. Michael was right, 'them lot' were back. Struggling desperately, he was pulled into their room. In the background he could just make out Jim and Tracy. Both turned away and tried not to look at him. No help from that quarter. Alone. At the mercy of the mob. Not tough guy John now, but terrified little wimp John. The John that peed on the Bishop's carpet.

Kev pulled him up to his chest. 'Liddell nark, ain't yer?'

'No, I'm not, honest!' Oh. heavens, has Bob gone and spilt the beans? How to get out of this one?

'Yer grassed us up didn't yer?'

'No I didn't!'

'Yer did an' all!'

Vicious punch in the face. Blinding flash of light. Pain. Salty taste of blood as it pours out of his nose.

'Oyer!'

A token attempt at resistance was impossible as both his arms were firmly pinioned. God, what are they going to do to me now?

'Yorra rich git ain't yer?'

'No, I'm not!'

A hefty punch in the ribs made him gasp. Remember Bob's instructions about being robbed. Resistance pointless. Give them what they want. 'You can always get a new camera on the insurance, but you won't be able to get a new stomach or liver that easily.'

'All right, what do you want?'

'Nikka! That's what! We needs it like!'

'OK. Let me get it out!' At least they're not going to take my pants off; the shame of that in front of Jim and Tracy!

They released him and he unbuttoned his shirt and, unzipping his money belt, handed over his remaining dihrams.

'Is that all? Howay, yerv got more!'

'No, I haven't, honest!'

'Liar!'

Another punch in the ribs sent him sprawling onto the floor. Fighting back tears, he was hauled to his feet. Hairy paws ripped open his shirt and pulled off his money belt.

'What's them things then?'

'They're travellers' cheques. They're no use to you!'

'Crap!'

Another punch in the face. Another blinding flash of light.

'Oyer!'

'We'll 'ave 'em anyway!'

Kev returned the money belt. 'An' we wants a bit off your mate Steadman. Gerrus twenny quid. Tomorra mornin' sharp, mind, else yer's gerrin it!'

A final punch in the ribs sent him sprawling on the floor for the second time.

Picking himself up, he scuttled off down the stairs. Looking into his money belt, he found his passport was still there. At least they hadn't taken that. That, at any rate, was something. But, oh God, how pathetic he'd been! Trembling and snivelling when he should have lashed out at them! If it had been at Beaconsfield he would have done, but this was different. These were wild animals – Greenhill again. But, oh, the shame of it all! And in front of Jim and Tracy too. He had to make a big effort to stop the tears trickling.

'It Should be Interesting'

He crept back into the bedroom.

Steadman was there. 'What's up with you? You've been through the wars, haven't you?'

'Oh, nothing.' How could he explain this away? It was all so degrading! Beaten up in a fight! As bad as shitting yourself.

'Oh come on! Your nose is bleeding, your shirt's ripped and you've got a corker of a black eye. Don't tell me you just

walked into a door. You've run into Kev and his mates, haven't
you?'

'Well, yes.'

'And they've mugged you, haven't they?'

'In a way... yes.'

'I knew they would,' said Michael.

'I'm afraid that was inevitable, sooner or later,' added
Steadman with a sigh. 'Did they take your money?'

John was silent for a moment. Eventually he forced himself
to tell some of the truth. It was like squeezing hardened
toothpaste out of an old tube.

'Yes, they took all my money and all my traveller's cheques
too. But I put up quite a fight and managed to keep my
passport. But there were six or seven of them... and I couldn't
do much.'

'Oh, don't start trying to apologise. It wasn't exactly your
fault, was it? But we can't let them get away with this. It'll be
Michael next, and then maybe Jim.'

'They said I'd grassed on them. Did you tell Dobson about
the drugs?'

'No, it wasn't me. It was Jim, but they don't know that.
They think it was you, and Jim was too scared to say it was
him.'

'Well, what's Dobson going to do about it?'

'If he's any sense, he'll tell the poliss and they'll pack 'em
all off ter the nick,' said Michael vehemently. 'Them's nowt
but trouble, them lot!'

'I don't know what he'll do,' said Steadman. 'We'll just
have to wait and see. It should be interesting.'

A Drug Dealer? Consequences

A little later, but not quite on cue, Dobson appeared outside
the room, looking like thunder.

'Mr Steadman, a word, please.'

Steadman went outside to meet him while John and Michael stationed themselves by the door and listened to the ensuing dialogue.

'I'll come right to the point,' said Dobson. 'I'm taking your two extras down to the nearest police station and I want you to accompany me and act as interpreter.'

'Why, for heaven's sake?'

'You obviously haven't been noticing things. But I've been reliably informed that when they went into the town last night, they bought drugs and then tried to sell them to my people.'

'Who on earth told you *that*?'

'Kevin Bartlett.'

'And you believe him?'

'Why not? He's a good lad.'

'That's not what I heard. Drug pusher. Two convictions for robbery with violence. Hardly a squeaky clean innocent.'

'We've been through this before. He's a *deprived* kid. He *has* to do a bit of robbery to get the cash for his everyday needs. Anyway, it's not robbery. It's only recovering what society's taken from him. Not like your two that's just after money.'

'That's as maybe, but —'

'No buts. Let's see what your little friends have to say for themselves, shall we?'

'John, Michael. Can you come here a minute?'

John who'd heard every word of the dialogue had become two people: one, the Greenhill version, wanting to shrivel up and hide under the blankets in sheer despair at the craziness of things: the other an incandescent bundle of fury, ready to charge, Kamikaze-style, at the enemy, regardless of the consequences. When he emerged from the shadows with Michael, he was visibly trembling.

'Right, you two,' said Dobson, putting on his 'official expedition leader' voice. 'You're coming down to the police station with me.'

John screwed up his faltering courage. 'Why?' Curled lip, adolescent defiance.

'You know perfectly well why.'

'Don't.'

'All right then, I'll remind you. Last night you went into the town and used your privileged education and superior wealth to buy drugs, which you then tried to sell to my people.'

Flabbergasted stare. Blind fury. Tears trickling.

'Crap! Get Tracy and Jim. They were with us. They'll tell the truth.'

'They already have.'

'Can't have done. Michael, you tell him.'

Michael turned away. 'John, yer canna dee owt, son. He's got it all sewn up like.'

'Oh, for fuck's sake, don't be a wimp *now*!' John turned on Dobson in a blaze of temper. 'I *never* bought fucking drugs! You *know* it! It was those hippies that Kev was with.'

'Oh, it's hippies now, is it? Think that one will wash, do you?'

'But they *were* there! I *saw* them! They were all smoking dope. Sandra was being screwed in the corner.'

'Don't try to lie your way out of it.'

Steadman intervened. 'That *is* true, Brian. I saw them at it.'

'Can't have done, because it never happened.'

'Are you calling me a liar?'

'*Yes* he *is*!' shrieked John. 'Because that's what you are! You're a *cunt*!'

'John, that won't do you any good,' said Steadman trying to restrain him.

'Nobody calls me a cunt,' said Dobson slowly and deliberately.

With that, he stepped forward and punched him hard in the ribs. He was big, muscular, powerfully built and far stronger than John who, for the third time that evening, crumpled up.

'Just remember, sunshine, that I'm a boxer,' he declared triumphantly.

'That's assault!' said Steadman, as he lifted the panting bundle off the floor. 'And in front of two witnesses, as well.'

'Law's different here. I can get away with it. That I *do* know.'

'Look, if the adults can't sort things out without violence, how do you expect the kids to?'

'There's nothing to sort out. We're taking these two down to the police station now.'

Despite his most valiant efforts, John slid into helpless child mode. Tears came. 'Why? Why? *Me*? I've done nothing wrong. Mad! Mad!'

Michael, who had fewer illusions about human goodness and expected far less out of life, remained calm. Resigned.

'Come on, John,' said Steadman, grabbing John's shoulder, 'You've nothing to worry about. I'll stand by you.'

How he was relishing the situation! The youth totally dependent on him, wide open to… well, just *what*? Also, it was a glorious chance to parade his underused linguistic and anthropological skills, a chance to demolish that pretentious buffoon, Dobson. The adrenaline was pumping. This was *war*!

They filed their way through the exotic anarchy of the Jemaa el-Fnaa and eventually ended up outside a modern two-storey building in the newer part of the town. Uniformed men ushered them into a small office where a dapper little man, all gold braid, gold shoulder pips and medals, sat behind a large desk. A picture of the King of Morocco occupied the wall behind him.

Immediately Dobson went onto the attack. 'I've brought two young men who have been dealing in drugs.'

The man behind the desk looked blank.

Dobson repeated the sentence in a louder voice. *'I've brought two young men who have been dealing in drugs!'*

A blank look was followed by an offended scowl.

'He doesn't understand English,' said Steadman. 'I think I'd better handle this one.'

As he launched into fluent Arabic, the man seemed to visibly melt. The hard-lined military face broke into a broad grin. He stood up and rang a bell on the desk. Chairs were brought in for everybody – including the two supposed miscreants – to sit on, glasses of steaming tea were handed round. Steadman continued his speech, and eventually the man stood up and shook everybody's hands.

'Well, that's settled,' declared Steadman. 'John and Michael, you can sleep easily tonight. You're in the clear.'

John's sullen and grubby face dissolved into a dazzling smile. 'Thanks Bob! Thanks!'

In a rush of emotion he embraced him. With more restraint, Michael followed suit.

But Dobson wasn't convinced. 'What the hell have you been telling him?' he growled.

'Simply the truth, old man. These two had nothing whatever to do with drugs. It was those hippies who got them.'

'You mean you just soft-soaped him to get your two off the hook. I might have known it! Well, this'll have to go higher up. We'll have to go to the British Embassy to get justice, then. Obviously I can't rely on you. Anyway, what about that cafe they visited last night? That's where Jim says they got the stuff.'

'All right, we'll check it out, if that's what you want. We'll bring a policeman along to help us. John, can you describe the cafe you visited last night?'

John did so.

More Arabic conversation from Steadman. A young policeman arrived. Together they left. The policeman obviously knew the way and they soon reached the cafe.

'Yes, this is it,' said John.

As they parted the beaded curtain and entered the little den, they were overwhelmed by an effusive welcome. John and Michael were embraced and kissed by the grave old man in the white robe. Tea was brought. A vigorous Arabic conversation began between him, Steadman and the policeman. Hands were shaken. Kebabs were brought.

'What's all this, then?' growled Dobson.

Deftly switching languages, Steadman explained. 'This man angrily denies selling drugs to these two. He praises them for their good manners and adult attitude towards the local culture.'

'Huh! Well he would, wouldn't he?'

'Maybe, but he says he knows about a group of hippies who were using drugs and who were staying at our place. This policeman happens to be the brother of the owner, so you'd better be careful. If it came to a court action here, it would be a Moroccan word against a British word, and I hardly need tell you who would be believed.'

'Well, it looks if you've got it all nicely sewn up, doesn't it? This'll have to go further. A lot further.'

They left and walked in silence through the darkened alleys.

Eventually Steadman broke the silence. 'Look, Brian, we really can't go on like this.'

'Huh!'

'I mean, we've got an expedition to run. Don't get me wrong, old man, I fully support you're aim to get your down-and-outs to achieve big things. I admire you for trying to do it. But they've landed you in a spot of serious bother. We must pull together to sort it out. Ignoring obvious facts and trying to blame my two won't solve anything. It'll just make matters worse. And I hardly need tell you that if we don't get *somebody* up a mountain and into the desert we're going to look pretty bloody silly when we get home. The papers will have a field day for starters.'

Silence.

'The expedition will continue,' declared Dobson eventually. 'But without your two. They've done quite enough damage already.'

'In that case,' replied a weary Steadman. 'It goes ahead without me. You do things your way. I'll do things my way.'

'As you wish, but there will be consequences when we get back home. That's insubordination. The committee won't take kindly to that.'

'Yes, there will be consequences, all right,' replied Steadman grimly. Then in desperation he made one final plea. 'Oh, for heaven's sake, Brian! We can't go on living on this level! It's so childish!'

There was no reply. Not even a 'Huh!' No attempt at conciliation. Not the slightest hint. The truth had to be faced: Dobson was an incorrigible idiot and he'd just have to cut his losses and face the consequences whatever they were.

'John, Michael,' he said, calling them over to him. 'We're on our own now. Tomorrow we'll go for Toubkal without the others.'

The Tale of a Messiah – of Sorts

Back in their bedroom, John was too hyped up to sleep. 'Why is Dobson going on like this?' he exclaimed. 'He's mad! Off his trolley!'

'No,' replied Steadman with a voice of sad resignation, 'He's not mad. He's just desperate.'

'He doesn't look it.'

'You see, his whole world's coming unstuck and you, my man, are part of the unsticking.'

'What do you mean?'

Steadman lay back on his bed and stretched out.

'Let me tell you a little story – but don't ever say that I told it to you. Once upon a time there was a little boy called Brian. He grew up in a bleak mining village called Chopwell. His father was a coal miner. A hard life had made him a bitter and driven man and he had become a communist. He was determined to change the world for the better. Class war was everything.

'His little boy, Brian, was all he could have wished for. Big, strong and a good boxer – which, as you must know, goes down well in Geordieland – he was , also, clever. He was the pride of the village. He would assert the rights of the working class. He would expose the pretentious vapidity of the middle class exploiters. "Be the best, son," his father would say to him. "Don't let the middle classes do you down. You're far better than any of them!" If he had been a Christian – which he wasn't! – he would have claimed he was some kind of Messiah.

'But when he passed his Eleven Plus and went to the local grammar school, he found that the middle-class kids were just as clever as he was – sometimes cleverer – and just as good at football and boxing. That hurt. He and his father rationalised this. Class prejudice. Not any lack of ability on his part. He passed his A Levels all right, but not, alas, well enough to get to university. He had to make do with a teacher training college instead. Class prejudice again.

'He was a brilliant teacher. Kids feared him; he was handy with his fists, as you have doubtless noticed! But he won their respect. He began to see himself as a sort of Messiah, destined to fulfil his father's hopes and lead the working class onwards and upwards and get rid of all those middle-class snobs who were holding them down.

'He became head of maths at Morton Hill Community College. But he wants more. He wants to be a headmaster, but without a degree, that avenue is blocked. He could, of course, do a degree with the Open University, but he doesn't see why he should. That would be giving in to class prejudice.

'Youth expeditions, however, have provided an alternative. The local politicians like his pedigree and he has wangled himself into a strategic position. He can make or break his subordinates, and doesn't poor little Morris just know it! But he can't touch me. I've got Don Mackay behind me. I'm immune. But the problem is that he hasn't actually done any expeditioning before. He has the form, but not the substance, and it's been noticed in influential quarters.

'Hence this expedition. He's out to prove to the world that he's a groundbreaking youth expedition leader who can do what nobody else can do. He wants to show County Hall that he can handle inner-city desperadoes and get them to achieve big things in ways that nobody else can. Think of it, Jonny boy, what a feather in his cap! Hence the presence of Kev and his merry men.'

'But, oh dear, in his pride he's gone and bitten off more than he can chew! He can't handle "abroad", let alone Morocco. Worse still, Kev and his gang have taken him for a colossal ride. They've no intention of climbing Toubkal or going into the desert. They're here to get drugs for their minders back home, and poor old Brian can't do a thing about it! Right now his worst fears are being realised and, as you would put it, he's shitting bricks.'

'But why can't he come clean?' interrupted a bemused John. 'Admit it and get us to help him out?'

'You've got a lot to learn! Admit to County Hall that he's a fraud who can't handle inner-city thugs after all? Admit that they've run rings round him? No way! He needs a scapegoat, and that happens to be you. Under his charismatic leadership Kev and co. couldn't possibly have been buying dope. It could only have been provided by you.'

'But that's rubbish! He must *know* that!'

'He does, but to *admit* it to himself would destroy his whole conceptual universe.'

'What do you mean by that?'

'Dobbie's a Marxist. Know what that is? Yes? Good! But he's a very simplistic Marxist. Kev and co. are the proletariat and that means that they are good and clever. You are the bourgeoisie, which means that you are bad, stupid and a stuck-up little snob. But the trouble is that you aren't stupid, you're good, and you're not a stuck-up little snob either. You don't fit. You're not what you should be. Nor is Michael.' Here he pointed to the gently snoring heap under a sheet. 'Michael's pedigree is better even than his: alcoholic, drug-dependent single parent on social security. Can't hope to beat that. But he's at a private school, which means that he's a rich bourgeois! Doesn't fit!'

'Poor man! He's like a scientist whose pet theory has been disproved by simple facts. Should be banned. Like you. Can't admit that Kev's a crook. Proles aren't crooks. Only bourgeois exploiters are. You should pity him. He's in a right fix!'

'But why doesn't he clout Kev? Give him a bit of fist and bring him into line?'

'I'd like to see him try. Kev beat you up, didn't he?'

'Not really. I did put up a fight...' All defensive here! Like Dobbie, there's some things you can't admit, even to yourself!

'Oh come on! Look at yourself in a mirror. You've got a lovely black eye coming up. All I can say is that you're lucky that's all he did to you.'

'How do you know all this?'

'I've told you. I've got second sight.'

Silence for a while.

Eventually John spoke up. 'I can't sleep. I must have a shower. I'm all yukky.'

'Wash yourself in the fountain down here. Don't go upstairs, not for a while anyway.'

'Why so?'

'There's things going on.'

'What *things*?'

'You'll find out soon enough.'

'Things Going On'

He crept out into the darkness of the courtyard and duly splashed his battered face with the deliciously cool water. Murmuring and Geordie voices floated down from the balcony above along with the familiar pungent smell.

As he slipped quietly back into the room, Steadman raised his head from his pillow. 'Be sure you write all this down in that diary of yours – chapter and verse, if you don't mind.'

'Even the business of Kev and Dobson thumping me? I mean, it's so embarrassing.'

'Especially that. It could come in very useful. And I hope you're taking lots of photographs. They, too, could come in very useful. Now, try to get some sleep. There's going to be quite a day tomorrow.'

'Oh?'

'Just wait and see.'

As John lay down he heard more Geordie voices and the sound of feet scurrying over the courtyard. 'Things' were obviously going on.

Crisis

Another hot morning came with waves of mounting heat flooding in through the open door. John woke up brimming with excited anticipation.

Steadman took over. 'Sort your rucksacks out, lads. Anything you don't actually need leave on the bed here and I'll give it to Madame for safe keeping.'

Breakfast in the courtyard followed.

'When we've finished we'll go to the bus station and look for a bus to Imlil,' said Steadman.

But hardly had they finished their coffee before loud Geordie voices began to boom out from the balcony above them.

'Any of you bastards seen me fuckin' boots?'

'Who's got me bloody cagoule?'

'Yer haven't seen me sweater, 'ave yers?'

A seething and aggressive Jim came stumbling down the stairs. 'Have any of you lot got me boots?'

Blank stares. 'No.'

'Sure? Mind if I have a look?'

'Feel free,' said Steadman. 'Search our room if you like. We'll help you.'

The room was duly ransacked. Rucksacks were opened, the neat pile of excess baggage on the bed demolished, bedclothes removed, dark corners scoured. Nothing was found.

'Well some bastard's nicked them!' snarled Jim. 'And how the fuck am I meant ter climb a bloody mountain without me boots?'

He stomped angrily back upstairs.

More voices. 'Anybody seen Kev and Jakie? Worraboot Sandra an' them lot?

'Room's empty!'

'Looks like they've scarpered!'

'And taken half our kit with them, the bastards!'

'Berra fetch Brian.'

'Looks like he's scarpered an' all.'

Steadman winked at John. 'Just as I said: things have been going on in the night.'

'Come on, Bob!' exclaimed a frenetic John. 'Let's get going. I want to climb Toubkal. Let's not get tangled up in their mess.'

He shouldered his pack and marched purposely towards the door.

But just then a flustered Morris burst into the courtyard. 'Bob, we've got a crisis on our hands!'

'I'm afraid that's your problem, and not mine,' replied Steadman.

'What do you mean? You're part of the expedition, aren't you?'

'Not any more, Joe. Brian said so last night.'

'Oh come *on* Bob!' cried John. 'Let's get going!'

'Going?' asked Morris, 'Going *where*?'

'We're going to climb Mount Toubkal,' declared John defiantly. 'Without you lot or bloody Dobson! So there!'

Morris turned to Steadman with desperation in his voice. 'But you can't just walk off like this! Please Bob, we *need* you!'

John looked on with mounting frustration. He could almost see the thoughts flickering through Steadman's brain, like the flashing images of a video being fast-forwarded. Christian duty. Forgiveness (or was it merely weakness?). Let them see the error of their ways by leaving them to stew in their own juice. That would be justice all right! But not all of Brian's lot were bad; there were good people there, too, like Jim and Tracy. They'd been badly let down. They deserved justice. And if he simply abandoned them, think of the repercussions when they got back to Britain! Vicars were in exposed positions: they had to set an example. Only one answer.

'Don't worry, Joe. I won't let you down.'

John stamped his foot in an incipient tantrum. 'Oh don't just give in! What about *us*?'

'Cool down, John,' replied Steadman. 'Don't worry. You'll get up Toubkal all right, but we can't just leave these people in the lurch!'

John wasn't convinced. He felt his dream dissolving and relapsed into a villainous sulk.

Steadman went into avuncular mode and turned to Morris. 'All right, Joe, what's all this about?'

'Kevin Bartlett and his crowd have disappeared.'

'Well?'

'But this is serious. They seem to have taken half the expedition kit with them.'

'Any idea where they might have gone?'

'Jim says they'll have gone off to Agadir with those hippies that were here.'

'That figures. They'll have taken the expedition kit to sell in the souk and buy drugs with the proceeds.'

'You don't seem surprised.'

'I can't say that I am.'

A pregnant silence.

'But Bob,' spluttered Morris eventually, 'What the hell are we going to *do*?'

'Better fetch Brian and have a conference.'

'But he's gone down to the police station.'

'In that case, we'll have to wait till he returns. In the meantime we'd better muster the remaining troops before anything else happens.'

'Oh *shit!*' groaned John. 'What about our trip to Toubkal? I mean, you promised...'

'Be patient, young man, be patient!'

Steadman Takes Charge

One by one, four sullen and dishevelled youngsters trickled down the stairs and sat down under the tree in the middle of the courtyard. A calm Michael and a seething John joined them.

Steadman went into crisis management mode: the infantry officer on active service, his alter ego, and so much more fulfilling than his dreary parish duties back in Boldonbridge! He seemed to visibly enlarge.

'Jim? Tracy? Rob? Maureen? Is this all that's left of you? So the others have all gone with Kev and co.?'

'Yes, it seems that they have,' sighed Morris.

Full of confidence, Steadman forged ahead: 'Now listen to me, all of you! We've got a big problem on our hands. First point: we're all in this together, so I don't want any more of this nonsense about these two lads, Michael and John, not being part of this expedition. If you think that just because they are at a private school they are upper-class snobs, let me tell you that *this* one' – pointing to Michael – 'has been sent there because he is a ward of court and *that* one' – pointing to a squirming John – 'is there because he has been abandoned by his parents. They're just as deprived as any of you lot. So no more of this upper-class snob stuff. Got it?'

'It weren't us what didn't want them, like,' said Tracy. 'It were Kev an' them lot! Aye, an' Brian an' all!'

'Good. Well you know the position.'

Murmurs of assent.

'Next point. To put you in the picture. Your mates have absconded. Frankly, I've been expecting this to happen. I may be a silly old vicar, but I wasn't born yesterday. I've seen what's been going on. They've made a bee line for the local hippies – of which there are many round here – and they've been shooting dope with them. Now, apparently, they have bunked off with them. They'll probably be heading for Agadir – that's a seaside resort where the druggies hang out, in case you didn't know it already – and they seem to have taken most of your kit with them. That'll be to sell in the souk to pay for their pleasures- which can get pretty pricey, I can tell you!'

'But just in case any of you have similar ideas, let me tell you that many of the hippies round here are police plants. They'll sell you the stuff and then get a big reward for shopping you. It's a nice little earner if you know the ropes. And I happen to know that there's at least one plant among the lot that were here.'

'So when Kev and his merry men *are* caught – and they soon will be! – they'll be right in it, right up to their necks and beyond. Penalties for possessing narcotics are savage here. They'll land in prison and, believe me, the screws round here aren't exactly lily-white softies either. Don't think that just because they're British they can't be touched. They regard all foreign tourists as rich and pampered; yes, even people like you! And they'll just *love* to put the boot in!'

Stunned silence.

Steadman continued, 'So, if any of you have been in any way involved in the drug dealing, now's the time to make a clean breast of it. Before any of you, also, land in trouble. I am waiting.'

Silence. Then agitated whispers. Finally Rob, a big thickset youth with a downy chin and mousy hair, spoke up. 'I knew it were gannin' on me, like,' he said.

'But why didn't you tell somebody?'

'How could I? I mean Kev woulda done us ower like. I mean, jus' look at John here.'

All eyes turned on John and his luridly polychromatic black eye.

'Yer was lucky ter gerroff that lightly, Jonny lad,' observed Jim. 'Knowin' what Kev can do like.'

John blushed bright red at the public revelation of his reprehensible weakness.

'We couldn't of said nowt to Brian, neither,' declared Tracy defensively. 'I mean, he just wouldn't listen him.'

'All right,' said Steadman. 'Point taken, but we're going to have to wait here till this business is sorted out.'

'But what about our expedition?' exclaimed Jim. 'I mean, that's what we came for, weren't it?'

'Oh, that still goes on. Don't worry. In the meantime I suggest that you get your kit together and see how much you still have. But wait a minute, here comes the Great Man himself.'

All eyes turned on Dobson as he entered the courtyard. He looked somehow shrunken, not thunderous, nor even baleful. Just diminished, emptied. Despite himself John felt his hatred start to trickle away. The voice of Gentle Jesus, Meek and Mild, or simply congenital weakness?

'Well Brian!' boomed Steadman. 'What's the sitrep?'

'Sitrep?' Michael whispered into John's ear. 'That's an army word, ain't it? He just loves playin' soldiers, don't he? Mebbe that's why you an' him gets on so well. Yer both liddell kids like.'

'They're all down in the police station,' replied Dobson in a soft and slurred voice.

'Cor,' hissed Michael, 'He's right pissed, him.'

'Anything else?' asked Steadman.

'That's all I know, Bob. You'll have to come down and talk the lingo. I don't know the half of what's going on.'

'Right we are. I'll come down now!' Steadman seemed to glow, to radiate even. He was obviously wallowing in his rival's humiliation and relishing another chance to parade his linguistic and anthropological skills.

'Listen, chaps,' he added jauntily, 'I'll have to go down to the police station with Brian. I've no idea how long I'm going to be so you'll just have to be patient. Joe, can you see that nobody leaves the place? And, maybe, you can get Madame to rustle up a bit more breakfast for everybody?'

As he prepared to leave with Dobson, John rushed up to him. 'Please, Bob.'

Irritated glance. 'John, this is urgent. Can't it wait?'

'But I've no money. Kev nicked it all, and all my traveller's cheques too.'

Steadman produced his wallet. 'All right, here's eighty quid. Change it at the bank later on. But please don't wander off, now!'

'But what about Toubkal?'

'That's going to happen, *do* try to be patient!'

Not easy for a hyped-up John Denby.

Frenetic Boredom, and Alliances

A long, boring wait followed. After a while Jim approached John and Michael. 'Looks like we'd berra be proper mates now.'

They duly shook hands. One issue had been solved. A desultory game of cards followed with Rob and the two girls.

'I *knew* this would fuckin' happen!' sighed Tracy. 'But you just couldn't tell Brian bloody anything!'

'Now we're *all* in the shit!' added Jim from the sidelines. 'I came here to climb mountains, not to be a bloody prisoner in this place!'

The sun got higher. The temperature rose as waves of soporific heat reverberated off the tiled floor of the courtyard. The game of cards died and they retreated to the shade of their bedrooms.

Seeing Steadman's *Guide to Morocco* and his map of the Toubkal area lying on the bed beside his rucksack, John picked them up. There it all was: bus from Marrakesh to a place called Imlil high in mountains; trail from Imlil to a mountain hut called the Neltner Hut; trail from the Neltner Hut to the summit of Jebel Toubkal. All so straightforward. But beyond his grasp!

To calm himself he tried to read one of his books, but was too worked up to focus on the page. For dreary hour after dreary hour he just lay there, fuming.

Hopes Dashed

Round about two o'clock Steadman and Dobson returned. Deliverance at last! John's spirits soared. Shouldering his pack, he rushed out to meet them.

'Bob! Let's get started now!'

'Wait a moment!' snapped Steadman testily. 'There's one or two things that need to be sorted out before we can think of climbing mountains.'

The lad's self-absorbed tunnel vision was beginning to grate on him. He was not quite the paragon of selfless virtue that he'd allowed himself to think he was.

'Brian,' he added, ' can you gather everybody together?'

They duly assembled under the limited shade of the palm tree. Steadman opened the proceedings. 'Well, chaps, here's the sitrep. It's not good news, I'm afraid.'

Expectant silence. Dobson looked even emptier than before.

Steadman continued, 'Just as I predicted, Kev and his crew *were* getting drugs off those hippies.'

'What about all our kit?'

'What about me boots?'

'All gone, I'm afraid. They sold it all to some crook in the souk, who paid good money for it. Things like boots and rucksacks are very valuable here, you know. With the proceeds they splashed out on drugs, and not just hash, either, but the hard stuff as well. But what they didn't realise was that one of their hippie friends was a police plant, just like I said! Well, he shopped them and got a big reward for it. So, if any of you have similar ideas, *be warned*! The police picked them up at the bus station as they were waiting for the bus to Agadir. The upshot is that they are now in the nick.'

'Will they be sent home?'

'Probably not. They'll be charged under Moroccan law.'

'They won't be sent to prison will they?' asked Morris in an anxious tone. 'I mean, they are British, aren't they?'

'That won't make a blind bit of difference. In fact, it could make things worse for them. They'll be made an example of.'

'Good!' cried John vindictively. 'We're well rid of them!'

The mugging rankled deeply. At long last some thugs at any rate were getting their just deserts! 'Now for heaven's sake, can we start the expedition?'

'Not just yet, I'm afraid.'

'Oh God, *why* not?'

'Because Brian and I will have to go to the British Embassy in Rabat – that's the capital, by the way – to see the British Consul, who won't be exactly overjoyed to see us, I can tell you.'

'How long will that take?'

'At least five days, maybe even a week.'

'*Five days? Oh fucking hell!*'

'Temper tantrums won't get you anywhere, John. There's nothing I can do about it.'

'Aye, but warraboot the rest o' us?' demanded Jim. 'Do we just have to hang round in this dump?'

'I'm afraid that's the sum of it. You'll just have to wait till Brian and I get back.'

'And Joe,' added Dobson, 'I want nobody leaving this place. Everybody stays here – *here!* – till we get back! I want no more daft buggers buggering around with undesirables. Get it?'

With that, he glared at John and then he and Steadman turned and left.

'*Bloody fucking Kev!*' shouted John, beating the air with his clenched fist. Hopes dashed. Dreams of glory in ruins.

Fizz in an Overheated Coke Can

John passed the rest of the rest of the day in a state of suppressed fury, like fizz in an overheated Coke can that threatened to explode at any moment. He was frantic to climb Toubkal. It was more than just an adventure. His very self was at stake. Vindication before Major Allen. Proving to Dolly and Mekon that, despite their doubts, he really was tough and reliable. Avenging his humiliations at the hands of Kev: he'd show him who was the real tough guy all right!

It had all been within his grasp, only to be snatched away by Kev and his brain-dead Neanderthals! They were so *thick*! Couldn't they have seen what would happen when they started buying dope? Oh no! They couldn't see beyond the ends of their snotty, puke-spotted noses. They just *had* to land everybody in the shit, didn't they? 'Leaders' Dobson called them! Christ, that man was such a *dork*! Such a meathead! Bringing a gang of hardened criminals along and so fucking thick and big-headed that he couldn't see them for what they were. He had to stop himself weeping from sheer frustrated anguish.

Tentative Plans

The hot day wore on its tedious way. As evening was closing in, Jim and Rob entered the room.

'John,' said Rob, plonking his large backside on the bed, 'we can't just hang round in this hole. We gotta do sommat!'

'There's nowt yer can do,' said Michael, emerging from the sweat-soaked sheets of his bed at the far end of the room.

Ignoring him, Jim launched forth. 'I came here ter climb mountains an' that, not jus' ter sit roond deein' nowt!'

'Yeah!' added Rob. 'I'm gonna look pretty bloody thick when Ah gets home like an' folk asks me what Ah did. Just sat on me arse an' did nowt else.'

John's gloom lifted a little bit. He wasn't the only one who was frustrated. He had potential allies here, and, maybe just a chance... But those two beefy young Geordies alarmed him. They almost certainly thought he was an upper-class poofter, and, if they hadn't already heard of – well, that business in the shower – in all probability they soon would hear of it. To win a little protective street cred he thought it best to go into 'Dirty Denby' mode: the big, bad lad of the Beaconsfield corridors.

'Exactly what I feel!' he exclaimed. 'I mean, back home they'll start saying we're a bunch of benders who just lay about bumming each other.'

'There'll be naebeddy sayin' that about me!' growled Jim with an aggressive snarl. 'But with the likes o' you, mebbe folk'll think different!'

Ploy's not worked! Back off quickly before things turn nasty! These blokes will need careful handling.

'I wasn't being serious.I am just that pissed off! But, I mean…'

The appropriate words just wouldn't come. Silence ensued.

After a while he picked up Steadman's *Guide to Morocco* and opened it at the chapter headed 'Marrakesh and the Atlas Mountains'.

'Look,' he said, 'It's all in here. Bus to that Imlil place. Then just follow the path up Toubkal. The book says it's easy. We could do it. No sweat.'

More silence.

John finally spoke up again. 'Why don't we ask Joe to take us up Toubkal?'

Jim's hostile scowl broke into a broad grin. 'Good idea! But, Jonnie, lad, I'll do the talking, so don't you start.'

'Oh?'

'Well yer'll just fuck things up! I mean Joe thinks you're a bad influence on us like.'

'How the fuck could I influence the likes of you?' (Sprinkle your conversation with F words: that should squash the 'poofter' burr!)

'You wouldn't believe it, but Joe's ower scared o' yers!'

'He's not, is he? What the fuck's he got to be scared of? I mean I'm not exactly Mohammed fucking Ali who's going to beat him in, am I?' (More F words in the hope of getting that elusive bit of street cred!)

'It's not that. It's because you're posh and can talk Frog an' read maps an' that. Wor Joe's not exactly a brain box, yer knaa. Why, he's pretty clueless him!'

So they went to see Morris.

'It's a Question of Safety'

They found Morris in his little cubicle at the far end of the balcony. He was sprawled on his bed, staring at the ceiling with a half-empty bottle of wine on the table beside him. He seemed to be sunk in a listless torpor.

'Jesus!' muttered Rob. 'He's pissed!'

Jim spoke up. 'Joe, there's no point in us just hanging round in this dump.'

Semi-comatose flicker of the eyebrows.

'I mean, why don't we all go off and climb the Toubkal? It won't take that long, like.'

At that, Morris seemed to return to consciousness. Uncoiling himself, he sat up and put his feet on the floor.

'Absolutely out of the question.'

'But why?'

'Brian's instructions were to stay here till he returns from Rabat.'

'But that could take a whole week.'

'So?'

'But we're just wastin' time hangin' round here doin' nowt. I mean, it's dead borin'.'

Morris levered himself into a higher level of consciousness: 'Look, young man, you don't seem to understand the situation.'

'Yes I do.'

'No you don't. It's a question of safety. Mount Toubkal is a dangerous mountain over thirteen thousand feet high. Far higher than anything in Britain. I can't possibly let you go. Brian has said that I am personally responsible for your safety.'

'But we're not askin' yers ter lerruz gan by ourselves like. We want you ter take wor, like.'

'Out of the question.'

'Why?'

'I'd need another properly qualified adult leader with me. And Toubkal's a difficult climb, you know. There's cliff bands and snowfields.'

'No there ain't! John's guidebook says there's an easy path up it.'

'That's not what I've heard. Anyway, you haven't any kit. Most of your climbing kit's been stolen. No, we stay here. Those are Brian's instructions.'

'Well, that seems to be it, then,' sighed Jim, reluctantly accepting defeat.

Morris cast a sharp, hostile lance at John. 'I knew *you'd* be mixed up in this!'

They left in silence.

Inspiration

'Well that were a reet waste o' time!' declared Jim as they sat disconsolately under the palm tree in the courtyard.

Sullen silence.

Suddenly inspiration came to John. Electrical storm in the brain? Flash of light? Spark of genius? That voice from Heaven on the Road to Damascus? Or simply common sense stating the obvious? Don't waste your time on youth leaders, 'qualified' or otherwise. You'll just get tangled up in a jungle of petty rivalries and rampaging egos. Anyway, you're not the sort of person who gets selected for things. You'll go nowhere with them. No, Jonnie, my lad, if you want to climb mountains and the like, you'll just have to get on and do it yourself.

'Jim,' he said, 'Why don't we just go and climb Toubkal ourselves? We don't need Joe. I mean, Toubkal's not hard.

Bob's guidebook says there's a path up to the top. We can get a bus to Imlil and start walking from there. Why not?'

Pregnant pause. The notion was tasted, chewed, swallowed and digested. Metaphorical buzzes and clicks as cumbersome computers registered the data.

Then Jim spoke up. 'Jonnie, me bonnie lad, yerra a genius!'

'Just what I were thinkin',' added Rob.

Fervent Plotting, Intrigue, Conspiracies Hatched

John wallowed in it. Bonding. One of the lads at last. Recognition. Acceptance. The thrill of anticipated adventure. Fletcher Christian against the tyrannical Captain Bligh. 'Christian's taking the ship. Are you with us?' The escape committee at Stalag Luft. Whatever it was.

Throughout that hot and steamy night and on into the sweltering day that followed, detailed plans were honed and put into action. Deception. Cunning. Keeping Morris in the dark, but at the same time keeping him sweet. Making sure that everybody was present at roll call. Showing willing when you were asked to sweep out the bedrooms or wash up the mess tins after lunch. Making sure that Morris didn't see you when you sneaked off into the town. One by one the items were ticked off the list.

Personnel? Tracy and Maureen were recruited. No problem there: both were eager and willing.

Not so Michael: 'Yer daft! Yer'll never gerraway with it yer knaa! We'll all get done. I mean Brian'll blow a fit on us like.'

Brute force sorted that one out: 'Belt up Mike! If you don't come along, we'll do you over! And don't go crawlin' to Joe neither. Not unless you 'ave your face rearranged for yous.'

Money? John had the £80 Steadman had given him. The others said they had nothing. Kit? Rob and Jim needed boots. Tracy needed a sleeping bag. Jim needed a rucksack. A secret foray into the souk enabled John to change his pounds in to Moroccan dirhams and buy two very inferior pairs of boots and a largish shoulder bag, all for about £20 in British money.. As part of his 'Christian duty' he willingly paid for all this. Keep God sweet in the hope that he'll sort things out for you; and, maybe, even sort *that* out! He couldn't find a sleeping bag anywhere and had to make do with a threadbare old rug that he got for 50 dihrams from a stall. One corner of it was stained with a noxious brown substance, which on closer examination turned out to be of a repulsively organic origin. However...!

Stoves? Jim still had a Trangia and three bottles of meths. Food? There were twelve packets of dried soup which Kev hadn't managed to steal. The guidebook said there were shops in Imlil where they could buy bread and fruit.

John sussed out the bus station – all in his faltering French – and discovered that there was a bus to Imlil at six in the morning. He bought tickets and booked seats.

'Mean Bastards Wins Wars'

By evening everything was in place. A conspiratorial meeting took place in John's bedroom. Adrenaline was pumping.

'All packed up and ready?'

'Right. When do we go?'

'After midnight. Wait till he's asleep – or pissed!' (Giggle! Giggle!) 'Then scarper – quietly, mind... '

'Ain't this a bit hard on poor old Joe?' said Michael. 'I mean, he's a decent bloke what's doin' his best like. He'll wonder where we've gone. Brian'll get him done.'

'We'll leave him a note,' replied Jim. 'I've got it here. Take a decco.'

He handed a piece of paper to Rob who read it out aloud to the assembled conspirators: 'Dear Joe, Thank you so much for letting us go and climb Toubkal. You've taught us well that nothing will go wrong. You're a great youth leader. We really mean it. See you in four days' time. Signed, Jim.'

Rob handed it round for the others to sign.

'But it's all crap!' exclaimed Michael. 'It's a lie. He ain't given us permission!'

'Who's to know that?' replied Jim with an evil leer. 'It's his word against ours. Six against one. Besides, I've got a little present for him.' He brandished a bottle of brandy he'd bought in the new town with money John had given him. 'This'll keep him occupied, especially when I've added the flavouring like.'

He pulled a small blue bottle out of his pocket. Undoing the top, he poured the contents of into the brandy.

'What's that you're puttin' in?'

'Just milk of magnesia. Me mam gave it us as a laxative. She's always on aboot keepin' regular, her.'

'Poor bloke!' exclaimed Tracy. 'He won't half be gerrin' the squits, him!'

'Yeah!' grinned Jim. 'He'll be so fuckin' busy that he won' have no time ter gan lookin' foprrus. I'll leave the bottle at the top o' the stairs with our letter an' another note tellin' him that it's a present ter show our appreciation for all he's done, an' that.'

'Cor, yer mean bastard!' sighed Michael.

'Mean bastards wins wars,' replied Jim. 'Nice blokes don't.'

The Brotherhood of the Hunted: Escape
Midnight came. Zero hour. Pumping adrenaline. Hushed whispering.

'Is he asleep?'

'Yeah! And reet pissed too by the look of it! He's drunk half that bottle of brandy you gave him.'

'Jesus! He's gonna suffer sommat wicked him!'

'Yer shouldn't of done it, yer knaa!'

'Belt up, Mike!'

Opening the front door, they slipped quietly out into the dark and silent street.

An Ancient Bus

A long and anxious wait followed in the bleak, deserted bus station.

'Christ, I hope he ain't gonna send the fuzz ater us.'

A hot, yellow dawn came. Slowly the place began to fill up with bustling crowds: veiled women carrying bundles, white-robed men, young men in jeans, dark-skinned women bare-headed and wearing slacks.

Six o'clock came.

'Where's the bus you promised us, Jonnie lad?'

'Dunno! Dunno what's happened to it.' Panicky thought: *is* there a bus? I've bought the tickets, but bloody hell, have I been done? What'll the lads say if I have?

Seven o'clock came. Still no bus.

'Where's this fucking bus got to?'

'It berra come soon, else the fuzz'll be here!'

'Yeah, Joe'll have woken up and read that note.'

'Poor bloke! You shouldn't of done it! Ain't right!'

At eight o'clock a battered old bus finally spluttered up to the stand. Saved! John felt the kind of relief that you feel when a painful boil is lanced.

A souped-up rugger scrum followed as a seething mass of bodies piled into it. Somehow the bewildered and buffeted gang of fugitives managed to secure seats. More and more people piled in: men in robes and turbans, veiled women with babies, ragged street urchins, even a couple of goats. A flustered young man clambered over the crouching bodies, collecting fares.

John showed him the tickets he'd bought.

'Non! Non! Non!' the man said. 'Trente dihrams!'

John gave him a 50 dihram note and he clambered off to the front end of the bus. No change was forthcoming.

'But you paid for them tickets already,' said Michael. 'You've just lerrim lift fifty dihrams off yer.'

'Well, what else could I do? I mean he'd have booted us off the bus if I hadn't.' Michael could be so irritatingly unperceptive at times.

Eventually, like an asthmatic old camel, the bus staggered off. They had escaped. The journey passed slowly. It was too crowded to see out of the windows which, anyway, were caked over with years of grime. After two sleepless nights they felt drowsy and soon dozed off into a semi-coma.

Images of another escape flickered through John's mind: a shamed and deluded little wretch boarding a train on a black autumn evening. He quickly banished them. This escape was different. This time he was a big, bold lad on the threshold of an adventure, which would show the world what *really* lay under his small and scrawny exterior.

'What Do We Do Now?'

Hours later the bus ground to a gasping halt. It was as if the old camel had given up its unequal struggle against the odds, and had lain down and died. Everybody piled out. Blinking blearily in the bright light, they found themselves in a large square, sun-blasted and surrounded by low, flat-roofed buildings and market stalls. It was noticeably cooler than Marrakesh, and not far away were grey mountains, wrinkled and snow-streaked, rising imperiously into a clear blue sky.

'Is this that Imlil place, John? What do we do now?'

John fished the guidebook out of his rucksack and turned to the chapter about Imlil. This place doesn't seem to fit the description in the book: no gorge, no river, no single street.

'It's not Imlil,' he eventually said. 'It must be a place called Asni. The bus seems to have stopped here. But getting to Imlil shouldn't be a problem. There seem to be plenty of buses.'

He indicated a ragged line of vehicles, some new and flashy, others in a seemingly terminal state of dilapidation. 'One of these must be going up to Imlil. In the meantime we'd better get some nosh. We can't survive on a few packets of soup.'

Money was the problem. 'I'm down to fourteen hundred and fifty dihrams,' he said. 'Has anybody else got any dihrams?'

Nobody had.

'We're not rich like you, yer knaa,' said Rob with just a hint of aggression.

'All right, I suppose I'd better pay. But I'll have to go easy.'

Going round the stalls with John struggling at the outer limits of his French, they managed to buy eight honey melons, six loaves of bread and some flat Moroccan stuff which was also called bread, but looked like sheets of cardboard.

'We'd better get some Coke too, it's going to be pretty hot when we start walking.'

The price came to 250 dihrams.

'That were pricey,' sighed Michael. 'They did yer over them melons.'

'Probably did,' replied John. 'But there was nothing I could do about it. Now let's find a bus to Imlil.'

That proved easier said than done. A wearisome traipse round the square followed.

'Autobus Imlil?'

'Non! Non! A Marrakesh!'

'Imlil?'

Dismissive gesture. 'Non, Fez!'

And so on for over an hour.

'We seem to be stuck in this dump,' sighed a hot and sweaty Jim. 'So what yer gannin' ter do like, Jonnie lad?'

What indeed? John began to get desperate. Marooned in

this dreary hole? Stranded for the duration? Toubkal slipping away? Achievement evaporating?

Then he saw a tractor bouncing across the square pulling a large, empty trailer. Frantically he waved, and it stopped. He approached the swarthy and bejeaned young man in the driving seat.

'Allez-vous à Imlil?'

'Peut-etre, si vous voulez?'

'Nous allons à Imlil et nous avons besoin de transport.'

The man smiled. 'D'accord! D'accord!' He signed to them to get into the trailer.

'All aboard, team!' cried a triumphant John. 'He's taking us to Imlil!'

They clambered into the trailer and with a roar of the engine and amid a cloud of dense, oily exhaust fumes, they lurched off.

'Did you fix a price?' asked Michael.

'No, he just said he'd take us.'

'Like fuck he will! You'll get done again, John. And how do yer know he'll take wor to Imlil? I mean he could be takin' us anywhere, couldn't he?'

'God, you *are* a mingy old git, aren't you!' snorted John. 'Always looking on the black side of everything!'

At the same time, he had a nagging fear that just possibly Michael could be right. Then what? It was with profound relief that he noticed them pass a signpost with 'Imlil' on it in both Arabic and Latin script.

With mounting excitement he observed the rapidly increasing drama of the landscape as they bounced up a narrow, dusty road. A wooded valley narrowed into a gorge where a babbling river ran between plunging mountainsides, which swept down from beetling crags. Ahead were hints of vast mountains, grander than anything he'd ever seen before; huge piles of twisted and contorted rock. The explorer fantasy grew. He was about to penetrate an unknown mountain range. He was one with Burton, Speke and Livingstone.

Then Imlil came, a straggle of flat-roofed houses lining a single dusty street and thronged with minibuses and crowds of what were obviously foreign tourists. The explorer fantasy dissolved. No, John Denby, you're not the first. Others have got here before you.

The tractor juddered to a halt amid clouds of dust. Mission successful.

'Good on yers, Jonnie lad!' said Jim. 'Yer've gorrus here, like!'

They tumbled out of the trailer.

Doin yers one Minute and Entertainin' Yers the Next.

'Merci bien, Monsieur,' said John to the driver, as he shouldered his rucksack and set off up the street with the others.

'Moment! Moment!' the man cried aggressively. 'Cent dihrams!'

'Eh? Eh? Cinquante?' John pulled out a 50 dihram note and handed it to him.

'*Non! Non! Cent!*

'A *hundred*? Oh shit!'

Ruefully he handed it over.

'Cadeau! Bakshish!' cried the man.

'Mais j'ai vous payee…'

'Je suis pauvre! Une femme! Quatres enfants.'

The man began to get aggressive and to shout. A small crowd gathered and began to gesture threateningly. In desperation, John opened his rucksack and pulled out a sweater. Grumpily the man took it and drove off.

Crestfallen, John joined the others. 'God, he was a crook. He took one hundred dihrams off me and then had the cheek to demand a sweater!'

'Yer didn't give it him, did yers?' said Jim. 'Ah mean yer shoudda told him ter fuck off like!'

'Yeah? And get done over by that crowd? No way!'

'I knew this would happen,' declared Michael with a hint of triumph. 'Yer shoudda fixed a price first, like what I said.'

'Well, it's done now!' sighed John. 'And I'm down to twelve hundred dihrams now!'

'Well, what now?' asked Rob.

'Let's go to that cafe there and see if we can get some breakfast,' replied John. 'If they won't do us that is!'.'

They clambered up onto a shaded terrace and sat down at a table. A little bald-headed man with an unshaven chin and luxuriant black moustache greeted them effusively and, before they could say anything, brought them plate-loads of fried eggs, chips and bread.

'Combien l'addition?' asked a flustered John, desperate to avoid another financial humiliation.

'Rien!' replied the man bowing, 'Rien. Vous êtes jeunes et l'hospitalite a la jeunesse est la loi d'Islam.'

'What's he sayin'?'

'He says it's the law of Islam to be hospitable to young people and he's not charging us anything.'

'Eee, that's ever so kind o' him!' said Maureen. 'They's not what Brian said they would be, is they?'

'Funny blokes, them Pakkies,' said Jim. 'Doin' yer one minute and entertainin' yer for nowt the next.'

Council of War

Next came a council of war. John produced Steadman's map of the Toubkal area and spread it out on the table. Confidently he expounded the plan which had been simmering in his mind for the past two days. Like a photograph being developed, it just emerged from his brain.

'We're here at Imlil. Six thousand feet up. It'll take a day to get to here, the Neltner Hut, which is at over ten thousand feet. That's four thousand feet to climb. It'll be a sweat. The guidebook says the hut's expensive so we'll have to bivvy up next to it. It'll be cold, but it won't rain. Next day, final assault. To Toubkal. Back here. Next day, down again.'

He was the leader, the General expounding his plan of campaign to his assembled staff officers. He wallowed in the role. If only Major Allen could see him! If Mekon, if Dolly, if Bob…! Gone was the snivelling little wimp who'd let Kev do him over.

'Agreed!' said Jim, 'But what about today? It's two o'clock already. We'll not reach that Neltner place. Where'll we kip like?'

'We'll have to find a hidey-hole,' replied John. 'Somewhere where we can't be seen.'

'Yeah!' added Rob, 'We're escaped prisoners on the run, ain't we?'

'You've said it!' added John. 'We're like guerrilla fighters in the mountains. We'll walk along the track there, find a suitable place, doss down and have a brew. At dawn we'll start for the Neltner Hut.'

Into a New and Exciting Landscape

They began to organise their packs. The boys ostentatiously took the heavier items from the girls. Maureen, plump and obviously not very strong, was given the shoulder bag. The melons and the large bottle of Coke caused especially difficult loading problems. To counter the 'upper class poofter' burr, John insisted on taking five of the honey melons, which meant that there was no room in his rucksack for some of the extra sweaters, shirts and trousers he'd brought along. After several unsuccessful attempts to wrap them up in one of his bivvy bags and strap them on to the outside of the rucksack, he simply draped them over his shoulders.

So they set off, stepping out of the shade of the café into the blinding glare of the afternoon sun. The hill that led out of Imlil was brutally steep and soon they were panting and sweating copiously.

'Jesus! Me sack's bleedin' heavy!'

'How far have we gotta lug this lot, John? Four thousand fuckin' feet, did yer say?'

A brown-robed figure ambled down the hill, leading a donkey laden with baggage.

'We could do with one o' them donkeys, Jonnie lad!' said Rob.

'Yeah!' replied John, 'But I just haven't got the dosh. They'd probably do us and we'll have to have some money for a bus back to Marrakesh.'

'Hadaway man!' said Jim, 'Yer could pay if really wanted ter. Yer rich ye!'

John winced. That stung. They still thought he was a rich poofter who could dole out the dihrams if suitably pressured. All because of his southern accent. Could he *never* break through the carapace of distrust in which they encased themselves?

'Well,' he replied defensively, 'we'll see about that tomorrow.'

Luckily the track soon levelled off and the donkey question was postponed; for the moment, anyway.

All at once they found themselves ambling through a new and exotic landscape. There were green, terraced fields climbing up steep mountainsides to ancient villages of mud brick houses, flat-roofed and stacked up one above another, like old and mellow bricks. Behind them were huge mountains, grey and wrinkled, surging up into a brilliant blue sky. Still and apparently timeless, this was a world which seemed to speak to John – if not to the others – of eternal truths. It reminded him of pictures of the Holy Land that he'd seen in his long-lost Children's Bible. His spirit soared. Here was exploration, adventure, the challenge of the unknown.

Guerrilla Fighters in the Mountains

After about an hour the encroaching mountains on either side of the valley came together, almost like a monstrous vice squeezing out the trees and the level ground between their massive walls. The track turned abruptly to the left and began to zigzag up into a narrow gash. Down to the right, the last remnants of the wood washed up against a tumbled mass of huge boulders.

'Let's kip down there,' said Jim. 'Nobody'll see us.'

Crossing a small, dusty field, they stumbled into the wood. Right next to the boulder field they found a patch of green grass, lush and smooth, almost like a pond. Hemmed in by the protecting rocks, it made a perfect den.

'This'll do! They won't find us here!'

Dropping their cumbersome packs, they spread their sleeping bags, the bivvy bag and the blanket on the grass. Jim produced his bottle of meths and the Trangia set. Filling a bowl with Puritabbed water from John and Michael's water bottles, he brewed up the soup. Then they attacked the bread, which was fresh and filling. The feast ended with them demolishing two of the honey melons.

The hot sun, the lack of sleep, the hard exercise and the food... all produced a deep drowsiness.

'Time to catch up on a bit of kip!'

Spreading themselves out on the grass with their rucksacks as pillows, they settled down.

'This is great!' exclaimed Jim. 'We're just like guerrilla fighters!'

'Yeah!' added Rob. 'Just like the S.A.S. in the Falkland Islands!'

'Mind, there's gannin' ter be a reet stink when we gets back!' sighed Michael. 'If we ever does get back, that is!'

'Oh belt up, yer mingy old git!'

Snuggling down, John felt a warm glow of acceptance: one of the lads at last! Just to reinforce his position, he donated his sleeping bag to Tracy.

'Eeee! Yorra proper gentleman, you!' she chortled.

Suddenly she embraced him and kissed him effusively. A whole kaleidoscope of emotions flashed through him. Sheer physical revulsion at the big, slobbery mouth and the cold, wet tongue combined with the animal thrill of close contact with a warm, pulsating body, the child snuggling up to its mother. A cool, detached analysis: kill the shit-stabber thing by being seen to snog a girl. Yes, lay it on double thick, roll her over, squeeze her tits. The message will get round. It can only do you good... unless, horror of horrors, she starts asking you to actually perform! Luckily she didn't, and they disentangled themselves.

He then wrapped himself in the thin apology of a blanket that he'd bought in the souk. The brown, organic stain on the bottom left-hand corner soon fulfilled his worst fears. However...!

Silence fell, but for the low murmur of the nearby stream. For a long time he lay on his back, gazing up at the dome of the sky that peeped through the lattice of leafy branches above him. Slowly the blue deepened and turned purple as the light faded and the shadows of the night crept over the rugged landscape. He felt a sense of contentment, of liberation; the strangeness of the place he was in, the thrill of being on the threshold of great things. Sleep descended quickly.

The Demon Again

He began to dream. The Demon possessed him. As usual it was boys. Not Danny Fleetwood this time, but Mark Ramshaw, a dark-haired and elfin little Beaconsfield first year, cavorting round naked. In that wild, glorious exultation which surpassed all possible joys, it happened...

He opened his eyes to see a friendly blue sky beaming down through the branches above him. The blanket had slipped off him and a sticky wet stain was right down the left leg of his jeans, there for all to see! Oh bloody hell!

Jim had also woken up. Hw stared at him and his foxy face twisted up into a lascivious leer. 'Eeeee, Jonnie lad, yer sexy arld basstadd!'

Discovery! Christ All bloody Mighty, if he knew what I'd *really* been dreaming about! But turn it to your advantage...

He grinned back. 'What do you expect when you're sleeping next to a bird? Makes a bloke right horny, you know!'

'Aye, yorra reet lad, ye!'

Ploy's worked! Acceptance. Bonding. The 'Dirty Denby' act pays dividends. Keep it up!

'Hang on a moment. I'd better go down to the stream and wash this out before anybody thinks I've pissed myself.'

Morning

The others woke up. In the cool of the morning they brewed up the last of the soup on the Trangia and finished off the loaves of bread. Then they attacked two more honey melons.

'That leaves four melons,' said Jim. 'We'll need ter stock up at the next village – Cham – whatever-it-is we's gannin' ter flake oot like. There *will* be a shop there, won't there, John?'

'Yes,' replied John. 'That's what the guidebook says.'

'Well there bloody well berra be. Else we's in the shit! Yer've got the guidebook, so you lead the way, me bonny lad!'

Slight threat here! Hope there *is* a shop at Cham – whatever-it-is!.

'OK. But first we must clear up the bivvy site so that nobody knows we've been here. Joe'll have found the note by now and could have sent the fuzz after us. We're hunted fugitives in enemy territory. In *Combat Survival* it says the S.A.S. never leave any traces behind them when they are on active service.'

The military fantasy went down well and all the rubbish was duly picked up and placed in a black polythene bag, which John stuffed into his already overloaded rucksack.

Shouldering their packs, they stumbled back to the track. All around them were dark blue mountains, vast and mysterious, their ragged summits brilliantly red in the slanting rays of the rising sun. 'Come!' they seemed to say to John, 'Come with us! Here is where you really belong!'

Like Something out of a Children's Fairy Story

The track zigzagged a broad and easily graded way up a steep, rocky slope and into a deep gash between huge, plunging mountainsides. John surveyed the brutal anarchy on either side of him: a great sweep of enclosing crags, screes, tumbled boulders and far-off airy summits, harsh, barren and merciless. He felt a twinge of anxiety, amounting almost to panic. These mountains were something new to him: vastly bigger, steeper and more serious than anything he'd ever seen before. More hostile even than Sgurr na Ciche in the remote and rainswept Knoydart. *Was* there a way up Toubkal? Or would they have to crawl back, defeated and humiliated, to a judgmental I-told-you-so Morris? Quite possible! Was there even a village at Sidi Cham – whatever-it-was? If not, with only four melons between the six of them they were going to have problems. Also, Jim and Rob's still precarious acceptance of him would turn to rejection; and when that happened, Jim's fists would go into action.

But then, topping a rise, they came upon the promised village. John's spirits leapt. What a place! It was something quite beyond his experience, like something out of a childhood fairy story: a straggle of rough stone shacks, flat-roofed with lumps of turf and squeezed into a narrow defile, seemingly cringing under the massive threat of the soaring mountainsides above them. One small shake and it would all be flattened by the enormous boulders poised precariously above it. Biblical-style robed figures strolling round completed the vision.

To his profound relief there was a shop: a little cubbyhole of thing piled high with assorted tins. His French went into action and he managed to procure ten tins of tuna fish, four large bottles of Coke, a tin opener and ten tins of some weird Moroccan stuff: stuffed vine leaves or something, but as the label was in Arabic, it could have been anything.

'What the hell's this?'

'Dunno! But it's all he's got so we'll have to make do with it.'

The bill was predictably horrendous.

'That's me down to eight hundred dihrams.'

Before setting off, John ran round photographing everything, relishing the idea of the illustrated journal he planned to produce. Maybe he could get it published in book form. There was a thought! Eagerly he snapped a bearded and robed exotic walking along the street.

'Dix dihrams!' growled the man.

Obediently he coughed up, consoling himself with the thought that he'd recoup all his expenses when the book was published.

'Done again!' sighed Michael. 'Yer jus' won't learn, will yer?'

Donkeys

They duly set about the problematic task of loading the recent purchases into their already overloaded packs. Finally they attacked the stony track that wound its way out of the village and up the steep slope ahead of them. The sun was now high in the sky and the heat was building up. The heavy rucksack bit deeply into John's shoulders and he began to feel as if invisible hands were pushing down upon him. But, by getting into a slow rhythm, he made steady progress.

Soon the two girls were falling behind. Long waits and long rests ensued.

'I canna dee this!' declared Tracy eventually. 'I'm knackered, me!'

'Me an' all!' echoed a sweating Maureen.

Quick consultation.

'We canna dee owt in this heat,' declared Rob. 'We'll just flake out!'

'Aye,' said Jim. 'We'll not make Toubkal at this rate, so what's we gannin' ter dee, like?' He looked aggressively at John. 'You got any ideas?'

'All right,' replied John, 'I suppose I'd better try and get a donkey.' Whatever happened, he was going to get up this mountain! If it meant donkeys, then so be it.

'It'll be pricey, though,' he added. 'But if worst comes to worst, I can always sell my clothes.'

'And walk round in the nuddy then,' said Jim with a leer. 'You'd look great on the front page of *Gay News*, you! Just what the benders want!'

Barb here? Did Jim suspect what he *really* was behind that carefully constructed laddish exterior? Back off quickly!

'No, on second thoughts, I'll not go that far.'

While the others waited, he hurried back to the village. In the shop he met the man who'd served them.

'Nous avons besoin d'un âne pour transporter notre baggage au Neltner Hut. Combien?'

The response was immediate, like switching on a light. Two robed figures soon appeared leading two donkeys. 'Cinquante dihrams chaque.'

He quickly doled out the 100 dihrams and they set off up the track. Reaching the others, he was greeted like a hero.

'Good on yer, me bonny lad!'

Both Tracy and Maureen hugged and kissed him. The ego blossomed. John the lad! Dirty Denby with his girlfriends!

Each girl was hoisted onto a donkey and the rucksacks and bits of extra baggage distributed between them.

'Vous allez à la cabane Neltner?'

'Oui, à sa cote!'

Progress – at a Price

They set off, ambling slowly up the stony trail. Without his rucksack pressing down on him, John felt liberated. Set free from gravity, almost floating upwards. A renewed burst of hope!

The going was surprisingly easy – easier even than Scafell Pike! – and they soon reached the top of the steep lip of the valley. Before them, a broad, rock-strewn trough opened out between towering mountainsides. To their right a huge wall of jagged rock surged upwards, jerking along the skyline like a giant scribble. To their left, bare, rocky peaks reared upwards like gnarled and twisted old tree trunks. Morale rose.

In a ridiculously short time – scarcely more than three hours – they arrived at the head of the valley. Amid the anarchic swirl of mountains walling it off, there was what seemed like a lake of green grass hemmed in by screes. Above it, perched on a rocky spur, was a small European-style stone building.

'Qui est cela?'

'La cabane Neltner.'

'Vraiment?'

'Oui, vraiment!'

'Team, we've made it!' cried and exultant John. 'There's the Neltner Hut! Do you realise we're over ten thousand feet up?'

'Christ, that were quick!' said Jim. 'It's not even twelve o'clock!'

'Well,' said John, 'we'd better make a base camp. We'll basher up, army style, among those boulders there.'

'"Basher up?"' said Michael. 'That's another of yer army words, ain't it? Yer never stops playin' soldiers does yer?'

'Yer knaa,' he added with a sigh, 'yers nowt burra greet big kid, ain't yers?'

John ignored him and continued his military-style orders. 'We'll rest here. Tomorrow morning we'll make the final assault on Mount Toubkal.'

The donkeys were duly unloaded, but instead of departing, the two men hung around, looking aggressive.

'Au revoir et merci beaucoup!' said John, holding out his hand.

'Bakshish! Cadeau!'

'Mais nous avons vous payee!'

'Bakshish! Cadeau!'

'Oh shit! Now they want presents.'

'Don't listen to them!' said Michael. 'You'll only get done!'

John turned away and began to walk towards the nearby boulders. The two men followed him, gesticulating angrily. 'Cadeau! Cadeau!'

Their threatening manner scared him; that Greenhill feeling which dissolved your bones and reduced you to jelly. There was nothing for it. It was a matter of survival. Reality! He rummaged in his rucksack and pulled out a spare shirt and one of his few remaining spare sweaters.

The effect was immediate. Warm smiles replaced hostile scowls. He was embraced and kissed effusively, and with friendly waves the two men departed.

'God, you are a reet softy!' sighed Michael. 'Them's just usin' yers, yer knaa!'

That stung. 'Well, Mike, what would *you* do?' he retorted angrily. 'Let them bloody knife us? We're not in Britain, you know!'

'It's no different there!' he replied. 'Jus' look at Greenhill Skyerl, like? Remember what *that* were like?'

The thrust went home. John *did* remember what Greenhill was like: only too well! It was a reminder that John, the big, bold lad, could only exist in a very sheltered environment. Beyond its narrow parameters he was a quivering jelly.

'Well, it's done now, Mike,' he said. 'No use crying over spilt milk, as they say. Let's get on and basher up.'

They soon found an ideal place, a sort of mini canyon

between two large, overhanging rocks. Drowning his humiliation in an orgy of militaristic fantasy, John rushed about creating his best shelter ever. The two bivvy bags they had were stretched between the rocks and secured with stones, they formed a roof. A dry stone wall was constructed, blocking one end of the canyon, and an elaborate doorway was created at the other. Tufts of grass lined the sandy floor. Every stage of the operation was photographed, culminating in a triumphant group picture celebrating its completion. Major Allen would positively *eat* it all when he saw the photos! They would all go to illustrate the book he was going to write. The lad was back in business.

'We could spend a week in this.'

'Where's the bog?'

'Broad and beautiful nature,' replied John, continuing in 'trained soldier' mode. 'Only please bury your produce. Camp hygiene, you know!'

Snigger, snigger, snigger at the scatology involved.

The Brotherhood of the Hunted

A long afternoon of waiting around followed. Lunch involved the exploratory opening of one of the Moroccan tins and the tentative testing of its weird contents, which turned out to be rice wrapped up in oily green leaves.

'Pretty yukky!' said John. 'But, well, it's fuel for tomorrow.'

'It's that slimy, like,' replied Jim, 'that it'll jus' gan straight through yers and yer'll have ter start all over again.'

Visits to the bog. Crude laddish comparisons. 'I'm a bit liquid, how about you?'

'Ah shuddup!' exclaimed Tracy. 'You lads is ever so coarse! There's ladies here, yer knaa.'

Isolated amid the sprawling mountain grandeur, the disparate little group started to bond. Jim's haughty reserve melted – just a little. He began to reveal something of himself;

not much, but just a few little nuggets. His father was a Geordie miner who'd served in the Durham Light Infantry in the war and won the Military Medal. A tough, hard-bitten and fiercely masculine character, he expected his son to be the same as himself, if not better. 'Proper blokes' didn't waste time on 'the arty-farty academic crap' that they taught in school: they got proper men's jobs like going down the pit and joining the army. Jim had to prove he was a hard man like his dad. That was why he'd volunteered for this expedition.

He eyed John: 'Yorra funny blerk, you! Ah canna make yers oot like. Yer talk posh, but Mikey here talks Geordie like, so what's yer deein' at the same school? Divvent make sense.'

John gave a severely edited version of his life. His parents had been too busy to look after him as a baby so they'd sent him to live with his grandparents down south; that was why he talked posh: 'That's the way they all talk down there.' But when they'd been killed in a motor accident he'd been sent to Boldonbridge to live with his mum and dad. All true so far! But they'd sent him to Greenhill School.

'Hadaway man!' snorted Jim. 'They didn't! Posh git like ye? Why, they woudda kicked the shite oota yers.'

(A bit near the bone, this! Too true, they did… and even worse – *much* worse! But I can't possibly mention *that*!)

'Well, they tried, but I hit a teacher and got expelled. No school would have me, so that's why I ended up at Beaconsfield.'

'*You* hit a teacher? Hadaway man, yer never did! They chucked yers oot because them lads was kickin' yer in, more like.'

'No, it's true.'

'Well, I suppose I'd berra believe yer like. Yer looks reet soft like, but mebbie yer's hard underneath. Anyway in this place we's all mates. We gorra be, like.'

They all shook hands: Tracy, Maureen, Jim, Rob, Michael, all of them. John revelled in it. The final breakthrough. Total unconditional acceptance. The Brotherhood of the Hunted – just as in the Lake District all those years ago.

'You Shouldn't be Doing This by Yourselves'

Groups of European hikers passed them. A large French party appeared at the head of a cavalcade of laden donkeys. Seeing the newly constructed shelter, they stopped.

'Êtes-vous Français?' asked a tall, dark-haired man, intimidatingly professional-looking with his closely cropped hair, sunglasses and immaculate climbing breeches.

'Non,' answered John. 'Nous sommes Anglais.'

'Ah, you're English!' exclaimed the man, breaking into an excellent and well-pronounced English. 'So, where are you going?'

'Up Toubkal. Is it difficult?'

'No, it's easy. Just follow the path up to the hut there,' the man replied, indicating the way. 'And then up to those two big boulders, over the stream, and on up into the *cirque* you can see. But you're very young, aren't you?' he added with a strong hint of suspicion. 'Where's your guide? You shouldn't be doing this by yourselves, you know.'

Alarm! Momentary panic! Discovery! Quick thinking required.

'We're on a training exercise. Our teacher's down at Imlil at the moment. He sent us up here to make the shelter to test us. He'll be coming along to inspect us this evening.' (Hope he's daft enough to swallow this one!)

'I see. Well, goodbye. Bon escalade, as we say in France!'

The cavalcade flooded past them.

Profound relief! Narrow escape. Suppose he'd found out that we were alone and escorted us back to Imlil? Just shows how precarious our position is. We'll *have* to succeed in climbing Toubkal!

John looked across the valley and studied the route the

man had indicated. Squeezed between two massive and frighteningly steep mountain bastions was an unwieldy avalanche of screes and boulders, pouring down from a big hanging valley in a monstrous flood of brutal rock. It was a kind of gateway leading up to an unexplored beyond. 'Easy', the man had said? It certainly didn't look it! Fear began to nibble away at him... that 'cloud no bigger than a man's hand', but seemingly destined to grow into something frightful.

The Beyond World

The long day finally faded into evening. The cool air became colder. It was time for sleep. As the others settled down in the shelter, John went out for a final pee.

Immediately he was awed by the mountain grandeur that was enfolding before him. The sun was setting. The savage ridge that formed the western boundary of the valley was now a black mass, an imprisoning and threatening wall. Opposite it, on the other side of the valley and ablaze with golden light, was the gateway leading to Toubkal. The massive, enclosing bastions seemed to be almost pulsating, as if the brilliant light had actually breathed life into them, with each tiny wrinkle and knobble was lovingly illuminated, caressed even, by the warm rays of the sinking sun. The avalanche of scree between them glowed a gentle yellow and seemed to have become a staircase, which spoke to him in soft and friendly tones: 'Come on, John! Come on! See what lies beyond.'

And what *did* lie beyond? An easy path leading to the summit as the Frenchman had said? Or unclimbable walls of rock and snow, as Morris seemed to think? Triumph or humiliation?

As he gazed at the gateway something happened to him. A strange and beautiful exaltation filled him, like that exaltation which had filled him during that midnight Christmas service back in '81 when he'd heard that carol 'O come all ye faithful':

'Yea, Lord, we greet ye, born this happy morning'. Like that wonderful and comforting exaltation that had filled him during that memorable high summer dawn in the Lake District the following July. He was looking at the gateway to the Beyond World, the place where everything was rational and good, where his perfect gran and granddad were waiting for him, bathed in the glow of... well... God. 'Come to us, John, we're waiting for you. Come. But not yet. It's not time.'

Tears trickled down his cheeks. For a long time he remained sitting on the rock above the shelter. Slowly, majestically, the light faded. The mountains disappeared into a dense blackness, but the sky still glowed: orange, red and purple, before dissolving into a deep blue. Then in the cold, clear air there emerged a dazzling display of stars; shimmering, subtle, immense. A vision. But a vision of what? Humbleness? Submission? The vision seemed to become a part of him. He seemed to dissolve into Mind. 'In the beginning was the Word and the Word was God.' Time, his time, was so utterly insignificant. The mountains seemed so fixed and eternal, but their time was equally small and insignificant. They were destined to be ground down to nothing. The stars and the galaxies above him, so seemingly infinite, but they too, destined to fade into nothingness. To be swallowed up in God's time. 'We wither and perish like leaves on a tree, but naught changeth thee.' God's inexplicable plan. The Mind of God.

Loud Geordie voice: 'Howay, Jonnie lad! What's keepin' yer? Got the shits or sommat!'

Jerked back to normality. The contrast between grandeur and squalor. But wasn't the Crucifixion like that? Repulsive animal degradation: pus, urine, excrement, stink, stark nudity, hideous pain, and jeering raucous yobbery alongside the ultimate in beauty and grandeur? There was a thought for the diary.

He returned to the shelter and snuggled down beside Tracy, who gave him a long and sensual kiss.

'Try not to get too horny!' whispered Jim.

'Not possible!' he replied. 'Just can't manage it!'

Too true! He couldn't 'manage it'. But not in the way that Jim thought; or, rather, the way he *hoped* that Jim thought. Lies, deception, more lies: lying about his real sexual wants – nay, cravings! – lying to Morris, lying to that Frenchman ('Our teacher'll ... be coming along to inspect us in the evening'), lying to himself in the diary he was writing ('Snogged Tracy. God, she was horny!') Crap, wasn't it? All crap. His lies were like an octopus weaving its slimy tentacles round him. Could he ever cut free? Maybe, in that Beyond World he thought he'd glimpsed. But how could he possibly tell the others what he'd seen sitting on that rock?

Grandeur and Banality

A half sleep followed. A sort of in and out of consciousness, waiting impatiently for a morning that never seemed to come. In the end he could stand it no longer and crawled out into the cool and silent night. The moon had set leaving a velvety blackness, speckled by a glittering immensity of stars. Again he had had that sense of time, of eternity and the inscrutable mind of God.

Of the mountains there was nothing, just a deep, black nothing. Then came an Act of Creation, as if the old Bible legend really was true after all and the fully developed world had just emerged out of nothing. Slowly – ever so slowly – the blackness above him lightened and became blue. The stars faded and out of the black nothingness below rugged mountains emerged. Boulders and cliffs appeared. The sky became red and then blue. Suddenly the mountain wall to the west blazed up with a fiery red as if it had been set alight. Away at the head of the valley the tangled, snow-streaked peaks burst into a warm orange.

Stirred by the sheer wonder of the sight, he dashed back to the shelter. 'Hey guys! You must come and see this!'

There were a few grunts and wriggling of semi-comatose bodies as he rummaged around in his rucksack and extracted his camera. Scampering outside again, he began an orgy of photography.

Eventually Jim joined him. 'What's happened? What's up?'

'Just look at those mountains! Have you ever seen anything like that?'

'Is that all?' snorted Jim. 'Well, I suppose it is a canny bit pretty, like.'

With that he returned grumpily to the shelter.

John felt deflated. Couldn't Jim *see* the sheer magnificence of the sight before him? Probably not. Probably he, John Denby, was a freak who saw things that other people didn't see. Or maybe he was just a nutter. Set alongside that 'other thing', he wasn't exactly normal was he? A depressing thought.

Back at the shelter he found the others getting up and sharing out the melons for breakfast. Greedily he ate his four big slices, the sweet, sticky juice dripping down onto his shirt.

'Well this lot'll be gannin' straight through wor!' said Jim with a scatological leer.

'Still got yer bog paper, Jonnie lad?'

John winced. At that moment he was still on his ethereal plane and far above mere animal functions. That Gateway that led into the heart of Toubkal, the coming Day of Judgement, glory or ignominy. But... conserve your street cred, Jonny boy, be a lad.

'Yeah, just a bit,' he replied. 'But when it's finished, I guess we'll have to do what the locals do.'

'And what's that?' asked Jim.

'Well, Bob says they use water and their left hand. That's why there's no paper in the bog at Marrakesh.'

'Stick your fingers up yer bum!' snorted Rob. 'That's dessgustin'!'

'Them Pakkies!' sighed Jim. 'They do 'ave some funny ways, don't they, like!'

The Great Ascent

Things were made ready for the Great Ascent. Rucksacks were packed up and the rubbish religiously put into a poly bag.

'No point in carrying our rucksacks up to the top of the mountain.'

'Aye, it'll fuckin' kill wor! Thorteen thoosand feet do d'yer say, John? Yer get mountain sickness at that height, don't yers?'

'Yes, you do. That's what the climbing books say. You know, headaches and spewing.'

That was another worry. Suppose mountain sickness hit them and they just flaked out? You could just see Morris's complacent, I-told-you-so grin.

'Well, we can't leave the rucksacks here,' said John. 'They'll just get nicked. We'd better leave them at the hut there. There's sure to be a warden. He'll look after them for us.'

'Aye,' sighed Michael, 'and fleece us right proppa an' all!'

'Well, have you got a better idea?'

Michael hadn't. It was decided to leave their baggage at the hut. The shelter was duly dismantled and John took another group photo.

'That must be the tenth one yer've taken!' said Jim. 'Yer'll have no film left!'

'No sweat, I've got two more rolls.'

They shouldered their packs and attacked the stony trail ahead of them.

'Cor, I'm knackered already!' said a panting Tracy.

'It'll be better once we're rid of our rucksacks,' said John, assuming a cheerful 'good expedition leader' role. But, under the forced heartiness, he was fretting about mountain sickness. All the climbing books said it could be a killer – literally! Suppose Tracy collapsed and died of pulmonary oedema? Appalling thought!

They soon reached the hut, perched on its spur. It was a neat, beautifully built, stone affair; very European and in stark contrast to the Biblical world further down the valley. John felt a pang of disappointment. This thing could have been in a suburb of Boldonbridge. The explorer fantasy took a knock.

'Why does they call this thing a hut?' asked Michael. 'It is more like a hoos?'

The door was open and they went in to find a spacious dining room that could have been in an English youth hostel. A large group of European hikers was having breakfast at a long wooden table. Replete with expensive boots, climbing breeches and sweaters, they exuded a confident opulence. They stared disapprovingly at the intrusion. Among them, looking especially inquisitorial, John recognised the Frenchman he'd talked to the previous afternoon. Youthful anarchy did not seem to be welcome in this orderly place.

A long, gaunt man in a skullcap and a white robe approached them, aggressively, a bit like a terrier. 'Quoi? Quoi? Quoi?'

John tried to explain the situation: 'Excusez-moi, Monsieur, mais est-il possible…'

Here his French gave out. How could he explain that they wanted to leave their rucksacks here while they climbed Toubkal? Theoretically possible, but faced with the hostile stares of the hikers, his brain just ceased to work.

'Where's your teacher?' asked the Frenchman in his impeccable English. 'I think you'd better wait for him.'

Problem! Has he sussed us? Quick thinking needed. More lies.

'He's outside. He sent me in to talk French as a test. I don't want him to see me making a mess of my French, so please, *please*, don't ask him in! I'll get a bollocking.' Pleading voice. Flash the ingratiating smile and hope it works.

The man seemed to melt a little. 'All right,' he said. 'It's good to see the English actually trying to learn a foreign language for once. It doesn't always happen, does it.'

He turned and spoke in French to the gaunt man in the white robe who was obviously the warden. Then he turned to John. 'All right, leave them over there. But mind, don't you start climbing the Toubkal without your teacher. It's dangerous, you know.'

He didn't seem to be wholly convinced by John's cover story. However! Better get away quick before he starts asking more awkward questions. They deposited their loads and hurried outside.

'We'd better get going before he finds out that we haven't got a teacher with us.'

'But what if it's too dangerous?' said Michael. 'I mean, like what he said.'

'Well, we'll just have to turn back, won't we?'

John's anxieties were mounting. His prize, his whole being, was under threat. Just what *did* lie up in that corrie above the gateway? Please God, make it easy!

As they set off, however, an elation began to grow within him, tiny at first, but slowly, like that 'grain of mustard seed' in the Bible, swelling in imperceptible stages. Without his heavy pack, he seemed to glide up the trail. Plodding slowly and rhythmically upwards as Mekon had taught him, he led the way. Glancing behind him, he saw that the others were following him just as easily; the girls, too.

One after another they passed the landmarks – the two boulders, the river – and followed the cairned trail as it wriggled its way into the corrie and up the sun-swept avalanche of boulders before them. They were alone in the radiant dawn and all around them were harsh and rugged mountains. Bathed in the gentle morning light, they seemed friendly, affable even. Slowly and steadily upwards. Lots of rest so as not to tire the girls. Team work. Major Allen would just eat this! Photographs all the time. No hint of altitude problems. Rising hope.

Then, as they topped the lip of the corrie, a surge of elation! A broad basin opened out before them with easy screes sweeping down from an encircling, lumpy ridge. There were no impassable rock walls or lethal snowfields. Just a zigzag path snaking a carefully graded way up to a skyline on the right. Vindication! Breaking through the barrier!

'There, team!' cried John. 'What did I tell you? It's easy! We're gonna make it! We're mountaineers!'

'Jonnie, lad, yorra fuckin' genius!'

A delicious moment of bonding, togetherness and acceptance.

So, slowly upwards into the cool, welcoming sky. As they topped the ridge a vast panorama burst into view: wonderful, spacious, with a hint of that Beyond World. Wave after wave of craggy brown mountains rippling away into the blue distance like a boundless ocean of storm clouds. Far away to the south the rumpled ridges subsided, one after the other, into a vast sandy plain.

'Look team! There's the Sahara! Cor, this is *great*!'

To their left, a broad ridge, rocky in places, gravelly in others, led invitingly up towards a little plateau upon which they could see a large tripod: the top!

'There's the top! Not far now!'

'This is easier than Helvellyn.'

'A reet doddle!'

A walk, a little scrambling to add a bit of spice. Cool air, not a hint of altitude problems, a few slabby rocks… and they were there!

'We've done it!'

'And we're not knackered neither!'

It was one of those moments of delicious emotion that come to us rarely, if ever. Hand shakes. Hugs. Kisses from the girls. More than ever, that sense of bonding and togetherness, laced with the joy of achievement, and for John, of final acceptance and friendship. If only it could last for ever! Here was a tale he could tell Major Allen!

A group photograph. Then time to absorb the mountain drama that stretched away on all sides of them: those vast sinuous and craggy ridges snaking down into lonely, undiscovered valleys, those huge plunging mountain faces, that lordly panorama of rugged immensities, grey, black and brown, and fading into a hazy blue in the unknown distance. On the crest of a euphoric wave, John took an elaborate panorama, using up a whole film.

Then a sense of anticlimax. 'Well, I suppose we'd better be getting down,' he said, pointing to the easy-angled scree slopes that swept down into the corrie beneath them. 'It'll be quicker to go down directly.'

So down they plunged, almost wading at times through a veritable swamp of loose gravel. Clouds of dust. Grit in your boots. Tough on your knees. Covered in brown grime which clings to your sweaty face.

A rest among the boulders of the corrie floor followed.

Then they picked a careful way down towards the hut. As they left the corrie they ran into a party ambling slowly up behind a Moroccan guide. John recognised the Frenchman who spoke English.

'Nous avons fait le sommet!' he cried triumphantly.

'Well done, boys!' the man replied in his perfect English.

Then he frowned suspiciously. 'But where's the teacher you said was with you? I can't see him'

Alarm bells starting to tinkle. Plot discovered. More quick thinking.

'Oh, he had the gut rot and went down.'

'And he let you come up here without him? That's not right, is it?' The suspicious frown deepened. 'Or, perhaps, there is *no* teacher with you? I'm not sure that you have been telling me the truth.'

With that bombshell he rejoined his group and plodded on up the path.

'He seems to have sussed us,' said John. 'We'd better get moving before he gets the fuzz onto us.'

'Hadaway man! Divvent be daft!' snorted Jim. 'How the fuck's he gannin' ter fetch the poliss up here, like?'

'Well, he could have a radio in his rucksack. These big posh climbing groups often do, you know. We're hunted men on the run.'

Down to Earth

They stumbled back to the hut and retrieved their rucksacks from under the dining room table here they had been placed.

'Merci beaucoup monsieur,' said John to the gaunt, white-robed warden as he shouldered his pack. 'Vous êtes tellement aimable,' he added, extending his hand.

But to his bewildered dismay the man scowled back at him. 'Deux cent dihrams, soixant!'

'Eh?'

'He wants two hundred and sixty dihrams. I suppose I can just about manage it.'

John handed him a bundle of dihram notes and they prepared to leave, but the man blocked their way, gesticulating angrily.

'Cadeau! Cadeau!'

'Bloody hell! Now he wants a present!' groaned John.

With a resigned sigh, he pulled his last remaining sweater out of his rucksack and handed it to him.

'Nowt Burra Rich Snob'

'Well, he were a mingy old bastard!' growled Rob as they set off down the track.

'Yeah!' added Jim. 'He seemed to think we could *shit* money!'

'John, yer shudda told him ter fuck off!' sighed Michael. 'Ah mean, what the fuck's he done forrus like? Nowt! An' as well as the dosh yer had ter give 'im yer sweater! Yer daft, you!'

Still euphoric about climbing the mountain, John was fixed in 'charitable and forgiving Christian' mode.

'OK,' he said with a hint of defensive sanctimony, 'I take your point, Mike, but remember we're far richer than he is. Just by coming from Britain we're probably carrying on us far more money than he'd earn in a year. We're rich, you know.'

'Speak for yourself, Jonnie lad!' said Jim, with more than a hint of an aggressive snarl. '*You* may be rich, but I'm not!'

'Nor me neither!' echoed Rob.

Sensing a cleavage opening up in the previous warm bonding, John quickly backpedalled. 'Please, I wasn't saying you were rich. I was only saying that compared to the people here, we seem to be rich. Well, er…'

The complex legalistic hair-splitting required to clarify

what he had meant to say, however, was beyond him at that precise moment and he fell silent.

Sensing blood, Jim went onto the attack. 'Yer knaa Brian told wor that you was nowt burra rich snob? Whadda der yer say ter that? Eh?'

Inwardly John groaned. Not this one again! Could *nothing* break through that iron-hard shell of class resentment in which they encased themselves? He felt the ground sinking beneath him, that Greenhill feeling of utter helplessness in the face of blind, unreasoning brute force.

'But, I'm *not*!' he mumbled.

'Well, yer does talk posh and yer does gan ter a private school, like.'

'Aw give ower, Jim lad!' cried Maureen. 'Divvent start rowin'! I mean, we've all been such good mates! That's been the best part of it. Better even than climbin' the mountain.'

'Aye!' added Tracy vehemently. 'John's not a snob, him! I mean he's given all them things o' his away and paid out all that nikker an' all jus' ter help us out, like. Ah mean, you haven't done that much, have yers? Be fair! He's a loverly lad, him!'

With that she embraced John and kissed him. He reciprocated with interest – *compound* interest.

'Well,' declared Michael, when the two of them finally disentangled themselves. 'Yer've had yer smooch and we've 'ad out bitch, so warraboot 'avin' a birra lunch?'

'Thank God, some o' yer lads gorra bit o' sense!' said Maureen.

With that they sat down and shared out the remaining food. All the tins of tuna were duly opened and eaten. That left the nine remaining tins of that weird Moroccan stuff.

'Well, Ah'm not eatin' none o' that!' said Jim. 'It'll jus' gan strain through yers an' come oot the other end.'

'Nowt wrong wi' that!' replied Rob with a scatological grin.

'Nowt wrong with shittin', like! Ah mean, me arld granddad wot were in a Nip prison camp in the war, he always said to us bairns when we was having wor tea like, "Lads, if yer divvent eat, yer divvent shit. An' if yer divvent shit, yer dies. Yer gorra shit to live!" Ah mean, we's all the same inside, yer knaa!'

Scatological giggles. Back to being a group again. An inward sigh of relief from John. The little altercation had alarmed him. It had shown that under the apparently friendly surface of the bonding, old unbridgeable chasms still lurked. And yes, he'd snogged Tracy, all right. And yes, the girls had come to his rescue. But what if they sussed his *true* nature? You're not one of them. You never will be. So keep up your guard! But back to the present.

'Look,' he declared, 'we can easily get down to Imlil. It's only twelve o'clock. It'll be quick going downhill, and then we can get a bus back to Marrakesh.'

Knight in Shining Armour? All Good Mates

After reducing the girls' loads to a minimum, the little band set off for Imlil. By now the sun was beating down fiercely. A shimmering haze veiled the mountains, reducing everything to a monochromatic dullness, as if the land had gone to sleep and would only wake up in the evening.

After three hours of stumbling down the stony track, the two girls sat down on a rock.

'I'm bloody fucked, me!' declared Maureen. 'Me feet is killin' us!'

'Me an' all!' sighed Tracy. 'Ah canna gan nee further, me!'

'Well we can't just stay here, me bonny lasses,' said Rob. 'We got no food. We'll bloody starve!'

'Well, we've got them tins of Pakkie stuff,' said Michael. 'We ain't eaten that yet.'

'There's no way I'm eatin' that crap!' replied Jim forcibly.

'So what does we do, then?' said Rob.

They sat in silence for a while.

Then John saw his chance. Perform an act of heroic self-sacrifice and unstinting generosity. Like one of those knights of old, rescue the two damsels in distress! Then, surely, nobody could ever call him a rich, snobby git again – not even Jim!

'Don't worry, lads,' he said, 'I'll get some donkeys to take the lasses down to Imlil.'

'And get done again!' snorted Michael.

'Maybe! But I've got five thirty dihrams left. Tha should do. You wait here while I go down to that Sidi-whatever-it-is place and see what I can find. Guard my pack, will you, while I'm gone.'

'How long will you be?'

'Not that long. Can't be far.'

But, complications... It was now three o'clock, and the round trip to Sidi-whatever-it-was would probably take three hours. That would mean starting off with the girls at six o'clock. They would have to buy more food and spend the night somewhere.

'Eeee, John!' said Tracy as he set off. 'Yorra knight in shinin' armour, you!'

But he had hardly disappeared round a corner before he met two men coming up the track, each leading an unladen donkey. It was almost as if God had put them there on purpose.

Quick pleading conversation: 'Excusez-moi... Est-il possible transporter deux personnes à Imlil avec votres ânes?'

Atrocious and hideously accented French, but after a few moments the message seemed to get through.

'Oui, containment.'

'Combien?'

'Cent dihrams, chaque âne.'

'D'accord!'

He handed over 200 dihrams.

Saint Bloody George

In triumph he returned to the others.

'Great lad!'

'Worra tell yer, lads! He's Saint bloody George, him!'

For a brief moment he wallowed in the applause. Yes, truly, John the wimp, John the shit-stabber, bashed up by Kev and laid out by Dobson, had been swallowed up by John the tough mountaineer and resourceful explorer!

The girls were hoisted onto the donkeys along with their baggage. After two hours the group reached Imlil.

'Bakshish! Bakshish!' said one of the men.

'I'd better give him something,' sighed John.

He rummaged in his rucksack and handed over his one and only spare shirt to one of the men.

'Bakshish! Bakshish!' chorused the other one aggressively.

In desperation John handed over his spare pair of jeans. Apart from two pairs of socks and a pair of underpants, he now had no clothes except what he was wearing. Should he get wet or something, he was going to have problems. Of course, the Bible said you shouldn't worry about what clothes you were going to wear. God was supposed to see to that, just as he looked after the sartorial needs of the sparrows. And after all this Christian generosity of his, God bloody well ought to provide something. Part of the bargain. But would the mingy old thing honour it? Probably not. However!

'Right, team,' he said. 'Now let's see about a bus to Marrakesh.'

Happy Ending?

But there was no bus to Marrakesh, not even a minibus.

'Looks like we're stuck here for the night,' said Jim. 'Where does we doss down, lads?'

Just then John saw a lorry, with a group of rough, moustachioed characters climbing into the cab.

'Hang on!' he said, 'I'll try that lorry. Maybe they'll give us a lift to Marrakesh.'

He scampered over to it: 'Excusez-moi monsieur, allez-vous à Marrakesh?'

'Oui.'

'Combein pour transporter nous et notres baggages à Marrakesh?'

'Cent dihrams.'

He handed over a 100 dihram note and signalled to the others. 'Problem solved, guys! They'll take us to Marrakesh.'

Helped by one of the men, they clambered into the back. With a roar of the engine and a grinding of gears, they lurched off amid clouds of dust.

'Worra day! Worra set o' adventures!' said Jim as they bounced down the stony road.

'Hang on!' cried John. ' I've got one last shot in my camera. This'll make a good ending!'

Precariously trying to stand upright on the crazily vibrating platform, he managed to take the final picture and extract the film from the camera.

'That'll have to do until we get to Marrakesh.'

'If we ever does get there,' sighed Michael.

'Oh, for fuck's sake, we're halfway there already!'

'Ah mean, Ah divvent like the look o' them blerks in the cab, me. Ah mean, what's ter stop 'em pullin' over and robbin' us, like?'

'We'll 'ave a lot more ter worry aboot when we gets ter Marrakesh,' said Maureen. 'I mean, Joe'll play war wi' us, and why, Brian'll bloody *do* wor!'

'Not if Ah've got owt ter dee with it!' said Jim, flashing his wicked leer, to which his pointy, fox-like face was well adapted.

'How so?'

'Like what Ah said, Ah'll just say Joe told us ter gan, like.'

'But he didn't, did he?'

'Ah knaa he didn't, but who's ter prove it, like? It'll be our word against his word. Ah mean, jus' think. He's gonna look pretty daft for lerrin' us slip away without him noticin' like, ain't he? And then we can say he were pissed, an' he can't deny that! Pissed in charge of kids? He won't want that to come oot, will he?'

'Eeee, Jim lad! Yorra reet crook, ye!'

The lorry bounced on.

Soothed by the rush of cool air, John relapsed into a blissful torpor. He'd succeeded! What a tale to tell Bob! What a tale for his diary, and for the book he was going to write. 'One day I'll be famous.' It was going to happen. Chris Bonnington had made the first British ascent of the North Face of the Eiger. John Denby had led the first Boldonbridge schoolboy ascent of the Jebel Toubkal. Slightly different in detail, perhaps, the difference was one of degree rather than of kind.

The Red Badge of Courage

Suddenly the lorry lurched onto the side of the road and jerked to a halt. Four large, bristly-chinned and beefy men got out of the cab and approached them, signalling to them to climb down.

'What's all this?' said Jim. 'John, you berra talk yer frog and find out.'

'Mais nous allons à Marrakesh…'

There was no reply. Instead, one of the men climbed up and started flinging their rucksacks onto the ground.

'Hey! What are you doing?'

Then John was grabbed and bodily lifted over the side. The others were similarly bundled unceremoniously off the lorry. It all happened so quickly that there was no time to think. As they picked themselves up off the ground, one of the men grabbed Michael's arm and wrenched off his watch.

'You bloody thief!' snarled Jim, brandishing his fists.

Then he fell silent as he found himself facing a drawn pistol and at least three long, sharp knives.

The temperature dropped 30 degrees. The bewildering reality sunk in. This was for real. Not play. They were being robbed.

'Montres! Cameras! Argent!'

'What the fuck's gannin' on, John?'

'They want our watches and money and cameras.'

'Well they're not gerrin' mine!' said Rob grandiloquently as one of the men seized his arm.

Immediately, another of the men grabbed him and pointed a long knife at his throat. Bigger and obviously stronger, he towered over him: an unequal contest.

'Oh, for God's sake give it to him, Rob!' cried John. 'I mean, you can always buy a new watch, but you can't get a new liver if he sticks that knife into you!'

Crude reality triumphed over adolescent bravado. Reluctantly and shamefacedly, they handed over their watches. John handed over his camera and his remaining dihrams. Jim let them take the Trangia from his rucksack.

John felt physically sick. This was the one thing that, above all else, he dreaded: crude physical strength ruthlessly applied against weakness. He felt himself go limp and soggy, that Greenhill feeling. Then his innards began to churn round. Any moment now he was going to shit himself. The shame of it! And in front of the girls, too! Despite himself, he began to tremble violently and visibly. Not the budding Chris Bonnington, but the pathetic little wimp who'd been done over by Kev in front of everybody and everything.

One of the men seized Tracy's arm and brutally wrenched off her bracelet. Suddenly John saw a chance for redemption. Redeem yourself! Like that soldier in the American Civil War, win the Red Badge of Courage. Damsel in distress! Ride to the rescue. Maybe they'll stick a knife into you, but that's better than shitting your pants. And if they kill you, you won't have to worry about that, will you?

So, wild Kamikaze charge. Mad. Crazy. *'Leave her alone, you bastard!'*

Colossal thump. Flash of light. Searing pain. Second thump. Fierce pain in the stomach. Gasping for breath. Hurtling to the ground. Thump into the dust. Blind terror. Curl up into a ball like a small kid. Wait for the agony of the knife thrust. Eyes closed. Feeble body taking over completely. Oh God, I *am* shitting myself! Total squalid humiliation.

A long silence. Slow emerging consciousness. How to handle this one?

He opened his eyes. There was no sign of the men or the lorry. Wave of relief. He was safe. Looking up, he saw Tracy and the others standing in a circle around him.

'Are you OK, John?'

'Yeah! Yeah! I think so.' Play the wounded hero. Might get you a bit of street cred.

'Eeeeee, John!' exclaimed Tracy. 'You're ever so brave! Yorra knight in shinin' armour what sacrificed hissell for ter save a lass!'

So the hero act had retrieved something out of the disaster. But what to do about the disgusting – and expanding! – mess in the 'nether regions'? Soon it'll be horribly visible. That's hardly very good for the St George image, is it?

He got up: 'Hang on guys, I'd better slip behind that rock. I think I'm going to spew. That punch in the guts, you know.'

Luckily the rock in question was big and capacious enough to conceal him while he completed the emptying operation and embarked on the cleansing operation. He was able to remove and bury his disgusting underpants, and scrabbling round with his handkerchief, he managed to wipe himself down. Situation saved. Dignity intact. But, oh God, did this sort of thing happen to Hector when he fought Achilles?

Or to Bonnington when he'd climbed the North Face of the Eiger? Or, indeed, to old Mekon when he'd won his military medal? Certainly not, because they were proper people, not dirty little shit-stabbers like John Denby. Message received: no, John Denby, you're not a budding Chris Bonnington. Not by a long chalk!

Helpless

He returned to the group.

'Well done, John,' said Jim. 'You were great.'

'Sorry, team,' he replied, 'I shouldn't have got that lorry. But how the fuck was I to know they were bloody bandits?'

'Bloody Pakkies!' snarled Jim viciously.

'Hadaway!' said Tracy. 'They're not all thieves, yer knaa. Ah mean, that man in the cafe, he were ever so kind him.'

'Aye,' added Maureen, 'an' warraboot Kev an' them lot? It ain't just the Pakkies what's thieves, yer knaa.'

Silence.

'So whadder we do now?' said Rob eventually.

'I suppose we'll have to wait till a bus comes,' replied John.

'And how the fuck are we gonna pay the bus fare when we've no fuckin' dosh?' said Jim.

Silence. John couldn't answer that question. As the reality of their predicament slowly sunk in, a feeling of utter helplessness descended on him. How to get back to Marrakesh? How to explain this catastrophe to Morris? And when Dobson heard about it he would have a field day. So now what? Dreams of glory shattered.

The Brotherhood of the Helpless

The shadows deepened. Night fell. Darkness overwhelmed the rocky, barren land, pierced here and there by the flickering lights of distant villages. Above them the sky blazed out with its infinity of glittering stars. The moon rose and bathed the distant mountains in its soft ethereal light. The silent majesty of eternal verities, far removed from the forlorn little group huddled on the roadside.

By way of compensation, John felt a sense of togetherness. That underlying cleavage of different accents and different backgrounds withered before the reality of their shared predicament. Here, stranded and penniless beside that empty road, they were all the same. Naked before the blunt facts of existence.

Rescue

Hours later a white minibus drew up beside them, dazzling them with its headlights. A neatly dressed and very modern-looking Moroccan got out.

'Que faites-vous ici? Vous êtes tres jeunes. Êtes-vous Français?'

Instinctively they cowered away. Christ, not another set of thieves?

'Talk to him, John,' said Jim eventually.

'Non, nous sommes Anglais.'

'Oh, you're British!' exclaimed the man breaking into fluent and well-pronounced English, 'But you're all very young. So what are you doing here at this time of night?'

'We want to get to Marrakesh. That's where our teachers are.'

'It's too late for buses now and it's not safe to stay here at night, especially for girls.'

'We know that,' said John ruefully. 'We were on a lorry, but the men held us up and robbed us. That's why we are here. They took our watches and our money.'

'And they obviously attacked you as well, by the look of you.'

'Well, yes, but you see they were attacking the girls and, well, I had to come to their rescue.'

'A word of advice, young man. Don't ever try to resist. These thieves are far stronger than you are and they're quite heartless. They're perfectly capable of knifing you if it suits them.' Pause. 'Look,' the man eventually said, 'I'll take you down to Marrakesh.'

Bewildering Kindness

A bizarre roller-coaster experience followed. They found themselves enveloped in kindness and generosity. Nothing was too good for them. They were taken down to Marrakesh and escorted into a neat modern house in the new town. There they were introduced to a very European family consisting of a mother, two small boys and a little girl. A vast meal was prepared for them and they were allowed to have a shower before being ushered into a large bedroom and bedded down for the night.

The man and his wife were doctors who had worked in France and visited London. Before John joined the others in the bedroom, they carefully washed his bruised face for him.

'You're so kind,' he said, as they examined his chest to see if he had any broken ribs.

'God wants it,' replied the man. 'It is the tradition of Islam to welcome foreigners and protect young people.'

The next morning he took them to a police station where they told the story of the robbery and got the necessary stamped certificate for their insurance claims. Then the man drove them to the Jemaa el-Fnaa and they parted amid effusive thank-yous and exchanging of addresses.

'Odd folk, these Pakkies,' said Jim as they strolled down the narrow alley towards the pension. 'Cheatin' yers and muggin' yers one minute, and being right decent the next. I doubt if yer'd find a blerk as canny as that back home! Don't make no sense.'

'But we doesn't make that much sense, neither,' said

Maureen. 'Ah mean, we've got Bob what's great, and Kev what's a bastard.'

Michael shook his head dismissively. 'Hadaway lass, it's just folk, yer knaa.'

A Teacher at the Mercy of his Pupils

They reached the door of the pension.

'Now forrit!' chortled Jim, 'Ready for the explosion, lads? And Jonnie me boy, you jus' leave all this ter me an' Rob. Gerrit?'

They ran into Morris in the courtyard. John felt he could actually read the emotions that flashed through the man's mind, almost as if they were being displayed on a big television screen.

First was immense relief: a tidal wave of tsunami proportions. 'Thank God you're back! I've been so worried about you!'

Second was blind fury, a whole pile of rage that had been accumulating, bit by fiery bit during each of the past four days. '*But where the bloody hell have you been?*'

'But,' replied Jim, flashing his evil leer, 'we left yers a note. Didn't yer read it, like?'

The dam burst and the pent-up torrent of rage poured out. 'Sneaking off like that without permission! Appallingly irresponsible behaviour! Downright criminal! God alone knows what might have happened to you! No end of worry...'

Eventually the torrent dwindled into an exhausted trickle. 'Well, when Brian comes back I'll have you all sent home.'

Exhausted silence.

'But,' said a calm and still leering Jim, 'Yer *did* give us permission ter gan. Yer said it were a great exercise in self-management, didn't yer?'

'No, I did *not* and you *know* it!'

Jim's leer deepened. He was hugely enjoying this. He'd felt upstaged by John's ability to talk French. Now was his chance to even the score. Like a seasoned barrister in court, he delivered his punch line. 'Oh yes, yer did. Didn't he, Rob, you was there, you heard him?'

'Aye, Ah did so.'

'And John, you was there. Ye heard him 'an all?'

'Yes, I did.'

'Yer see, old man,' said Jim, 'it's us against ye. Our words agin thine. Six against one. In a court o' law that's what counts, like. There's nowt yer can dee aboorit.'

Morris's rage and frustrated resentment turned on John. 'I knew *you'd* be mixed up in this business, Denby! You should never have been allowed to come on this expedition. You've been nothing but trouble.'

'*Aw belt up yer rotten bastard*!' shrieked Tracy. 'Wor John's a loverly lad, him. He's a knight in shinin' armour what sacrificed hissell for ter save us lasses!'

With that she hugged and kissed him.

'Don't you dare to speak to me like that!' spluttered Morris.

'Look, Joe,' said Jim, adopting a calm and gentle voice, 'let's sort this out like grown men an' not like liddell kids shoutin' an' that.'

'There's nothing to sort out. Just you wait till Brian comes back!'

'Yeah, just *you* bloody wait, Joe Morris! Brian'll 'ave yer balls for breakfast. Lerrin' us gan away without ye noticing it! An' we can tell 'im that you was drunk an' all. Drunk in charge o' kids? That won't go down that well with the Committee or whatever it is back home, will it, like?'

'Now look here, young man —'

'But Brian's in the shit an' all, ain't he? Lerrin' Kev and them lot buy drugs an' that, and him not noticing.'

'That's nothing to do with you.'

'Oh yes it is! What's the Committee back 'ome gannin' ter say if they learns that we never climbed no mountains an' that despite all the nikker they doshed oot? Yers all gannin' ter look reet daft, ain't yers?'

John observed the unequal contest with a bemused awe. Coarse, philistine and horribly ignorant of many things: Jim was all of this. Yet he was clever too, and bold with it! *He'd* never have dared to speak to a teacher like this. Talk about being streetwise! Jim would go far. He felt humbled before abilities that he, John Denby, just didn't have. But, at the same time, he began to feel sorry for Morris. Poor bloke! He was a decent man at heart, but he really had landed in it. Between them, Jim and Dobson had him on a skewer.

A pause.

'You do make things difficult for me,' said Morris eventually.

'But,' replied Jim in his gentle voice, 'there's an easy way oot for all of us.'

It seemed to John as if Jim were now the adult and Morris the wayward youth who needed straightening out. He'd become caring and paternal. It was a side of him he'd never imagined was there. Jim was... well... multifaceted.

'What do you mean?'

'You just tell Brian that *you* led us up Toubkal and that, due ter your great leadership an' that, we all got ter the top, like, and had a great time. He'll thank yer forrit, because it gets him off the hook and you 'an all! We'll all be happy then!'

'But that's not true.'

'Who's ter know that if we all sticks to the same story, like?'

John felt even more sorry for Morris. Poor, poor bloke! A teacher, a leader, at the mercy of a clever and wholly unscrupulous pupil. The sheer humiliation of the situation!

After another pause, Morris surrendered to the inevitable. 'Let's call it quits, then. It's no use crying over spilt milk, is it? You're all safe and sound and that's what matters. And, on reflection, you've all done very well.'

He turned to John. 'Sorry I snapped at you. I didn't mean it. You're a great lad, really, you know. But what's happened to your face? Have you been in a fight?'

'Well, sort of... Some locals tried to rob us, but well, with the help of the lads I managed to drive them off.'

'Well done! Yes, you really *are* quite a lad, aren't you!'

John glowed with satisfaction. He'd broken through another barrier. Acceptance at last. But then came a warning bell: not a shrill alarm, but just a faint tinkle. Be careful! You're not through the woods yet, Jonnie boy. This could be a tactical withdrawal. Morris needs you at the moment, just to save himself. Later on he won't need you, and things could change. You should *know* that!

Three Different Truths

John spent the rest of the day writing up his diary. A cliff band was placed in that corrie on the Toubkal with a few desperate moves needed to wriggle up the only crack in its sheer face. But as he wrote this an awkward thought flitted through his mind. Hope nobody who reads this has *actually* climbed the Toubkal! The ascent of the Toubkal really *was* a doddle, wasn't it? You'll have to climb a harder mountain than this if you're to prove yourself, Jonnie, my lad!

He came to the robbery. He'd boldly confronted the thieves and, after a vicious punch up, they'd fled. A black eye and a bleeding nose? Honourable wounds gained in battle! Indeed, that coveted Red Badge of Courage! No mention of being sent sprawling on the ground and shitting yourself with fright. That hadn't happened.

Another pause for reflection. There seemed to be three truths in the offing. The 'official truth' agreed with Jim, with a highly competent Morris leading them to the summit of the Toubkal. The sanitised and heroic 'truth' in his diary. And what had *actually* happened in all its stringy banality. So just what *was* the truth about John Denby? Fantasising wannabe who was in reality just a shit-stabbing little wimp? Or a bold and enterprising mountain explorer? Who knew? He certainly didn't.

Expedition Saved

At nine o'clock the following morning, Steadman erupted into the courtyard.

'Hello, people! How are we? Still alive, are we?' Beaming away, full of heartiness and bounce, clearly relieved to have been released from an onerous burden.

Hearing the booming voice, John scrambled out of bed and dashed out to meet him. All through the night, tedious hour by tedious hour, the tale of his adventures had been waxing ever more dramatic. He just had to release the head of accumulated steam.

'Bob!' he spluttered. 'We've had a great time! We've actually climbed the Toubkal and I led the way!'

'Tell me about it later, John,' replied Steadman. 'I've got to see Joe Morris, first. Keep to the modalities, you know.'

'Where's Dobson?'

'He's at the airport.'

'He's not going home, is he?' Hopefully, *yes*! Gone for good! Hooray! Hooray!

'Be patient, young man. All will be revealed.'

With that, Steadman disappeared upstairs.

Half an hour later he and Morris emerged and a meeting took place under the palm tree in the courtyard. Steadman spoke first.

'First of all, chaps, congratulations to you all on your splendid ascent of the Jebel Toubkal, and especial congratulations to Joe Morris here for leading the way. Very well done all round!'

There was a hint of irony here. Clearly Steadman had swallowed the 'official version' of events.

'Now the sitrep.'

'He's still playin' soldiers, ain't he?' Michael whispered into John's ear.

'Kev and his merry men are being sent home. The British Consul managed to swing the lead on their behalf.'

'What about Brian?'

'He's got to go home with them. They're all at the airport now.'

'And good riddance to the lot of them!' exclaimed John with a malicious glee, 'Hooray! Hooray!'

'John, that's quite inappropriate!' snapped Morris.

Steadman continued, 'We can now get on with the expedition. Because of the extra expenses – like going to Rabat and getting our erring bretheren back home and out of harm's way – money's a bit short. So it'll have to be public transport from now on. No more taxis, I'm afraid. Still, that won't stop us. Tomorrow morning at six o'clock sharp we'll catch the bus to Zagora. That's over the mountains and into the desert, where you are all going to do your Lawrence of Arabia act and ride camels for three or more days.

'After that we'll come back here, rest a bit, and then we'll go off into the mountains and do some *real* mountaineering in places where few foreign tourists ever get to. That should satisfy some of you would-be Bonningtons.

'In the meantime, you can spend today getting yourselves ready for the desert. We'll check your kit at eight o'clock this evening.'

Reimbursement

As the meeting dispersed, John sidled up to Steadman. 'Bob, please can I have some more money?'

'So you managed to blow the eighty quid I gave you? That must have taken some doing.'

Shamefaced look onto the ground. 'I'm sorry, Bob. And I lost my camera, too. It was nicked by some thieves.'

'That doesn't surprise me. I suppose you want me to buy you another one?'

'Well, yes. And I'll need to buy some film, too.'

'So fairy godmother here will have to provide? That's your little game, is it? Well, here's fifteen quid. That'll have to do. Can't give you any more, I'm afraid.'

'But what about the camera? I was so looking forward to taking photos of the desert. I mean, it wasn't my fault that my camera was nicked. We were held up and robbed.'

'Were you, indeed? Joe didn't say anything about that.'

Pause.

'Well,' declared Steadman, 'I suppose you'd better borrow my camera. What with all the recent comings and goings, I just haven't had the urge to take pictures. You can be the official expedition photographer from now on. Off you go, then and buy yourself some more film. Here's a few dihrams.'

'Cor, thanks, Bob! Thanks a bomb! You're so kind.'

'A great big softy is what you *really* mean.'

Versions of Truth: Objective Reality versus Factualism

A foray into the town with Michael, Jim and Tracy followed. They returned towards evening, and while the others went upstairs to see Rob, John slipped into his bedroom to load Steadman's camera with one of the films he'd bought. Inside, he found Steadman reading the diary he'd been so avidly writing up the previous day.

'You seem to have had quite a time climbing Toubkal.'

John swelled with pride: this was the first of the many rave reviews he was going to get. 'Yes, we did! I'm thinking of writing all this up as a book and sending it to the publishers along with the photos I've taken.'

'I'd be a little careful about that, if I were you.'

'Oh?' Unexpected deflation here! Not the accolade he'd been expecting.

'Well, before you let anybody see it, you'll have to do a bit of editing. Quite a lot, in fact.'

'But *why*? It's all true. It all happened. Like Stephen Crane in the *Red Badge of Courage*. I've written it as it was.'

'"As it was?" That's what you think, is it?'

Pouty expression. 'Yes!'

'Well, what's all this about climbing up a four hundred foot sheer cliff to reach the final knife-edge ridge, which led to the fifteen thousand foot summit of the Jebel Toubkal?'

He began to read from the open notebook: 'We had to squeeze our way up the narrow crack. It was really scary without ropes. One false move and we would be hurled to our deaths on the brutal rocks far below. Clambering along that terrifying knife-edge ridge towards the summit, our feet were dangling precariously over a sheer thousand-foot drop. Just one slip and we would fall into the fiery furnace of the Sahara Desert.'

Steadman paused and looked him full in the face.

'Well it *is* true!' protested John. 'It *did* happen.'

'Oh come on, young man!' Steadman retorted. 'And piggy-wiggies can fly! I've done the normal route up the Toubkal three times. There're no four hundred cliff bands or knife-edged ridges. It's just an easy path. You've written a load of rubbish, haven't you?'

Sussed. Sussed to a crust. John blushed bright red.

But Steadman was relentless, remorseless. Turning a few pages he continued to read. 'Very horny. Knocked Tracy off that night. What a bang!' Once more he stared him in the face. '*That* never happened, did it?'

'Yes it did.'

'Look, young fellow, I know all about all your proclivities. It couldn't have happened, could it?'

Squashed like a buzzing fly! The 'great climber' reduced to a pathetic retard. How were the mighty fallen.

Steadman shifted gear from inquisitorial judge into avuncular friend. 'Let's have the truth, shall we? Did you really climb Toubkal, or have you made it all up?'

'Yes we did, honestly we did.'

'And did Joe Morris really lead the way?'

'Yes, he did.' Be loyal to your mates! Don't shop them! Stick to the agreed story or Jim and Rob'll do you over.

'Well, that's not the impression I've been getting. Morris seems to know next to nothing about the route up Toubkal; so little, in fact, that I don't think he can ever have been there. So exactly what *did* happen?'

Long pause.

'All right, I'll tell you. But *please* don't tell the others or they'll do me over. But, well, we sneaked off without Joe's permission and did it ourselves. I've got photos to prove it.'

Bit by bit the story came out. Even the robbery by the road. But not, of course, the bit about shitting his pants with fright. Out of pure self-respect, something has to be hidden from prying eyes.

'I see,' said Steadman when the confession finally petered out. 'But, tell me, were you the ringleader?'

'Yes, but Jim and Rob were in it too. It was Jim who wrote that letter to Joe. And it was Jim who laced Joe's brandy with milk of magnesia to give him the gut rot so he wouldn't come chasing after us.'

'Yes, I get you.'

Another pause.

After a while, John spoke up. 'Will I get my Duke of Edinburgh's Silver Award for it? After all it *was* a four-day, self-managed expedition in wild country, wasn't it?'

'No, I'm afraid you won't.'

Sulky adolescent pout. 'But why not?'

Steadman got up, closed the bedroom door and locked it.

'This is strictly between you and me. Understand? We don't want big ears flapping and rumours being spread around.' Sitting down on the bed, he became conspiratorial. 'Now, just listen to me. Things aren't nearly as simple as you think they are. I'm going to have to write a full report to the Committee when we get back home. There's going to be a pretty good stink, I can tell you. What with the antics of Kev and his crew, Dobby's got egg all over his face and he doesn't like it. So when he gets back to Boldonbridge he's going to look for scapegoats, isn't he? It wasn't his fault, was it? And it wasn't Kev's fault either. Nor Jakie's. Nor Sandra's. Nor any of them. They're deprived proletarians and in Dobbyland proletarians can't sin. So whose fault was it?'

Theatrical pause.

'No prize for guessing who was to blame?' he eventually said.

'You?' replied John.

'Yes, and you too, young man.'

'*Me?*' exclaimed John. 'But I had nothing to do with Kev and his drugs. You *know* that!' The old dread was reigniting.

'*Of course* you hadn't. I know that. So do the police here. But the literal truth is irrelevant.'

'What do you mean? Facts are facts. You can't alter facts.'

Steadman shook his head and smiled in a condescending way. 'I'd better give you a little lesson in Marxist philosophy,' he said. 'There's "Factualism": that's what you think when you just look at the proven facts. And there's "Objective Reality": that's the reality behind the observed facts which is only apparent to trained Marxists. Follow me?'

'Not really, but go on.'

'Well look at our situation through Marxist eyes. Just think of the scenario. Simple, good-hearted, proletarian youngsters, deprived children to boot, are taken to Morocco

265

by a correct-thinking proletarian leader. All are above sin. But, posh, moneyed, upper-class public schoolboy, John Denby, inveigles his way onto the expedition, despite the correct-thinking Marxist leader's worst fears and in open defiance of the left-leaning Committee's express instructions. Being bourgeois, he is only able to think in terms of petty financial gain. It's wired into his genes. Inevitably he uses his privileged education and superior wealth to buy drugs and sell them to the poor, innocent deprived kids, and when his bourgeois iniquity is unmasked, he uses the corrupt capitalist system to oil and grease his way out of trouble.'

'But that's a load of crap!' exclaimed John. 'It's just not true!' That Greenhill feeling of helpless dread before wild, irrational forces was rising fast.

'Of course it isn't true,' said Steadman. 'But that's Factualism. Objective Reality says it *is* true. You try to convince the Sociology Department up at Boldonbridge University that it's not true! What people *think* is the truth is more important than the real truth – whatever that is.'

'Oh God!' groaned John, 'But what the hell am I supposed to do?'

'Don't worry!' replied Steadman, adopting a paternal and comforting tone. 'The whole world isn't as daft as Boldonbridge University. At least not yet. There are still plenty of sane people around who know fact from fiction. That's why you'll have to be very careful with the truth when push comes to shove. Now, this diary of yours. They'd want to see that, and the first thing they'd jump on would be the lies you've told about cliff bands and knife-edged ridges on the tourist route up Toubkal. And if you tell lies about that, you're perfectly capable of telling lies about buying drugs, aren't you? Get it?'

'And another thing,' he added. 'That nonsense about having sex with Tracy. That's another thing they'd jump on. Upper-class seducer of innocent proletarian girls. Thinks he can use deprived kids as sex objects. And they'd start investigating. You wouldn't want that business with young Fleetwood in the shower to be made public, would you? But let me tell you, that's just the sort of juicy tit-bit they'd love!'

Steadman paused again and shook his head. 'You're landing yourself right in it with your self-serving fantasies. And if you go up to the Duke of Edinburgh's Award people and demand a Silver medal on the strength of your Toubkal effort, what do you think would happen? Deliberately deceiving your teacher, sneaking off on an unauthorised and hair-brained adventure up a dangerous mountain and getting yourselves robbed into the bargain? They'd have a heart attack. They're already up to their eyes in the safety thing. They'd disown you. You'd be labelled as untrustworthy, deceitful and, above all, a dangerous liability. Dobson, of course, would have a field day.'

John felt crestfallen. Crushed. Down came those airy castles he'd been constructing.

'But,' he eventually managed to say, 'I thought I was doing something *good* when I went up Toubkal. You know, showing initiative, being positive and adventurous and that.'

'So you were, young man, so you were,' replied Steadman in a kindly tone. 'And, you know, I'm proud of you. You're a splendid lad. You're brave, enterprising and creative. You've probably saved this expedition. But you'd better start saving yourself. Now, we'll rewrite this whole Toubkal thing in your diary, shall we? First, though, we'd better clean it up a bit.'

Deftly he tore out the offending pages and ripped them to shreds.

'Now get your biro,' he said, 'and start writing. The truth this time: the truth, the whole truth, and nothing but the truth, if you don't mind. Oh, apart from one thing. You'd better include Joe Morris in your ascent of Toubkal.'

'But it's not true!'

'Of course it isn't, but it's what we call "necessary

expediency". It'll solve a lot of problems. You look bewildered? History, my man, history! After all, does anybody know what *really* happened when Henry Tudor beat Richard III on the field of Bosworth?'

A Ghastly Reality

So John lay on the bed and began to scribble furiously. Steadman looked at the youth as he lay sprawled across the sheets, and his mind began to seethe. Something was happening to him, something he couldn't control and that he'd long dreaded. Something he'd desperately wanted not to happen. That exquisite young body in the full bloom of adolescent youth, that fleeting moment before the onset of manhood coarsened it. And that eager, enthusiastic nature, so full of good things, and yet so vulnerable and so much in need of a defender. And 'one of us'. Too good to be true. A gift from heaven to a lonely, isolated and unfulfilled man who longed for marriage and a family, but knew he could never have it.

But go down that road, go where your body tells you to go, and shame, degradation and ruin await you. Exposure, ridicule, prison, the paedophile register, the hunted life of an outcast, a social leper.

A time for bitter reproach. He should never have brought him here in the first place. He'd deluded himself into thinking that his animal lusts were Christian compassion. Now he knew. There was only one solution: keep away from him. Cut loose *now* before the temptation overwhelms you. He had fallen in love with John.

The 'Commanding Officer'

So to the Sahara Desert. That morning, things were different. Steadman seemed to have changed: to have physically swelled up, become straight-backed, taller and openly military. He was now the 'Commanding Officer' who made all the decisions, quickly and decisively. It was, perhaps, what he'd always really wanted to be, thought John. Not a suburban vicar, but a soldier on active service.

Everything went with an exaggerated military precision. It was early parade, check kit and off to the bus station. When the archaeological relic of a bus eventually condescended to crawl up to the stand, a planned assault went into action to ensure that everybody got seats despite the frenetic rugger scrum that ensued.

Tracy insisted on sitting next to John, and, to bolster the 'Dirty Denby' image, he ostentatiously smooched the whole way over the mountains. The bus was crammed to the roof — young men in jeans, veiled women, white-robed exotics, even four goats – and the windows were filthy. As a result he only fleetingly glimpsed the unfolding grandeur as they wriggled their way over the dry, stony mountains and trundled down a long valley, following a dried-up river bed – a relic of wetter times long gone by – which eventually lost itself in an immense yellow emptiness. In dribs and drabs he became aware of a Biblical land of mud brick fortresses, palm trees and crushing heat.

Not the Sort of Place a Vicar would Know About?

Finally they staggered into the little town of Zagora. Squeezing themselves off the bus and disentangling themselves from the jostling crowd of passengers, they found themselves in a desolate, sun-blasted dump of a place, which struck John as an uneasy blend of a one-horse Wild West town and a set for the film of *Lawrence of Arabia*.

'Cor, worra hole!' exclaimed Rob.

'We'll be spending the night at Madame's place,' declared Steadman as he shepherded the cavalcade down a dusty, litter-strewn alley and ushered them into a low, flat-roofed building. A battered neon sign above the door, half in English and half in Arabic, said 'Garden of Paradise Billiard Saloon'.

'Who's Madame?' asked John.

'Never you mind!' growled Steadman aggressively.

John recoiled at the unexpected hostility.

'Howay, Bob lad, tell wor like!' said Rob, continuing to talk the ostentatious Geordie he'd been using all day and obviously sensing something deliciously dirty.

To John's bewildered surprise, this semi-insolent request was greeted with a big, friendly grin. 'All in good time, young man. You'll learn soon enough.'

Inside was a shabby reception hall decked out in the gaudy splendour of a run-down amusement arcade. A few beaded curtains concealed little cubicles whose dim red lights gave a hint of the precise nature of the 'Paradise' on offer.

Behind a big dusty desk was a vast and voluminously fat white woman with a shock of brilliantly white peroxided hair and lurid red lipstick. Her rolls of pale elephantine flesh seemed to ooze out of a short and barely adequate skirt, while her huge, balloon-like breasts were only nominally concealed by her scanty, unbuttoned blouse. A damp cigarette hung from her lips. This, it seemed, was 'Madame'.

Steadman addressed her in fluent German.

'Where on earth's *she* sprung from?' asked John.

Steadman ignored the question and went on talking German.

'Hey, Bob!' said Jim. 'Ah thought all the women roond heor went roon in veils an' that an' were locked up in harems, like?'

At which Steadman turned round with a big, beaming smile and a knowing wink. 'Not *all* women, Jimmy lad. Some women have – shall we say? – a different role to play.'

'Where's she from?'

'She's from Hamburg.'

'That's in Germany, innit? So what's she doin' heor then?'

'That's a long story.'

'Hamburg?' echoed Rob. 'Me uncle when he were in the army, like, knew all aboot that place. Why, it's not the sorta place I thought a vicar would knaa aboot.'

'I know a lot more than you think.'

'Howay, tell us, then!'

'All in good time, lads! Meanwhile, just think what Brian's going to say when he hears that we stayed in this place.'

Oh, Bob Steadman, *do* watch it! (This little exchange was to be the genesis of a 'Dirty Vicar' legend, which was to grow exponentially with every telling. What was a vicar doing in the red light district of Hamburg where the likes of 'Madame' hung out? And just how did he get to know her so well? Brian Dobson *did* hear about it and, in due course, was to make full use of the unexpected windfall.)

A little later they all settled down on cushions around a low table and drank glasses of hot, sugary mint tea. Steadman went into a tight whispering huddle with Rob and Jim. John tried to join in.

'*Do* let Rob have his say!' snapped Steadman. 'There *are* other people in the world you know!'

'But —'

'Yes, John, I know what you're going to say, so just keep quiet for a change!'

Another hostile rebuff.

Hurt and bemused, John stood up. 'I think I'll go outside and take some photographs.'

Hostile growl. 'No you won't! I'm not having you wandering about and getting into trouble. You just stay here.'

A New Dispensation

The sun went down in a pink glow and a velvety darkness descended on the dusty land. They spent the night sprawled on the flat roof of the house. As Tracy prepared to spread herself out beside John, Jim grabbed her arm and pulled her away.

'Howay, lass that's enough o' him! Geordie lads not good enough, eh? Gorra 'ave a birra class 'ave we? Well, not any more!'

For a long time John lay on his grubby rug, staring at the stars. A new dispensation seemed to have emerged; one which he neither liked nor understood. Things had changed, as if a box had been shaken up and its contents rearranged in a different pattern. On Toubkal he'd been the leader who'd made the decisions, and on whose ability to talk French they'd all depended. But now, with Steadman firmly in charge, he'd been demoted. Made redundant. More, indeed, than merely made redundant: he'd been discarded.

Jim and Rob had changed. With Kev and his gang safely out of the way, they seemed to have swelled up and taken over the positions they'd left vacant. They were no longer allies, but a dominant and excluding group whose exaggerated Geordie talk proclaimed their aggressive elitism. Michael, with his keen eye for the flow of things, had joined them and so apparently had the two girls. That left him isolated. The camaraderie that he thought he'd built up in the course of the Toubkal adventure had mysteriously vanished. It was all a bitter disappointment.

And just what *had* got into Steadman? He was no longer the protecting father figure he'd so depended on before. He'd become a sarcastic bully, openly ingratiating himself with the others and getting cheap street cred by continually snubbing him. Obviously he had offended him in some way or other, but *how*? What had he gone and done to deserve this?

His one remaining ally seemed to be Morris. He too was a discarded pariah, continually snubbed by Steadman, who treated him as an unwanted piece of baggage to be publicly humiliated at every opportunity.

Bitter Sweet in the Desert

Three days of camelling in the desert followed. For John it was a bitter-sweet experience; good and bad entwined like a coil of multicoloured string. There was the sense of adventure and challenge. Perched uncomfortably on the swaying back of his camel, his increasingly sore backside, the ferocious and deadening heat, the continual thirst, the taste of the chlorinated water in his mouth, the noise of the camels: a deliciously scatological 'organ concert' in every meaning of the phrase.

And there was the harsh beauty of the desert: The gravel, the dust, the sand dunes, the vivid green of the oases with their rustling palm trees and timeless mud brick walls. Hazy and leached of colour as it cringed under the afternoon heat, in the cool of the evening it seemed to awaken from its torpor. Under the long rays of the setting sun, it burst out into a blaze of glowing colours: the rich brown of the rocks, the warm yellow of the sands, the vivid blue of the distant mountains. Then came those wonderful silent nights under the brilliant immensities of the universe. Here was the world of the great explorers: René Caillié struggling over the Sahara, Lawrence of Arabia braving the sun-blasted hell of the Nefud. This was what he wanted.

At the same time, there was the bitterness of his rejection by the others and, especially, by Steadman. Isolated, he gravitated towards the Moroccan camel drivers and to the blue-robed, turbaned Tuareg guide in particular. He carefully observed him as he made his 'desert bread' every morning, assiduously photographing the whole complicated process. While Jim and the others disdained eating the finished product – 'Ah'm not eatin' no Pakkie crap, me!' – he gorged himself on it and profusely thanked the man. He watched fascinated as he performed the elaborate and alien ritual of his Muslim prayers. Using his now superfluous rags of French, he asked about Islam. What did Muslims think of Christians? How did they view Jesus Christ? The man seemed flattered by his attentions and replied in a torrent of badly accented and almost incomprehensible French.

A bond seemed to develop. The man let him help with cooking the desert bread and boiling up the tea. At night he was invited to drink tea with the Moroccans. Seated cross-legged on the sand under the glittering stars, they conversed. 'Vous êtes different. Peut être vous êtes destines d'être Islamist.'

John glowed. It was a deep compliment. Destined to be a great explorer like Burkhardt or Richard Burton? That *would* be something!

'Gannin' Pakkie, are yer?' sneered Rob as John settled down to sleep.

'What's Up Wi' Bob?'

On the evening of the third day they returned to Zagora. Leaving the camels with the Moroccan drivers, they strolled back to Madame's place. Michael sidled up to John, and for the first time in three days, began to talk to him.

'What's up wi' Bob?' he said.

'Oh, has something happened?'

'Well, 'e's gone all funny, like. Not 'is normal self. Ah mean, 'e's being ower rude ter you, like. Ah divvent knaa why. Ah mean, Ah thought you twos were proppa mates, like. Now 'e's not talkin' ter the rest o' us. Seems 'e's reet arsed off wi' the lotta us.'

John turned round to see Steadman walking behind him in vigorous conversation with the Tuareg guide. Just then Tracy walked up to him and tried to interrupt him, only to be brushed aside with an unfriendly shove.

Michael was right. Something *had* got into Steadman. But what was it?

Inner Crisis; a Curse, not a Blessing

The fact was that Steadman was having a mental crisis. The desert, that far-off yellow blur to the south where the ancient river lost itself in the scorching sands, that ferocious environment with its strange and fearsome people with their alien culture and complex languages, *there* was something worthy of him! Vicar in a dreary north country suburb, fighting a losing battle to ignite a tiny flame of spirituality in silly old women and inadequate adolescents? What a waste of himself! And these kids he'd been landed with in Morocco? So crushingly banal! So petty and trivial! Raise their snouts from the muck they wallowed in? Fat chance! Pie in the sky!

Christianity in Moorside! At best a trough of glutinous treacle, a vague sort of do-goodery. You were always having to apologise for being a Christian, always having to kow-tow before the supposed 'superior wisdom' of the scientific atheists at the university. To think about the realities of death and the transience of life evinced a psychotic lack of mental hygiene. So you airbrushed them out or smothered them in that glutinous treacle which passed for 'post-religious enlightenment'.

But here in the desert it was different. Uneducated, bigoted, crassly superstitious, unbelievably narrow... these Muslims here were all that, but nevertheless wiser than all the 'liberated sophisticates' of Boldonbridge. They weren't embarrassed to talk about God. They knew that death and eternity were realities that had to be faced and not drowned in a barrel of treacle.

The wild was calling him. Telling him to break out of the cloying cocoon of Moorside and be true to his real self. But there was an even more pressing need to cut loose and flee. It was there, two yards in front of him. John Denby.

John the ridiculously beautiful... that fleeting culmination of adolescent beauty before adulthood coarsened it. At this precise moment, that gorgeous body obsessed him! Those delicately muscled legs, that glorious backside rippling so seductively under the tight jeans. That shock of blonde hair. Those lustrous eyes. And not only the body. There was nothing petty or banal about him! That developing mind, so full of curiosity and wonder. He could see things that the others simply couldn't see. In all the dross around him, he was the nugget of gold. A soulmate.

His whole being seemed to light up when he approached John. He knew what he wanted to do. But go down that road, let your iron self-control slip for just a moment, and ruin and shame would follow. John Denby was the Forbidden Fruit of the Garden sent to test his resolve. The glorious Song of the Sirens luring him to shame, squalor and degradation. In olden times he would have thought he was the Devil incarnate, deliberately luring him to destruction.

Once more, just as four nights ago in Marrakesh, he was

filled with self-disgust. He'd allowed himself to flatter the youth, build him up; yes, bring him to Morocco at his own expense. He'd wilfully deceived himself into thinking that it was an act of Christian charity, whereas it was no more than pure lust, perverted and sordid lust. Now he was paying the price. The message was clear: push the tempter aside before he destroys you.

Yet at the same time, he felt pangs of remorse. Shame at the hurt he was causing an innocent youth by his sudden rebuttal. Shame at the obvious bewilderment and upset at the sudden and inexplicable rejection. Poor innocent creature, who needed his help and guidance and instead got the crazy lurching of a perverted lust! John Denby's beauty was a curse, not a blessing.

Discomfort

Back at Marrakesh, tired, dusty and sweaty after an acutely uncomfortable bus journey.

'Well, that were a reet waste o' time!' declared Jim as they stumbled back to the pension.

John winced. It had been a wonderful experience, a dip into a colourful world of challenge and fulfilment. The only bad bit had been some of the people he'd been forced to go with.

A bad-tempered wait for the shower ensued. A wretched apology of a thing at the best of times, the sudden demand for its services was too much for the spindly old contraption. A trickle of tepid water dwindled to a few drops, and then stopped altogether.

'Jesus!' snorted Rob. 'Can't them Pakkies do anything proppa, like?'

'Now He's Really Gone Nutty'

Then Steadman called everybody together for a meeting in the courtyard. Hair all awry, wild-eyed and with bushy eyebrows quivering, he looked to John as if he'd just had an encounter with the electric chair.

'Cor,' muttered Michael, 'now he's really gone nutty! That's all we need!'

To John he seemed to be putting on a show and hamming it up badly, as in 'high melodrama' mode, he launched forth.

'Well, chaps, we've had our little jolly. Now it's the *real* thing!' Pause. 'Yes, the *real thing*!' He spat these words out as if he were a venomous snake spitting poison at its prey; the prey, perhaps, being the despised idiots with whom he forced to deal? 'We're going back in time. Back to the third world. Back to the *real* world! ! Another pause as he fixed his X-ray eyes on Morris. 'So, if you're into dried food, professionalism and safety... *well just forget it*!' More metaphorical poison spat at Morris. 'Because from now on there's going to be *no* concession to suburban prissiness. Are you up to it?' Melodramatic and hammy pause. 'Because all I can offer you is exhaustion, fear, vile food and the gut rot.'

After an even longer and even more hammy melodramatic pause, he continued in a gentle tone. 'And, for those of you who survive the ordeal, I can give you the honourable title of "Mountain Explorer". Any questions?'

'Bloody hell!' said Jim. 'We're not gannin' fuckin' Pakkie again, is we?'

'Yes we *is* gannin' fuckin' Pakkie again!' replied Steadman, picking up the challenge with relish and consciously imitating Jim's rich Geordie accent. 'And, my boy, it's like it or lump it!'

With that, he screwed up his eyes and flashed a withering beam of metaphorical X-rays in the direction of Morris, who squirmed uncomfortably as if he were a small boy who hadn't done his homework properly. John felt a pang of sympathy for him as a fellow pariah.

Then Steadman went into 'Commanding Officer' mode as

he reeled off a stream of orders, in a staccato machine gun style.

'Still playin' soldiers, him!' murmured Michael. 'Jus' like a liddell kid.'

'Tomorrow morning. Zero nine hundred hours. Got that? Synchronised watches? Good! Zero nine hundred hours, bus to Imlil. Then march to Tacheddirt. After that, two groups. Hard men will climb Angour Mountain and cross Aksoual Mountain. That's going to involve some *real* climbing.'

He glared at John. 'So, Jonny boy, you might be seeing some *real* cliff bands and not the imaginary ones you wrote about in that ridiculous diary of yours! Cliff bands four hundred feet high on the doddle route up the Toubkal? Did you *really* expect anybody to believe that kind of infantile rubbish? Well, we might just see if you really *are* the great rock climber you seem to think you are. The north face of Aksoual will be rather more than strolling up an easy path. Will you be able to hack it? I wonder. I really do!'

While Jim and Rob sniggered, John blushed bright red. What had he done to deserve *this*? Handle those cliff bands? Yes, he bloody well would – and *how*!

The staccato stream of orders resumed. 'The others will follow the path over the Likempt Pass. I'll do the hard stuff. Joe, you deal with the weaker bretheren.' He cast a contemptuous glance at Morris. 'You might just be able to manage that, I think.

'Then we'll go down to Amouzeate and back to Imlil over the Ouaanoums pass. Six days. All we have time for. Because of the antics of Kev and his merry men, we'll have to go home early. I'll wangle a flight home. We're strapped for cash, so no taxis. Local bus: cheapest going. One donkey. No guide. Now go and organise yourselves. Be ready at zero seven hundred hours.'

Morris got up and tried to speak.

'Nothing useful *you* can add, Joe Morris!' snapped Steadman. 'I've said all that needs to be said.'

Visibly infuriated, Morris stalked off, muttering to himself.

'There's gonna be shit flyin' roond one day soon,' Michael whispered in John's ear. 'Bob canna gan on treatin' Joe like that. Joe's norra liddell bairn, yer knaa!'

Yes, sighed John to himself, Steadman *has* gone nutty all right! And *why*, for Christ's sake? Still, here, at any rate, was his chance to do some *real* climbing! He prepared himself with vigour that night.

Geriatric Bus

A grumpy trail to the bus station early in the morning. This time the bus was even more dilapidated than before. It was as if Steadman had used the black arts to conjure up a machine that did justice to his masochistic mood. Probably he would have preferred a camel, but this seemed to be the best he could manage. It reminded John of an old Roman helmet that he'd once seen in a museum: so ancient and corroded that it was only held together by congealed mud; wash it, and it would fall apart.

Hideously overloaded, the contraption groaned and spluttered its way up the road like a moribund camel in the last throes of some repulsive intestinal disease. At increasingly long intervals it stopped to belch and gasp. In a final paroxysm of doomed effort it just managed to stagger up the last steep hill before expiring in the middle of Imlil, like some geriatric marathon runner heroically defying the odds. A frenetic rugger scrum ensued as they extracted themselves from the anarchic throng of passengers.

'Jesus Christ!' sighed Jim. 'How much more o' this Pakkie crap are we gonna have ter take? Let's get a shift on wi' the climbin'! That's what I came for.'

Humiliation

Steadman hustled them up to the cafe, where the owner recognised them. Greeting them effusively, he brought along a tray-load of mint tea. A scrawny and cadaverous local in a brown robe and white skullcap was summoned. A long and boring hiatus ensued as he and Steadman began an intense conversation in Berber. From the figures they kept scribbling on a scrap of paper, John guessed that they were haggling over the price of a donkey and a driver.

As the negotiations dragged tediously on, the youngsters grew restive.

'Cor, look what's comin' up the road!' exclaimed Rob suddenly.

They craned their necks over the balcony and saw an enormously fat European woman waddling up the street beneath them. Only nominally clothed, her vast, wobbling backside was stuffed into a minute pair of shorts, little more than an upgraded G-string, which disappeared up her cavernous bum crack and only belatedly emerged at her waist. A tattered suggestion of a bra scarcely concealed her huge, flabby breasts, which flapped around like overloaded shopping bags. Probably she was a Dutch or Danish tourist making a 'sexually liberated' statement. Backwards and forwards under the balcony she went.

'What the fuck's she on aboot?' said Jim. 'Walkin' roond showin' her tits an' that?'

'Probably wants a birra shaftin',' replied Rob.

'Yer'd 'ave ter be pretty bloody horny before yer went up that!' snorted Jim. 'It'd be like shaggin' a rubber mattress.'

'Ever done that, Jonnie lad, yer arl porvort?' he added.

Delighted at being included in the group again, John responded with gusto. 'Only once when I was desperate.'

'Aw give ower, yer dorty pigs!' cried Tracy. 'Can't yer talk about oot else but sex?'

But the intervention had come too late. A kind of resonance had begun, with each young male having to prove his sex cred by capping his mate's obscene remark with an even fouler one. In the end, the more articulate John outdid them all with a peculiarly repulsive comment, enhanced by vigorous gestures with his fingers. He even managed to shock Jim.

'Cor, you *are* a sexy 'ard porvort, ye!'

Raucous peels of laughter duly exploded. John glowed with satisfaction. He'd scored big time. 'Dirty Denby' was back in business.

Suddenly the old Berber sitting next to Steadman let fly a tirade, waving his arms about and thumping the table in front of him.

'What's all this then?'

'I'm being given a dressing-down about Western decadence,' growled Steadman. 'He's saying that one day all Muslims, good and true, are going to smite you lot down with the sword of Islam, if you must know.'

He glared angrily at John. 'And you, young man, by your eloquent gestures have caused him to double the price of the donkey and driver, which I thought had just been settled.'

John grinned furtively at the others. 'Oh, er, sorry. But, well, a bloke's a bloke, you know.'

'Bloke, are we?' replied Steadman with an angry sneer. '*Bloke*? For heaven's sake shut up and stop showing off!'

He paused for a moment, as if he were reloading his gun for a second salvo, and then let fly. '*You* may think you have impressed your mates, but you haven't impressed *me*! Stop pretending to be what you're not! I know what you are, even if the others don't!'

There was a frosty silence as everybody stared at John, who blushed bright red.

A leering Jim dug him in the ribs. 'Ah knaa what yer really are an' all!'

John's carefully constructed image was in ruins.

'Cor, John,' whispered Michael, 'Bob really has gorra a down on yers noo. Ah mean, what 'ave yer gone an done ter him, like?'

John didn't reply. He seethed with anger and went over and sat down by Morris, who'd remained silent throughout the dialogue. The lame duck alliance was renewed – and with interest.

Going Native

Eventually Steadman scooped them up and led them out of the village and into the Biblical land beyond. The green, terraced fields, the ancient mud brick villages, the vast wrinkled mountains beyond them, the silence… it was a gentle ointment that soothed John's wounded ego. 'Here is a deep reality,' it seemed to say. 'What do your petty squabbles really matter?'

His spirit soared when Steadman led them to a large mud brick house, which looked like a miniature castle. Clambering up a ladder, they entered an upper chamber. Richly carpeted and with cushions surrounding a low table, it could have been a picture out of one of his exploration books. It was the sort of place that Richard Burton would have stayed in when he so famously went to Mecca.

After an effusive welcome from an old man in a robe and turban, with his entourage of similarly attired exotics, they all sat down on the cushions round the table. Supper consisted of a vast tagine eaten with spoons out of a communal bowl.

While Steadman and the old man began a vigorous conversation in Berber, the others began muttering among themselves.

'How's we gannin ter climb bloody mountains if we's 'avin' ter live on this Pakkie crap, eh?'

'Can't we 'ave a proppa place ter kip, like?'

'Me mam wouldn't half dee her nut if she knew Ah were kippin' in a Pakkie hoos.'

John remained silent. He loathed this racist talk, but he didn't dare to say anything in case Steadman flew at him again and accused him of being a selfish little prig. And suppose that, like poor old Morris, he was banned from climbing the mountains? He would simply go bananas! It was all so crazy. Daft. But that was the way things were turning out. Steadman, the one-time friend, sponsor and protector, had turned into a primed hand grenade that might at any moment explode with devastating consequences. Why? He was damned if he knew.

They spent the night on the roof of the house, stretched out under the stars.

'No petting or snogging please, chaps,' said Steadman as they snuggled down together. 'They don't like that sort of thing here.'

'Them Pakkies!' groaned Rob, 'No booze, no sex, eatin' shit all day! Worra life!'

'Yeah!' added Jim. 'They can keep it!'

John winced again.

Gut Rot and Culture Clash

Morning came, lighting up the ancient world in a blaze of brilliant light. But John's spiritual ecstasy was short-lived. Suddenly his innards began to churn up and down as if he had a spin drier inside him. A frantic dash down the ladders ensued. He only just managed to reach the disgusting little toilet at the far end of the garden in time before an explosion of liquid squitter blasted out of him. It was a narrow escape, and a timely warning. A few seconds delay, and disaster would have struck, and he had no spare clothes to change into if he messed himself. Then what? Didn't bear thinking about. As a precaution he swallowed a double dose of his anti-squitter pills.

That day saw an easy ramble along a broad trail, which led to the little village of Tacheddirt. Ambling over a gentle pass, they left any lingering remnants of tourism behind them and entered an ancient and unblemished world: more green, terraced fields; more ancient mud brick houses piled up on each other like cardboard boxes in a warehouse; more wild and craggy mountains surging up behind them, grand, snow-streaked and seemingly inviolate.

They were a compact little group: the donkey laden with the rucksacks; the donkey driver, brown-robed, bearded and sullen; then Jim, Rob and the girls; then the lame duck group, Morris and John; and striding out in front, Steadman. That morning he had gone ostentatiously native, with a blue Tuareg turban round his head and his large muscular body draped in a white Moroccan robe.

'What's yer dressin' up like this for?' asked Jim aggressively. 'Ah mean, yer looks reet daft, like!'

Pure insolence. John braced himself for the inevitable explosion. But, oddly enough, it just didn't come.

Steadman smiled back from his, by now quite substantially bearded face: 'Pure commerce, my man, pure commerce! If they think I'm like one of them, they won't charge us too much. After the antics of Kev and his merry men, we're pretty short of cash.'

Again, John seethed at the way that the others could be as cheeky as they liked to Steadman without getting the stinging rebukes he was constantly getting. It was all so unfair! All part of the inexplicable change that had come over him. And this new sartorial display of his? It was more than just a commercial ploy: it marked a change of his whole identity. But change into what?

When they stopped for a rest, Steadman made a little fire, and producing a little teapot and some glasses from his rucksack, brewed up some mint tea which he duly dispensed.

Then he handed round some hunks of dry Moroccan bread. While John devoured it ravenously, the others nibbled a few bits of their slabs and then tossed them contemptuously aside.

They soon reached Tachddirt, another timeless collection of mud brick houses, piled up against the mountainside, cardboard box style. Robed men and veiled women working in the green, terraced fields completed the Biblical scene. Steadman immediately dashed ahead and hailed an old man in a brown robe. An emotional embrace was followed by another of his fervent conversations in Berber.

'Not another Pakkie love-in!' groaned Jim. 'Jesus, what the fuck does 'e think 'e's bloody deein', like?'

This was too much for John, who felt compelled to retaliate. 'He's an explorer, like Burckhardt and Burton.'

'Who the fuck's them?' Dismissive sneer.

John withdrew. It was no use trying to argue. After a brief taste of an alien culture, Jim and Rob seemed to have rebounded back into a truculent Geordie shell. Impenetrable and impervious. Don't even think of reason here. After a tiny, tentative opening, the blinds had come crashing down. It was all so sad.

Steadman beckoned to them and the old man led them into the bottom storey of one of the mud brick houses that climbed up the hillside like a giant staircase. Inside they were assailed by a faecal animal stench, and through the darkness they dimly glimpsed some big and very greasy sheep. Huddled on a pile of straw in a far corner were a couple of old, veiled women.

'Is this where they put their women, like?' exclaimed Maureen. 'Why, me mam wouldn't half be playin' war if she saw that!'

'What do you expect?' sneered Jim. 'They're Pakkies, aren't they?'

Steadman grinned broadly, apparently relishing their discomfiture.

They were ushered up a ladder to the next storey where they found a relatively cosy den with carpets on the walls and the floor and a big picture of the Kaaba in Mecca prominently displayed. Animal stink wafted through the gaps in the floorboards and there was no glass in the window.

'I wonder how the Committee's going to take this sort of thing,' Morris muttered to John. 'That ladder's not exactly safe, and as for the hygiene… It's risking the health and safety of young people, you know.'

He was clearly gathering ammunition for a devastating counter-attack when they got back to Boldonbridge.

John sighed inwardly. Why, oh why, did Steadman have to so deliberately antagonise poor old Joe Morris? He could so easily have made him into an ally. He seemed blatantly to be sailing into trouble. He was like a small boy sticking his tongue out at the teacher and wondering why he landed in detention. Crazy!

They duly squatted down on the cushioned floor and waited. Eventually a side door opened and some veiled women entered, carrying a large earthen bowl and some sheets of dry, unleavened bread. Having with considerable difficulty placed the steaming bowl in the middle of the group, they handed everybody a metal spoon and then shuffled out. The old man who was sitting cross-legged next to Steadman signalled for everybody to start eating.

'Worraboot his women?' exclaimed Maureen. 'Divvent they get owt ter eat?'

'Women don't eat with men here,' replied Steadman. 'Their job is to prepare the food and look after the house. They eat what the men leave over.'

'That's one thing the Pakkies *have* got right!' declared Jim aggressively. 'Woman gets yer tea and parts her legs!'

'Eeee, yer male chauvinist pig!' sighed Tracy.

More Gut Rot
After an hour the panting and gasping women cleared away the bowl and the spoons and everybody settled down to sleep on the floor. Soon night descended and imprisoned them in an impenetrable pitch-black darkness. John dozed off.

Suddenly the room seemed to erupt. Unseen bits of blackness were crashing round. A big foot landed painfully on John's stomach. Angry voices stabbed the darkness.

'Gerroff me bloody legs!'

'How the fuck dee yer gerrot o' heor?'

Clunk! Crash! Thump! Then deep-throated coughs and gurgles.

'Jesus! There gans the tag-whatever-they-calls-the muck!'

A torch beam picked out a woebegone Jim.

Steadman's voice boomed out, 'Oh, Jim, you *idiot*! You've thrown up all over the rucksacks!'

'No I ain't! Ah gorrit all oot the windee! Wanna take a look?'

'No thanks, I'd rather not. Good shooting, anyway!'

A few more bumps and crashes and silence returned. John tried to resume his slumbers.

A little later there was another earthquake. Crash! Clatter! Clunk! Bang!

'Oyer!'

'Watch oot yer basstadd!'

Then an almighty crash.

From the unseen depths below came the bleating of sheep and a raucous, *'Fucking hell*!'

Steadman's torch flashed again to reveal a missing Rob.

'What's up now?'

'Rob's got the shits.'

Light off. Darkness again. Then more clumps and crashes. Unseen feet squashing squelchy bodies.

'Mind oot will yers! Yin's wor legs!'

Torch on again. Rob revealed in the spotlight.

'Christ! Worra do! There's nowt left in us!'

Steadman, obviously relishing the situation, went into 'tough explorer' mode: 'No problem, old thing! All explorers get the shits. You're not a proper explorer unless you've had the shits. If you die of the shits, you're in distinguished company. Livingstone died of it and so did Francis Drake.'

'Thanks for nothing!'

The torch went out and semi sleep was resumed.

'Usin' Up His Nine Lives'

Suddenly there was yet another earthquake.

Steadman's torch went on again. 'Right, chaps, who's for Angour Mountain?'

John spoke first. 'Me! I'll go!'

An anxious, nail-biting wait followed while Steadman

stared him in the face. Oh God! Is he going to reject me? I'll go crazy if he does!

Then came the blessed reprieve. 'OK. Anybody else?'

Rob and Jim spoke up. 'Me!' 'And me!'

'How's your guts, Rob?'

'Nae frets. Nowt left inside. It's all oot, like!'

'Girls?'

'Na!' said Tracy. 'Me an' Maureen's stayin' here today.'

'I'll stay with 'em an' all,' added Michael.

Emerging from his sleeping bag, Morris spoke up. 'I'll come too. I need a few hard mountains for my CV.'

'No you won't!' replied Steadman in a hard and aggressive voice. 'You'll stay here and look after the weaker brethren. That's your role!'

He could have been squashing an irritating fly.

Michael nudged John. 'Bob's usin' up his nine lives reet quick! He'll 'ave ter pay for this, yer knaa!'

A Real Explorer Now, But Still the Odd Man Out

It was into the dim blue world outside, a cool place where vast, black mountains reared their anarchic heads into a mass of glittering stars. They formed up into a line and Steadman led them slowly up a broad, stony track that wound its way up the valley ahead of them. The flood of the morning found them on top of a high pass. All around them was a pageant of rugged mountains, seemingly restored to life by the friendly rays of the rising sun. Resurrection. Life after death.

Here Steadman announced breakfast, made a little fire and brewed up sweet, sugary mint tea. Extracting a roll of dry, unleavened bread from the depths of his rucksack, he tore off strips of it and handed them round.

'Is this all we're gerrin?'

'Yes. We're real explorers now, not pampered suburbanites

on a jolly!' Revenge being taken by proxy on the dreary suburban inhabitants of Moorside?

'Time for a dump,' declared John. 'Anybody got my bog roll?'

In an effort to be a 'good expeditioner' he'd donated his last remaining one to the community.

'Na. Used it all up!' replied Rob.

'Bugger!'

'You don't need bog paper!' snorted Steadman dismissively. 'Just do what the locals do.'

'What's that?'

'Use water and your left hand.'

'Ugh! That's disgusting!'

'Too precious, are we? I can see you're not a proper explorer!'

Another put-down. But don't argue. Don't want to join poor old Morris in the detention class, do you?

'Well, get on with it, boy! We haven't all day to waste on your *toilette*!'

John slipped behind a convenient boulder. Luckily there was some coarse grass available for the 'cleansing operation'.

'Got the shits?' asked Jim as he returned.

'Not yet. Solid as a rock!'

'Thought so! Some blerks is privileged, eh?'

He was still the odd man out.

Mountain Grandeur

Steadman led them down the other side of the pass for a short way and then turned left and entered a deep, gloomy canyon, which wound its contorted way into the heart of a huge, flat-topped mountain, which loomed over them. As they squeezed their way between the enclosing walls and heaved themselves up the numerous rock steps, John felt a rush of excitement; that childhood thrill of secret passages in ruined castles.

'Cor, this is better than Toubkal!'

A scramble up a cliff face followed, and they emerged onto a flat, windswept plateau hemmed in on three sides by plunging crags. It was a bit like the flight deck of a gigantic aircraft carrier.

'Lads!' declared Steadman. 'You've just climbed eleven thousand foot Angour Mountain!'

He then led them to the southern rim of the plateau which ended suddenly in a sharp edge, almost as if the world was flat after all and they had inadvertently discovered its edge. The boys sat down with their feet dangling ostentatiously in the empty nothingness, each young male trying to outdo the others in a display of nonchalant bravado.

Away to the south, beyond the void, a wall of mountains surged upwards with an arrogant disdain. To the left was a high, pointed, but seemingly accessible peak.

'Is that Aksoual?' asked John.

'No! No!' snapped Steadman. 'Aksoual's the peak to the right!'

With a sweep of his arm he indicated a great, craggy spire that leapt skywards in a tumble of slabs and cliffs.

'Christ!'

'You didn't imagine that I was going to let you have it easy, did you?' The bearded, turbaned face broke into a supercilious grin: 'You'll be getting your sheer cliffs all right, Jonnie boy! Are you sure you will be able to handle them?'

'Yes.'

'Well, we'll have to see, won't we?'

A mix of fears welled up in John: fear of the appalling mountain in front of him, fear of failing, and worst of all, fear of being forbidden to even try.

Lunch followed. More sweet, sticky mint tea. More sheets of dry unleavened bread; cardboard, it seemed, masquerading as something edible.

Then Steadman led them down an airy and precipitous ridge that swept off the southwest corner of the plateau and plunged down towards Tacheddirt.

Kamikaze Mission?

In mid-afternoon, dusty and tired, they stumbled back to the house.

Morris met them. 'Well, did you make it?'

'Of course we did!' snapped Steadman.

A faint look of disappointment flickered across Morris's face. Michael, standing next to him, winked at John.

'Right, men!' declared Steadman – now, apparently in 'Victorious General' mode, 'You can have a brief rest, and then get yourselves ready for Phase Two, the assault on the North Face of Aksoual Mountain. We leave in an hour's time.'

'All of us?' asked Morris.

'No, just the mountaineers.'

'But oughtn't I to come along too?' said Morris. 'I've been studying Aksoual and, frankly, it looks pretty dangerous. You'll need two trained adults with you if you're thinking of taking a group of youngsters up there.'

No response from Steadman.

Hesitantly, Morris persisted. 'I could send the two girls over the Likempt Pass with Mahomet and the donkey. Michael could go with them. He's a steady and sensible lad. Responsibility would do him good.'

'Don't bother! This is a serious mountaineering expedition. I don't want to be burdened with incompetents!'

The stinging rebuke was visible to John and Michael, if not, perhaps, to the others.

Morris was moved to a barbed retaliation. 'You *do* know the way, don't you? Taking untrained youngsters up a dangerous mountain face is downright irresponsible, you know. What if there was a serious accident? You wouldn't have a leg to stand on at an inquest.'

Steadman didn't deign to reply.

'Bob's pushin' it!' Michael whispered to John.

John remained silent. Fear was welling up in him again. Fear of the vast, precipitous mountain looming up before him. Fear, also, of Steadman: no longer his avuncular protector, but a primed land mine, requiring the skills of a bomb disposal expert to defuse. Fear that Steadman might suddenly consign him, shamed and disgraced, to the rearguard. He climbed up the ladder to the carpeted living room and sorted out his rucksack.

A little later Michael sidled up to him. 'Are yer sure yer's gannin' up that mountain with Bob, like?' he whispered with an anxious look on his face.

'Yes, why not?'

'Well, Ah mean, Bob's gone nutty, yer knaa! Joe says he don't know the way an' that he's jus' wantin' ter show the folks back home that he's a proppa climber, like, an' not jus' an ole vicar. But he's norra a proppa climber, Joe says. It could all end in sommat right rotten, yer knaa. Ah wouldn't gan, John, really Ah wouldn't.'

'Don't be such a wimp, Mike!' snorted John. 'I'll be OK.'

But beneath the adolescent bravado, he wondered if Mike were right. He wasn't the brightest light on the tree – not by a long chalk! – but he was gifted with sound common sense. For a moment, he hesitated. But then he had no choice, had he? Supposing he chickened out now, and the others succeeded in climbing the mountain? He'd be confirmed as a posturing poofter. He went down the ladder and joined the climbing group outside.

'Right, men!' boomed Steadman, looking more manic than ever. 'Final briefing! Tonight we climb a third of a way up the mountain. Early tomorrow morning we make the final assault on the peak. Then it's down the south face to rendezvous with the rearguard at seventeen hundred hours.'

'Oh yes!' he added as an afterthought. 'I've told Mahomet where to meet us. He knows the spot.'

With that, the little group shouldered their packs and followed him through the green terraced fields. John felt like a Kamikaze pilot taking off on his final suicide mission: a tangle of exaltation and dread.

A Night of Awe and Dread

Steadman led them into the jaws of an immense canyon that seemed to slash the mountain ahead of them into two clumsy halves. It was a savage, unfinished sort of place, full of huge, brutal boulders and crude, overhanging crags.

After a while, he turned to the right and clambered up a stony gully, which cut its way through a maze of slabs and cliffs. Above them a colossal rock face lurched crazily skywards towards terrifying and seemingly unclimbable heights. It was vaster and more hostile than anything John had ever seen before. Fear mounted: were Joe and Michael right after all? But keep going and try not to show it.

Eventually they emerged onto a broad shelf, as if the mountain had taken a little breather from its relentless, puritanical steepness. Here they settled down for the night. Producing some twigs and tinder from his rucksack, Steadman brewed up some mint tea and then handed round more sheets of dry, unleavened Moroccan bread.

Wrapping his threadbare old rug around him, John snuggled up against his rucksack and tried to keep warm. His nagging fears were absorbed – indeed, positively sucked out of him – by the sheer grandiose immensity of their situation. The fading light. The great peaks glowing a fiery red as they caught the rays of the setting sun. The wild, improbable towers of rock thrusting their insolent way into the darkening sky. The enormous mountain face above him, cascading crazily down like a waterfall of rock, threatening to sweep away their little perch in a riot of anarchic boulders.

Then the oncoming night, the wave of blackness, the deep, slow silence. The closing down of life. Far above them the myriads of stars. This was not for humans, but for God. Up there was God's inscrutable purpose. The others seemed to fall asleep, but he couldn't. He was too stirred up. Again, he felt like a Kamikaze pilot taking off for his final suicide mission.

A Desperate Venture – and Redemption?

After a seeming eternity, Steadman stirred and began to shake the others. 'Three o'clock, men. Time to go!'

For John it felt like the hour of doom: the condemned criminal wakened to face his execution.

They packed up, and after nibbling a few pieces of dry bread, shouldered their packs and followed Steadman into the threatening blackness above them, clambering up easy but precarious gullies, which sliced their stony and crumbling ways through the cliff bands.

Slowly the dawn came. To John it seemed as if the world was being reborn in a new and evil form. Crudely formed, cruel mountains emerged from the blackness. It was almost like resurrection on the Day of Judgement. Waking up and finding the green, comforting world of your earthly life transformed into a grim and brutal world where there was no hope of Redemption, but only awe and dread. The mountain face seemed to be getting steadily steeper and ever more malignant as it curled above them like a gigantic wave on a windy day, hanging momentarily in the air before crashing down and hurling them to oblivion.

The little gullies degenerated into little more than large cracks, and they found themselves clambering up increasingly smooth slabs which led up towards a sheer overhanging cliff. Running right across the mountain face, it barred all further progress. A narrow gully slicing down through it seemed to be the only breach in its formidable defences. That, apparently, was what Steadman was heading for. To John, however, it seemed impossibly difficult.

Then, glancing to his left, he saw that, some way below them, a series of broad, rubble-covered ledges led into the top of the canyon, which by now had degenerated into little more than a big groove. Beyond it, further to the left, easy-angled slopes swept up past the edge of the cliff and reared gracefully up to a sharply pointed summit.

'Bob!' he called out. 'Oughtn't we to be going that way? I mean, it's much easier!' The words just slipped out of his mouth.

Steadman rounded angrily on him. 'John, *do* stop showing off for once in your life! We're on the correct route, so just *shut up!*'

'Yeah, sussed!' sneered Jim.

John blushed bright red. Squashed again.

Up they went, scrambling up a narrow crack and then teetering up a knobbly slab at 45 degrees. John looked down and felt a spurt of terror ripple through him; a bit like an electric shock. A huge void had opened out beneath them; one slip, one careless move, and you'd go tumbling down... to what? Horrible, unthinkable pain and injury... death... oblivion. He began to feel sick. It was that awful Greenhill feeling of utter helplessness before brute force, that feeling of paralysis that seeped into you like a blinding headache.

He glanced at Rob and saw that he was white and visibly trembling. Big, beefy and uncoordinated, Rob was made for fighting, not for delicate rock climbing. Here was an ally in fear.

'Rob!' he called out. 'Are you OK?'

'Fuck off, will yer!' In his extremity of humiliating fear Rob was not prepared to confess to weakness in front of a poofter. That was just too much for an already wounded ego to bear.

They clawed their way up an even steeper slab and reached a broad, rubble-strewn ledge. The cliff loomed over them, smooth and relentlessly hostile. The gully they'd been aiming for was revealed as a mere groove which petered out into a blank, holdless overhang.

'No way we're gerrin' up that!' exclaimed Rob in a high-pitched falsetto squeal, quite unlike his normal deep bass.

Wild-eyed and looking even more manic, Steadman eyed the scene. Then he spoke in a soft and gentle voice. 'Chaps, I seem to have made a boob.'

'Where now?' asked a tremulous Jim, not quite terrified, but obviously badly shaken.

'We'll just have to go back down those slabs and try to work our way round to the left,' replied Steadman, in an unconvincing 'put-a-brave-face-on-things' voice.

Rob cast a horrified glance at the slab they'd just negotiated. 'Ah'll niver get doon that, me! No way!'

John noticed that he was shaking and that tears were trickling down his cheeks.

'Come on,' said Steadman in his gentle voice, 'I'll rope you up. You'll be perfectly safe.'

He pulled a climbing rope out of his rucksack, uncoiled it and tied it round the trembling youth's middle.

'Now, down you go. You're perfectly safe. I've got you.'

'No you fuckin' ain't! There's no fuckin' belay! If I slip I'll jus' pull yers off!'

'Oh come on! You'll have to go. We can't stay here.'

A wild, panic-stricken yell: '*Yer fuckin' clueless bastadd! We's fuckin' stuck, ain't we?*'

John studied the wild-eyed, violently shaking lump. Not since 'Army Barmy' Martin's celebrated freak-out on the Isle of Rhum three years before had he seen anything like this. Fear was like an acid, which dissolved you. Here was big, hard man Rob, reduced to a Martin-style lump of jelly. How were the mighty fallen.

Impasse. Now what?

Just then he glanced to the right. The ledge they were on led in an erratic way towards a protruding rocky rib, which plunged down from the cliff and shut off any further views in that direction. Unlike the cliff, it was not smooth, but was a tumble of big boulders, full of easy footholds and handholds. The ledge, itself, though poised over a terrifying void of steep slabs and vertical cliffs, looked negotiable. There were plenty of conveniently placed footholds and firm handholds. He had a sudden inspiration.

'Bob!' he called out. 'I think there could be an easy way over there. Could I go and have a look?'

For a moment, no reply came. The humanoid landmine seemed to be ticking ominously away. He braced himself for the coming explosion and humiliating put-down.

But instead, there came a calm and reassuring voice. 'Good lad, John. Well, off you go and have a look.'

John glanced at the awful void beneath the ledge. It was like the slobbering jaws of a Tyrannosaurus waiting to gobble you up. One careless mistake, one wrong move and… oblivion! Fear began to well up within him.

'Bob!' he said. 'Can you tie me onto the rope and give me a belay?'

'You don't need a belay,' replied Steadman in his now gentle voice. 'You're a good rock climber. You can manage without. Here's your chance to prove yourself. So off you go!'

Steadman seemed to *want* him to cross that ledge unprotected. Why? It was like one of those section attacks at the army camps when the Sergeant ordered the 'Mongs' to stick his head out of cover to draw the enemy's fire and reveal his position. 'Mongs' were the expendable idiots. So was *he* expendable? He hesitated.

'Go on,' said Steadman. '*You're* not scared, are you?'

Yes, he was scared. Bloody petrified, if the truth were known! But then, this was the way that Mekon had won his Military Medal. So, no choice!

Heart thumping, all senses acute, everything hyped-up to super infra red alert, he picked his way carefully along that ledge. Don't look down! Fight down that fear which will turn you into a wobbling jelly! It's easy, one firm hold following another like the sentences in a book.

So to the rib. An easy clamber up the big, tumbled boulders. Footholds and handholds like a gigantic staircase. On to its wobbly top, and on to the far side where a crumbly slab abutted against the cliff band… and then, *salvation*! Here the sheer face was slashed by an easy-angled gully, rocky, boulder-filled and, with its mass of big hand and footholds, little more than a glorified ladder. Clearly visible above it were broad and easy slopes sweeping up to an airy, tapering summit cone.

He felt a wave of sheer exultation flash through him. 'Thank you, God!' he muttered, 'Thank you! I should have known you'd come to my rescue!'

With infinite care, he clambered back over the rib and along the ledge to where the others were waiting.

'It's OK!' he called out, 'There's an easy way to the top over that rib!'

'Right lads!' said Steadman in a strained voice. 'Follow John along the ledge!'

Rob, however, refused to move and clung desperately to his stance. 'I'm not gannin' along that!'

Steadman immediately took charge of the situation. 'John, tie yourself onto the rope. You know, bowline, the way I taught you... that's right! Now, go over to the rib and give us a belay.'

Promotion! Restored to favour! John obeyed with alacrity. Reassured by the rope, he crept carefully along to the ledge. Reaching the rib, he found an almost perfect knob of rock. Testing it out, he found it was firm and slipped the belay over it. Hauling the rope in, he called out, as he had been taught by Steadman. 'Climb when you're ready!'

'Climbing now!' replied Steadman. 'Come on Rob, old man, you're perfectly safe! John's holding you and so am I.'

With that, he heaved the protesting adolescent lump to his feet and gently shepherded him along the ledge. 'This hand here... Now left foot there... Right foot here. We're winning! We're winning!'

Reaching John, Rob collapsed in a sullen heap. Steadman returned along the ledge to collect Jim, who refused to tie himself onto the rope and clambered deftly over to John, ostentatiously scorning the void beneath him. Obviously, he resented John's success.

Clambering over the big, inviting boulders of the rib, they reached the bottom of the gully. Steadman eyed it and let out an audible sigh of relief. His craggy face broke into a broad grin.

'Right, Jonny boy,' he said. 'You shin up that and give us

a belay. It shouldn't be difficult, but *do* be careful! Give us a shout when you're ready!'

While a silent Jim glowered sullenly at him, John began to clamber up the gully. It was reassuringly easy with big, comfortable hand and footholds within easy reach and plenty of room for his body. Only at the top was there an awkward bit. An especially large boulder had wedged itself between the enclosing walls of rock, but a big, jagged gap to its left offered hope. Squeezing himself into it, with his back pressed against the smooth wall of the gully, he found himself faced with a multitude of little knobs and ledges. It was almost like a climbing frame in a kids' playground back home. Wriggling his way upwards, he duly emerged from the shadow into brilliant sunshine. There before him was... the promised salvation: the easy, gravelly slopes leading up to the sharp, rocky summit. He'd done it!

In a burst of excitement, he pulled out the camera and indulged in an orgy of photography. Then, finding another conveniently placed rock spike, he went through the elaborate belaying routine he'd been taught.

'Climb when you're ready!'

'Climbing now!'

Slowly and gently, Steadman coaxed the nervous, complaining Rob up the gully. 'Left foot there... Here's a good handhold... Careful now! You're all right! John's holding you on the rope.'

This was hardly soothing his wounded ego! Hauled up by an effin' poofter? Fuckin' 'ell!

A predictable crisis occurred when they reached the big boulder. Rob was too bulky to fit easily into the gap. 'Ah can't fuckin' move! Fuckin' stuck! Crap route this, Jonny lad!'

'Go on, try!' said Steadman.

'Ah'm fuckin' stuck!'

His large backside wedged sideways between the walls of the gap, Rob's arms and legs thrashed wildly in the air. Ignoring the torrent of obscenities, Steadman grabbed a flailing right foot and firmly placed it in a large hold and, seizing a thrashing right arm, he manoeuvred it carefully towards a big jug-handle handhold. Then, wriggling underneath the quivering body, he pushed hard on the elephantine backside that was wobbling above him.

'Go on! I've got you! Pull hard, John!'

Grunts, gasps, obscenities, frantic wriggling and thrashings about, and then almost like a cork in a bottle, Rob burst out into sunshine above and lay panting on the gravel.

'Well done, Rob!' cried John. 'You've made it!'

'Trust you to choose a crap route!' growled Rob when he finally recovered his breath.

Jim arrived next, romping up the gully with a positively aristocratic disdain for any difficulties. Without even looking at John, he sat down next to Rob. Steadman followed.

'There's the summit!' cried John. 'Lads, we've made it!'

Rob didn't reply. Jim flashed a ferocious scowl. John felt a bewildered despair. They seemed to resent his success. Could he do *anything* right with them? Still at square one.

An easy walk up the gravelly slopes and a short scramble up some steepish rocks brought them quickly to the top.

'Well done, lads!' exclaimed Steadman, beaming and shaking hands vigorously.

'Well, John,' he added. 'So you managed to cope with a *real* cliff band after all! Satisfied now, are we?'

'Yeah, Bob! You bet! Thanks, Bob! Thanks!'

For a glorious moment of enhanced life, John wallowed in blissful euphoria. A real mountaineer now! Bob had returned to normal and was his surrogate dad once more. Things were back on track.

He beamed at Steadman and began to speak. 'I —'

But without a word Steadman turned away and began a huddled conversation with the other two. John tried to join in, but was simply ignored. The euphoria dissolved in a flash. He was still out in the cold. Things were still crazy. Why, for Heaven's sake? He'd proved himself tough and brave – or so he thought, anyway! But even that wasn't enough! What *more* did he have to do to be accepted?

Disconsolately he looked around him. Almost immediately the sheer enormity of the prospect before him softened his bruised feelings. How petty human squabbles were! Up here he was in the presence of something far bigger than himself. All around him was a stormy sea of jagged mountains, a harsh and brutal riot of rampaging rock. Contorted, unformed, unfinished, untamed… it surged away and lost itself in a dim, blue distance. 'You're nothing,' the mountains seemed to be saying. '*We're* what matters, not you. We're far older than you are, but we're still in our early childhood. When you're gone we'll still be growing up. One day we'll be bigger even than the Himalayas, but all you'll be is a heap of dust, or maybe even a fossil if you're very lucky.'

A soft wind caressed their lonely perch. Far away to the south was the yellow emptiness of the Sahara Desert. Here, beneath the immense blue dome of the sky, the solitude was the solitude of the open sea.

Alpha Males

The opposite side of the mountain was very different. Broad, stony slopes swept easily downwards, speckled here and there by the odd crag and cliff band, all readily bypassed. Having driven them almost to their limit, the mountain seemed willing to let them go with a minimum of fuss.

They met the others in the brown, sun-baked valley below. Morris seemed almost disappointed to see them. Michael seemed relieved. The two girls screeched and whooped and smothered Jim and Rob in a deluge of hugs and kisses.

When Tracy finally disentangled herself from Rob's

amorous tentacles, she rushed over to John and hugged him. 'Eeeee! Yorra real hero, ye!'

John responded with a flurry of kisses. But as they extracted themselves from their mutual embrace, a surly Rob approached him.

'Leave her alern! Yin's not for poofs!'

That stung. 'I'm not a bloody poof!' he growled. 'I got you up the mountain, didn't I?'

Rob clenched his fists. 'Wanna fight, son? I'll take you any day!'

John backed off. Discretion, he decided, was the better part of valour. He knew he couldn't fight Rob. He would only be sent sprawling on the ground. Memories of that ghastly playground at Greenhill flitted through his brain. At the same time, a feeling of hopelessness filled him. He desperately wanted to be friends with Rob and Jim, but whatever he did, nothing seemed to work. He'd led them out of danger, found the way to the top of the mountain… yet that only seemed to enflame their hostility still further. Mad!

He remembered a film he'd seen about mountain gorillas in Africa. They went round in small gangs each led by a big macho male, what was officially called an 'alpha male'. Other alpha males weren't friends: they were rivals to be seen off. Slowly the dismal penny dropped. It was the same here. Rob and Jim were the alpha males and he was the outsider to be seen off. They were Geordies, and toughness was their exclusive property. People with posh accents were poofs. Always had been, always would be. If they happened to be as tough as you, they were rivals that had to be squashed. End of argument.

Madness?

A short way down the valley they found a broad pool of green grass beside a small stream. Here they settled down and made a fire. Mahomet, the donkey man, produced a cornucopia of meat, vegetables, dates and almonds out of a bag, and pouring it all into a big earthenware bowl brewed up a vast, spicy tagine.

As the sun went down and the shadows lengthened, Steadman seemed to go into a kind of trance, staring ahead of him and snapping at anybody who tried to speak to him. Suddenly he got up and marched resolutely over the brow of a nearby spur.

'Now Bob's got the shits!' declared Rob. 'An' serves him bloody right an' all for eatin' all this Pakkie crap!'

Night fell, the moon rose and they settled down for a night under the stars. Steadman didn't return.

After an hour of semi-sleep John returned to full consciousness. The tagine and the long day's exercise were having their effect and the internal traffic was on the move. Getting up, he scrambled over the adjoining spur.

The mission successfully accomplished, he ambled back towards the bivouac. Rounding a big rock, he was confronted with what seemed to be a vision from the distant past. The brilliant moon bathed the vast, shadowy mountainside in a soft, silvery light. There on his knees, his hands locked in an attitude of fervent prayer, was Steadman.

As he beat his breast and gazed intently at the sky, he seemed, for all the world, like a picture out of a history book, a medieval knight at vigil or a crusader taking his vows. 'Oh Lord,' he said in a loud and clear voice. 'Accept me as I am. Forgive my weaknesses. Calm my wild and evil passions. Show me the right path.'

John just gaped. Just as Michael had said, Bob really *had* gone nutty! Just *what* had got into him?

Crisis and Remorse

Had John but known it, the answer was: quite a lot. The Reverend Robert Steadman, M.A. D.D, Ph D. – and all the rest of it! – was having an identity crisis. His life had reached a turning point. More than ever, the wild places were calling him. His suburban parish on the outskirts of Boldonbridge was not for him. It was a bowl of sticky treacle which sucked him down into a deadening nullity. Here, amid the harsh mountain crags and scorched desert wastes, was the reality he sought: hard, unforgiving nature, which alone provided a test worthy of him. Only when your body was pushed to its uttermost limit could you experience true spirituality. At heart he was a desert anchorite, not a suburban social worker.

And, again, there were these wild Berbers. Ignorant, bigoted, crassly superstitious… they were all of this, yet they had a deeper sense of reality than the suburban sophisticates of Calderbridge. You didn't have to apologise for mentioning God. To them, God was simply reality. You didn't airbrush death and eternity out in the name of 'mental hygiene'. You accepted them face to face.

And there was something else which continually tormented him. John, the ridiculously beautiful. John, his soul mate. For days now he'd tried to banish him from his presence. Rudeness, cruel cutting remarks, rejection, he'd tried it all, but still the youth hung around him, unable to take the hint. And it wasn't only a physical presence: John invaded his sleep. He was there in his dreams, every night, cavorting round, bewitching him. 'Be true to yourself! You'll never be able to marry a woman, so marry *me*. Consummate the marriage. It's perfectly normal. It's what the Spartan warriors used to do with pretty young boys. Why not?' That path, he knew, led to catastrophe; to shame, ridicule, prison and the squalor of paedophile register. It was the Song of the Sirens luring him to ruin.

And it was all so petty and sordid. He'd done his share of 'Paedophile Awareness' courses. Long-term strategies: be kind to your prey; become a father figure in whom they will confide and then, when you've softened them up, pounce! By befriending him and bringing him, he'd done just that! By now he'd come to hate the youth for exposing him for what he really was. Not spiritual, but a mere paedophile all but consumed by his animal lusts. In his dreams, he saw him jeering at him.

A Demon?

The events of the day shamed him. In his desperation to find a physical challenge worthy of him, he had deliberately chosen an unknown and dangerous route up Aksoual Mountain, regardless of his responsibility for the safety of his youthful charges. And when confronted by failure in the shape of that overhanging cliff, what had he done? The true answer pained and horrified him so much that he hardly dared to admit it even to himself. He coaxed and flattered John Denby, an innocent youth, into crossing a dangerously exposed ledge, without the protection of a safety rope, in hope that he might stumble and fall to his death.

In that way he would rid himself of the tempter that was luring him to destruction. Of course, an appalling row would follow, but he could soft-soap the coroner into believing it was all a terrible accident, beyond his control. An undisciplined and hyperactive John Denby had wilfully ignored his entreaties and dashed off along that ledge. After all, he'd disobeyed his teacher, Joe Morris, and charged off up the Jebel Toubkal without permission, hadn't he? He was just that kind of a lad, wasn't he? Perhaps he shouldn't have taken him mountaineering, but, well, he'd given him the benefit of the doubt in a good Christian way and he would make a great show of sorrow over the tragic death of such a promising young man.

A coroner would swallow it – and so would a jury – but

God wouldn't. You couldn't soft-soap God! Alone on that moonlit mountainside, he was filled with shame and self-disgust. The Publican in the Temple. 'Oh Lord, forgive me for what I am! Make me a better person.'

Trouble Brewing

An anti-climax day followed. It was a gentle amble over a big mountain pass and then a matter of following an ancient trail down a long valley. A stream bubbled noisily down through a land of large, rounded mountains, sun-bleached and increasingly dry.

As the glorious photo opportunities appeared, one after the other, John indulged himself in an orgy of photography. It was partly to illustrate the book he was planning to write, and partly to take his mind off the increasingly unpleasant tensions within the group. Rob and Jim were more hostile than ever and had corralled the girls into a tight-knit clique from which he was excluded. Michael had joined them. And to crown everything, that morning Steadman had been viciously rude to him, for no apparent reason. At long last he had come to hate him. That left him with only one possible friend: the other excluded pariah, Morris.

'You mean to say that Bob took you up the wrong route and lost his way, and that you, a minor had to rescue everybody?'

Clearly Morris was gathering ammunition for a long-planned counter-attack, just as Michael had predicted. Full of bile, John supplied all the juicy details, chapter and verse, and with compound interest.

'Yeah! When Rob collapsed, I had to find a way out of the mess we'd got into. Bob just hadn't a clue. I mean he'd led us into a mess and then... Well, he just gave up.'

Spiteful? Full of malice? Yes! But true? That depended on what you called 'the truth'.

Plots. Intrigue. Revenge. Trouble brewing.

Human Frailty: Gut Rot

Then the long-heralded gut rot struck, followed by a frantic dash for cover. Which, by Sod's Law, happened to be conspicuously lacking at that precise moment. The net result was being observed in full squat by a jeering Jim.

'Your turn at last? Mighta chose a berra place like? Or mebbe's yer likes showin' us yer bum? Figures doan it?'

'Fuck off!'

'Watch yersell, son!'

John seethed with anger. Bloody hell, he'd tried to be sympathetic when Jim had got the gut rot! So sympathetic, in fact, that he'd given away all his anti-squitter pills. And small thanks he'd got for that act of altruism! There seemed to be one law for him and one law for them. He comforted himself by slipping in a 'heroic explorer' fantasy. David Livingstone dying of dysentery in the wilds of Africa. If you wanted to be a *real* explorer then you had to suffer like him.

More Culture Clash

And so to Amsouzeate, an oasis of bright green fields and the usual scatter of flat-roofed, mud brick houses amid bare, brown hillsides. The now familiar routine ensued. Steadman went into a huddle with the bearded, berobed local men, talking vigorously in Berber. Meanwhile the rest of them hung around in two muttering and mutually hostile groups.

Eventually they were ushered into one of the houses, through the bottom storey with its dung-soaked straw and greasy, stinking sheep, and up a ladder into the cushioned living room above. The usual mantras occurred.

'Jesus, not *more* Pakkie crap!' growled Jim.

'Ah can't take much more o' this!' sighed Rob.

Wearing an expression of affronted professionalism, Morris muttered to himself about 'appropriate safety standards'.

John winced and bit his tongue.

Supper followed: tagine, dates and dry Moroccan bread. Old women in veils cleared it all up and disappeared down the ladder to their proper place among the animals. Then they all snuggled down to sleep on the cushions. The window shutter was closed and the oil lamp turned off. A seemingly solid blackness enveloped them.

An Ancient Pagan Rite, or Plain Depravity?

Almost at once, John began to dream strange and violently coloured dreams. He was part of a traffic island in the middle of Boldonbridge, full of brilliant flowers. All around him was a maelstrom of roaring motor cars and lorries. Indeed he, too, was a motor car. Then he emerged into semi-consciousness. The traffic island and its roaring traffic was inside *him*… the screeching of the tyres, the frantic revving of the engines as the cars surged away from the traffic lights. Up and down, careering round the corners.

Then came a ghastly realisation. A massive internal eruption was imminent, at any moment now! It was get out quick before the explosion blasted out of him with appalling consequences. A crazy kaleidoscope of events followed, one after the other, so fast as to be almost simultaneous, a video fast-forwarded at lunatic speed.

Stagger through the black void, treading on unseen human obstacles. Uproar.

'Gerroff me legs!'

'What the fuck!'

'Mind yersell!'

Stumble to the ladder. Go crashing down into the soggy straw below. Tangled up with stinking, bleating sheep. Still, by a desperate hair's breadth, managing to keep the tidal wave at bay. But pressure mounting with every second… Dam creaking… See the door, a jet black rectangle outlined by the dark blue frame of the night sky. Oh God, it's fucking *locked*!

Bang furiously, '*Lemme outa here*!' Angry old woman emerges from the blackness. Screeches in some unintelligible lingo. Get on and open the door, you silly old cow! Door finally opened. Out into the night.

Then suddenly an appalling, irredeemable catastrophe. The dam burst. Out poured the tidal wave. On and on it went. A disgusting brown slurry all down his jeans, onto his trainers, all over the back of his shirt... stinking and repulsive, squalid and utterly degrading. The worst had happened.

Now what? He couldn't go back inside like this. He had no spare clothes to change into. He'd given them all to the greedy, grasping, effing, bloody locals on Toubkal. Jim and Rob wouldn't have done that. No way! Only posh, poofter, soft-as-shit Denby would have been that stupid! Final destruction faced him. Jim and Rob would rip him to pieces, revelling in his degradation; the girls would laugh at him; Steadman would jeer at him. He'd gone back to that nightmare of early childhood: the small boy who'd messed himself in the classroom and dared not tell the teacher and who could only wait in dread for the awful mockery that would come when his classmates found out. The pitiless cruelty with which children attack helpless prey. He sat down on a nearby rock and desperately tried to stop himself crying. Minutes turned into hours.

Suddenly, Steadman's angry voice boomed out of the darkness. 'Who's there? What's going on?'

A torch beam picked him out. Discovery. Final doom! Accusing voice.

'John! What the hell *are* you doing? Is this another of your little games?'

He didn't answer – what *could* he say?

'Come on back to bed! Can't have you wandering around at night and causing trouble. There's been quite enough of that already!' Had Morris been getting on to him about expedition discipline?

'Can't!'

'Don't you "can't" me, young man! We've had more than enough of your oversized ego in the last few days! Move!'

'Can't! Won't!'

'Look, do I have to get physical!'

The tears finally trickled. In his utter degradation it was unconditional surrender.

'Oh, for Heaven's sake, Bob!' he spluttered. 'Give over! If you must know I've shat myself, big time. Dunno what to do! I'm so ashamed. So ashamed!'

He waited for the inevitable crushing sneer. But oddly enough, it didn't come. Instead, Steadman became gentle and reassuring. Back, indeed, into his former paternal mode.

'I see. Well, you'd better get changed into some clean clothes.'

'Haven't got any. I gave them all away to the locals on Toubkal. I thought I was being Christian.'

'So, indeed, you were, young man. But don't worry, I'll give you some of mine. In the meantime you'd better clean yourself up.'

'How? Where?'

'There's a stream down there. I'll help you. Come on, get up.'

He staggered to his feet and winced in horror as the obscene slurry slithered down his legs and spilled out over his trainers. Taking him by the hand, Steadman led him into a grassy, tree-lined gully where a small stream glimmered in the soft moonlight.

'Come on, don't be shy. Get these filthy things off.'

In his state of total dependency – as helpless as a sick child or a bed-ridden old man – he obeyed, appalled at the disgusting mess that was revealed. How illness humiliated you and reduced you to the level of a baby in a pushchair! Had he ever fallen quite so low? No. At least, not since…. well, Greenhill! Starkers, like a baby having its nappy changed.

Seemingly unconcerned by their sheer awfulness, Steadman put the mephitic objects into the water downstream and rinsed them out. Returning to John, he laid them out on the grass.

'Now you wait here while I get you some clothes. Don't go wandering.'

Stark naked, John waited on the grass. As he gazed at the moonlit world around him, blue and mysterious, something began to stir within him. He no longer felt ashamed of his nakedness. A soft wind caressed him, soothing him as if some unseen spirit was wafting gently down from the shadowy immensities of the mountains above him, calm, timeless and infinitely wise. His naked body was not something shameful to be hidden, but a natural part of things. 'Come with us! Come with us! Let the spirit enter in… Be one of us.' A deep, quiet thrill welled up with in him. He gloried in his nakedness.

Steadman returned with a bundle under his arm. 'Here's the things. But first, we'd better wash you down. Into the water.'

In a peaceful daze he obeyed; not something the normal John would have dreamt of ever doing. But here it was… different!

The cool water soothed him. The thrill increased as Steadman's sponge moved over his body. A tingling excitement grew. Steadman seemed similarly affected. The sponge caressed the forbidden zone. Not forbidden now, but holy.

Then it happened, in a wild, ecstatic explosion. The Demon – or was it the Mountain Spirit? – finally entered him, taking over his whole being. A deep, frantic joy, which surpassed all possible joys, wild, anarchic, yet at the same time deeply peaceful. It all happened… Then penetration… Not a violation, but something wholly natural. Meant to happen. A union of souls.

In passionate embrace they rolled out of the water and onto the grass, kissing each other effusively. He was no longer John Denby, a fifteen-year-old schoolboy, but a primordial spirit, under a glowing midsummer moon in an ancient Thracian forest, dancing with a holy frenzy of a Demon-possessed satyr before Dionysus, the God of Ecstasy. A different and higher being.

The moment passed. As he dressed himself in Steadman's spare clothes, he felt a sudden spasm of utter shame and disgust. Flopping round and decidedly ridiculous in the oversized shirt and shorts, he became John Denby, the schoolboy, again.

'We'll keep this a little secret between ourselves, shall we, John?' said Steadman. He, too, seemed shamed by what had just happened.

'Of course! Of course! I'll never tell!'

There was a pause as they sat down in the moonlight.

'Please,' said John after a while, 'Why were you being so horrible to me recently? I mean what had I done?'

An awkward silence.

'Well,' said Steadman after a while, you won't believe it, but I was testing you.'

'Testing me?'

'Yes, testing you. Have you read the Book of Job?'

'No.'

'Well, you should. It's deep stuff. God has given Job everything: wealth, a good family, the lot. Then, just to make sure that he loves him for his own sake and not just because he's showered him with goodies, God takes it all away from it and gives him horrible diseases instead. That's what I did to you. To see if you could still be good when things were going against you. Also, I was protecting you from the others.'

'What do you mean?'

'Well, they don't like you, and if I openly favoured you they would hate you all the more.'

'But why do they keep calling me a poofter? I mean, you haven't gone and told them about...?'

'Of course not.'

'Then what's it all about?'

'Look, it's *who* you are, not *what* you are. Even if you were James Bond himself, they'd still call you a poof. Why? Because Geordie males are the toughest and most macho people in the world. You're not a Geordie. You talk posh. Therefore you can't possibly be as tough as they are. You are – shall we say – *ex officio*, a poof whatever you do. Don't think they respect you for taking them up Toubkal or getting up that cliff on Aksoual. You were better than them and that shamed them. You destroyed their conceptual universe – Dobson again, I'm afraid – and they can never forgive you for that.'

Another silence.

Then Steadman continued, 'Don't think that I have violated you, John. What we've just done has been a religious act, a sort of Holy Communion. The physical expression of a deeply spiritual relationship. You've heard of the "disciple that Jesus loved?" Well, in that sort of way you are my disciple. All that I want to achieve, I see in you.'

A pause.

'You're homosexual, John,' continued Steadman in a calm, yet oddly ecstatic voice, 'and don't try to deny it. But it's not a disease. It's a gift from God to increase your spirituality. Among the North American Indians, homosexuals were regarded as shamans, men with special spiritual gifts denied to other men. And homosexuals aren't poofters, either. Alexander the Great was homosexual. He and Hephaestion were lovers. In Ancient Greece the Sacred Bands of Thebes were some of the most formidable warriors of all, but many of them were homosexuals. The older men took younger men as lovers, and together they formed couples dedicated to prowess in war. That's our relationship.'

Another long pause.

'But, I'm afraid, John,' he said at length, 'that this must be our secret. Other people will not understand it. If they found out, they would debase it. So let it be your secret initiation into the highest level of an ancient mystery religion.'

They embraced and kissed again.

As they disentangled themselves, Steadman switched to practicality mode. 'Leave these wet things out to dry. Collect them in the morning. When you meet the others, tell them that you tripped up and fell into the stream on your way to the bog. Rob may have been a chicken on Aksoual, but at least he hasn't done anything as daft as that. It'll make him feel a bit better. By the way, take these pills. Double dose. We don't want any more disasters. I haven't any more spare clothes to give you. Now come on. Back to bed.'

Normality Again?

Back in the house, John was unable to sleep. His mind was a whirling tumult. The whole episode seemed so improbable. Unreal. Out of joint. From another dimension unconnected with his normal existence. In the normality of the darkened room, squeezed up against the gentle snoring heaps of Jim and Rob, the physical reality of what had happened filled him with shame and revulsion. He wanted to erase it from his mind: never happened, never could have happened! Yet that strange spiritual exaltation lingered on, whispering, it seemed, of the unspeakable joys of what one part of him found detestable. Was it an angel or a demon? How on earth was he to know?

Eventually, he crept out into the night again. After a long time, slowly and majestically, a brilliantly coloured world emerged from the darkness, that seeming miracle of a Biblical-style creation out of nothing. Under the friendly rays of the rising sun the familiar landscape of rolling mountains, valleys and villages took shape. The dark and unreal world of the night gave way to normality. And not just a physical normality either: his relationship with Bob was back to where it had been. Things were on track again.

Triumph for Some, Revenge for Another
That day saw a magnificent hike. It was past a brooding lake lurking in a deep rubble-strewn canyon, and then up into a world of towering crags and wild, convoluted rocks. Then came a high, windy pass, a place of stupendous views of an unfolding sprawl of mountain grandeur and distant yellow deserts. And then it was precipitously down into the familiar valley beneath Toubkal, the Ourika Valley it was called.

It was like being welcomed back by an old friend. It was down past the Neltner Hut on its rocky spur, past the scene of their memorable bivouac, home again into a land of glowing memories. The adventures, the warm comradeship of shared adversity, the improbable Toubkal triumph. 'Welcome home, young heroes, we all remember you!'

The old bond between the escaping vagabonds revived. Jim and Rob seemed to melt. The girls became effusive. They were friends again. Steadman was his old self again. Excitedly they all babbled out the tale of their great shared adventure, pointing out all the familiar landmarks. For John it was intoxicating.

Only Morris was left out. There were no warm memories for him. Only a shamefaced reminder of failure and inadequacy that had to be expunged from his mind. Worse even than that, a guilty secret that must not come out. For the sake of form he had to pretend that he had been there; and also for the sake of his self-esteem and his future career. He knew that the youngsters knew, and he suspected that Steadman also knew. And he'd come to hate Steadman.

Silently, he prepared his defensive position. Insanitary Berber houses, weird and unsavoury food, youngsters needlessly afflicted with debilitating and degrading stomach problems, a flagrant disregard for elementary safety on the Aksoual Mountain, John Denby's revelations about getting stuck on a potentially lethal cliff band… it all added up, didn't it?

And there was more. There were hints – and more than hints! – of something not quite normal in Denby's relationship with Steadman. He'd seen the lad going out at night. He'd seen Steadman going out after him. He'd seen Denby returning dressed up in Steadman's spare clothes. They'd been out in the darkness for a long time. Again, it all added up, didn't it? And added up to precisely what? There was 'Madame's Place' down in the desert. It was quite obvious what sort of a place that was, wasn't it? And taking a bunch of youngsters there? And just how did a supposedly holy vicar get to know a woman like Madame? There was plenty of ammunition here. The more Morris thought about it, the stronger his position seemed to become.

Back Home. All Well?

So, back to Marrakesh. A final two days of washing dirty clothes and scraping up the last remaining dihrams to buy a few souvenirs in the souk ensued. Then it was off to the airport and onto the plane.

It was back to Heathrow, through the customs and into the frenetic hullabaloo of the Arrivals' Hall. Here the expedition finally ended; for the time being, at any rate.

Before they finally parted, Steadman and Morris went into a seemingly friendly little huddle. A little horse trading, thought John: don't shop me and I won't shop you. Then came friendly handshakes with Rob and Jim. Old enmities seemed to have been buried. 'It were a great expedition, weren't it, lads.' Jim even allowed the girls to kiss John goodbye. With that, Morris led his group off to the minibus that was waiting for them in the car park outside.

5

Aftershocks

Repercussions and Fallout: Something's Up

As Steadman led John and Michael over to meet Dorothy at the previously agreed rendezvous point by the currency exchange desk, John walked on air. He had so much to tell her. He had proved himself worthy of her trust. More than that, he had excelled himself. He was a proven mountaineer, a proven rock climber, a proven leader.

Certain things, of course, had been carefully expunged from the prepared report, and, more especially from his conscious mind. They didn't happen, couldn't have happened, never had happened… at least not in this dimension.

'Mrs Watson!' boomed Steadman. 'Here's your baggage, all home in one piece!'

Dorothy gave a start as she saw his bearded, sunburned face enclosed in its ragged blue turban.

'Well,' she eventually replied, eyeing the ragamuffin group with an unexpectedly disapproving air. 'How was it?'

'Great!' replied Steadman, flashing a toothy grin. 'Just

great! Your lads were magnificent! They've really done you proud. John here is a real mountaineer.'

'I'm glad to hear it,' she replied in a coldly measured tone with more than a hint of sarcasm.

A frost descended. This wasn't quite the effusive welcome that John had been expecting. Bloody hell! What *had* got into the old thing now? Not a storm brewing up? You never quite knew with these old trouts, did you?

'Right,' continued Dorothy in the same measured tones. 'Let's go to the car.'

'I'd better be off now,' said Steadman as she led them through the jostling crowds.

'You're not coming with us? I thought you were.'

'I was, but I've had a last-minute change of plan. I've urgent business here in London. I'll see you later in Boldonbridge.'

With a few perfunctory handshakes he darted off and was soon lost among the seething mass of returning holidaymakers.

'Cor!' sighed Michael. 'Ah wonder what's gorrinta him?'

Dorothy looked grim and didn't reply.

They climbed into the car and drove off. John tried to defuse the oddly unsettling atmosphere by setting up an enthusiastic babble. Out came the tale of their adventures, with all the heroic bits suitably embellished: 'Getting up that cliff on the Aksoual Mountain was a desperate struggle. I don't mind admitting that I was scared rigid… sheer drop of thousands of feet…'. So it went, on all the way up the A1.

Dorothy nodded and emitted an occasional 'I see. Very interesting.' Otherwise she maintained her icy reserve.

Something was up.

Adolescent Tantrum

Back at Boldonbridge, Michael was dropped off at a Residential Care Home. 'Developments with Darren' had made residence with his mother 'inadvisable for the present'. Dorothy and John returned to Fern Avenue.

He wallowed in a long and luxurious bath and then, clean, fresh and glowing, went into the kitchen for supper. Throughout the meal Dorothy remained monosyllabic and taciturn. Clearly something was brewing. But *what*? Anxiety mounted.

They washed the dishes and then she said, 'Now, John, can you come into the sitting room, please.'

It was that cold and formal voice which she had employed on that awful Wednesday two years ago. This was not the triumphant homecoming he'd been expecting. Obediently he followed her. Motioning him to sit on the settee, she sat down in the armchair opposite him. Switching into 'enhanced Mrs Watson, Headmistress' mode, she fixed him with her X-ray eyes.

'Now, John, I want you to tell me the *truth* about what you did in Morocco.'

He sat in a stunned silence for a moment. That sinking, despairing feeling when a supposedly sane world suddenly goes insane. Eventually, a bewildered protestation. 'But I *have* told you!'

'That's what you think. Perhaps you should read this letter which I received from the Youth Outreach Committee.'

She handed him a very official-looking letter with 'Boldonbridge Youth Outreach Committee' embossed in dark blue letters on top of it.

'Dear Mrs Watson,' it began. 'We on the Committee fully appreciate the strenuous, sincere and highly professional work that you do on behalf of your pupils.' A long ramble through a jumble of emollient official platitudes followed. 'However, we are unfortunately constrained to point out' – at long last the meaty bit – 'that the inclusion of your pupils John Denby and Michael Connolly in what was intended to be a highly selective venture explicitly aimed at the deprived youth of Boldonbridge, was most irregular and wholly against the spirit of an enterprise dedicated to the achievement of excellence... Sadly their subsequent behaviour... John Denby... purchase of illegal drugs... exploiting his privileged background in the furtherance of criminal aims... avoiding the punishment unjustly incurred by innocent and less privileged youngsters... Investigations in train... legal proceedings...'

He read it over twice, struggling to make sense out of the turgid and convoluted phrases. Why couldn't these people get on and say what they *meant* instead of filling a whole page with this kind of stuck-up waffle?

As the meaning slowly dawned on him, he felt the blood drain from his face. This was... mad! Fucking crazy! What the hell was going on? He seemed to be sinking into the floor. Then the penny dropped. Dobson. Dobson had obviously made full use of his early return home to blame him for the drugs disaster that had befallen his cherished protégés. The bastard! The stinking pile of newly laid turds! He began to tremble, not from fear, but from blind fury.

'Well?' The X-ray eyes were boring into him.

Silence, and then a sudden explosion. 'It's *crap*! Lies! It's all *fucking Dobson*!'

'Bad language won't help you. Now be so good as to tell me just what *did* happen in Morocco.'

He was too steamed up to focus his mind. Thoughts were whirling round like rocks blasted out of an erupting volcano. 'I've fucking *told* you!'

Increased dose of rays from the X-ray eyes. 'Mind your language, young man.'

Silence. Contest of wills developing.

'Come on, I'm waiting.'

Eventually, bit by incoherent bit, in spurts and flurries, the story dribbled out. Nothing in order. No sequence of events.

Just a disorderly pile of bricks waiting to be properly arranged by a more disciplined mind. The hippies... Kev and co. stoned on the dope... The sale of the kit in the souk... Sandra being screwed by a hippie... And, by the way, Kev getting drunk on the plane and throwing up... Yes, the trip to the police station... His and Michael's complete absolution... Toubkal... (But be careful here... Include Morris in the trip. And, of course, not a word about what had happened that night at Amsouzerte.)

'So that's your version of events. And you expect me to believe it, do you?'

'Well, yes. I mean, why not?'

'But can you prove it? It's not what I've been told.'

He felt himself sinking into a swamp. It was that old Greenhill feeling of utter helplessness in the face of blind irrationality. A lunatic world where nothing made any kind of sense.

Suddenly his temper blazed out. 'I've fucking *told* you the truth! *Why do you never believe me? Always the same, isn't it?*

'John Denby, that's no way to talk to me.'

(Get real, woman! You of all people should know better than this. Standing on your dignity in these situations gets you nowhere.)

The torrent poured on: 'You're ashamed of me. Ashamed, that's what! People like Dobson say you're a softy for helping me. Big headmistress mustn't be soft, must she? What would fucking Briggs think? Must suck up to Dobson, mustn't we! Can't do a fucking thing right, can I? Even when I pay for the bus to Imlil and for all the fucking donkeys.'

'When you've quite finished, you might apologise for your filthy language.'

'*Oh fuck off you old cow! Get the fuzz! Go on! Chuck me in the fucking river if that's wat you want!*'

He rushed out of the room. Violent slamming of doors. The whole house shook.

Just an Emotional Woman?

For a while, Dorothy sat fuming in the armchair. Spoken to like that by a pupil! And in her own house, too! The sheer *outrage*! Well, this couldn't go on! She'd have to get rid of him. She'd been a fool ever to have to have taken him in. It had all seemed so easy then. A lovely and friendly little boy, so polite and so creative... and, yes, as pretty and cuddly as a kitten. But what had he turned into? A homosexual who did repulsive things to other boys in showers. A devious two-faced manipulator who was always having to answer back and argue. God alone knew what he was getting up to behind her back. That letter from the Committee had confirmed her very worst fears. Nasty, underhand drug dealings and using his oily charm to put the blame on others. How was she going to explain all *this* to the parents, let along to the Director of Education? It could sink her whole school. What with all the exhausting business of the new academic year about to burst upon her, this was all she needed. Why, oh *why* had she let her sentimentality get the better of elementary common sense? 'Just an emotional woman?' Too true!

Poor Little John?

But then other thoughts seeped in. That 'still small voice of calm', perhaps? She'd been through all this before. It was a recurring theme: that famous Christmas party four years ago, that furore over the 'shower affair' two years later. And each time, things had sorted themselves out.

Prominently displayed on the wall in front of her was the expensive plate he'd given her last Christmas. Yes, he *was* big-hearted and generous, paying for buses and donkeys with his own money. And there before her very eyes was her treasured picture of Margherita Peak in the Ruwenzori Range. He'd been the only one to appreciate it. And it wasn't *his* fault that he was homosexual, was it? Besides, Meakin had warned her about Dobson's crew: 'Kevin Bartlett? Well-known drug pusher? He'll have his work cut out with that baggage.'

Poor little John! He had been pitched headlong into a thieves' kitchen. Even so, he *had* stuck it out, and in spite of everything he *had* achieved big things. And now to be falsely accused of drug dealing! What a welcome home! Dolly, mend those fences before it's too late!

Still a Little Baby?

She hurried out into the passage with her heart thumping. Gently opening his bedroom door, she was profoundly relieved to find him lying face down on his bed. Thank goodness he hadn't gone storming out of the house and off into the big, blue beyond!

'John,' she cooed, 'I'm so sorry to have upset you. Of course I believe you.'

To her further relief, he turned round and spoke to her.

'Sorry, Miss! Sorry I swore at you. I was so *angry* at being falsely accused like that.' He stood up and continued, 'You see, I was disappointed. I really thought I'd been selected for the expedition. And, you know, I tried so hard to do well. Nobody would have got up Toubkal if I hadn't talked French and paid for the donkeys. I really tried to be Christian... you know, giving away clothes and that. Dobson's such a liar.'

'Don't worry, we'll put things right. I'm proud of you, really proud of you.'

Then she hugged him. Despite himself – and to his enormous embarrassment – he burst into tears. Dorothy loved it; yes, he still was the stray kitten that needed her protection. He loathed it. Bloody hell, could he *never* stop being a little baby that had to be cuddled by a soppy woman?

Counter Attack

Next morning, Dorothy telephoned Meakin. Having collected Michael from the Care Home, the four of them went to see the school solicitor. The Committee's letter was produced and John's story was duly trotted out, chapter and verse, and confirmed by Michael. Further possible evidence was cited in the form of police files in Marrakesh and records in the British Consulate at Rabat. And there would be more to come when the Reverend Bob Steadman returned to Boldonbridge. In the meantime a weighty letter was composed and dispatched to the Boldonbridge Youth Outreach Committee.

'They really have landed themselves in it,' sighed Meakin as they left the solicitor's office. 'Putting that ass Dobson in charge of a thing like that! I mean, taking Kevin Bartlett to a place like Morocco! Part of the biggest gang of drug pushers in town. What did they *think* would happen?'

Dorothy shook her head silently.

Meakin continued, 'And trying to wriggle out of it by pinning the blame on poor old Jonny boy, here? Doesn't do. Doesn't do.'

'By the way,' he added, 'what's happened to Bob Steadman? We could have done with him today. And if their lordships at County Hall start playing silly buggers, we'll be needing him.'

'I haven't heard from him since we parted at Heathrow,' replied Dorothy. 'But he should be turning up any day now.'

'Well, he'd better turn up. Doesn't do to leave the lads to carry the can on their own. Scarpering off like that: not on! Anybody would think *he* had something to hide.'

John stayed silent. Steadman *did* have something to hide. Indeed he, John Denby, had the power to destroy him, land him in jail, label him as a social pariah for life. But if *that* were to come out, then he too would be destroyed. Blown away in the blast. Just think what Dolly would say! And what about

Danny Fleetwood? It didn't bear thinking about. Truth was a luxury that not everybody could afford.

Five days later a letter arrived from County Hall. In view of the evidence provided, it declared, it was best to let the matter drop. Meanwhile, any distress that had been caused to John Denby was deeply regretted ans quite unintentional. So file closed. Skeleton locked in its cupboard. At least, for the time being.

'So Talented'

Dorothy was profoundly relieved. Now at last she could use the expedition to promote her school. John was back in favour again. Normality was resumed.

John sent his ten rolls of film off to be developed. When they came back the slides were magnificent: more magnificent that he'd dared to hope. Carefully he ordered them and, unearthing Dolly's projector and screen, gave her a show in her sitting room.

As, one after another, the exotic scenes flashed out in the darkened room, she was swept away by their sheer colourful splendour. The long-buried embers of her wanderlust were reignited. When the show was over, she engulfed him in an emotional gush.

'John, that was simply wonderful! You are *so* talented!'

Excruciating emotional hug.

'Now you must give a talk to the school!' she added. 'I'll invite the parents, and Major Allen of the Cadet Force, and we'll make a real show of it, shall we?'

'Great! I won't let you down!' he replied, disentangling himself from the octopus-like envelopment.

The gush continued, this time slightly conspiratorial. 'Now, John, there's something I want to say to you.'

There was a dramatic pause while the bombshell was prepared and primed. Tense wait. Then it was detonated.

'I'd like you to be our Head Boy next term. It's a great honour.'

With a warm glow of pride, John accepted. 'Cor, thanks, miss!'

'And,' she continued in the same hushed, conspiratorial vein, 'there's another thing.'

Another pregnant pause.

'This is your exam year,' she finally said. 'You're down for seven O Levels and eight CSEs. You must concentrate on your work. Give it all you've got. Because, if you do really well, we can get you a place at the Stirling Academy to do your A Levels. That's the most academically prestigious school in the North of England. Nobody could call you stupid then!'

'Wow!'

It was like luxuriating in a warm bath. Security. Acceptance. Hidden talents revealed. Head Boy. Academically brilliant. In the old Rickerby Hall days, this would not have been possible. The new John Denby walked on air.

What about Bob Steadman?

There was only one fly in the ointment: Steadman; or rather, the lack of Steadman. After that hasty goodbye at Heathrow he seemed to have vanished into thin air; dematerialised, even. Dorothy made enquiries, wrote letters which went unanswered. Eventually she learned, via the Bishop, that he'd had a 'personal crisis' and had been received into the Catholic Church. Secretly, he had returned to Boldonbridge, cleared his things out of his Moorside flat and then departed like a thief in the night. He'd now got a job in a remote part of Paraguay where, in the far reaches of the Grand Chaco – wherever that was! – he was rehabilitating Guarani Indians with drug problems and combating criminal narcotic gangs.

That left a big gap to be filled. His replacement was about

as different as a person could be. The elderly couples and widowed old ladies of Moorside found him a welcome relief after his wayward and incomprehensible predecessor. But with the Beaconsfield kids it was exactly the opposite. Fat, balding and well into his sixties, he found youngsters – and especially teenagers – an irrelevant irritation to be endured rather than enjoyed. Mutual hostility quickly developed and Dorothy had to take over the RE lessons.

John was both bewildered and hurt. That deep, hidden part of him had been expecting great things: companionship, a father to guide him, even discipleship and spiritual development, 'the disciple that Jesus loved'. But all that had gone. The one person who really knew him and understood his guilty secrets had scuttled off like a criminal escaping from the police.

Unpleasant thoughts surfaced. 'The physical expression of a deeply spiritual relationship?' Hadn't that poor, sex-crazed acid-head Cedric said similar things? In the end all amounted to the same thing: a good bum fuck. Indeed, the more you thought about it, the more sordid the whole Steadman business seemed to become. Help you when you are desperate. Ferret out your innermost thoughts. Flatter you. Build you up. Shower you with kindness. Pay for you to go to Morocco and fulfil your dreams. Protect you from your enemies. Get you into a state of dependency. Play cat and mouse with your emotions by pretending to reject you. Then, when you are your most vulnerable, take advantage of you – and in you go! Lard the whole thing over with a lot of high-flown guff about religion. Then, when you've got what you wanted, scuttle off and leave you in the lurch.

Yes, it all added up: the carefully planned strategy of the clever and cynical paedophile predator that he'd read about in those 'Paedophile Awareness' pamphlets that the sex education people were giving out!

Desperately he tried to persuade himself that it hadn't really been like this. At night, in the privacy of his bedroom, he prayed secretly and earnestly. 'Bob! Bob! Why have you deserted me? Come back! I need you! The boys at Beaconsfield need you! Why have you run away?'

There was no response. When he wrote a letter, it disappeared into the void. No reply came. Nothing. In the end he had to face the blunt truth. He'd been led up the garden path. Exploited. Used and then discarded. Face facts, Jonny boy, it wasn't you he liked, it was only your bum. He felt dirty and deeply ashamed.

Meanwhile he wrote a fulsome letter to the Boldonbridge Youth Outreach Committee, thanking them for organising the expedition to Morocco and offering to give them a slide show, and even to write a newspaper article for them. He got no reply. Odd, wasn't it?

Blaze of Glory

Term began in a blaze of glory. Head Boy. Captain of the rugby team. Brilliant academic prospects. The 'Morocco Expedition Evening' was a triumph. Parents and school governors rolled up. The dining hall was packed. In the interests of fairness and even-handedness Michael was wheeled out to act as second fiddle alongside him. Apart from a few inarticulate mumbles, he shuffled about, picking his nose and looking vacant. John had to carry the can alone. After an intensely nervous start, he got into his stride, and as a sympathetic audience warmed to him, he launched forth into his carefully rehearsed oration. Soon he was going from strength to strength. Showing off again, Denby? Most emphatically *yes*! After all, it came naturally to him. When the show ended and the lights came on again, he was greeted with tumultuous applause. He wallowed in the momentary adulation.

Major Allen approached him. 'Good show, John! Good show! Now, you must give a talk to the cadets on Wednesday night.'

That talk was an even greater success.

'How about writing an article for the *Cadet News*?' said the Major, shaking his hand afterwards. 'You can illustrate it with some of your first-class photographs.'

There was nothing that John would have liked better, and when he got home he set to work with gusto.

That week he was promoted to Corporal. So onwards and upwards, soaring into the bright blue sky.

A Special Sort of Person?

But then was into schoolwork with a vengeance. He had to achieve and get good exam results; and not just for Dolly and her school, but for himself. It was a matter of self-esteem and his survival as a tolerable human being.

Projects had to be submitted for C.S.E. history and geography. This wasn't a chore, but his big chance. So, pull out all the stops and go for broke. Not just 'good', but the best ever! For his history project he chose the exploration of Africa. It was off to the library and into old books: Livingstone's *Missionary Travels*, Stanley's *Through the Dark Continent*. Photocopies of old maps and diaries. René Caillié struck a deep chord within him: the lone, poverty-stricken Frenchman, weak and unprepossessing, who defied all the odds to reach the fabled city of Timbuktu and cross the ferocious wastes of the Sahara. He illustrated that chapter with his photographs of the desert and the Tuareg guide. For the chapter on Stanley he got prints of Dolly's slides of Uganda and the Ruwenzori Range.. His geography project was about Morocco. He devoured guide books and illustrated it with a cornucopia of his photographs.

The O Levels were a big challenge. This meant extra

one-to-one lessons with Mekon, practising the arcane art of writing examination essays; boring, but a vital part of his exam-passing kit.

Work, rugby matches, weekends with the Army Cadets: it was a full and productive life. The article for the *Cadet Journal* was duly published, lavishly illustrated with his photographs. It was plaudits all round. Major Allen crowed, Dolly cooed. He began to think he was a special sort of person – gifted, talented and being groomed for big things. 'One day I'll be famous!' On course for that, more than ever, through the black and buffeting clouds and up into the dazzling blue dome of the sky.

Not That Simple

But, alas, it wasn't that simple. One Wednesday morning in early November an article appeared in the *Guardian*. 'Expedition for Deprived Youngsters Hijacked by Middle Classes' ran the headline. A 'dedicated investigative reporter' had apparently uncovered yet another example of 'perfidious middle-class machinations'. As part of its ongoing 'commitment to equality and social justice', etc., etc., etc., the Boldonbridge Youth Outreach Committee had organised an expedition to Morocco, specifically aimed at 'deprived inner-city youngsters'. The expedition leaders were all 'experienced and properly qualified' and their 'rigorous selection procedures' had produced a team of 'first-class young people dedicated to the pursuit of excellence'. But, unfortunately, an 'ambitious middle-class teacher from a privileged private school' had managed to short-circuit the selection procedures, and 'in direct contravention of stated procedures' had slipped two of his 'moneyed protégés' onto the expedition. Worse still, the said 'moneyed protégés' had got involved with drug dealing, which had resulted in 'innocent members of the expedition being falsely accused and sent back to Britain'. And – as if that wasn't enough! – they and their 'totally unqualified teacher' had taken over the expedition and, 'blatantly ignoring the sound advice of a properly qualified youth leader', had indulged in 'antics of the most irresponsible folly' by climbing 'dangerous mountains' and 'wantonly risking the lives of children'. In short, a whole can of worms had been uncovered.

Because nobody at Beaconsfield read the *Guardian* – they did not aspire to such lofty heights – the bomb remained undiscovered for a couple of days.

Future Criminal Charges?

Then, on the Friday morning Dorothy received an 'official notification' from the Boldonbridge Youth Outreach Committee. All the old scabs were unpicked. With interest – indeed, with compound interest. The proven mendacity of her pupils who had bought drugs, dumped on deprived inner-city youngsters and then used their 'middle-class social skills' to foist the blame onto these poor, unwitting dupes. 'New and disturbing revelations' had emerged of how a 'totally unqualified Beaconsfield teacher' had ignored the advice of a 'properly qualified youth leader' and wantonly involved 'the children in his care in all kinds of quite unacceptable dangers'. A list of appalling expeditional misdemeanours followed: 'sleeping in unhygienic and disease-ridden local houses'; 'forcing British children to eat unpalatable and filthy local food' which had been the cause of 'serious intestinal disorders'; 'outrageously dangerous antics' on high mountains onto which 'only highly trained and properly qualified mountain leaders should be permitted to venture'.

And to cap it all there were 'strong hints' of a 'grossly improper relationship' between the said teacher and a Beaconsfield youth who, incidentally, had been 'a thoroughly bad and disruptive influence' throughout the expedition and who was 'almost certainly the chief instigator of the purchase of illegal drugs'. In short it was a whole mountain of iniquity meriting 'further investigations… and future criminal charges'.

The Vampire Rises from its Grave

Dorothy reeled. She'd confidently assumed that all this nonsense was dead and buried. Yet here was the corpse, climbing vampire-style out of its grave. Dracula himself could hardly have done a better job.

This was all she needed. She'd just had an exhausting few days. Recently a new boy, named Kenny Merrick, had arrived in Form Two. Having been bullied almost to extinction at his comprehensive, he'd set himself up as a 'hard', distributing cigarettes and porno mags to Form One. Then he'd found a suitable target in the shape of a scrawny little fellow named Freddy Monks. On Wednesday evening he'd urinated in Freddy's school bag and tried to flush it down the toilet.

For much of Thursday mornings she'd been bombarded with furious telephone calls, first from Freddy's mother and then from his father, complaining at vast length about 'the complete lack of discipline' in her school and about her enrolment of 'nutters who ought to be behind bars'. Later investigations, however, had shown that young Freddy was not quite the squeaky clean innocent that his parents fondly imagined him to be. On Wednesday morning, during the PE lesson, he'd stolen Kenny's underpants and dropped them into the changing room urinal. At times like these Dorothy felt as if she was swimming in a sewer.

Now it was John Denby again! A 'thoroughly bad influence' … 'purchase of illegal drugs' … 'foisting the blame onto innocent deprived children' … and, especially alarming, that 'grossly improper relationship'. All her old fears revived. She could almost *see* a grinning James Briggs standing in front of her and saying, 'I told you so, didn't I?'

Then the countervailing force: *her* child, who, inspired by her high pedagogic standards, and against all the odds, had done great things in Morocco. The young man who this summer was going to get a clutch of brilliant exam results, which would prove to all the doubters that her school was not a dustbin for deadbeats, but was, in its own way, a centre of excellence which got the very best out if its pupils, able and less able alike.

No, like it or not, far too much of herself had been invested in John Denby for her to abandon him now. But subconsciously, she muttered a prayer: 'Please John, *please* prove that you are innocent!'

'Not in the Eyes of the Law'

Somehow she managed to get through the rest of the day. That afternoon was yet more trouble to sort out. This time it was a fight between two Fourth Year boys, which had resulted in one of them having to be taken to see the doctor. Did the kids at her school *ever* stop being vile to each other?

And it wasn't only the kids who had a problem. With the school inspectors descending in less than a month's, time she *still* hadn't got a scheme of work out of Clarkson's English Department.

After school, she summoned Meakin.

'Roderick, just look at what I received this morning.'

Meakin perused the document and proceeded to light his pipe.

'I really thought we'd sorted all this nonsense out last month!' sighed Dorothy anxiously. 'What with the solicitor's letter and all that evidence! So just what *is* all this about?'

A long pause. Billowing pipe smoke. Then Meakin pronounced, 'It'll be Dobson and Morris getting their revenge on Bob Steadman.'

'But it was all settled.

'Not in their eyes. For both of them the expedition was a pretty good disaster. Dobson's great scheme of being a proletarian Messiah went pear-shaped, and if what Jonny boy says is correct, Morris didn't exactly cover himself with glory either.'

'But what are they hoping to prove? They can't alter *facts*!'

'That all depends on how you define facts.'

'But facts are facts.'

'Not in the eyes of the law. A fact is only a fact if it can be proved in court.'

Pause. Puffs of acrid smoke.

'I mean, all we've got is Jonny boy's version,' said Meakin eventually.

'But what about the police records in Marrakesh and the records in the British Consulate at Rabat? Won't that put things straight?'

'We never actually contacted them. We don't really know if they *have* any records of what happened.'

'But what about those other youngsters who were on the expedition? The ones who weren't sent home? They can support John's story, can't they?'

'In theory, yes. But we'd better check them out. I suppose that – shall we say? – a little *pressure* has been put on them.'

'And what about John? I do hope he *has* been telling the truth.?

'I'd leave His Nibs out of this for the present. If you're not careful you'll go and have a temper tantrum to deal with. And *that* won't do anybody any good.'

Dorothy shook her head. 'Oh, Roderick, what *are* we going to do?'

'Don't you worry,' replied Meakin amid an extra large cloud of pipe smoke. 'I'll handle it. It should all sort itself out.'

For a brief moment Dorothy became the 'emotional woman' she so despised. Meakin was so *strong*, so *masculine*! So like her long-lost Lawrence at his best. If only he wasn't married to that ghastly Molly woman!

'Don't Get Him Involved, Please!'

The next few days saw comings and goings. Meetings with Acroyd, the school solicitor; exchanges of letters with the Youth Outreach Committee; a letter dispatched to the British Consulate at Rabat. It all drew a blank. The Outreach Committee merely reiterated what they'd said in the letter. No reply was forthcoming from either the Moroccan police or the British Consulate at Rabat. Telephoning in that direction got nowhere. Jim, Rob and the two girls all appeared to support Dobson's story; and so, alarmingly, did Michael Connolly.

'It all looks pretty bleak!' sighed Dorothy.

Meakin stayed silent for a while, enveloped in the usual cloud of pipe smoke.

All the old doubts resurfaced in Dorothy's mind. 'Well, it seems as if John *could* have been involved in drug dealing after all! And I don't like that 'improper relationship' business one little bit. Teenagers can be so *deceitful*!' Pause. 'Frankly I wish we'd never got involved with that wretched Morocco business!' she added vehemently.

Pause. More clouds of tobacco smoke.

'I wouldn't jump to any hasty conclusions if I were you,' replied Meakin eventually, 'I mean, look at the situation. Jim, Rob and the two girls are all at Morton Community College. Who's just become the Deputy Head there? Our friend Dobson. Who wants to be head of the PE Department there? Our friend Morris. That Morocco business was their big chance to prove themselves. They're hardly likely to admit that they made a dog's dinner of it, are they? They need a scapegoat. As I expected, pressure has been applied in certain quarters.'

'You mean bullying young people into telling lies?'

'Not exactly bullying. Dobson's a very charismatic figure; at least, with those youngsters who have the correct pedigree. Charming. Very persuasive.'

'But what about Michael Connolly? He's not at Morton. He's with us!'

'They'll have got at him through the Care Home.'

'But why did he agree with everything John said before?'

'I should forget about Michael.' replied Meakin shaking his head dismissively. 'He's a poor lost soul. Hardly knows his front end from his back end, that one. I mean, just look at the kerfuffle over his Mum's new partner, Darran. Darran does him over good and proper and flings him out of the house. But what does he go and tell the Probation Officer? He says it was *he* who did the attacking and not Darran. Gets himself a criminal record just to please his mum who doesn't want her mate to get into trouble. Count him out of this.'

Silence.

'But, Roderick, where do we go from here?' exclaimed Dorothy eventually.

'We'll have to get chapter and verse from John,' he replied. 'Find out just what *did* go on. I suspect that there could be a few skeletons lurking in that particular cupboard that we don't know about.'

Dorothy took a deep breath. 'I'm afraid, you're probably right. But this *would* go and happen just when the inspectors are coming!'

'Sod's Law, I'm afraid,' said Meakin gravely. 'But we'd better handle His Nibs with kid gloves. He's our prize exhibit and we don't want him going doolally just when Their Lordships arrive.'

'But what about Bob Steadman? Can't we get hold of him?'

'That *would* solve a few problems, I agree. Not exactly right for him to swan off like that and leave us to face the music. Makes you wonder if there aren't any skeletons lurking in *his* cupboard.'

'But how on earth do we get hold of him? He's in... where? Paraguay or somewhere.'

'That's a problem, yes. The only person likely to know is the Bishop.'

'Oh, for heaven's sake!' cried Dorothy. 'Don't let's get *him* involved! *Please!*' The alarm bells were ringing as humiliating memories flooded back of his bullying, and of how he'd reduced her from a Headmistress to an incompetent schoolgirl.

Meakin stayed silent and relit his pipe.

'Yes,' he finally said, 'I quite understand your sentiments. But, frankly, he's our best hope. And, you know, he's the one who could winkle a reply out of Rabat for us. They might just take notice of a big noise like him. He's quite a force in the land, you know.'

Dorothy stayed glumly silent.

'All right,' continued Meakin, 'Let's consider the alternative, shall we? Jonny boy gets done for drug dealing and being a rent boy. Lands in a Young Offenders institution. Newspapers hear of it. School pilloried as a place which turns a blind eye to juvenile crime and child abuse. Parents start to remove their kids. Council stops sending us new boys. School forced to close; which is exactly what a lot of people at County Hall and up at the university want.'

More silence.

Eventually, a resigned and weary Dorothy capitulated. 'Yes, Roderick, you're probably right. But, *please*, can *you* deal with the Bishop and not me. I really couldn't go through all that again!'

'Not Your Little Wonder Boy Again?'

Meakin duly arranged a meeting at the Bishop's house. For a tense moment he thought he'd stepped on a landmine. In the depths of the big, leather armchair the massive brow wrinkled, the eyebrows quivered, the hairs coming out of his ears bristled.

'Not your little wonder boy again? What's it *this* time, eh?

Not another little *accident*? Some people never seem to learn, do they?'

'Not quite. Please hear me out.'

As the tale unfolded the great craggy face broke into an avuncular smile. Yes, of course he was willing to help. Yes, he'd rustle up young Steadman. 'I'll put a bomb under him all right. Yes, send it all the way to the St Francis Xavia Mission Station at wherever-it-is in the back end of the Chaco Grande!'

The mere mention of the British Embassy at Rabat set off an explosion of almost nuclear dimensions. 'No reply to your letter? For heaven's sake, man, did you seriously think that their Lordships of the FO would actually condescend to reply to a letter from a mere *schoolteacher*? What planet are you living on? The Foreign Office!' He spat the words out as if they were some noxious fly he'd inadvertently swallowed. 'You know, when I was in Uganda...' There followed a venomous five minute rant. The Foreign Office was one of Donald Mackay's pet hates. You pronounced those two words at your peril.

'Yes,' he finally concluded, 'I'll sort that lot out and with *pleasure*! But,' he continued with a conspiratorial wink, 'we'd better keep the whole thing under the wraps for the time being. And when we've gathered enough material we'll set a trap for little Jonny! We'll find out just what he *did* get up to when backs were turned.'

'You don't think he's guilty, do you?'

'Of course not! He's much too naïve. Young for his age. Immature. Still living in a *Boy's Own* adventure world. He's just the lamb caught in the thicket. But he must know things we don't know. Incidentally, don't breathe a word of this to my wife. Great lass. Great Christian and all that. But, well... she's a little too *emotional* for this business!'

Delicious Undercover Operation

In fact it was just the sort of undercover operation that Donald Mackay loved. All those forensic skills which had lain unused since his Ulster days were unearthed and lovingly repolished.

A missive was dispatched to the now devoutly Catholic Steadman in his sun-blasted Paraguayan outpost, hinting at 'unfortunate and potentially damaging rumours' which needed to be 'firmly squashed' before they resulted in 'prurient and most unpleasant publicity'.

'That'll set the cat among his pigeons!' chortled a gleeful Bishop.

A prompt and decisive reply was all the more urgent as the 'well-being of an innocent schoolboy' was at stake.

A war began – or, rather was renewed! – with the Foreign Office. Peremptory letters to Rabat. Letters to influential politicians. Telephone calls to Foreign Office mandarins. Hints about possible 'embarrassing disclosures to a sensation-hungry press'. Donald Mackay was not above applying a little judicious blackmail where he felt it necessary in the pursuit of justice. War was war, and there was no place for wishy-washy sentimentality.

Next, he paid a visit to Morris at Morton Community College.

'I'm writing an article for the *Diocesan Journal* about youth work in Boldonbridge. You, I gather, led a group of youngsters to the summit of the highest mountain in North Africa. Quite an achievement, I might add. Could you tell me all about it?'

There was nothing Morris would have liked better. Public vindication. Vital ammunition to bolster his campaign to become head of the Morton PE Department. Long and enthusiastic reply. Copious notes taken. Secretly, too, the Bishop taped the conversation; something he'd remembered from his Ulster days.

Then he cornered Tracy; but not at Morton College where she could be influenced by Dobson. Instead he chose the more relaxed venue of the council house where she lived with her single-parent mother. The three of them went into a huddle over the teacups in the cosy little living room.

He opened the proceedings by speaking in Geordie so as to sound reassuring and not ecclesiastical. 'I've got this article to write aboot youth work in Boldonbridge. Noo I'd like the feminine angle on the Morocco expedition. Can't 'ave been that easy bein' a lass among all them lads, like?'

Long reply. More copious notes taken.

'And noo the awkward bit, like. Sorry an' that. But warraboot this business of drugs an' that what the newspapers is on aboot?'

Immediate defensive bristle. 'That weren't us lot! It were Kevin Bartlett an' them lot! Rotten bastards!'

'Tracy, lass! Watch yer language!' exclaimed her mother.

'But, Mam, it weren't us, yer knaa!'

'But weren't one o' yer lads – John Denby or sommat? – into drugs an' all?'

'Why no! Weren't 'im! Weren't that sort. Too posh like!'

'But weren't he a canny bit daft an' that?'

'Why no! He were reet canny him! Mind, wor Brian 'ad it in forrim, jus' cos he talked a bit posh like. Weren't right! But me... why, man, I fancied him, like!'

'Eeeee, Tracy, yer naughty lass!'

'But Mam, he were a loverly lad, him! He were the one that gorrus up Toubkal, yer knaa! Ah mean that Mr Morris, like, he weren't nivver there! It were John Denby what gorrus there all on his own, yer knaa! Paid for the busses an' that hissell.'

'That's news to me!' chortled the Bishop. 'Now tell us all aboot it.'

Tracy prattled away for the next ten minutes.

'That John, he were ever so Christian, yer knaa. Spent

all his money on donkeys an' that for me and Maureen. An' yer knaa, he were givin' all his things, clothes an' that, to the poor Pakkies. Yer knaa, like what the Bible says. An' when we was robbed, why he sacrificed hissell for us lasses. He were a knight in shinin' armour, him. Mind, the lads didn't like 'im! Treated 'im sommat rotten like. Kev did 'im over an' Jim called 'im a poof. But he weren't no poof! Knight in shinin' armour.'

As well as taking copious notes, again the Bishop secretly taped the conversation.

Finally, he managed to run Jim to earth. They went to a little cafe on the edge of the dingy estate where he lived. There, among the sauce bottles and plastic tablecloths, they talked over mugs of Nescafé. Or, rather, tried to talk. Guarded and suspicious and with his pointy face twisted up into a fixed scowl, Jim was surly and monosyllabic. Getting anything out of him was heavy going. But eventually, bit by bit, a story unfolded…

'John? Him? Brainy. Ah'll gee 'im that much like. But always showin' off an' that. Had ter be the star, him. Soft as shit, mind. Kev did 'im over. Set 'im crying like a liddell kid, yer knaa. Poof? Yeah, not 'arf! Why he were dressin' up in Bob Steadman's clothes, yer knaa? Couple o' homs the pair o' them if yer asks me!' Drugs? No way! Too soft for that sort o'thing!'

Long silence.

Then a final lunge. 'What the fuck's all this aboot like? What's yer game, eh?'

A mature, streetwise young man, this, the Bishop decided, bold beyond his years. The hard product of a hard environment. He'd seen his like before. In Ulster he would have been a paramilitary. Here he'd end up in the army. One of those military machines you found in the Parachute Regiment. The sort of phenomenon the likes of Isobel would never understand. But he'd got what he wanted out of him, and taped it for good measure. So back off. Don't push it any further.

A Little Dinner Party

And now for 'soft as shit' John Denby. Dorothy was telephoned and given her orders. 'About your little protégé, John Denby. I intend to get to the bottom of this Morocco business. Need to talk to him – what in the army they call interrogation… No, you silly woman, there won't be any third degree. No hooding or water boarding, just a little gentle inducement. Arrange a little party where he can show us his slides and get talking… I'll bring Akroyd along, too. This Saturday at six o'clock. Got it? Good. I expect a properly professional performance. Goes without saying.'

Dorothy shuddered, but had no choice. Orders were orders.

Slipping into 'shaggy sheepdog' mode – indeed, to a practised eye, the performance was a hammed-up caricature – she duly approached John.

Sweet smiles and maternal gush. 'John, I've got a special task for you. Can you stay at Fern Avenue over the weekend and give a slide show on Saturday night?'

'Huh? But I've already given you a slide show.'

'But this is special. The Bishop's coming to supper!'

'Oh God! Not *him*! He freaks me out. Scares me shitless! Oh, er, sorry about the bad language! What does *he* want?'

'No need to look like *that* about it!' Every need, in fact! The Bishop scared her rigid, too! 'The Bishop's a fan of yours. You of all people should know that! He wants to know all about your exploits in Morocco.' Yes, but not quite in the way that *you* might think! 'You're quite famous, you know. And, by the way, Mr Akroyd, the school solicitor's coming along, too. He's an assessor for the Duke of Edinburgh's Award Scheme, you know, on the Wild Country Panel, and he's thinking of fast-tracking you for a Silver medal, and also for Gold.' Lies, this: blatant lies! But gild the honey trap! Those are your orders...

John's pouty adolescent face broke into a broad grin. 'Wow! Yeah! I'll do my best!'

Hooked! Soaring up into the stratosphere. Yes, I really *am* a special person. A high-achiever whose brilliant talents are being recognised by high up, influential people. But *this* time I'm not going to grovel in front of that great gorilla, the Bishop! I'm not taking any crap out of him! I'm not a little shit-pants kid any more. I'm a *lad* – and a fucking great lad, too!

A Silly Adolescent

Saturday morning found Dorothy crashing round in her kitchen. She was all on edge, nerves taut, dreading the evening that lay ahead. At the very least it promised humiliation at the hands of that ghastly humanoid gorilla, the Bishop. Then there was Ackroyd, a typical lawyer who always had to score points off her, nit-picking away, finding fault with everything and continually having to put her *down* into her proper place. Worst of all were the excruciating revelations that would doubtless emerge about John had *really* got up to on that wretched Morocco expedition! What with the coming school inspection, she had an enormous amount paperwork to get through. Yet here she was, thrashing round trying to create a quiche sophisticated enough to satisfy the pretentions of a couple of gastronomic snobs. The whole charade was so infernally exasperating.

And, just to cap it all, John's recent successes had gone to his silly adolescent head. He had puffed himself up into a callow and pompous juvenile arrogance. He was right into the 'I've outgrown you: I'm better than you are' thing. It was contrived confrontations all the time.

'John, could you wash these wine glasses while I deal with the oven?'

'But I'm sorting out my slides and they're much more important!'

She went into the living room to set the dinner table, only to discover that he'd drawn the curtains and rearranged the furniture.

'John, we're supposed to be having supper in this room.'

'But I've got to give a proper slide show. This isn't just a cosy little family get-together, you know. They're really *important* people.'

Then she realised that she hadn't got enough cheese. 'John, could you watch the kitchen while I slip down to Millwards?'

'Oh hell! Do I *have* to?'

So it went on. She bristled. She really wanted to slap his silly, sulky face for him; or, better still, put him over her knee and spank his bottom. But with a gangling fifteen-year-old, neither was a feasible option. The fact was that there was nothing she could do. Except grit her teeth and grin and bear it.

Poor, silly, deluded mite, she thought as he strutted pompously round the house. He hadn't the first idea of what was really going on. Well, he'd soon find out! In the meantime it all went to show just how limited a schoolboy's view of the world really was.

A grudging compromise was eventually reached. The living room was organised to accommodate the dining table – albeit squeezed uncomfortably up against the window – and he agreed to watch the kitchen while she panicked off to Millward's in search of cheese.

A Ghastly Evening
Put-Downs
Evening came. Dorothy dressed up in her available Marks & Spencer's off-the-peg finery. Not, of course, that finery was

exactly her line; indeed, her lack of dress sense was notorious. The Bishop arrived in scruff order, looking as if he had just stepped off the footplate of one of his beloved steam engines. This was a subtle put-down: *you* may have to obey dress codes, but, as your superior, I don't have to! He was unusually affable and avuncular; a mode that set the alarm bells ringing with people like Dorothy who knew his true nature. Hidden booby traps were obviously lurking for the unwary.

A little later Ackroyd turned up, dressed to a tee in an elegant pin-striped suit and one of those shirts which sported a different-coloured collar. A subtly patterned tie proclaimed his membership of some esoteric and elite legal society. Here was another sartorial message for Dorothy: I know what real sophistication is, even if you don't, and what is more, I have been successful enough in life to be able to achieve it.

True to form – and right on cue – he started to nit-pick. He eyed the photograph of the cloud-wreathed peak of Margherita on the wall, Dorothy's pride and joy.

'Fine photo that, really artistic. I congratulate you. Pity it wasn't better printed, though. Where did you get it done?'

'I think it was at Boots.'

'You *didn't*, did you? Well, that explains the fuzziness.'

A PR catastrophe?

Supper began.

Showing off like mad, John scuttled about serving the quiche and vegetables.

'I see you've got him well trained,' observed the Bishop.

'But in future you might tell him to serve from the right-hand side and not the left,' added Ackroyd.

Without asking Dorothy, John dashed into the kitchen and emerged with an open bottle of red wine. With an elaborate fuss he started to fill the glasses.

'What's this?' asked Ackroyd.

'I think it's Burgundy... or it could be claret, I think,' replied Dorothy.

'Think? I thought you would have known!'

Dorothy didn't know. Wine was not her forte. She'd just rushed into Millward's Deli and grabbed some suitably exotic-looking bottles off the shelf.

'Where did you get it?'

'Millward's.'

'Then it's probably some cheap plonk that they've put into a fancy bottle. That's how they con gullible customers, you know. Galbraith's in Blackhouse Lane is where you should go if you want the real stuff. You might remember that in future.'

Meanwhile John had sat down and poured himself a tumbler-full of wine. Dorothy seethed. This was an open defiance of her specific orders about not drinking alcohol. It was bad enough being lectured to about the purchase of wine. This was much worse. Her credibility as a controller of teenagers was at stake.

'John,' she said quietly, 'I thought we'd agreed that the wine was to be for the adults only.'

'Oh, come on! I'm not a little kid any more!'

'Oh, let him have it!' grinned the Bishop. 'He's got to start sometime.'

'*In vino veritas*,' added Ackroyd with a wink. A not-so-subtle hint of the hidden agenda of the gathering.

Dorothy writhed.

John drained the tumbler and then helped himself to another even larger dose, and to another after that, and to yet another... which finally drained the bottle. The results were soon embarrassingly apparent – at least to Dorothy. He became loud and giggly and dominated the conversation, hectoring on in a shrill, rasping voice about rugby matches and the screwed-up section attack at the recent cadet weekend camp.

When the first course ended, he scooped up the plates and

vegetable dishes and bundled them into the kitchen. A loud crash and a horribly audible 'Oh shit!' followed.

'There goes your dinner service, Mrs Watson,' said Ackroyd.

Dorothy squirmed. The horrible evening was fast getting out of hand.

After a while John returned with a trayful of cheesecake, which he dumped unceremoniously in the middle of the table.

'Sorry about the crash, folks!' he giggled. 'But my bloody foot got caught on the table.' Snigger! Snigger! Splutter!

Once more Dorothy squirmed, but before she could say anything, he had disappeared into the kitchen again. Another crash and a loud 'Oh fuck!' followed.

'There go the remainder of your plates, Mrs Watson,' said Ackroyd. 'That'll mean another visit to Millward's.'

'John, *do* be more careful!' snapped Dorothy as John returned, brandishing a large Stilton cheese.

'Weren't my bloody fault!' he giggled inanely as he plonked the cheese in front of Ackroyd. 'It was that bloody chair.'

'And where did you get this cheese, Mrs Watson,' asked Ackroyd. 'Not at Millward's again?'

'Where else?'

'You get better stuff in a little place down by the quayside. And, by the way, you ought to add a little port if you really want to appreciate the true subtlety of the flavour.'

'There's a bottle of port on the kitchen shelf,' spluttered John. 'Hang on, I'll get it!'

'No, John, you *won't*!' exclaimed Dorothy forcibly. 'You just sit down and try to behave yourself while I get it!'

With that she disappeared into the kitchen and returned a minute later with a large bottle labelled, 'Millward's Special Christmas Port'.

'Ersatz, again, I see,' observed Ackroyd, superciliously as she poured the bright red liquid into a hole in the cheese.

'But, still, we might as well drink a little toast to our young hero, here.'

'Young hero' was hardly how she would have described the smirking John in front of her as she began to pour the port into the wine glasses.

'Excuse me,' interrupted Ackroyd. 'But isn't it customary to drink port from special port glasses?'

'Oh, sorry!' spluttered Dorothy, 'I must have forgotten. Wait a minute while I get them.'

'I can get them!' said John, standing up.

'No, John, *I'll* get them thank you!' she replied testily. 'You've done quite enough damage for one night!' Those port glasses were a treasured gift from her long dead father, lovingly preserved, but never used. The last thing she wanted was an oafish teenager getting his clumsy – and sacrilegious! – hands on what, to her, amounted almost to a sacred relic.

When she returned with them she found to her embarrassed fury that John had poured himself half a tumbler of port.

Worse and worse! Her prize pupil, the carefully furbished exhibit who was earmarked to prove her pedagogic excellence to a disbelieving public, behaving like *this*! What must her distinguished guests have thought of him? And not only of him, but of *her*? That she couldn't control a whole school of them? What a PR catastrophe!

A Slide Show, With Consequences

Eventually the gruesome meal ended and she managed to clear the table without too much trouble, apart from John spilling the remains of the port onto the carpet. The lights went out and she gritted her teeth as the long-prepared slide show began.

Well-oiled with the wine and the port, John gave what he thought was a bravura performance. Sniggering and burping, he played up to his seemingly admiring audience and revelled in his position as the centre of attention. Once more, Dorothy writhed and squirmed. Had he the first idea of what an idiot he was making of himself?

Finally the excruciating show ended and the lights went on. The Bishop and Ackroyd gave a round of applause.

'Well done, John, that was most informative,' beamed the Bishop.

John stood up and gave a little bow.

'I do think our maestro deserves a glass of Cointreau,' added Ackroyd, with just the hint of an evil grin. 'Don't you agree, Mrs Watson?'

Dorothy didn't agree, buy felt duty bound to oblige.

John winced as he sipped the ferocious liquid. He was in paradise. The Bishop didn't usually give compliments, so he must have given a really professional show. It was his first serious encounter with alcohol and he had the blissful feeling of floating up into the stratosphere in a balloon. On and up. Leave frowsy old frump Dolly behind.

There was a pause.

'Now then,' said the Bishop looking earnest, 'There're one or two things I need to know for the article I'm writing about youth activities in Boldonbridge. That ascent of Toubkal. Where was Mr Morris? Why wasn't he in any of your photographs?'

An unexpected bolt out of the blue! A sudden drop in the temperature. John fumbled for something to say – and coherent thought wasn't easy when you were squiffy.

'Well... Well, er... Well, he just didn't want to be photographed.'

'Didn't *want* to be photographed?' replied the Bishop, twitching his huge eyebrows. 'Don't you think that's a bit odd, Ackroyd? Up and coming PE teacher? I'd have thought that a photo of himself on top of Toubkal was just what he needed for his CV.'

Uncomfortable pause.

With a big benign smile the Bishop continued, 'I've been talking to Mr Morris. I have to say that he doesn't seem to know a thing about the route up Toubkal. Not a blind thing! A bit *strange* for a fellow who claims to have led you lot up to the top, isn't it?'

Another strained pause.

Sip of Cointreau. Continuation of benign smile. 'I don't think you have been telling me the whole truth, young man.'

Sinking feeling. The balloon plummeting down from the stratosphere. Panicky look round the room: no help anywhere. Cornered.

'Mr Morris wasn't there at all, was he? You're covering up for him, aren't you?'

'No! No! No! He was there, honest!'

'That's not what your friend Tracy told me, last week.'

Helpless stare.

'Shall I tell you what *really* happened? You got bored hanging round in Marrakesh while Bob Steadman was away in Rabat, didn't you? You'd been beaten up by Kevin Bartlett, hadn't you? He set you crying, according to your friend Jim, who witnessed it.'

'No! No! No! That's a lie!'

'But he *did* steal all your money and travellers cheques, didn't he? And there was absolutely nothing you could do about it, was there?'

'John!' cried Dorothy, as the mounting fury finally burst out of her. 'You *never* told me about any of this!'

'But I wasn't a little kid who had to go running to the teacher, was I?' replied a red-faced John. 'I could handle it myself! Anyway, I didn't start fucking crying!'

'*Mind your language, young man*!' Dorothy's exasperation was getting the better of her.

The Bishop signalled to her to be quiet and continued with

an ominous Cheshire Cat grin. 'All right, I'll believe that bit. But "little kid" was what it was all about, wasn't it?'

Embarrassed silence. The stratospheric balloon was hitting the ground now.

'Not very nice being mugged,' purred the Bishop. 'Bad for the tough guy image. Needed a bit of compensation, didn't you? Had to prove yourself by climbing the highest mountain in North Africa. But Mr Morris refused to take you. So you hatched a little plot with your mates and went off on your own without permission, didn't you?'

John stared at the floor and avoided eye contact.

'Yes,' he finally mumbled in a barely audible whisper.

Dorothy's worst fears seemed to being realised. The lying, deceitful young toad! Her pent-up rage exploded. '*John*! That was thoroughly *deceitful* of you! If I had *known*...!'

John looked up and confronted her. An outburst of teenage temper.

'But it wasn't only *me*! Jim and Rob were in it, too! So was Michael! I mean, we couldn't have just sat around in Marrakesh, could we? We'd come to climb mountains, we'd have looked right bloody dicks if we'd just sat around doing nothing.'

Dorothy was about to reply when the Bishop signalled her to stop.

'But why didn't you tell Mrs Watson about it?'

'Couldn't! Me and the lads had made an agreement with Mr Morris. I mean, he was a good bloke really. He wanted to come, but Dobson had told him to stay in Marrakesh. Dobson was always bullying him something wicked. We said he'd come with us to make him feel better. I mean, he couldn't tell that lot back home that he'd lost control of us, could he? He'd get sacked as a teacher.'

Silence. All eyes were on the floundering John.

'I mean I felt *sorry* for him!'

Desperate plea. 'I was trying to be *Christian*!'

Ackroyd spoke up. 'But wouldn't it have been better if you'd told Mrs Watson the truth?' Legalistic pause. 'After all,' he continued, 'You'd nothing to be ashamed of. Getting up Toubkal on your own like that, coping with a strange country and having to do everything in a foreign language. It was a splendid effort which showed real spirit. Surely you agree, Mrs Watson?'

Dorothy nodded silently, but was not fully reassured. There could be worse revelations to come. *Much* worse!

'And, what's more,' continued Ackroyd, in his smooth, patronising-the-stupid-client voice, 'you saved the credibility of the expedition. The Youth Outreach people would have looked rather foolish if, after spending all that money, nobody had climbed a mountain. And your concern for Mr Morris is most commendable. Very mature, in fact.'

Some relief. With his battered ego partially restored, John clutched at a straw.

'Will I get a D. of E. Gold Medal for it?'

'We might think about that,' replied Ackroyd.

For John this meant a firm 'Yes'. For a practiced lawyer, however, it meant almost certainly 'No'.

The two men smiled knowingly at each other while Dorothy's X-ray eyes bored into her wayward protégé. She sensed that there was something else in the pipeline – and it wasn't going to be very nice, either.

'One other point,' said the Bishop quietly. Threateningly, thought John, not unlike Giles when he was about to go ballistic. 'About you and Bob Steadman.'

Oh, God! Not *that*, *please*!

'That business at Am – whatever-it-was-called.'

Not crashing *onto* the ground now, but sinking *into* it. Blood draining from his face. He actually felt it happening. How much do these people *know*? Had Bob gone and spilled the beans? Gone all soppy and repentant? That'd be why he'd buggered off to fucking Paraguay…

'What were you doing in the middle of the night, walking around in Bob Steadman's clothes? A bit *strange*, wouldn't you say?'

'I… I wasn't! I never!'

'That's not what your mate Jim says. He told me that he saw you.'

There was a pause while the Bishop's large, ugly face twisted up into a hungry grimace, not unlike a grizzly bear eyeing a succulent salmon it had just caught.

'You weren't tarting around, were you?' he eventually said. 'Flashing your charms in the hope that Bob might be a little *susceptible*?'

Silence.

Dorothy gritted her teeth. This was the bit she'd been dreading. Another 'homosexual accident'. Rumours had been circulating among the senior boys about the 'dirty vicar bumming little Arab boys and having to do a runner'. She'd dismissed this as low-grade teenage smut. But maybe there was some truth in it after all. Not 'bumming' little Arab boys, however, but the British boy sitting in front of her! This was going to take some explaining away when the school inspectors arrived! The squalid, deceiving young…!

Her X-ray eyes glowing with deadly radiation, she broke the silence with a hard, headmistress voice. 'Tell the truth, John. And I mean *the truth*!'

John squirmed and said nothing. What *could* he say? He'd have to tell the truth… but *not* the *whole* truth. No way! That would amount to a form of suicide.

'Well,' he eventually spluttered, 'It's, well, a bit embarrassing.' Back to being a squalid little shit-pants again! Could he *never* grow out of it?

'The *truth*, John.'

He felt his blood starting to flow in the opposite direction this time, not downwards and out of his face, but upwards and into it. He blushed bright red.

'Well I had the gut rot. Everybody got it. Not just me. I was... er... caught short in the middle of the night.'

The Bishop grinned, baring his teeth and looking, this time, like an oversized piranha fish. 'But that was no reason for dressing up in somebody else's clothes.'

Pause. You've no choice. You'll have to admit it. Come on, get it over with.

Eventually a red-faced splutter. 'Well, if you *must* know, I shat myself. Big time. Couldn't help it. It just poured out. Bob had to give me some spare clothes while mine were washed and dried.'

Pause.

'I mean, I could have walked round in the nuddy, could I? That *would* have been tarting around!'

'But where were your spare clothes?'

'Hadn't got any.'

A burst of hostile radiation from Dorothy. 'John that's *not* true! I gave you plenty!'

Desperate plea. 'But I'd given them all away. To pay for the donkeys on Toubkal! For the girls. They wouldn't have got there without donkeys to carry their rucksacks, and to carry them, too.'

'But couldn't any of the others have helped out?' said the Bishop. 'I mean, what about Jim and Rob? Why only you?'

'Well they said I was a rich git and that they had no money.'

'And you believed them, did you? You let them bully you into giving all your things away?'

Worse and worse! Not just a dirty little shit-pants, but a pathetic little wimp as well!

He wriggled and squirmed for a moment and then said in a frantic, pleading voice, 'I thought I was being *Christian*!

That's why I gave them away. The Arabs were poor. They hadn't got anything. I was trying to be *Christian*!'

Only very partially true, this. In reality, you had them lifted off you and there was sod all you could have done about it! But, well… gild the lily, as they say.

'Perhaps you were, John,' said Dorothy guardedly. 'Perhaps you were. I'll believe you this once.' At least she'd been spared the dreaded 'homosexual accident'. That was a big relief… but what else was lurking in the pipeline?

'So you have been taking my wife's words to heart, have you?' purred the Bishop. 'Nothing improper about that. Quite commendable in fact! But, oh dear, you *do* seem to be afflicted with these "downstairs problems", don't you? Just like two years ago, isn't it?'

John winced. Same old Bishop, this! Always had to pick on this sort of thing. Always had to make you feel small and pathetic!

He let out an angry retort. 'But I'm not the only one! After all, David Livingstone died of it!'

'Yes,' smiled the Bishop. 'You're in distinguished company, I'll grant you that.'

A ripple of laughter followed. The tension seemed to ease a bit. But he was not out of the woods yet; there was more to come.

'One final thing,' said Ackroyd, beaming indulgently. 'You're a wired-up young man. Streetwise. You'll know things I don't know.'

That's more like it, thought a bruised John. At least *he* appreciates me, which is more than you can say for Dolly or that great caveman of a Bishop!

'Yes?'

'I've got a young client who's in deep trouble with drugs. It's not something I know much about. He keeps on talking about things like 'acid' and 'coke'. Maybe you could help me out?'

John, of course, hadn't a clue. The world of drugs was a blank, an empty space on his map, a 'terra incognito' perceived, if at all, as an evil emanation from the nether regions of the Greenhill world. But, well, none of these bullying old Neanderthals knew anything about it either. So here was his chance to restore a bit of street cred to his battered ego. Just invent! Use your imagination! They'll swallow it!

For a full five minutes he gabbled away. The audience nodded gravely, obviously profoundly impressed by his profound worldly knowledge. So easy to take people like this for a ride! And good fun, too!

The flood eventually dried up.

'Anything else you want to know?'

'No,' replied Ackroyd with the barest hint of a grin, 'you've told me all I want to know.'

Another silence followed as the two men looked knowingly at one another.

Floating on his sea of alcohol, John's inhibitions were relaxed and his awareness intensified. Slowly, the penny began to drop. Things weren't quite what they seemed to be. Something he didn't know about was going on.

'What the fuck's all this in aid of?' he eventually blurted out in a slurred voice. 'Why are you asking me all these questions?'

'I think we'd better tell him, Ackroyd,' said the Bishop, flashing his toothy, piranha-style grin.

'Here, read this, young man.'

He handed him the official letter from the Youth Outreach Committee.

John read it. Again he had that awful Greenhill feeling of utter helplessness. Enhanced by his alcoholic haze, it was an actual physical sensation of falling into a bottomless pit. He could almost hear the blood draining away from his face, like bathwater gurgling down the plughole.

'But… But…' he gasped. 'This is all lies. I never!'

The appropriate words wouldn't come.

'Don't worry, we know that,' purred Ackroyd in his smooth, cultivated voice. 'You've just proved that you weren't involved in drug dealing.'

'Oh?'

'You know absolutely nothing about drugs. You don't even know the difference between hash and coke. You've never seen heroin, have you?'

'Oh?'

'You've just talked a load of rubbish, haven't you? You made it all up, didn't you? You thought we'd be impressed. Well, we were impressed, but not quite in the way you thought we'd be.'

Awful deflation. Not a lad. Just a silly kid who'd shot his mouth!

'But, don't worry,' added Ackroyd, slipping into his patronising-the-client voice, 'you're off the hook. Exonerated. And, what's more, we've got all the evidence we need on tape.'

'God! If I'd known you were taping me…'

'Normal intelligence practice, old thing!' chortled the Bishop with an ugly leer.

'And when we get that report from the Embassy at Rabat – which better come pretty soon or I'll have to twist arms in influential places! – you'll be untouchable,' he added. 'Innocent as a newborn babe, in fact. Not a bad metaphor under the circs, is it, Ackroyd, old man?'

A drained Dorothy heaved a deep sigh of relief. 'Well, that's something achieved, anyway!'

Yet another awkward silence.

'Come on, laddie!' Ackroyd eventually said to John. 'Don't look like that about it! You've nothing to be ashamed of. Quite the opposite! You did very well in Morocco; better, perhaps, than the expedition – if you can call it that! – deserved. Mrs Watson, he's a real credit to you.'

'One last thing,' added the Bishop. 'Just watch your mouth, young man. One day somebody might go and believe you. And, whatever you do, don't even think of trying to compete with the likes of Kevin Bartlett in the macho stakes. You're just not in their league. Keep away from them.'

By now, John was drifting helplessly on the heaving ocean of alcohol, which was wildly enhancing the ups and downs of the emotional roller coaster he was riding. He was fast losing control. To his embarrassed horror, he suddenly started to cry like a little boy.

How are the Mighty Fallen

The guests left. Dorothy returned to the living room. Seeing a woebegone John slumped on the settee, she lost control of herself and tumbled right into Emotional Woman mode. Decent honourable youth, desperately trying to do what was right, but, through no fault of his own, tangled up in a mesh of juvenile criminals and rampaging adult egos! Horribly wronged! And how she, too, had wronged him by believing his traducers! Oh the remorse! Oh the deep sense of inadequacy! She was *so* unworthy of such a treasure!

She sat down and hugged him.

'Oh John!' she cooed, 'I'm so *sorry*! You're so *good*! I'm so *proud* of you!'

John writhed. To his utter dismay he began to cry again. Christ, he couldn't bloody help it! It just happened. It was like shitting yourself when you had the squitters. The utter shame of it!

Dorothy loved it. He was no longer the defiant teenager, but had gone back to being the vulnerable little boy who needed her. It was just like that night in Scotland four years ago when he'd crept into her tent crying because he'd had a nightmare and wet himself. Things were back to where she liked them.

'Come on, dear,' she said, 'I think you'd better go to bed. You've had a difficult evening, darling, and you've drunk rather too much.'

('Dear'! 'Darling'! *Ugh*!)

In the full flood of Mother Hen mode she led him slowly to his bedroom. Without bothering to undress, he collapsed in a heap onto the bed. For a time he lay there while the whole room seemed to heave up and down as if he were on a ship in a hurricane.

Suddenly he threw up all over the eiderdown and the carpet. The final humiliation. Couldn't even hold a little booze! How were the mighty fallen!

A Lad Again

On Monday morning, however, John became a lad again. It was back to school, back to being the brilliant young scholar and the dashing *condottiere* whose deeds of derring-do in the Army Cadet Force and in the mountains of Morocco made him a hero; at least, among the Beaconsfield juniors. The humiliations of Saturday evening were consigned to oblivion. Stuffed into another dimension where they could do no harm.

Christ! If They had Known!

A couple of weeks later the school inspectors arrived. The whole school was on parade. Polished. Garnished. Drilled by the right. Everything positive was highlighted and burnished. Especially prominent were John's paintings, history essays and burgeoning history and geography projects. His Morocco photographs formed a dazzling display that occupied the lion's share of the exhibition in Geography Room. His only serious competitor was Fred, who'd produced some fine woodwork – West Indian-style chairs – a geography project about Barbados and had cooked some exotic Caribbean food, which was duly served up for the inspectors' lunch.

Washed, scrubbed, groomed, honed and resplendent in his red blazer and Head Boy badge, John led the inspectors on a conducted tour of the school. It was a bravura performance: showing off, flashing his ingratiating smile, playing up to an appreciative audience. It was the sort of thing he was really good at.

The climax came when, accompanied by a crowd of admiring juniors, he ushered them into the model railway room in the attic. The model railway had come a long way since the early days when an anarchic Danny Fleetwood had adorned the maths teacher Polly's upended rear with an RAF-style roundel. It was now a miniature world of hills, trees and villages with tunnels, embankments and stations, much of it created by John himself and a team of willing juniors. The juniors duly rose to the occasion, shepherding three long trains simultaneously round the fearsome curves and through the multitudinous hazards of the marshalling yard.

Prominent among them was a quite ridiculously beautiful little new boy, named Mark Downing. Physically uncoordinated and an academic disaster area, under John's tutelage he'd managed to make a big castle which crowned one of the hills. Grabbing an inspector's arm, he pointed to his castle. 'Look, sir. Ah made that all by meesell, didna, Mr Denby!'

The inspector duly responded with an appropriate accolade. 'Did you? Did you *really*? Well done! Very well done!'

In a short life chiefly marked by disasters Mark had had few – if any! – such accolades. Intoxicated by the new experience, he embraced John. 'Me big bruvva! Me hero! Ta ever so!'

The inspectors were suitably impressed. 'Most impressive. All the work of the youngsters? Magnificent', etc., etc., etc.

John walked on air. Artist, scholar and now Leader of Men.

Then suddenly – out of the blue – came a visitation from the 'hidden world'. As Mark pressed his little body against him, he felt a wild electric thrill surge through him. Crazy, madly exciting 'stirrings' erupted in awkward parts of his anatomy. The Demon was there and, bold and insolent, was taking possession of him. It was like one of those slaves who stood beside victorious generals when they entered Rome in triumph. 'Remember, you are only a man.' Here, it was: 'Remember that you are not a real man, but a fraud. You can't do the proper thing. Never will be able to.'

Thankfully, neither the inspectors, nor the juniors, nor little Mark, noticed the embarrassing effects of the arousal. Instead they pronounced themselves 'deeply impressed by the excellent relationship between the senior and the junior boys and, especially by the mature leadership evinced by the head boy'. Christ! If they had *known*!

Contradicting the Historical Dialectic

Dorothy duly received a glowing report: 'Dedicated staff… excellent relationship between staff and pupils… a school which fulfilled its stated aims by caring for and nurturing each individual pupil, whatever their background and native ability… high standards of work from some very unpromising pupils…', etc., etc., etc. Hidden among the jargon of the concluding paragraphs was a coded message: if only some of the local comprehensives were as successful as Beaconsfield School.

Dorothy luxuriated. Vindication! All her trials and tribulations had not been in vain: she'd won through in the end! And, indeed, what a missile to fire at her traducers up at the university! She couldn't resist sending a copy of the report to Professor Stimpson.

The net result was a series of seminars in the higher reaches of the Education Department about the way in which the Inspectorate was 'riddled with inappropriate middle-class prejudices'. Later the theme developed into a session on Factualism as opposed to Objective Reality. Factualism was the seeming success of a private school like Beaconsfield; while Objective Reality was the underlying truth – apparent only to the 'properly aware' – of how such places were actually undermining, not only education, but the whole of society by contradicting the 'Historical Dialectic'.

EPISTOLARY WARFARE

Militant Mother Hen

Meanwhile the Morocco saga rumbled on. The British Embassy at Rabat eventually produced a report which stated quite unequivocally that Kevin Bartlett and his gang had been caught drug dealing by a carefully prepared police sting operation. The Bishop duly sent a photocopy of it to Dorothy, who wrote a massive letter to the Youth Outreach Committee.

Marshalling this and all the evidence so laboriously amassed during that gruesome Saturday evening, she demolished their accusations point by point, especially the business about drugs. As for the 'grossly improper relationship' of one of her pupils with an adult leader, she waxed indignant. The youth concerned had had 'an unfortunate accident' while suffering from a stomach upset. Having given all his spare clothes away to destitute locals in 'a spirit of genuine and mature compassion', he had none to change into and had, of necessity, to borrow some from the adult leader. To elevate his 'excruciating predicament' into an act of homosexual soliciting was 'quite unacceptable'. Adolescents were 'especially sensitive'... and as for 'the sheer hurt and anguish' engendered by such 'prurient and unfounded allegations'…! Here her indignation blazed up into a fury, fuelled by her desperate need to do penance for having so gratuitously wronged him before. Militant Mother Hen, not just fending off the marauding fox, but aggressively savaging it.

Faced with this, the Committee backed off a little. They duly wrote a letter thanking her for 'supplying useful information'. A final resolution of the business, however, awaited 'further clarification'.

She also wrote a lengthy letter to the *Guardian* in a similar vein. To her bewildered anger it was neither published, nor even acknowledged. Not, of course, that she should have expected otherwise. The *Guardian* was a serious newspaper with properly informed views on education. It did not have time to waste on the semi-literate prejudices of petty bourgeois teachers in private schools.

A Very Different Matter

It was a very different matter, however, when a week later Dr Giles Denby chose to comment on the issue. Ground-breaking historian, Labour member for Boldonbridge West, member of the Shadow Cabinet, 'Conscience of the Party' and 'tireless campaigner for equality and social justice' etc., etc., etc., he had to be taken seriously; *very* seriously. Ever vigilant – as always! – he submitted a closely reasoned diatribe castigating the way in which the 'middle classes' exploited the welfare state for their own devious ends, and in particular 'altruistic initiatives' aimed at 'deprived inner-city youngsters'.

Waxing indignant with righteous fury and with a multitude of precisely ordered facts and figures, he mercilessly exposed their machinations. The recent Boldonbridge Youth Expedition to Morocco was a classic example of this perfidy. Step by step, he detailed the way in which this 'bold and generous-spirited socialist initiative' had been subsumed into the 'commercial interests of a small private school' which was 'a petty bourgeois money-making racket of the worst sort'. It was, of course, merely a microcosm of what was taking place nationwide within the N.H.S.

Those in the know were deeply impressed by Dr Denby's sincere incorruptibility in refusing to spring to the defence of his wayward and overindulged son who had weaselled his way onto the Morocco expedition and had been implicated in drug trafficking and other less mentionable activities.

Naturally, such 'compassionate and well informed' views had to be taken seriously. The lengthy missive was published in its entirety, not merely as a Letter to the Editor, but as a leading article on the editorial page.

It was a welcome shot in the arm for the beleaguered Youth Outreach Committee. They felt vindicated and began to explore the possibility of legal action against Beaconsfield School.

Letters from Paraguay: A Bolt Out of The Blue

Then, like a bolt out of the blue, came a clutch of letters from Father Robert Steadman in Paraguay. A 'Very Personal and Confidential' one was for the Bishop's eye only. What revelations it might have contained were anybody's guess. Its contents remained hidden from prying eyes.

Another very public letter went directly to the Youth Outreach Committee.

No, the two Beaconsfield boys had *not* been involved in drug trafficking. That had been confined entirely to Kevin Bartlett and his gang, who had been caught red-handed in a Moroccan police sting operation. Photocopies of the police report and a statement from the British Embassy at Rabat – which, unknown to everybody, he'd secretly kept with him – clinched the issue. Indeed, a glance at the police records of Boldonbridge would show that the said Kevin had convictions for GBH and was believed to be deeply involved in the local drug scene.

While 'sincerely applauding the earnest endeavours of altruistic youth leaders' to induce the likes of Kevin Bartlett to embrace a better way of life, the 'scapegoating of innocent youngsters' was 'to be deplored'. And no, Mr Morris had certainly *not* climbed Jebel Toubkal. That had been an entirely self-managed effort by the youngsters themselves, masterminded by the said John Denby. As for being a 'thoroughly bad and disruptive influence', the reverse was true. Without his drive, energy and linguistic skills, the whole expedition would have ground to a halt.

As for 'wantonly involving the children in his care in all kinds of unacceptable dangers', he, Father Steadman, had done alpine training in Austria and had climbed extensively in the Atlas Mountains. Morris may well have had a Mountain Leadership Certificate, but he had never climbed outside Britain and couldn't speak a word of any foreign language, and was thus 'unfitted to lead a group of youngsters in the Atlas Mountains'. And as for 'sleeping in unhygienic and disease-ridden local houses' and 'forcing British children to eat unpalatable and filthy local food', wasn't the whole point of the expedition to get away from the tourist trade routes and experience a different culture at first hand? One after another the allegations were demolished, buried indeed, under an avalanche of evidence; chapter and verse, the lot. Insinuations about an 'improper relationship' with one of the boys, if not immediately withdrawn, would end in court.

State of The Art Missile Strike

Another letter went to the *Guardian*. While 'applauding sincere and altruistic attempt to reach out to deprived youngsters', wasn't it 'just a little naïve' to take 'young offenders known to be drug abusers' to a place like Morocco?

Everybody knew that was where the hippies went to get their dope. Photocopies of the documents, which he enclosed with the letter, proved their guilt beyond doubt. And as for trying to foist the blame onto innocent youngsters...! This was a 'monstrous abuse of authority' and 'quite unworthy of any teacher of youth leader with the slightest claim to professionalism'. Youngsters were not responsible for their social backgrounds, and 'to victimise them for it' amounted to 'racism'. Even so, the youngsters concerned could hardly be described as a 'privileged elite': full details were given of Michael Connolly's domestic circumstances.

As for 'wantonly involving the children in his care in all kinds of unacceptable dangers', a bombardment of evidence and justifications followed, chapter and verse, the lot; indeed, a strike by metaphorical guided missile with all the devastating precision of state-of-the-art technology.

And then the 'improper relationship'. Said youth had had a stomach upset and was in a 'state of some distress'. Was helping him out any excuse for malicious and filthy insinuations? Indeed, readers might just care to consider 'the sheer hurt and mental injury inflicted on a sensitive and wholly innocent youngster'. This sort of thing was 'child abuse of the worst sort'. The letter was published and, moreover, got pride of place on the Letters to the Editor page.

A Question of Pedigree

Dorothy, it was true, had said almost identical things in her letter. But this time it was... well, a bit different! It was not, after all, *what* was said that was important but, rather, *who* said it. Father Steadman was a devout Catholic. That, by itself, was a bit 'iffy' in a post-Christian world. But, then, the Catholic Church did have intellectual credibility – if only of a limited kind – but, more to the point, it *did* have claims to being a 'victimised Oppressed Minority', as was evident in Ulster. The clincher, however, was his first-class honours degree, his PhD from Cambridge, and his working among the downtrodden and deprived in a struggling Third World country. For what could possibly be more respectable than working among exploited, alcoholic and drug-abusing Guarani Indians? Che Guevara himself could hardly have been more socially and intellectually worthy of attention! It was, after all, a question of *pedigree*, and apart from the religious bit, Father Steadman's pedigree was pretty watertight.

Men Among Children. Children Among Men

In the face of this unexpected counter-attack, a meeting was convened at County Hall. The lawyers were all for going to court. 'It's all bluff. After all, they're only *teachers*. Men among children. Children among men.Legal action will scare them rigid.'

This induced a baleful stare from Dobson. 'Huh! I suppose you're saying that *I'm* a child, too, are you? Thank you for nothing!'

He advised caution. He knew – if the lawyers didn't! – that there were just too many skeletons lurking in his cupboards for comfort. Those police reports from Morocco could blow a fatal hole in any case he could fabricate. And Heaven alone knew what else the Beaconsfield lawyers might rake up. Besides, he didn't trust middle-class lawyers: they were money-grubbers on the make and on the take. Even if the court case failed they would still be laughing all the way to the bank. He, on the other hand, could face crippling legal bills.

So a truce was declared. 'Sincere apologies' were issued 'for any hurt caused to innocent youngsters by some unfortunate misunderstandings'. The matter was officially dropped.

All Faces Saved; Judicious Rearrangement of Facts

Finally, the Bishop published his article in the *Diocesan Journal*. Those who thought they knew him were bemused by the strangely emollient tone of the article: so unlike the notoriously contentious bull in the china shop!

'Sincere and praiseworthy' efforts had been made to 'reform hardened young criminals'. Unfortunately, however, on this occasion the venture 'had misfired somewhat', but nevertheless, 'great praise was due to Brian Dobson' for the 'utterly unselfish' way in which he had abandoned 'his lifelong ambition to explore the Atlas Mountains' and escorted his erring charges back home to safety. The fact that 'on this occasion things had come a bit unstuck' was no reason for not repeating similar ventures in the future. Indeed, it was to be hoped that 'the dynamic and altruistic Brian Dobson' would not be put off by this unfortunate setback and would try again as soon as possible. As St Paul so rightly said.... etc.etc....

Meanwhile, 'inspired by the true leadership qualities' of the 'highly qualified PE teacher, Joe Morris', who had 'an exemplary faith in young people' and 'the praiseworthy courage to let them plan the venture with a minimum of adult interference', the remaining youngsters had made a 'truly splendid self-managed ascent of the Jebel Toubkal, the highest mountain in North Africa'. Furthermore, Joe Morris had 'unselfishly volunteered to take charge of the less able members of the expedition, shepherding them carefully over high and dangerous mountain passes, thus enabling Father Steadman, an experienced alpinist, to lead the young tigers up an appropriately challenging mountain peak'.

In fact, the whole venture had been a triumph, which conclusively proved to any doubters 'the excellence and the high professionalism of the expedition leaders' and, also, 'the wisdom of the Youth Outreach Committee in appointing so excellent a leader team'. In all it was 'an inspiring beacon of hope for the future'.

So, prizes all round; at least, for the people who mattered. All faces saved. No direct lies, just a judicious rearrangement of the facts.

A Load of Garbage?

A little later Meakin ran into the Bishop in Boldonbridge. 'That article of yours,' he blurted out in an unguarded moment. 'It was a load of garbage, wasn't it?'

Instead of the expected explosion, however, the Bishop grinned wickedly. 'Of course it was! But then, so is most of the history you read. Call it diplomatic oil on troubled waters.'

It was a side of the Bishop that Meakin hadn't seen before. It seemed that Donald Mackay was rather more than a tactless old bull in a china shop. Perhaps it all had something to do with his intelligence work in Ulster and his ability to control the prickly-proud, testosterone-crazed young Mburong warriors in that remote corner of Uganda.

'We'll Lay This One to Rest'

The big loser was John. There was no mention of his bold effort of leading a band of escapees up Toubkal. No mention of how he had beggared himself to pay for the donkeys that had enabled the girls to make the ascent. No mention of how he alone had found a safe way through the cliff band on Aksoual when even Steadman had been at a loss. His great achievements had been airbrushed out. Indeed, that was the fate of the whole Morocco saga at Beaconsfield. Airbrushed out.

'In future, Roderick,' declared Dorothy, 'I think we'd better leave these big, official youth expeditions well alone. I really couldn't go through all that again.'

'Quite agree,' replied Meakin, 'there're just too many

interested parties and big egos involved. Next time we'd better do something ourselves. We'll lay this one to rest.'

Monster or Angel?

So, laid to rest it was. John's Morocco display was quietly removed from the Geography Room. 'That's all in the past, now,' said Dorothy when he protested. 'You must look to the future.'

'Look to the future and forget about the past': that became the standard response whenever he tried to talk about it to any of the teachers. The Morocco Expedition just didn't seem to be something you mentioned in polite society. Not unless you wanted to be labelled as a boastful, self-obsessed, ego-manic.

Why? Things were all so topsy-turvy. Two years ago when he'd alerted the fire brigade about the fire in the Bishop's house he'd been acclaimed as a hero, even though he'd messed himself with fright and hadn't done a quarter of the things Isobel said he'd done. Yet now, when he really *had* done great things, he was pushed aside. Odd, irrational, perplexing.

And Steadman? His hero who'd rescued him from disaster two years ago, who'd stood by him, who'd taken him to Morocco, paid for him when all his money had been stolen, praised him to the skies? Why had he run away like a thief in the night? Why, after all those honeyed words, had he discarded him? Later that term he had an answer of sorts.

As part of its, Ongoing Sex Education Initiative, the Boldonbridge Education Committee sent teams of trained counsellors round the schools – and even to the private schools! – to 'raise Paedophile Awareness among young people'. All the old chestnuts of the 'Paedophile Awareness' pamphlets were brought out, polished and exhibited: warnings about those paedophile strategies that he knew so well.

Once again, it all seemed to fit Steadman like a glove. Textbook case. Forget all the guff about being 'the disciple

Jesus loved'. Face facts, Jonny boy, it wasn't you he loved, it was just your bum! Yet, one part of him insisted that he hadn't been abused. He'd been given something he'd wanted; indeed, he'd experienced a wild and seemingly holy *joy*!

Strange. Perplexing. What was he? Depraved monster or specially blessed angel? How could he possibly know?

Authorised Version

As time passed an 'authorised version' of the Morocco Expedition took shape both in the Youth Outreach Committee and in the Education Department of the University. 'That Morocco thing... Great idea... Pity it had to be hijacked by self-interested petty bourgeois elements... Pity the lawyers were too chicken to go ahead with the court case. They could have exposed the whole racket.'

But secretly, Brian Dobson knew better. By not going to court, certain embarrassing skeletons had remained firmly locked in their cupboards. More importantly, however, he had a grievance, to be preserved and lovingly polished up over the years. John Denby wasn't to hear the last of the Morocco Expedition.

6

Lost Childhood

A Friend Departs

The months passed. Vital exams loomed. All John's group were involved. Even bumbling old Sam Hawthorne was down for a few exams: R.S.A. exams in basic English and maths, a CSE in art. Dorothy declared herself satisfied by the 'mature and positive attitude' of the group; so different from Billy Nolan and his mates of evil memory!

The only blemish was Danny Fleetwood. Over the year a downward spiral had gathered momentum. He'd become increasingly obsessed with street culture: 'hards', motorbikes, fights, knives, screwing birds. To him, this was an alluring world, much more real than school. He set his heart on becoming a punk.

One day he turned up at morning assembly with his head shaved and sporting a quiver of red, blue and green Mohican plumage. Dorothy sent him home with orders to come back with his hair properly cut, and in his school uniform. Whereupon his father angrily protested and threatened her with the European Court of Human Rights. But she stood firm: school rules were school rules..

The net result was that Danny dropped out of school. Rumours abounded. He'd become a Hell's Angel. He was 'on drugs'. He'd been involved in a recent spectacular burglary in Moorside. Somebody said they'd seen him cavorting round with Kevin Bartlett and his 'hards' in the nether regions of Greenwood.

What Am I?

John was saddened by the spectacle. He remembered his one-time friend, so full of life and interests, with whom he'd made model aeroplanes, played with trains and formulated plans for recovering the Falkland Islands from the Argies back in '82. It was a loss. Like a bereavement: his best friend dead. Worse than dead; changed into something else, something he found repellent.

At the same time he found himself increasingly isolated. It became less and less easy to relate to his schoolmates. They inhabited different worlds. Not for them, explorers struggling through steamy jungles, the three hundred Spartans at Thermopylae or the undiscovered ruins of long-lost civilisations. Not derring-do on far-off mountains, and certainly not the sheer wonder of seeing the crags of the High Atlas emerge from the darkness into the brilliant light of dawn. Their world was football, pop music, motorbikes, who amongst them was 'hard' and, above all, sex. Bonking. Having it off with this or that bird on Saturday night. Their latest 'bang'.

It was all so *boring*! Of course, he had to take part in it, just to keep his macho image intact. That meant inventing 'conquests' that had never happened and, indeed, never *could* happen. Like that 'horny bird down in London' that he'd finally managed to 'have'. As always, it was a matter of getting yourself to actually believe your fictions.

But he feared discovery, especially when a resentful Army-Barmy Martin started up. 'Yeah! Great! But how come we never gets to *see* yer birds? Is they too good for the likes o' us? Or mebbe you ain't got no birds!'

Then it would have to be, 'Belt up Martin! Want a fight, do you?'

'No! Just kiddin' like.'

The threat of violence always worked with a self-indulgent fantasist like Martin. For the time being, at any rate. The trouble was that Martin almost certainly knew the truth about him, but was too chicken to say so openly. But one day the time would come.

And always at the back of his mind was the dread of another 'accident' like that one with Danny Fleetwood in the shower three years ago. This time, he knew only too well that he would not get off so lightly. Rejection, ridicule and, almost certainly, gross humiliations worthy of Greenhill were there waiting for him should he drop his guard for even a moment.

But if only the Demon would stop tormenting him with those unmentionable, but intoxicating visions! If only it would let him have desires that he could actually talk about instead of forcing him to tell lies all the time; let him do something that was acceptable and not shameful and disgusting. Every night he prayed for it. But it made no difference. God just didn't seem to be listening. Either that, or more likely, there was no God at all. Indeed, with the departure of Bob Steadman God was slowly dying within him, to be replaced by... *what*? A seeming emptiness, where nothing made sense and where, he, John Denby, was only a statistical quirk.

Very Different People

Among his classmates, of course, there was Fred. Fred was a big cut above the others. He could talk about more than just sex or 'being hard'. But they moved in different worlds.

He didn't want to penetrate remote and exotic jungles to test himself to the limit on high mountains. When John had suggested a hiking and camping trip in the Lake District, Fred had hummed and hawed, and when his parents had firmly squashed the idea as 'too dangerous', he'd meekly complied with their decision.

Fred was a decent and kindly lad and John wondered if he could possibly confide in him. Like his parents, Fred was a devout Christian, and John saw possibilities here. So one day he tentatively probed his beliefs. He read the Bible every night, but did he really believe that every single word in it was true?

'Of course,' replied Fred, 'it's the word of God, isn't it?'

'But what about that bit about Samuel hewing Agag to pieces before the Lord?' said John. 'That wasn't very Christian, was it?'

'But Agag was an unbeliever who had offended God, so of course it was right.'

Further probing showed that he'd hit a brick wall, so he backed off. He had thought of asking what he thought of that bit in Leviticus about homosexuality being an abomination. But he quickly thought better of it. It could well lead to awkward questions that were best left unasked. He and Fred, they were very different people.

Arrested Development?

The only people he could relate to were the juniors. Their world was still bright and exciting. They loved the model railway in the attic and were always willing to help him enlarge it. Together they made a great big papier-mâché Matterhorn with a spiral tunnel through it. They helped him create a big forest and a new village.

As Head Boy he was deputed to help out on the adventure weekends. While many of the seniors professed themselves 'dead bored' by these, the juniors wallowed in them. They were wildly excited when he took them on midnight walks through dark and creepy woods, conjuring up all sorts of grotesque monsters lurking in their Stygian depths. To them, Helvellyn was a grand and awesome mountain, a sort of Everest and Striding Edge, a dramatic challenge.

He came to relish these weekends. Here he was the king, the leader of the pack, his worth recognised. *They* weren't bored by him. They thrilled to his tales of Morocco and midnight operations with the Army Cadets. Among them he seemed to physically expand. Adolescence hadn't snuffed out their sense of wonder, nor sex yet thrown its drab monochrome blanket over their natural ebullience. They hadn't grown up; and, maybe, he hadn't grown up either and that was why he seemed to get on so well with them. They were all kids together. But wasn't it better to be a kid, if 'growing up' meant abandoning all that was fresh and exciting in the world? No, he thought to himself, I don't want to follow Danny Fleetwood, not *yet*, just let me feast a little longer in this Aladdin's Cave of wonders! Maybe he was a case of arrested development.

A Squalid Evolutionary Accident?

But that wasn't all. He *did* like supervising the juniors while they were showering after games – and in ways that he knew he shouldn't. The Wednesday afternoon rugby session became the highlight of the week: the chance to feast his eyes upon... hidden treasures! Briggs had been right; spot on, in fact, and didn't he bloody well know it!

Of course, he had to keep the Demon in check; more than just 'in check', locked up in an iron-bound cage. Let it out, even for the briefest moment, and it would ruin you. But was it *really* a demon? On that strange and, by now almost mythical, night in the depth of the Atlas Mountains, Steadman had talked of a visitation from the Holy Ghost. But where was Steadman now? Why had he deserted him?

Different, he certainly was. For a start, he now knew that he was a lot brighter than any of his schoolmates. And if Martin was average and Fred well above average, then he, John Denby, must be, at the very least, brilliant – if not almost a genius. Indeed, he'd read in a book he secretly got out of the library that many of history's most creative geniuses had been homosexuals: Leonardo de Vinci, Alexander the Great, Lawrence of Arabia, Richard Burton the great Orientalist and African explorer. So, maybe, John Denby was to be numbered among them?

Then came a more sober voice. At the Army Cadet summer camps he had to conceal the fact that he was at Beaconsfield because the other cadets said it was just a dustbin for thicks. So perhaps he was just average after all; or, more probably, below average. In the Kingdom of the Blind, after all, the one-eyed man was king.

Maybe the exams he was going to take would sort this one out. Do well and he would be vindicated. But *would* he do well? Maybe Dolly and Meakin were puffing him up when they had entered him for all those O Levels? The test would come. He might just succeed, and how wonderful it would be if he did! But it was much more likely that he wouldn't. Face reality, young man, you're nothing but a squalid evolutionary accident. Little more than a turd dropped by a dinosaur.

'I Know What I Am'

So what was he? Good or bad? Probably, very bad. One Saturday evening he saw a late-night horror film on television. It was about a youth who had discovered that he was a werewolf who killed people when the moon was full. 'I know what I am!' the youth exclaimed in despair. 'I know what I am!'

The climax of the film came when he'd met his girlfriend in a moonlit wood and had begun to rip out her jugular vein. In the nick of time, a silver bullet fired by a kindly policeman put him out of his misery and saved the situation. The distraught girlfriend duly wept over his corpse. It was a thoroughly bad film, creakily banal and embarrassingly awful. Yet, it made a deep impression on him. That's me! I, also, 'know what I am'.

Just Have to Soldier on

But what to do? Find a sympathetic listener and spill the beans? Fine! But who? Go to the vicar? Old Vicar Ainsley? He, the sixty-year-old who hated kids and couldn't abide teenagers? Forget it! Go to the doctor? Yes, and be classified as a dangerous loony who ought to be given drugs and locked up in an institution for his own and society's safety. No way! Ring up the Samaritans? But you only rang them up when you were about to commit suicide. They'd ring up the ambulance and you'd be carted off to a secure loony bin, certified and filled up with dope. Not on, either.

No, he would just have to soldier on, as if he had some dreadful, lingering disease. In a way it could almost be heroic, like the doomed Dr Livingstone struggling through the wilds of Africa.

Get Real!

All of a sudden the exams were upon him. Oddly enough, they were not the ordeal he'd been dreading. Instead it was an orderly and precise process, like executing a well-planned night exercise with the Army Cadets. It was matter of keeping calm and doing the right things at the right time. Nothing unexpected, the ground well reconnoitred, enemy position located, well-rehearsed plans calmly executed.

When it was all over he felt a shaft of seemingly irrational hope. That was *easy*! God, I could have done really well! That would be just *great*! But, get real! Dream on, deluded young man! In this life miracles don't happen; not to people like you, at any rate!

End of the Road

So, to the end of the summer term. Final Assembly. Praise. Glory. Special prizes. Given a special tie. A eulogy from Dolly: 'our most outstanding pupil' ... 'a tremendous asset to the school'... 'You *must* come back and see us!' Thunderous applause from the assembled juniors. Glory such as he had never known before.

Then emptiness. Long after the boys had gone home he went out of the front door. It was a glorious afternoon, the climax of high summer. A warm, friendly sun smiled down from a clear blue sky, seeming to caress the mellow red brick of the old Edwardian houses and the rustling leaves of the luxuriant trees. A rich and comforting world. 'Don't worry, you're safe here!' He hadn't realised just how much of it was a part of him, like his very hair and fingernails. It had taken him up when he had been at his very lowest ebb, restored him and given him everything. But it was all over now. It was his no more.

'Still a Liddell Kid Ain't Yer!'

And what next? Fear of the unknown waters that lay ahead. If only time would stand still and stop driving him relentlessly onwards.

Suddenly Martin breezed up to him, ostentatiously smoking a cigarette.

'Well that's me rid o' that dump!' he chortled, exhaling a cloud of blue smoke from his nostrils. 'I'm havin' me fag and there's fuck all Dolly can do aboorit, neither! Want a drag, Jonny?'

He pulled out a packet of Silk Cut and offered him one.

'No thanks, I don't smoke.'

'Still Dolly's liddell pet is yer?' sneered Martin. 'Scared Mekon'll catch yers and smack yer bum, eh?'

'Shut up, Army Barmy!'

Ever since that memorable ascent of Scafell Pike, four years ago, Martin had nursed a resentment against both him and the school. They just hadn't given him the credit he felt was due as a 'hard' and a 'military type'. Now, after John's apotheosis in the Final Assembly, his hatred was boiling over.

'Know what I'm gannin' ter dee tonight?' he said aggressively.

Without waiting for John to answer, he plunged ahead. 'First, I'll be shaggin' Meg.' John winced as the lengthy pornographic description poured out. It was all so childish – a small boy rehearsing all the four letter words he'd just learnt from his mates! And as if he, John, had never heard them before! 'Then I'll be off with the lads on me motorbike. We'll gan roond ter Jake's place and get proppa ratted on the vodka like. Worraboot you, eh?'

John walked away. He was too keyed-up to listen to this fantasising drivel. 'Shagging Meg?' That'd be the day! Martin was a notorious loser who'd never yet managed to score. That he *did* know!

Martin followed him. 'But you won't be doing nothing, will yers? Still a liddell kid, ain't yer!'

'No, I'm not!'

'Yes you is! You is goin' off ter Greece with Dolly an' all the liddell kids, ain't yers? Dolly's great expedition! Know what yer'll be doin'? Makin' liddell sand castles on the beach with all the liddell kids. And all the time Dolly'll be seein' that yoora a good liddell boy an' that. Else Mekon'll be pullin' yer pants doon an' smackin' yer bum. You'll *like* that, won't yer, yer poofter?'

'Piss off, will you!'

John hurried away and left him burbling away into the void. He really couldn't be arsed to get into a fight with a great lump of self-indulgent lard like Martin.

Trapped

Yet, as he ambled along the pavement through the dark shadows and pools of golden sunlight, he had the uncanny feeling that Martin, useless pile of flab that he was, had spoken the truth; or part of it, anyway. He *was* still clinging to Beaconsfield and his childhood. He *was* afraid of letting go.

That summer Dorothy and Meakin had finally taken the plunge and organised an 'Adventure Holiday' in Greece. They'd homed in on John. 'John we *need* you to help out with the juniors. You've been *so* good with them this year. You know, they *worship* you! Especially little Mark Downing. You're *such* a good influence!'

And who could resist a juicy massaging of their ego? Not insecure, fantasising, would-be hero John Denby. Yet, there were drawbacks. None of the top form had wanted to join him. Danny Fleetwood's 'rebellion' had inspired them with a guilty longing. If only they had had the guts to break out and be *real* lads like Danny! In the end the expedition consisted of two Third Years, four Second Years and one First Year: little Mark Downing.

Mark was really too young to go on the expedition and was only there by special dispensation. His parents were embroiled in a messy divorce and were far too busy sizing up their new partners to be lumbered with a rumbustious, whinging, attention-seeking little eleven-year-old.

When he had heard that John was going on the expedition, Mark had rushed up to him, bubbling over with delight, and embraced him. Another unmentionable electric thrill occurred. Once again, fortunately nobody noticed the embarrassing biological results.

So there he was. The honoured leader, the tough guy, admired and respected by the boys. But in reality, perhaps, the Mummy's Boy who was too frightened to leave school and face the real world. But, then, what else could he realistically do? For if Dolly ditched him – as she had so nearly done three years ago! – then who else did he have? Not Giles: he couldn't give a damn and, besides, they both hated each other's guts. Isabel? End up like poor, mad Jason? No way. He was trapped.

Clean. Sanitised. So Bloody Boring!

They drove out to Greece in the school minibus, spending each night at elaborate touristy campsites. It was a far cry from Morocco. No darkened and exotic alleyways in ancient Arab towns. No adrenaline-filled 'Great Escapes' into remote mountain fastnesses. No moonlit bivouacs on plunging mountain faces. It was all so tame and controlled.

'Are the boys bedded down in their tents?'

'Yes, miss.'

'Well you can go and read the younger group a story. But not a ghost story this time, please. Little Mark's scared of the dark. When you've finished you can join us for a cup of cocoa.'

A far cry from bedding down under the glittering stars of the Sahara.

Safe. Mundane. All the time Dolly's eyes were on him. Unobtrusively. Smilingly. But always there. Making sure that nothing 'awkward' happened. Bed early. No experiments with alcohol. No fags. No wandering off by yourself. Clearly no repetition of the 'Morocco affair'. Nothing for Dobson or the Youth Outreach Committee to get hold of. Coded message: 'You got away with it last year, but you're not getting away with it this time!'

All clean and sanitised. And so bloody *boring*!

Changed Into Exactly What?

They drove through Italy. Stopping at Rimini they spent a day in the 'fun park'. There he had a visitation: a sudden and painful flashback. He'd been there before. Long ago with his perfect Gran and Grandad in his previous incarnation before 'The Fall'. As he recognised the self-same carousel on which he'd ridden, he found himself standing in his lost Eden. For a beautiful and infinitely sad moment he seemed to hear his Gran and his Grandad calling him from the Beyond World: 'Don't forget us! We're still there, waiting for you to join us!'

Then the vision faded. There was no Beyond World. And, bloody hell, had he *really* found this tacky and cheesy place exciting? Yes, he was different now. Changed. But changed into exactly *what*?

Time for that Silver Bullet

The only remotely good bit of the trip was the ascent of Mount Olympus in Greece. It was a fine, craggy mountain, more a whole range of spiky summits than a single peak. Rearing up dramatically from the narrow coastal plain, its distant crests were often wrapped in dark clouds from whose depths there came the occasional flash of lightning and angry rumble of thunder. It really did suggest remote antiquity and ancient gods.

Yet, when they actually started the climb, it wasn't a patch on Aksoual. No mud brick Berber villages, no white-robed shepherds with their Biblical flocks of sheep, no adrenaline rushes as you wriggled your way up a cliff band to salvation. Little to compare with that great plunging face emerging from the nothingness of the night. No far-off deserts. It was just a matter of walking up an easy, well-marked path, staying in a spacious mountain chalet, helping Dolly cook the evening meal and getting the kids bedded down for the night.

Indeed, you were just a kid yourself, maybe slightly bigger, but a kid all the same. Coded message in Dolly's X-ray eyes: 'You got away with murder in Morocco, but not any more! This time I'm keeping an eye on you.

Even so, the final clamber up to the misty spire of Mykitas, the highest of the peaks, was exciting, especially when they neared the summit and became aware of the huge cliffs that plummeted down to the lingering snowfields that lurked in the gloomy depths of the far side of the range. This was a worthy mountain. His spirits rose.

But there was something else. While the Greek guide and Meakin led the way up the rocky gullies, Dolly had appointed him as 'back marker'.

'John, I want you to make sure that everybody reaches the top, especially little Mark. Poor soul, he's not much good at anything and climbing Mount Olympus will do wonders for his self-esteem. I know you can do it! You *will*, won't you?'

'Of course! I'll do my best!' Not much of a choice, have I, you manipulative old trout?

It was quite an assignment. Horribly dyslexic and quite excessively clumsy, Mark could barely cope with the steep, boulder-filled groove that swept down through the mist like a gigantic, badly made staircase. His feet just didn't seem to obey his brain, and always managed to miss obvious footholds, either thrashing round in mid-air or slithering off a smooth, fiercely angled slab.

'I canna dee it!' he wailed as he slithered into a deep cleft. 'I berra go down!'

Increasingly entranced by the perfection of Mark's little body, John found himself becoming paternal as he coaxed him upwards, step by awkward step.

'Come on, put your hand here and your foot there... Don't worry, I'm holding you... That's it! Well done! Now we'll have a little rest... Now we'll do the next bit.'

Taking hold of Mark's delicate little foot, he placed it

gently into a large scoop in the limestone. Then, grabbing the deliciously smooth skin of the boy's perfectly formed hand, he manoeuvred it onto a large jug-handle hold just above him. Finally, shoving on Mark's exquisitely shaped backside, bulging so temptingly beneath his jeans, he pushed him upwards onto the next stance. As he did so, a warm glow filled him. If only Mark wasn't wearing any clothes and would let him... A rich and terrifying thought! I'm in love with him! God, this is *awful*! Or is it beautiful? Holy Communion? The Theban Sacred Bands? The Holy Ghost? Or, more probably, the whisperings of the Demon that will lure you to destruction?

Eventually they emerged onto the airy summit.

'Well done, Mark!' exclaimed John. 'You're *there*! You're with the Gods of Ancient Greece on the throne of Zeus himself!'

Just then, almost on cue, as if Zeus himself had actually been listening, the mists rolled back, revealing the true grandeur of the range: the ragged cockscomb of the peaks, the immense precipices plunging down into unknown snowy depths, the soaring rocky spires, the sea of white clouds beneath them, the brilliant blue of the sky above. Truly, it seemed, the Throne of the Gods.

Mark gaped in what seemed to be wonder. 'Wow! Wow! I've climbed Moont Olly, me!'

Suddenly he hugged John. 'Ta, ever so! Ta a million! Yer wicked, you! Far berra than mingy ole Dad! I'll 'ave ye as me Dad instead o' him!'

A surge occurred in John's forbidden zone! Your Dad? I'd rather you were my bird and I could do what I long to do!

Full of emotion, Dorothy shook John's hand. 'Well done! That was wonderful! The best thing you've ever done for the school! So unselfish! So *adult*! John,' she gushed, 'You're a natural with the young! You really ought to be a teacher!'

For a moment he relished the accolade, almost rolled in it!

But then, like the mountain mists, dark thoughts swept down on the elation. God Almighty, if she *knew*! Knew that I'm not what I seem to be. That I'm a werewolf. When the moon is full, or when the Demon comes… same thing. Yes, I know what I am. God, if that kid knew…! Knew what danger he was in! Time for that silver bullet before 'something' happens?

Near Miss: The Demon Takes Over

Three days later 'something' did happen. Or, rather, very nearly happened. They were having a day on the beach. They were at a big, tacky seaside resort. It was sunshades, plastic tables and chairs, bars, ice cream, a constant trickle of pop music; everything that John found cloying and imprisoning.

The kids, of course, loved it. But for him it was a wasted day of excruciating boredom. While they went whooping off into the sea, he was deputed to guard their clothes. For a long time he sat disconsolately on the sand, gazing inland at the dull haze which blurred the distant and craggy mountains. *That* was where he longed to be, pushing the limits and probing the edges of his capability. Not stuck here like an overgrown kid! At this very moment, Martin was probably careering round on a motorbike. Useless, pathetic Army-Barmy Martin, the ultimate big, fat slob. Yet, not a little kid like him.

As he sat and sulked under the broiling sun, the Demon came. The juniors were running round on the beach, naked but for their minute swimming trunks which barely concealed their exquisite treasures. Among them was Mark, smiling and quite ludicrously lovely, plunging noisily into the sea. If only! If only!

Then, as if in a pre-arranged answer to his cravings, Mark emerged from the waves, wet and shining.

'Wanna ice cream me! Berra get me dry things on.'

Right in front of him, seemingly in slow motion, the

longed-for show began. Dressing was always a problem with Mark, and the business of extracting himself from his dripping wet trunks, finding his dry underpants in the anarchic heap of T-shirts, trousers and socks on the sand and, at the same time, keeping his towel securely round his middle... posed fearful difficulties for him. A desperately clumsy and hideously mismanaged dyslexic operation began. First he pulled down his trunks, and as they got tangled up with his feet, the towel fell off, leaving his pink, cherubic body stark naked for all to see with everything that mattered on display. Unconcerned and quite unaware of his surroundings, he began to rummage round in the heap of clothes in front of him.

Everything John had ever longed for was there before him. Ready. Waiting. Now's your chance! The Demon was in full command – his *all*. Wild, exultant joy, radiant ecstasy greater even than he had ever before! Holy joy! The Communion of souls! Doing what you're meant to do! The act of worship.

Biology was in total control. Total arousal. He got up and approached the unsuspecting Mark.

Just then he felt a hand gripping his shoulder. He turned round to see Meakin looking grimly at him.

'I know what you want to do,' he said in a firm, quiet voice. 'I know what you want to do, but for *his* sake, for *your* sake, and for the sake of *all* of us, *don't*!'

White-faced and trembling, John could only splutter defiantly.

'What do you mean? What are you on about?'

Still gripping his shoulder, Meakin led him away.

'Don't try to lie about it! I know what you are. You can't deceive me.'

'What? Lemme go!'

'It's not your fault. I don't think any the worse of you for it. But *don't do it*! Now go for a swim and wash out the evidence in your trousers. I won't tell anybody. Don't worry.'

John glanced down at his jeans.

'Oh, God!' he exclaimed. The 'evidence' was massive – all down his right trouser leg and hideously visible. The exposure! The shame!

He hurried, obeyed and plunged fully dressed into the sea.

No God?

That night in the tent, as the juniors snored softly and the waves gently caressed the beach, he prayed silently.

'Please God, stop it! Please make me normal!'

But, once again, God didn't reply. Or else there was no God at all.

'You're Such a Credit to the School!

Or, maybe, there *was* a God, after all. But a God who was playing a strange cat-and-mouse game with him: cold one minute, hot the next. He returned home to a clutch of brilliant exam results, far beyond his wildest hopes. Seven O Level passes. Grade As in English, history and geography. Grade 1 in all his CSEs. Special praise for his history project from the assessor. 'remarkable piece of work... masterpiece... promising young historian... best I've ever seen'. Only one query to Dorothy: 'What's a lad like this doing C.S.E. for? He's too good for it. It's not really meant for the likes of him.' What indeed? Why was he at Beaconsfield at all? But that was a long and very convoluted story.

In Morocco he'd done all the right things and had been covered in shit for his pains. But here his efforts had received their just reward. So there *was* rationality in the world after all. More than that, he now knew that really *was* as clever as he'd thought he was.

Dorothy was over the moon. She gave him a big hug. 'Oh, John, I'm *so* pleased! You've done *so* well! What with getting little Mark up Mount Olympus, and now *this*! You're such a *credit* to the school! What's more,' she added, 'they'll accept you at the Stirling Academy now! Think of that! The Sixth Form in the top academic school in the north of England! It's a real honour for you and for the school!'

She felt vindicated. Heaven alone knew, she'd taken a big enough risk in adopting him – and she'd had doubts enough about it! – but it had all turned out well. She felt a deep, maternal love for him. *Her* child. Her *good* child!

Now What?

Two days later John was at Gloucester Road recovering from the gigantic tea that Mrs Coburn had cooked for him. 'A growin' bairn like you needs buildin' up proper, like.'

Idly he glanced at his school blazer draped over his bed. There it was. There *he* was. His Head Boy badge. His rugby team badges. His Adventure Club badges. His Art Prize badge. His personality. His achievements. All that was best in him. Now it was all in the past. His Eden gone. Another Fall. And fall into *what*?

Casually he looked out of the skylight. It was a nondescript day with a greyish sky. Dust was blowing round the piles of rubble and the empty beer cans lying in the puddles. Above the obscene graffiti on the red brick walls, the newly built tower blocks stood crudely naked. South of the river the distant hills lost themselves in colourless haze.

Suddenly, from somewhere nearby, there was a coarse female shriek followed by an explosion of raucous male laughter. He shuddered. The predators were still lurking out there in that drab wilderness.

And, just what *was* waiting for him in the world beyond Beaconsfield?